For Skyla Dawn Cameron, who said, "Why the hell not?"

"Even a man who is pure in heart and says his prayers by night, may become a wolf when the wolfbane blooms and the autumn moon is bright..."

— CURT SIODMAK

PART ONE
INTO THE WOODS

1

ROSES AND TRASH

IN SUMMER, EVEN TAKING A SHORT HALF-HOUR LUNCH MEANT HITTING Quartz Avenue well after daybreak. In winter it was otherwise, and cold as shit too. The wind off the Marquette River was full of the silty stench of dead fish wheezing through pavement-floored canyons, and Zoe Simmons smelled ice behind it like a razor hidden in layers of folded quilt. The breeze tugged at her long dark braid; her brown coat with the ragged fake-fur collar reeked of cigarette smoke because she spent her breaks outside the receiving bays' fire door, shivering but refusing to light up.

Smokers generally had a better sense of humor than the non-nicotine folks. Zo said she was trying to quit and played with a pen; consequently, they didn't ask many questions. Most people liked talking about themselves more than anything else in the world, a fact well known to scammers, evangelists, and anyone with a legitimate reason to hide.

Zo crossed at 58th and turned north, stretching her legs; traffic was relatively light but no city ever really slept.

Not if you were in the right slice of real estate.

The heel of her left boot was loose, flopping in time as she strode along. This time of year in the Panhandle the temperature sometimes hovered a shade above zero, and her jeans were threadbare but at least nobody cared what a night stocker wore. You put in headphones and worked like hell, and that was enough.

Normally she'd already be at the squat, but every time she thought about crossing the street to get on the right track a cold little tickle slid warning fingernails down her back. Tiny light scratches, barely there but enough to keep her moving.

Two cities ago it might have been a prelude to an attempted mugging; last year in Akron it might've been Roy, but nobody knew her here. The satisfaction of a well-worked cereal aisle, the boxes flush and the bags of generics stacked in their wire baskets, faded before that chill tingle of danger. She couldn't even feel good about getting out the door before the first customers trickled in to root through her shelves like goddamn hogs.

No, not hogs. Pigs were nice enough, they ate what you laid down and largely had the sense to leave you alone when you weren't bothering them.

People were just the opposite.

The pachinko parlor on the corner of 62nd and Stark was lit up even this early, the proprietor reeking of body odor and layers of drugstore bodyspray, plopped like a mushroom on his folding chair by the front door. He barely glanced up as her shadow passed over the window. Zoe buried her chin in the coat's worn collar and thought about her options.

It couldn't be Royal. It couldn't even be Pastor Bea. Which left rape, theft, or just someone out for a good time.

The 28 bus chugged in the distance; if she timed it right, she could swing aboard just before it pulled away from the curb on North Pomoda. Not the best way to escape, but...

The feeling faded mid-block, and she only had to contend with the suspicion she was crazy instead of the undeniable feeling of shadowy pursuit. Her stomach settled, though a reek of diesel from a passing semi was hardly spring roses.

Mama liked pink roses. And rose soap, in those round little tins.

Thinking of Mama was a sure invitation to a day of fitful night-mares, tossing on the paper-thin single mattress she'd scrounged. *Up all night, sleep all day* was all right for a rock band, but when everyone outside was going about daytime business it was hard to get even five and a half winks, let alone forty.

At least in a squat the roommates weren't too nosy. The junkies didn't care as long as she didn't have any cash on hand or anything to sell, the crazies gave her a once-over and decided she was vaguely pretty but not interesting enough, and the predators were easy to spot and avoid.

God knew she'd had practice. And how Mama would hate her taking the Lord's name in vain, even inside her own blessed skull.

Blue eyes soft and thoughtful, Zo turned toward home with only a token doubling back on Harvey Avenue. The plywood flowers of boarded-up windows bloomed with increasing regularity, and broken glass glittered sharp and cold. The east was lightening; the sun died an early death behind the mountains and hauled itself up on the other side later and later until right before Christmas.

"Fuck Christmas," she muttered, hunching still further, and listened hard.

Nothing. Just the city breathing with traffic, a baby crying some-where, the half-heard stirring as those in shitty apartments woke up for another day of underpaid labor and squatters collapsed in what-ever blankets they could find after a night spent smoking, drinking, or eating whatever they'd begged during the day.

Maybe her instincts were off. Maybe Bea was right and she was possessed; maybe Mama was right and Zoe'd been marked by Satan from birth.

Angelina Simmons should know; she'd been present at the event.

Mama's cracked-sweet soprano, whimpering as the morphine did its best to blunt the pain of cancer raving through liver, blood, and bone, lingered in Zoe's brain. That sound pressed into walnut folds of grey matter, ran down in the dark wrinkles, dripped and filled like candle wax when the power got shut off and you needed some light to get ready for another day of backbreaking work for a handful of pennies.

Zoe turned down the alley, listening intently as she threaded her way between piles of black plastic bags, each a swollen egg. Where did they all come from? They never seemed to get hauled away or renewed, changing position only reluctantly.

There was never any shortage of trash. Like dandruff and pain, it collected in every crevice.

Two days to payday. Not even enough to get into a studio apartment, and forget a credit check. A hotel by the week was too expensive. There were other options, sure, but she didn't like any of them.

The condemned building's side door was still unlocked; she slipped through with a sigh of relief. It was just as cold, and stink-dark, but there was a certain relief in being *inside* your burrow. Everything sounded usual—the dealer and his girlfriend two doors down were having another fight. Pretty soon he'd hit her.

Depressing, and just like clockwork. It reminded her of Roy. *Get it through your head...*

Snoring rose from the end of the hall. It was the homeless man she'd christened Bartleby, the one who screamed on the street corner about the Second Coming when he wasn't deadass drunk and wallowing next to a rotting patch of wall. Frankly, his cries were like a little piece of home; Zoe's lip curled as she slipped past, her boots silent. The padlock on the outside of her door wasn't clipped, and she sniffed deeply as she slipped it in her pocket. Anyone watching might think she had a cold, but tasting the air was a survival mechanism.

Nothing out of place. Piss, shit, rotting food, misery. Everything just the same.

So why was she so unsettled?

Getting inside—a maneuver practiced in the dark, no electricity here, no sir—took only seconds. More hasps from the hardware store accepted the two inside padlocks she changed regularly just to be sure, and she moved around the tiny, gloomy room, a faint edge of dawn showing around the plywood boarding up the small, thankfully unbroken window.

She could light the Sterno and heat something up, but instead she chewed on a tasteless protein bar lifted from work, washing it down with mineral water, and dropped onto the bed. Batteries were expensive and she didn't feel like reading one of the mildewed books with her cheap LED lamp.

No tax returns. No rent. Nothing new, nothing flashy. No real address, no smartphone, no heating bill, no footprint, no trace. Mama would be proud, or maybe she wouldn't. Angelina Simmons's method—moving from man to man—wasn't an option for her daughter.

Not now, or not yet. She'd learned her lesson with Roy. Maybe when Zo got a little older and rough living took the bloom off the rose it wouldn't be a matter of pride anymore, but of no takers.

Even Mama had settled with Pastor Beaton, in the end.

That was twice in one morning thinking about roses and Bea, and that meant nightmares were coming, dismal and regular.

Zoe didn't even take her jacket off. She could shower at the gym tomorrow before her shift, if she could sneak in. If not, there was the racquetball club on Marbery Street. This city was beginning to be familiar, which probably meant she'd have to leave soon.

She stuffed the thin pillow under her head, curled onto her side, and tried to relax.

It didn't work. Still, she lay motionless, a long-limbed animal in its burrow, knowing goddamn well not to waste energy fighting until there was no choice.

Just show me where you are, the same soft, familiar voice said in the darkness, right before she fell asleep. *Just give me a sign.*

But she couldn't. The tingle was back at her nape. It wasn't the first time it had followed her home, and she *was* going to have to move on soon, God damn it.

More blasphemy. Mama would say it was the devil after them both. Well, he'd done caught up, as Bea might say, and carried in

Angelina's own body too. Maybe Zo had a brain tumor and metastasis would do to her what it had done to her mother.

When she did drop into fitful slumber, she dreamed of a full moon and soft singing voices. Hot tears trickled between her eyelids; her aching body shivered and shuddered, caught in the trap of living but unwilling to give up.

Yet.

2

PROPER CONTROL

HATE WASN'T EFFICIENT; TOO MUCH EMOTIONAL INVOLVEMENT MEANT A greater chance of mistakes. When fighting an almost-unstoppable collection of claws, sharp reflexes, hunger, and utter violence, errors were the last thing anyone could afford.

Especially a *demi* with a missing half, hunting alone. At least on a muggy-cool Miami night, sirens in the distance and wet darkness pressing against every surface, there was nobody around to witness him struggle.

Chasing the Broken away from populated areas was only moderately difficult. Simply impersonate good prey before turning on the thing with just enough calculated savagery to keep it baffled, rinse and repeat as necessary.

Jackson Rouje faded aside as the beast swiped for him, its snarl echoing in the alley's throat. He had it cornered; if he worked with a team they would be clustering, wearing the fallen Kith down before moving in for the kill.

Alone, he was forced to other methods. The change burned in him, bloodlust answering the call of combat, and his golden hair caught a random reflection of streetlamp light. A flurry of quick strokes, his own claws breaking free just enough to tear tough hide; there was a burning low on his left side where the beast got lucky and tagged him, and they were both bleeding now.

Which wasn't ideal.

The thing that had once been a proud Kith backed up, its lip lifting and fangs gleaming. Swaying fur rippled over muscle; all the power and glory were gone from its maddened gaze. Its hip brushed a lurking dumpster, crumpling metal—it was getting stronger the further it fell.

Stronger, yes. But also more stupid as its cannibalistic fury mounted.

An answering growl thrummed in Jack's chest, a sound too deep for his current, smaller, but still muscle-dense shape. He sank into an easy crouch, left fingers tented against cracked, filth-greasy pavement. This far south "winter" was still warmish, but the humidity clung to every breath and a man in jeans, heavy boots, a flannel button-up, a hoodie, and a hip-length leather jacket was overdressed.

The Broken lunged, halting in confusion when he didn't flinch. Jack simply waited, his breathing turning into deep easy swells, dark eyes half-lidded.

Come on. You're getting hungry again, we don't have all night.

It growled again, pacing from side to side. One hairy fist pistoned out, puncturing the dumpster's side with a hollow noise; its claws sank in and tore more metal as it lunged for him again, gaining confidence when he still didn't move. The bloodlust and smoking fury it radiated in waves almost overpowered his own scent; it might be thinking him too wounded for further battle or simply submissive, battered down by its fury.

As usual, when he wanted to be still, he thought about *her*. A black-haired toddler, her bright blue eyes closed and her lashes a charcoal fan against chubby cheeks as she slept, one hand outflung and her breathing filling his own chest. The end of the memory was always the same—he was lifted out of the crib and carried away, disliking the separation but having to endure it, the pediatrician's office a semi-familiar wonderland of cold antiseptic glare and his father's broad, safe, capable hands keeping him still for the examination.

Just a little irritation, nothing wrong. How's the other one?

And his father's reply. *Safe at home, healthy as a horse.*

Except she wasn't.

Any calm from that memory was always transient. Still, it worked, and he had to believe she was still alive. Somewhere, somehow.

The alternative was unacceptable.

The Broken flung its head back to roar, then darted for the alleymouth. Jackson unfolded, the spring performed with thoughtless, accurate speed very much like the thing's own, and his leap was precisely calculated to hit just before his opponent reached apogee. A crunch, a silver flash of pain as its claws sank into his side again, his fingers hooking just under its chin and a lunging, fishlike effort— he *twisted*, his boots kissing the brickwork on the left side of the alley.

His own claws sank deep, one of them finding the hot throbbing highway of a carotid, and he wrenched at exactly the right moment. A *crack* like a dead-dry tree snapped in half by a hurricane, a gout of warm crimson, and he landed, shaking slippery gore from his right hand and breathing deeply, wrestling the rage back into its home.

Control, his father said, his hand brutally hard on a young Kith's nape. *You are my heir, you are* demi, *and you* will *exercise proper control.*

The Broken slumped behind him, a hulk of fur and heavy bone, foxfire nerve-death twitching through muscles gone slack. It was finally at peace, after tearing through at least five skin victims; Trenckow the elder and his office were going to have a busy few days tidying this up. The shamans would mourn, and wonder if they could have halted such a disaster.

Sometimes skate—the only street drug that really affected his kind—didn't just kill its user, but others around them as well. But now it was over, and the Kith who had fallen from grace, control, and sanity was at peace.

Jackson shuddered, the change fighting him; nobody was supposed to hunt a Broken alone lest the rage go viral and ensnare them too, but who would take a chance at running backup when the analyst tracking the thing could fall just as quickly?

Still, he hadn't fallen yet. An analyst, even a *usanaugh* male with his *demie* absent, had a natural defense against the animalistic fury. The cold clarity of passionless logic simply became more difficult to employ every time it was used as a bulwark.

Jack was aware of a faint thrumming that was definitely *not* a growl, and when he opened his eyes, every edge in the dark alley stood out in sharp relief as if under noontide sun. Even the twisted paper garbage and rotting food bore a small measure of charm just by default of that clarity.

The sound was his phone, and there were only a handful of numbers that would ring through while he was occupied this way. Jack's jaw creaked as he forced himself fully into his smaller skin-form—still tall and broad-shouldered, but not likely to cause the skins any discomfort even on a subconscious level—and he fished the thin silver rectangle with its hard rubbery case out of a padded pocket with his left hand, glancing at its glowing face.

Shit. He thumbed the right spot to accept the call, glad his claws weren't out. The Broken's blood would degrade at high speed, becoming thin, viscous amber sludge as individual cells turned on themselves, not knowing or caring their bearer was gone to the heart of the Sun or the dark side of the Moon to be purified.

The hunger of a Broken went all the way down to mitochondria. Regular Kith flesh didn't degrade as quickly as the Broken did, but it still hurried to return to the earth's embrace.

The skins wouldn't get any forensics worth mentioning, as usual.

"Sir?" The word held a touch of Voice, just enough to make it stand up with a little starch.

"Hunting alone again?" Trevor Rouje's baritone, even translated through wireless and tinny speakers, was rich and resonant. "Whatever you're doing, stop. We have a location."

There was only one thing *that* could mean. "Where?"

"Texas. How soon can you get to the airport?"

Jack glanced over his shoulder. "Depends on if I run or get a car. I'll only need a light cleanup at this location before leaving; Trenckow's team is monitoring."

"Well, that's good news. Trenck's already dispatching transport to your location, they'll get you a flight and Hermann will meet you at the other end. It's the Howler's territory, so don't make any waves."

"Yes, sir." He had to ask. "Is it a confirmed sighting?" It didn't make any difference; Jack would chase even the faintest whisper.

He had before.

But Texas? That was news. They'd only gotten a break from Nebraska because some two-bit podunk pastor had filed for widower benefits using Angelina's Social Security number. The Bible-botherer was also suspected of burning down his own church for an insurance payout; a low-grade arson case was still wending its way through an investigative labyrinth.

The federal administration had processed the "widower's" claim, but let it hang fire without approval or denial since Trevor Rouje had applied a little judicious pressure to gum up the works.

Nobody, including Dad, had thought his vanished wife would be stupid enough to stay in the States. And the truly important person in all this mess was had vanished into the haze.

"It's double confirmed." The leader of the largest, most successful Kith family on the continent paused, and Jackson was already slipping past the shattered bulk of the dead Broken as it began to bubble into fast-forward decay. "Get going, son. Bring her home."

I'll do more than that. "Yes, sir." He thumbed the disconnect; there was nothing more to say.

Moments later, the alley was empty except for a twitching

corpse. Trenckow's crew was already en route to this location and would make certain of the scrubbing, and by sunup there would be no sign of the battle remaining.

And Jack would be in the air, winging toward Texas and hopefully, his salvation.

3
WORTH A SHOT

THE ONLY THINGS MAKING WORKING RETAIL EVEN FAINTLY PALATABLE WERE getting your biweekly check and the fact that night stockers didn't have to deal with customers. Sadly, Zoe's payday shift overlapped with opening the Greenfield Grocery's doors, and she was caught in front of a dairy case by an elderly woman with a cloud of bluish-grey hair and a tartan purse clutched to her once-ample but now deflated bosom like she was expecting a mugger to show up in the aisles.

"Miss? Excuse me, Miss?"

At least the lady was polite. Zoe straightened self-consciously, tucking a strand of black hair behind her ear. Her braid was coming loose, curls Mama had despaired of ever taming working free with a vengeance.

"Yes ma'am?" The right tone for dealing with biddies like this was carefully respectful; they spooked easy and got vicious if you barked too loud.

"I can't find them." The woman's mouth turned down at the corners and her wrinkled cheeks were paper-thin; when the wind came up the river it might blow her away. She'd probably married a roughneck and moved from the Midwest when she was a girl full of dreams. The faint hint of cologne touching her too-large leather boots said they were a dead husband's and the sourness of mild incontinence meant she was probably looking for the Poise pads today. "The eggs on sale, in the circular."

Lady, you think I know about the ads? I'm just night work. But Zoe was wearing a nametag—it said *Martha*, her own little joke—and an orange polyester apron because the doors were open, so that made her a walking store directory.

It wasn't this woman's fault, so Zo swallowed a hot rancid flare of impatience. "Let's take a look." *Since they're labeled on the shelf, too.* "This way." It was four steps, max, and Royal would have drawled *If it was a snake you'd be dead.*

Roy was an asshole. At least, Zoe hoped he still *was* and not *had been.* A shudder went down her back and she took a deep breath, trying not to wrinkle her nose at the reek of old dairy from the cooler behind the shelves.

"I can't find them, you see." Faded, bloodshot blue eyes blinked, and the old woman's shoes squeaked on freshly buffed linoleum. It always stank after the floors were done, and maybe that was why Zoe didn't smell trouble at first.

Patiently repeating that she was sure these were the eggs in the circular—the big bright tag on the shelf said so, after all, and if they weren't the checkers could handle giving a discount—ate up at least three and a half minutes. If she was late to clock off Nash would be on her ass; there was nothing worse than a good ol' boy with a little power, especially one who looked like a fat blurred copy of a minor movie star and knew it.

Still, the old lady got her eggs, and though it was against store policy Zoe stripped off her orange apron as soon as the biddy shuffled away with a carton in her slightly trembling paws. Zo also tore off her nametag for good measure and plunged into the stockroom, hurrying for the timeclock.

That was when the heel on her left boot decided to come off completely.

Oh, for Christ's sweet sake. It took everything she had not to hiss it aloud, because Steve Junior—everyone called him that, though his daddy didn't work here—was standing by the large freezer, his sandy-dark unibrow wrinkled with worry and a faint sheen of perspiration on his broad forehead.

"Martha? Over here." Low and urgent. He beckoned, and Zoe's temper almost snapped.

It wouldn't take much. She was much stronger than she looked. "What? I've gotta clock off."

"There's some guy looking for you." Steve stocked dairy and the hanging deli; he was built low and wide. He hunched, turtling his head, and the faintest twitch of his chin told her what direction the danger was coming from. "Nash is taking him around. Some bigshot, looks like a cop."

Holy fuck. For a moment she thought it was a practical joke, but there was no edge of malice to his scent. Instead, Steve Junior's sweat was adrenaline-greasy, relieved not to be in trouble but still taking the time to warn another soldier in the retail trenches.

The back end of Greenfield Grocery had a high bare ceiling sectioned by naked beams, a cracked concrete floor in the non-customer areas, and was full of several cold drafts in winter. At the other end, Tanisha and Harper argued good-naturedly over a couple pallets while Bubs ran the forklift. There was a fire door nearby, but the alarm on it was live. The receiving bays and the smoke door were closed at this point in the morning, since most of the freight had already been delivered.

Besides, Zo hadn't *done* anything, and though her ID wouldn't stand up to serious scrutiny she didn't make enough for the tax man to come calling, as Pastor Bea would say.

Of course there was Bea, and Royal. She should just run now and leave any questions for later.

But God *damn* it, she had a paycheck to pick up, and she needed it. Especially if she had to run.

The hesitation must have shown on her face; Steve glanced over his shoulder. "Last I saw they were looking for you out on the floor."

He was a decent enough guy, for all he stared fixedly at the tits of any female unlucky enough to end up in the breakroom with him. "You could probably get through Housewares and grab your check before, well. You know."

"Yeah." *Or I could just fuck off and get another job.* But she'd worked for that pittance and should at least try to collect it. "Thanks, Steve."

If the worst happened, well...she was fast. She didn't know just *how* fast, and it probably wasn't worth another Bad Incident to truly find out. But for God's sake, if they would just leave her *alone* she would be fine.

Everything would be.

Zoe turned and slipped through the swinging doors again, her left boot-heel flopping. The entire sole would come off if she had to move fast, but she'd run barefoot before. Not only that, but if she was going to do what she suspected was necessary, what stopped her from shoplifting a pair of sneakers on her way out the front?

Pastor Bea always said stealing was wrong, but there was a word for a man who mouthed a moralism while helping himself from the church coffers. Zoe tucked her nametag in the apron's pocket and dropped the entire bundle at the end of a Housewares aisle—stocking the appliances was fine but the dishes were a nightmare, bulky and fragile at once—and with that done she was just another customer, albeit moving more purposefully than most.

She made it to the front of the store without being noticed. Her purse was in an employee locker, but she was used to leaving things behind and always carried her current set of ID in a jeans pocket. If she could get in and get her check, she could cash it for an exorbitant fee at the place on Martello Avenue. She could be on a Greyhound less than an hour later, traffic and the stupidly slow public transit system notwithstanding.

It was a good plan, and she might have pulled it off except for the stench of the floor treatment deadening her nose at just the wrong time. She broke out of the shampoo-and-soap aisle and approached Customer Service, where employees could grab their checks from behind the counter if they hadn't signed up for direct deposit, just the store manager Nash rounded the other side. He brightened, catching sight of her.

And behind him was a tall blond man with dark eyes, in a very good tailored grey suit and a subdued blue tie far too expensive for a Greenfield Grocery just after dawn.

4
CONTROLLED
IMPATIENCE

IT WAS FAR CHILLIER THAN MIAMI, BUT THE LACK OF HUMIDITY WAS A
blessing. Jackson landed at a two-bit airstrip near the Marquette city
limits and Hermann—the retainer had landed just two hours earlier
—was there with the dossier, which was usual for any sort of hunt.

Jack settled against the back seat of the limousine, grateful to be
out of a fucking prop plane, and as he opened the manila folder a
shock went through him, toes to scalp.

The glossy 8x10 black-and-white was a telephoto shot, but you
needed that if your target was wary. Faintly blurred, it was still more
than enough. Whoever was behind the lens had captured her
midstride, a girl glancing aside before crossing a street. Very dark
hair pulled back, a few wavy strands escaping to frame her face, her
thin shoulders up and full lips slightly parted—at first blush she was
just a very attractive young woman, albeit heartbreakingly skinny.
Startling cheekbones, her chin too strong because the rest of her was
so pared-down, and her eyes large and very light.

He knew exactly what color they were. Blue, *bright* blue, lighter
than Dad's and sharing the essential vividness of Trevor's gaze. The
mouth was Angelina's, of course; their mother had been a stunner
possessed of some indefinable quality that made Dad take a chance

on a skin. Which she'd amply repaid by throwing a set of *usanaugh* twins, but then...well.

The recognition burned like the evanescent jolt of good brandy, and for a few moments Jack was barely able to breathe, staring at the photo.

Hermann, of course, caught the edge to his scent, and the chauffeur tensed as the limo negotiated a wide banking turn off the tarmac. "Sir?"

Which meant Jack had to swallow the shock and get going. An unsecured *demi* made everyone nervous. "Just fine," he murmured. "Where are we heading?"

The destination was a run-down chain supermarket; a few more moments with the dossier gave him the name she was hiding under —Martha Smith, camouflage or maybe even a joke. The file also gave him a series of startling mini-jolts; the Howler's pack had quite the competent security operation.

Her name was indeed a complete fake, as was the social she'd gotten the job under. There was no address, but she'd been sighted more than once in a certain neighborhood full of transients, junkies, and crumbling abandoned tenements.

Another few pages gave him the timeline; she'd been in town for four months. Anything between that and Nebraska was a mystery, but the Howler would know this stray was definitely Kith and just as certainly not any of the Howler's kin or clan. Of course the wet-nosed bastard had passed along the news to the Rouje pride as a courtesy since Dad was missing one of a matched set, but it wasn't like a pack leader to leave any Kith, especially female, roaming around unclaimed.

Which meant Jackson had to work quickly.

As a result, he was in a state of finely controlled impatience when Hermann piloted the limo into a barely paved parking lot beginning to fill up despite the early hour. The dingy Greenfield Grocery still bore ghosts of old seventies cigarette smoke, Muzak filtering through static-laden overhead speakers and a reek of floor wax heated by industrial buffing giving Jack a headache two steps through the door. Not to mention the thin, maddening thread of quite another scent, one rasping against every nerve he owned, anticipation pulling all his strings harp-tight.

The store manager, a blurred overweight skin bearing a distinct resemblance to a forgettable action-movie star, was almost comically vulnerable to a strong pheromone balance. It was the same old story; lots of aggressive skins got a whiff of a true predator and turned into putty. *Paper tigers*, Dad called them, often with one of his flint-hard smiles.

It was almost pathetically easy to playact law enforcement looking for a particular civilian, just wanting to ask a few questions. Unfortunately, Jack was more unsettled than he realized; he hadn't taken into account the speed information could be passed among skin retail workers. And of course she was sensitive.

All of which brought him to the moment he stepped around a corner, idly marking the position of a few half-asleep skin customers getting ready to bother already fatigued employees...

...and *she* appeared.

The "customer service" counter was a hollow rectangle, its back pressed against a six-foot nowhere-wall—to cut down on snatch-and-grabbers, of course. Plexiglass cubicles were supposed to protect the employees responsible for listening to complaints, dishing out refunds, cashing checks for obscene service fees, and wiring money orders; at the other end a slim shape was just reaching for the catch of a swinging door that simply kept the honest people from tiptoeing into space they shouldn't tread.

Glossy raven hair braided severely back, her blue eyes smudged with sleeplessness, the girl glanced at the store manager and hunched her thin shoulders. A threadbare blue T-shirt peeked from under a green and yellow flannel button-up; her jeans were a size too big and cinched tight with a distressed leather belt. She was absolutely and indisputably Kith, almost vibrating with nervousness, and utterly familiar. The breath left Jack in a rush, his heart gave a shattering leap, and his knees, usually perfectly adequate for whatever task he put them to, decided to stop working. He all but staggered, staring back at her, and a stray breath of forced air blew a tsunami draft of that gorgeous, maddening scent he'd been tracking all through the structure right into him.

The world narrowed to a single small point, the entire universe trembling upon a knife-tip. His mouth opened, he exhaled, and the last half of the breath shaped itself into a word.

"Zoe?"

Her pupils flared. A wine-red flood of fear passed through that glorious, intoxicating scent, and the beast in him answered, ready to kill whatever—skin, Kith, or anything else—was menacing his *demie*.

The girl whirled, one of her cheap boots giving a forlorn squeak, and ran.

5
SAME OLD STORY

IT WAS AN INSTINCTIVE RESPONSE, BUT SHE'D BEEN LIVING BY HER INSTINCTS for so long and so successfully—for a certain measure of *successful,* Zo supposed—that she streaked past the jewelry section with its reinforced display cases and the rubber-reeking aisles of the shoe section before she realized she was running. Once started, well, she had to continue, and she piled through the front doors, the shiny new antitheft sensors on either side moving slightly as she sped past. Glass shattered, her left bootsole disintegrated, and she barely registered the big glossy black limousine idling in the gravel-fringed parking lot.

A limo in North Marquette wasn't usual even during prom season.

She knew she was much faster than normal people, at least, and she made it to the edge of the parking lot in a blink, veering to the right to plunge through a tiny abandoned lot full of dry sand and winter-dead scrub. Apartment buildings on either side were no help; everyone would be at work. The buildings' backs and the tail end of the lot starred with junked cars and broken glass looked over the freeway. An anemic chain-link fence rattled under the chill early morning breeze, and if she had thought about it, she might have gone right over said fence and plunged across eight lanes of traffic, their assorted shoulders, and a broad yellowgrass median.

But you weren't supposed to do that, even if half-crazy from fear, so she hesitated. Which meant her pursuer hit hard enough to drive the breath from her lungs, and she expected them both to go rolling down the sage-starred embankment into the fence's rickety metal.

His own footwear dug in, leaving long furrows diagonally across the slope. They stopped with a jolt, and she was doubly surprised to find herself upright *and* trapped in a pair of iron-hard arms.

Plus, he was repeating her name. Not Martha, not Susan, not Carol or Amber or any of the other monikers she'd worn since fleeing the burning church, the night after after Mama's funeral.

Her *real* name.

"...Zoe, it's all right, it's okay, nobody's going to hurt you, just *calm down.*" He sucked in a deep breath, and her nose was full of exhaust from the roaring freeway, plenty of the cars still glimmering with headlights though dawn was now firmly past. A cold damp breeze swirled; she was used to people who smelled oddly washed-out, bleached except for when they were high on some strong emotion—fear, lust, terror.

But this guy smelled *real*, a deep wash of healthy brunet-male spice, an unfamiliar warmth spreading down her back and loosening her muscles. Zoe sagged, and his repeating of her name finally penetrated the fog of terror.

"Easy," he continued. "Just be calm, Zoe. Nobody's going to hurt you, I promise. I *swear*, nobody's ever going to hurt you again."

That's a lie. Why would a man say it unless he had some hurt planned? She surged one last time against his grasp, found it unbreakable, and went temporarily limp, her ribs flaring and collapsing with deep heaving breaths.

If he thought he'd won, maybe be would loosen up a bit and she could wriggle free.

"Good," he said in her ear, a brush of warm breath. "I'm from your father, Zoe. Whatever Angelina told you, whatever she said, it's not true. I'm from your dad. He wants to see you. We've been looking for seventeen years, ever since she took you."

What the hell? Zoe stared at the freeway—bright white headlights on one side, bloody taillights on the other, smearing as her eyes unfocused. If he was a cop...

Cops smelled of sour sweat, a rough edge of firearm metal and smoke, and oily aggression. This guy wasn't cuffing her *or* blathering about constitutional rights, nor was he getting a grope while he could like most any male she had to suffer being near. He simply held her immobile; Zoe's own scent, a constant shifting cloak insulating her from other people, frayed under the strength of his.

"What..." Her throat was desert-dry; a deep shiver passed through her and drained away. "Who the fuck are *you*?"

"I thought you'd never ask." A soft, amused baritone, his voice sent a shiver down her back. "But really, are you going to listen? I can stand here and hold you for as long as it takes to calm down."

Somehow, she believed him. The usual fear was trying to get through waves of strange relaxation, poking and prodding with sharp diamond claws, but it couldn't quite pierce all the layers. There was a weird humming sound, too, a deep purr rumbling against her back that wasn't the traffic. Was anyone watching from the apartments?

"My father's dead," Zoe said blankly. It was an article of faith, repeated over and over every time Mama had her medicine.

He's dead, and in hell. Don't you dare pray for him, either. He was bad, Zoe. He was a demon.

Which Zo'd always figured made her one too, or at least *half* demonic, but she had no truly funky powers and didn't burst into flame when she stepped inside churches. Even Bea's exorcisms were just an excuse for him to hit something that couldn't fight back.

But what about the church burning, and Royal's face? She was stronger and faster than regular people when it counted, and her senses were a lot sharper.

On the other hand, having psychotic breaks wasn't a superpower. It was just to be expected when people pushed you too far. Most of the time bullying worked out the way the pusher wanted, but sometimes, the victim simply had enough.

And *did* something about it.

"Is that what Angelina told you? We thought she'd left the country." He said it as if this were a normal conversation to be having, standing on an embankment in one shoe and a stranger's arms after she'd just lost her goddamn two-bit job, not to mention paycheck. "Then some guy in Nebraska used her original Social Security number to file for death benefits."

Oh, my God, of course Bea did that. The relief was deep and bright red, a flash all through her. Because it meant she hadn't killed the sausage-fingered, oily hypocrite when she burst out of the burning cellar.

Even if, to be absolutely honest, she'd wanted to. Oh, Zoe was going to hell for sure, but finding out her conscience wasn't *quite* as dirty as she thought was a gift. "Let go of me."

"Not until I'm sure you're not going to take off again." The stranger actually sounded amused now, like he had nothing better to do than harass her. "Seventeen years is a long time, Zo."

Don't act like you know me. "Who. The hell. *Are* you?"

"Didn't Angelina tell you?" He took a deep breath, the first intimation that he maybe wasn't as calm as he sounded. He was also really strong—she could normally wriggle free of just about anyone's grasp, but he held her like a butterfly on a pin. "You're Zoe Arcadia Rouje, daughter of Trevor Rouje. I'm Jackson Arcadius Rouje, your twin brother, happy to meet you and at your service." Deep, bitter amusement ran under the words. "I was born thirteen minutes before you, so you might want to listen to me."

Wait. "You can't…" She sounded like she'd been punched; there wasn't enough air with his smell all around her, wrapping her in unfamiliar warmth, turning all her muscles to cut strings sagging away from a cardboard bale. "She…Mama said…" Funny shadows clustered in Zoe's peripheral vision; the rushing in her ears was an old friend. Normally even the slightest whisper was loud enough to be a torment; right, now, though, she couldn't hear anything but his breath near her left cheek. Even her own voice was muffled, reaching her ears through layers of cotton wadding. "Mama said you were dead. And my father too."

"He's very much alive. We've been searching for you, Zoe." His arms loosened; she found herself set on her feet, her left bootsole gone and her sock toes touching bare dirt. A thin scrim of sweat lingered under her clothes despite the postdawn cold; the dusty sagebrush up and down the hillside knew there would be a slight spatter of cold sleet later in the day.

She could smell the impending rain too; her nose was still working as usual. This had to be real.

The stranger stepped away from her back, the warmth suddenly gone, and a wave of trembling spilled through her arms and legs. Zoe whirled, staring at this fantastical creature. "You don't look like me." *Great, Zo. Beautiful observation. Tip-top. Genius.*

He was tall, broad in the shoulder but narrow-hipped, and his hair was a manicured shock of honeygold. That was another sign he wasn't a cop; they liked high-and-tights, especially in this part of the world. Dark eyes—iris blending into pupil, like Mama's—and a strong chin, cheekbones like Zoe's, and a faint rasp of stubble; his blue tie was loosened and he didn't wear wingtips but boots that had to be either *very* expensive or flat-out custom to judge by their soles and the heavy buckles. The suit was tailored grey wool, and there was a bloody gleam on his third left finger—a heavy gold signet with a red stone, alive with its own inner light.

It didn't look like a wedding ring, but what did she know?

The young man—he was about her age, she decided, though that air of self-confidence made him seem older—studied her in return. Zo knew, miserably, what he'd see. Cheap T-shirt, tattered jeans, broken shoes, sloppy hair. It was the same old story, never quite fitting in.

"Fraternal twins. You've got Dad's eyes," he said, quietly. "The hair, though, that's hers. Angelina's. He always told me I looked like her a little." His hand came up; he pointed at his right eye, and a tentative smile curled up one corner of his mouth. *"Her gaze,* he says."

Zoe almost flinched, a short, guilty start at hearing her own thoughts spoken aloud. "Mama said you were dead," she repeated, stupidly.

"Well, I'm not." No anger, just a quiet statement of fact. His hand dropped, and he stared at her like gazing into a mirror, just like she was still gawking at him.

That's rude, Zo. But there was nothing in any manners manual that covered this. "I'm sorry." The same two words that followed her all her life, haunting every corner. "I just...I'm sorry."

"It's all right. Must be a helluva surprise." His right hand twitched, then he offered it, a short natural movement as if they were at a church social. "Truce? And maybe you'd like to come with me? I mean, unless you've got anything you want to stick around here for."

"I..." What did she have, really? Her last paycheck was useless now; she dimly remembered the sound of glass breaking as she pelted out the doors. Nash would absolutely dock her for that; it would make him happy as a clam. "I thought you were a cop."

"No." The blond guy just *stood* there, like it was normal to tell someone you were their long-lost brother with your hand hanging out in the air. "We should probably get out of here, though. Hermann'll drive us to the airport."

Who will do what now? It sounded like a comedy routine, and a jagged laugh shook up out of her ribcage. The guy smiled, uncertainly, and the thought that he might be just as nervous as she was turned out to be powerfully comforting.

"So?" he persisted. "If you've got something to hang around for, we can stay. But Dad's anxious to see you, Zoe. He's never forgiven himself."

That doesn't sound good. Maybe this was some kind of scam? But nobody in Texas knew her real name, and she was poor—like Roy would say, *so po' I can't afford the extra "or"*. Who the hell would want to scam *her*? And he was saying *we*, like he wouldn't go away even if she told him to fuck off and ran again.

Zoe could do a few things regular people couldn't, and it looked like he could, too. Her nose wanted to twitch, all her senses tingling. *Nobody* smelled like this, even Bea. Normal people were washed-out copies made over and over, diluted down to nothing.

"All right," she said. There was nothing else to do, really. Going back to the squat was stupid; he'd probably follow. "But I'm warning you..."

"Duly noted." He didn't move, still holding out his hand. "You've been on your own for a while, looks like."

Oh, if you only knew. Zoe reached out, tentatively, and laid her fingers in his. The sense of familiarity was probably a liar, but it came from the same deep place that had warned her about Royal.

The same instinct had told her *wake up now* the night after Mama's funeral, once Bea had gotten tired of doing...what he did and left her in the cellar with the police-grade handcuffs biting her wrists and tears streaming hot, slick, and unheeded down her face. The same deep place the flames had come from, and the tingle-aching in her wrists as her fingernails turned long and sharp.

Razor-sharp.

If this guy was lying, she'd find out soon enough, and that buried, instinctive knowledge would rise again.

She was very sure about that.

6

A MERCY

A LIMO IDLED AT THE VERY EDGE OF THE PARKING LOT, DRAWING MORE THAN one curious look from shoppers blinking against rainy grey winter light. She'd taken out a chunk of the glass doors at one entrance, and Jack was glad nothing had cut her; he was holding onto the change and his beast with deathly, icy control.

Even his chilly analyst's calm would break like sugarpane if she was so much as *scratched*.

She wasn't quite limping, but one of her boots had lost its entire sole. That would be attended to very soon, but the reminder of what she must have endured living among skins wasn't guaranteed to keep him calm, either. A cluster of orange-aproned employees was busy cleaning up glittering broken door-shards at the other end of the lot, dwarfed by the store's bulk. The skins babbled excitedly to each other and didn't notice her return; he was fairly sure the manager would be on the phone to actual law enforcement as soon as the pheromonal assault of a dominant Kith wore away.

It would take a while. Still, they were in another Kith leader's territory, and Jack never liked leaving any sign if he could help it. He could hope the security cameras were as ancient as everything else in the store, although the anti-shoplifting electronics had been brand-spanking-new.

It figured.

Jack held the limo's door open and his hand leapt to its proper place above her head, making certain his *demie* was protected as she bent, slipping into leather-scented dimness. He wasn't going to relax until he got her home, but it was a relief to settle on the seat beside her, close the door, and glance at the smoked glass partition curtaining Hermann, who had wisely stayed in the driver's seat.

If any other Kith approached her at the moment, Jack might do something...unwise.

"Get us out of here." Each word was edged with Voice, the subsonic rumbles passing through him attempting to hold her natural caution at bay. "How soon can we take off?"

"I suggest Houston instead, sir." Hermann's sleek dark head tilted slightly and the limo dropped into gear, moving smoothly for the east exit. "Bit of a drive, but proper transport's waiting for us there."

Shit. Jack considered this. His twin shivered—she was thin enough to feel the chill, but more likely it was pure shock. And of *course* Angelina had lied to her.

No skin was capable of raising a Kith on their own. What kind of damage had their so-called mother done with this bullshit?

Focus, now. Jack took a deep breath; his *demie*'s scent strengthened, stroking and soothing. He was almost, *almost* beginning to believe he'd found her.

For Hermann to suggest the hour-or-so drive to Houston meant that the retainer's cell phone had buzzed with a high-priority call, and the airstrip on the edge of Marquette wasn't sufficient. Put that way, it was obvious: Trevor Rouje had come himself, and was waiting on the tarmac. He wouldn't set foot on another Kith ruler's lands, but he could certainly stay on a plane waiting for his long-lost daughter, now proved beyond doubt to be alive. It was well within the codes, both the formal agreements governing inter-Kith relations as well as the practical, informal rules.

The Howler's diplomatic corps was probably losing their fur at the moment, though. Not nearly as bad as Fantome's people would be—Nebraska was Plainswalker territory, which was only a minor matter if they hadn't known Angelina was there.

The real thing they'd pay for was provably hiding a *demie*. Well, to be precise, either George Fantome's security was ineffectual because it hadn't caught wind of a stray on his turf, or they'd known and hadn't sent word to the Rouje Pride.

Both were bad looks on a Kith leader.

"Houston it is, then." Jack took care to keep his tone light and easy. The door on her side was probably child-locked, but a fear-maddened Kith could tear through in less than a heartbeat. The subsonic throbbing of Voice soothed injured Kith or calmed nervous ones; he let himself look at her again. "Sorry about the wait, but it's the closest real airport. There's a seatbelt, buckle up."

Seeing his twin was like staring at the sun. Seventeen years of wondering, of aching, of nightmarish solitude, and here she was. His *demie* buckled herself in like every good little girl was trained to, then she huddled on the seat, nervously attempting to look everywhere at once. Her fingernails were brutally short and ragged—maybe she hadn't discovered her claws yet—and those cheap boots hurt his own feet in sympathy.

"I don't even know where we're going," she muttered, and the sharp edge of fear under the words was a taunt all its own.

"Houston, then New York." He was going to have to be very, *very* careful not to unnerve her, to make his own movements as slow and nonthreatening as possible. "How long were you in Nebraska?"

"Too long." Zoe—at least their mother hadn't raised her with another name—knotted her slim fingers, squeezing until her knuckles turned white. "Mama said *your father and brother died in a car accident*. She called it a mercy."

"Did she?" Jack's face felt strange; he was grimacing. "She took you when we were three years old. Dad thought I might have an ear infection, though..." *Kith don't usually get them* was on the tip of his tongue, but instinct warned him against that little tidbit. Did she know what she was? "Though I was fine," he continued. "When we came back from the doctor's Angelina was gone, and so were you. He's been searching ever since, and once I was old enough I joined in."

"I never..." A red light brought the limousine to a stop and she glanced at the door on her side. If she was going to attempt fleeing again, now was a good time. But his *demie*, her blue eyes burning, turned back to him. "I used to lie awake at night, wondering what it would be like to have a brother. A living one." Now she was studying him curiously, and he was probably a bit rumpled. Twelve hours ago he was tracking a Broken in the mouth-wet mugginess of Florida, now he was sitting next to his lost sister. "I used to pray someone would rescue me."

He wondered if his own prayers, alone in the dark, had ever brushed against hers. "Well, here I am." *A little late, but I'll make it up to you. I swear.* "Are you hungry? We can get anything you want. Did you want to stop, you know? Pick anything up?" She didn't even have a purse, and though it was imperative to get the hell out of the Howler's territory...

Well, it hurt to see her so thin and forlorn, blue-black hair working free of a loosening braid and her shirts pulled off-kilter. The disarray made her even more heartbreakingly fragile, though each successive draft of her scent drawn into his lungs was powerfully calming.

Control, Trevor had always said, holding his son by the scruff. *Control is everything, especially when we find her again. You are still alive, that means she must be. You* must *have control, for her and for yourself.*

Dad was right, of course. But now Jack was in the uncomfortable position of wondering whether Trevor Rouje had really believed in her survival—or just *said* he did, to keep his son alive.

She was so thin, so nervous, and she was shaking like a wind-tossed branch. "It's fine." Did she sound despairing, or just resigned? "I travel light."

Apparently. "Good skill to have." *Say something soothing.* Once he got her on the plane, he'd feel a lot better. "This must be a shock."

"Yeah." She blinked several times, swallowed hard. "I, uh—so how long have you been following me?"

"I just flew in today." It had the advantage of being absolutely true; another Kith, if sensitive enough, would smell deception. How much information was too much? The dossier had vanished; it was probably up front with Hermann. "We haven't had much to go on. Angelina kept under the radar."

"It's so weird to hear Mama's name like that." A quick, bright blue glance, gauging his expression. Spots of dull color appeared high on her cheeks.

She wasn't any kind of mother. Look at me. Look at you, for God's sake. "I guess." It was work to keep his pulse controlled; his heart wanted to gallop. "Are you sure you don't want anything to eat?"

"I'm fine." Her shoulders tensed as if she expected a punch; she turned the movement into a supple shrug. Voice was working, smoothing the raw edges of her fear. Hermann was deadly silent in the front, concentrating on traffic. The responsibility of bringing Trevor's missing daughter safely to the pickup point was probably nerve-wracking; he was from the old country, and any failure, conscious or unavoidable, was harshly punished in his original Pride.

Trevor was unforgiving in his own way, but he was also known to be strictly fair. *Mercy,* Dad said, *can always be strained.*

In other words, leaving yourself room to escalate was always proper strategy. It was, Jackson thought with a sour smile, a very good thing Angelina was already dead. "You're doing really well, you know."

"For once." Zoe eyed the front of the limo, her fingers still tightly knotted. "Honestly, I'm just glad to be getting out of Marquette. This town sucks."

Yeah. "It's an hour to Houston, all freeway. We can talk, or just...I mean, whatever you want."

"Okay." She lapsed into silence, turning away and staring out the window. Cars swam by on either side; the sun peered from under a pall of cloud and flushed this slice of Texas with dusty winter gold for a brief few minutes. The silence stretched, thin and anxious as a worn-out *demie* except for the barely heard rumble of Voice, and Jackson settled himself, watching her breathe. He studied her shoulder, the raven-glossy rope of her long braid that had lost its elastic band at the bottom, the nap of her worn jeans. The limo's interior was warm, and according to the skin at the grocery store she worked the night shift.

She had to be utterly exhausted. It wasn't any wonder, with Voice wrapping around her and the terror leaching from her system, that his *demie* fell into deep, unnerved silence, glancing guiltily at him at intervals as if expecting sudden violence.

Which made him wonder about a *lot* of things.

7
PEACE AND QUIET

It wasn't like Zoe to relax where anyone else could see. But the car was warm and he didn't jabber at her, probably conscious of his own utter impossibility. The silence was full of a restful thrumming, wheels on pavement—it had been a long time since she was in a car instead of a bus, or just plain walking. Miles slipped smoothly away underneath her, easy-peasy, and the slick-haired driver wore a dark suit and tan leather gloves like in the movies. Tiny sneaking glances at the guy next to her—her brother, he said, and he knew Mama's name—always returned the same information.

Blond, dark eyes, good suit, heavy gold watch, red ring. He just... sat there, calmly, like this was a regular Thursday for him. A limousine, a driver, getting on a plane, New York.

Sure.

Life was all about adapting, but Zo figured an event like this would give anyone trouble. She eyed the door—it wouldn't be hard to unlock. She might survive a fall onto the freeway at seventy-plus miles per—or however fast they were going, since nobody obeyed the speed limit, especially in Texas.

It was a minimum, not a ceiling.

Someone would eventually get the padlocks off her door in the squat. Whoever it was would be awful disappointed, only gaining mildew-spotted books, a neatly folded pile of secondhand clothes, burned-down candles, her hairdryer, and a brush for their trouble. No jewelry, no money, no papers. Her purse had a handful of change in it, plus cheap ChapStick, a comb, and an extra pair of socks; now it would sit in the employee locker until someone took a bolt cutter to *that* lock too. Her Martha Smith ID was tucked in her pocket, along with the princely sum of eleven dollars in cash.

If this *was* a scam, they were going to be sorely disappointed in their victim choice. Unless they wanted to turn her out or something, but she'd escaped Royal. A richer version of Roy Petterson, even fast and strong enough to catch an exhausted Zoe after a long night-stocking shift, wouldn't be much difficulty.

But what if this guy was telling the truth? His eyes were just like Mama's, and he even knew Angelina's name. The signs started announcing Houston, counting down the miles, and Zoe found her hands had relaxed. She was drifting, thinking hard, because it was such a relief to have some peace and quiet.

"I'm sorry." There it was again, those two stupid words she had to repeat over and over. "I...this is weird, but...Mama never told me your name." The most she'd ever said was *your brother, dead with your father.*

He'd introduced himself, but she hadn't listened. If he was going to be sore about it, she'd know to bolt at the earliest opportunity.

The blond guy stirred. "No worries." No hint of anger in the words, just level calm. "It's Jack, Jackson Arcadius if I'm in trouble. Dad's Trevor, but he'll probably answer to anything that isn't *late for breakfast.* The last name's Rouje—you probably think you're Zoe Simmons, right? That was Angelina's maiden name."

Jackson. Trevor. Rouje. She didn't even know how to spell the last one. She'd never thought to ask Mama a dead man's name. "Jack, huh?" Now it was her turn to offer a hand. "Hi. I'm...well, you know. How do you do?"

"How do you do." His fingers were warm, and he didn't squeeze mercilessly like some men. Nor did he play any weird game, merely giving a couple businesslike shakes before letting go, and his smile was as easy and relaxed as the rest of him.

Sooner or later, men always got angry. Zoe and Mama agreed on that, at least. "Mama said I didn't have a middle name." *Since my father was a demon, right? Or maybe I am.* Which would make this guy demonic as well, but so far Zoe couldn't see any evidence. No speaking in tongues, no levitation, no lighting candles with a glance, not even a whiff of brimstone.

Not that she knew what brimstone was, even; Pastor Bea was always fuzzy on that point. Even with her nose working overtime, Zoe had never managed to smell it.

Of course, there was always the odor of bullshit, in many different forms and strengths. Bea had been full of it.

"Dad can dig out your birth certificate." The blond guy nodded a little, as if the information confirmed a private hypothesis. "Now that Angelina's...well, by now we should have most of the paper trail, how she hid. You can see it anytime you like. But your middle name's Arcadia. Old family name."

"Oh." What else was there to say? Traffic thickened, but the driver always seemed to know when to change lanes. "What about him?" She didn't quite point—it wasn't polite—but she did indicate the partition, with its smoked-glass window halfway open.

Every word was being listened to, and probably weighed.

"Hermann Barbu. Family retainer, been with Dad for ages." Jack leaned forward. "How's it looking up there?"

The driver took one hand off the wheel, lifting two fingers to his forehead as if touching the brim of an invisible hat. He didn't look at the rearview mirror, and his scent was oddly strong as well. "We should arrive in Houston shortly, sir." He had a pleasant voice, an even tenor with an accent dragging at every word. "Please give the young miss my thanks."

"He's old-fashioned." Jack grinned, a gleam of bright white teeth, a distinct warmth to his dark gaze. Mama's eyes had been like that sometimes when she was on her medicine.

But the thought of Mama's drugs, of her yellowed skin and slurred speech, and finally the monsters only Mama could see while the cancer ate its way through her body's cupboards, turned Zoe's stomach upside down. She hoped they'd be near a bathroom soon.

The silence warned her. She'd just drifted into thought, and brought herself back with a jolt. "I'm sorry." Those two awful words, again. "What?"

"It's all right. That guy—the manager—said you work nights. You're probably really tired." Jack deliberately wasn't looking at her, gazing instead at the front of the car.

Imagining Nash dealing with this fellow was a real joy, as Mama would say. "I left my paycheck there." It sounded like she was complaining, and Zoe slumped against buttery leather. She hadn't even known limos had seatbelts, and now here she was, learning all sorts of new things on a Thursday morning.

"We can send someone to pick it up. But honestly..." Jack paused, and of course she'd probably done something rude, because people who drove around in shiny black cars like this and wore custom boots didn't talk about money, ever. If you had to ask you couldn't afford, like Mama always said. "Honestly, you don't have to worry about anything like that ever again."

That could mean a lot of different things. "Oh," she managed, a cautious, propitiating syllable.

"I'm sorry." His profile had turned thoughtful. "I don't know what to say. I've been thinking for most of my life about what I'd do when we found you again, but here I am just...I don't know. Forgive me."

"It's a weird situation." That seemed to cover it, Zoe figured, and she should have been embarrassed. Instead, that strange relaxation was back.

The worst had happened, or just the most outlandish. Either

way, at least she wouldn't have to go back to the Greenfield, or the squat. Her whole life had changed in an eyeblink once more.

Frankly, it was kind of a relief.

8

ALL THE CONTROL

SHE DIDN'T ASK MUCH MORE. THE SILENCE, FULL OF HEAVY SEDATIVE VOICE-rumbles, would be dragging at her arms and legs. She was already tired, and those big bright baby blues held exhausted shadows underneath. Hermann was as good as his word—a little over an hour after leaving Marquette they were slipping through layers of security at George Bush Intercontinental, no ID needed above a certain income bracket, thank you and goodnight. If Jack hadn't guessed Dad was waiting and the Howler more than ready to get them off his pack's patch, the white-glove wave-through would have made it glaringly clear.

It was a miracle Jack's *demie* was still conscious; it pointed to a certain amount of raw willpower. Jack was sure she didn't have his talent for cold analysis—*usanaugh* twins, rare as they were, never shared the same affinity. It was impossible to tell just yet where her own talent lay.

Any of the secondary strengths—jäger, myrmidon, patterner—would be great. Best of all, of course, would be the Sorcerer's Gene. It didn't matter, she was his *demie*, and even if she showed nothing but the ordinary *usanaugh* dominance it would be more than enough.

But he wondered. She was altogether too quiet, not even shifting uncomfortably when the limo nosed between hangars and was waved toward the long white private jet crouching under a lead-colored sky. Houston didn't get much snow, but between Thanksgiving and Christmas it was an open question.

Dad was going to go nuts with the presents this year. There would probably be a mountain of brightly wrapped packages for every day she'd been gone, let alone year.

His twin stirred, seeing the jet, and glanced at him. She should have been somnolent, almost liquid, but instead she was tense and ready, her shoulders rigid and her cheeks drained of color.

God help me. He couldn't stand that look on her face; he was a goner already. "You ever flown before?" Maybe that was the problem. Jack bent slightly, peering out the window as if he shared her apprehension. A spatter of sleet touched the glass.

"Never." She shifted uneasily. "We always took the bus, Mama and I. But I wonder..."

"Wonder what?" *Ask me for something. Anything.* If she had a phobia he'd see about driving her north. It might even be enjoyable, but the paramount thing was to ease her fear.

She should never, ever look so frightened, or so lost.

Was this what other *demi*s felt? It wasn't spoken of, even by laid-back, dark-haired Dimitri who sometimes tried to ease a fellow *demi*'s agony, but there were hints in some of the old histories. Less than an hour in his twin's company, and Jack was ready to tell even Trevor Rouje to go fuck himself if it would make her less afraid.

She shifted again, anxiously. "Uh, this is all very nice, but...is there a restroom nearby?"

Oh. "Yeah, on the plane. As soon as we get aboard we can get you sorted out, all right? And look." Maybe it would distract her. "Top of the stairs. He can't wait to see you again."

A hatch yawned at the head of the temporary metal staircase wheeled up to the plane's side. In the mouth-shadow a mane of bright hair showed, its wave rigidly controlled, along with a hint of a plain but exquisitely tailored grey suit very much like Jack's own. The golden gleam was a ring on the man's right hand—the great Rouje signet with its vertical red catseye flaw, heavier than the heir's ring on Jackson's own third left finger; hers would be redone as soon as they could get her size. It had been locked in a safe at the main house, waiting for twenty years to glitter on a *demie*.

On his very own long-lost *demie*.

She leaned close, peering out his window, and the edge of her body heat married to a draft of her scent hit him hard. He hadn't truly sweated bringing down last night's Broken, and catching one skinny, exhausted Kith girl who probably thought she was a skin was nothing. But now salt moisture gathered under his arms, at the small of his back, behind his knees.

The girl had no idea of her power. "He..." Little Zoe retreated to her side of the seat, the shoulder-strap of her seatbelt wrinkling the green and yellow plaid shit. "That's him?"

"Couldn't wait to see you, so he flew down." Jack was trying to smile normally, hoping it wasn't a grimace. "Don't worry, all right? He's not very scary." *Not to you, at least.*

"I'm not ready for this," she muttered. Her hands were back to tangling together, graceful fingers clutching hard. "God." The faintest suggestion of a guilty flinch, and Jack was praying the control their father had insisted on would hold up.

"It's going to be all right." His throat was dry. "I promise." *And if it's not, I'll make it all right.*

A single hour in her company, and he was already giving unrestricted promises. It was flat-out dangerous.

She didn't reply. But she also didn't sneak a look at the door-lock on her side, and she obediently undid her seatbelt when he did, Hermann bringing the limousine to a feather-soft stop. Jack could still feel the buzzing of highway travel in his bones.

Or maybe it was, simply and solely, her.

9
TINY TOY

CLIMBING SLIPPERY METAL STAIRS UNDER FITFUL SLEET WITH ONE OF HER shoe-soles gone was another *real joy*, as Mama would have said. But there was no way out, and besides, this was a private plane. An honest-to-gosh jet, and the thought of how green Pastor Beaton would turn with envy, or how Royal would salivate over a trip in one of these, or how any of Bea's congregation would nudge each other and whisper behind cupped hands—well, it was almost hilarious.

Unfortunately, the world had taken on a strange wavering underwater quality, after a full stocking shift, the fact that Zoe hadn't eaten since before midnight, and sheer terror married to successive surprise-crashes like ocean waves.

Not that she'd ever seen the sea, despite Marquette being a single bus ride from the Gulf. But Zoe had seen videos, and could imagine.

"I'm sorry about your shoes," her new brother said behind her, and he really did sound regretful. A man in a black uniform suit with a weird pillbox hat was standing by the limousine talking to the driver, who had his leather-gloved hands folded before him as he nodded. The driver didn't smell normal at all—not as vivid as Jack, but not as washed-out as normal people either.

"It's okay," she managed. The anxiety in her demanded motion, escape; she used to run across flat prairie during lightning storms, daring God to hit her the way Bea thundered sinners were always struck down. Once she'd even done it during a tornado warning, the sirens stitching a bruised, yellowgreen sky. "I'm used to it."

"I could carry you."

A forlorn laugh tried to jolt its way free of her throat. The top of the stairs was approaching very quickly, and cold wind fingered her hair. There was a lot of wide-open space—well, it was Texas, and this was an airport. She'd thought flying involved security checks and baggage, but maybe it didn't matter because she had nothing.

Nothing except eleven dollars and a fake ID, that was, and she was about to see her father for the first time. Well, the first time she was old enough to remember.

Was that why her legs were trembling? They had good reasons to shake, really; what if this shadowy man didn't like her? What if she said something stupid and messed it up? What if he gave her a once-over, from boots to her tangled hair, and decided she wasn't worth the trouble? What if—

"Zoe?" Jack didn't sound upset, but she'd stopped midway up the stairs, clutching at the cold, skinny metal balustrade. There was a roaring in her ears, the same sound that filled them when she curled into a tiny ball and let the world go on without her.

Sometimes it was the only way to survive. And now she wondered who exactly had found her for these people, just how she'd made a mistake and left a trail. She'd been so *careful*, always paying cash, living below the radar, no real identification, nothing that could...

Her lungs refused to work. Soft black flowers bloomed in her peripheral vision, and the shaking had her like an excited dog with a tiny toy. It was no use, she couldn't get away, she was trapped on these stairs just like she'd been trapped all her life.

"Zoe?" His voice came from very far away. "You're radiating. It's all right. Calm down."

Oh, that's not gonna happen, Zoe Simmons—except that wasn't even her real *name*, apparently—thought, right before she crumpled into unconsciousness.

10

MORE THAN READY

Trevor Rouje exercised stringent control as a matter of course— his beast was powerful, extremely dominant, and he was the undisputed ruler of a Pride controlling much of the eastern U.S. seaboard, not to mention stretching inland. If he hadn't been cunning, strong, and savagely patient, he would never have survived.

For him to drop everything and rush onto another Kith ruler's territory, even without setting foot outside the plane, was unprecedented. But a daughter, especially a *demie*, was the most precious thing a Kith could have.

Jack's boots rang against wet metal strips that passed for stairs; he cradled his twin's limp, unconscious body. Zoe's braid hung over his shoulder; her scent would wash lesser Kith into submission like Dad's and his own. But amid that strength was a sheet of devouring sadness, anxiety, and something that wasn't strictly terror but close enough to raise Jack's hackles. His claws wanted to spring free, the crackle in the bones of his hands not quite audible.

Not to skin ears, at least. "Hello, Dad." There was just a touch of Voice to the words, enough to make them stand up for counting.

"Hmmm." A low rumble of controlled impatience. His father

stepped aside, into the belly of the jet. Despite visible impatience, he gave his son plenty of room.

Which was wise.

Inside, there was thick wine-red carpeting and pristine white upholstery, gleaming polished wood and the peculiar smell of a place that often lived under pressurized air. Jack laid Zoe on a couch and considered the seatbelts.

If she woke up disoriented and tied down, she might panic. She'd had a helluva morning.

And right now, he needed a goddamn drink. "Care for some rum, sir?" Easy, bored, he'd perfected the tone long ago. *Smile like it feels nice when the knife goes in.* The tension in his shoulders kicked up another notch as the words rumbled, his Voice-hold on her firm and complete; she didn't stir.

He was surprised she hadn't passed out before this, frankly.

"Too angry to drink just yet." A basso rumble; Trevor stalked to the intercom box. "We're almost ready, Markham. Hermann should be along soon."

No reply was necessary, or expected. Trevor hit the switch again and turned, examining Zoe. She moved restlessly, curled on her side. Her thin cheeks and ragged fingernails were all too evident. "So this is my daughter, my lost child." He approached cautiously, then crouched with quick, feral grace next to the couch, peering at her wan face. "Who would have thought, so close all this time. Why didn't Angel run further, I wonder? Was she more cunning than I expected, or did I simply overestimate her?"

So Dad wanted to test his son under conditions of high stress. The plane began thrumming with preflight preparation; soon they'd be in the air and that would do everyone involved some good. Jack poured himself a generous measure of brandy, downed it in a gulp, poured another. His back prickled—*somebody near her, someone with teeth.* "Dad," he said, conversationally, "you'll frighten her if she wakes up, and if you do, she may change. She's ripe for it."

"Point taken." Dad didn't move. "But you have a good hold on her. She won't wake until you let go." Still, the reminder leached some essential tension away.

Jack squashed the desire to insist Dad *back the fuck away from her*. It would be a long time before he could allow anyone else near his *demie* with any semblance of calm, but he *had* to, so he kept a tight grip on his beast and his own temper. "It took the entire ride here to get her sedated." And for all that, she'd collapsed on the steps, probably overwhelmed to the breaking point at the prospect of meeting a father she'd never known. "As for Angelina, it was overestimation." Amber alcohol glowed in the glass; he considered hitting from the bottle, even though it wouldn't do a damn thing. "Time enough to figure that out later. What I'm more concerned about is why my *demie* ran so hard, and so successfully. And just who she's so goddamn afraid of."

It was an elementary guess. You didn't hide like she had if you felt safe; you especially didn't take off through a glass door. She hadn't hesitated, just fled.

What had Angelina done to her?

"Skin, or otherwise?" Trevor's voice was quiet, restful, a deceiving purr. He was coiled tight as a watch-spring.

"I don't know if a human could inflict so much fear." Jack turned, leaning easy and hipshot against the bar, and regarded his father. He knew his eyes would be burning-bright, glittering, because his father's were. The air crackled and shifted uneasily between them. "I suppose it's possible, if she didn't fight back."

Father and son gazed at each other for a long moment before Hermann climbed the stairs and attended to the hatch closure. "Good afternoon, sir. Everything's handled, and the Howler sends his regards." The retainer conspicuously did not even glance at Zoe, looking at the floor instead.

"Well done, Hermann. Come on over and have a drink." Jack forced himself to smile, but closed-lip, no teeth to make anyone nervous.

Zoe stirred, her fingers twitching. The air thickened even more.

Their father stared quizzically at her, a peculiar mixture of tender-ness and concentration on his familiar face.

Jack realized he must be wearing the same expression. He firmed his hold, a deep subvocal growl, and she slipped back into uncon-sciousness—a respite from sheer exhaustion and what had to be a goddamn overwhelming situation.

"I remember her as a baby," Trevor said, softly. "Once we're airborne, you can let her wake. Or not, she looks like she needs the rest."

You don't say. Jack didn't let the sarcasm loose. It wasn't a good idea.

Hermann approached the bar; Jack poured him a generous dollop of his preferred whiskey. The sleek-haired retainer nodded his thanks and sipped, showing no emotion. Still, it was possible to tell he was pleased—participating in an event of this magnitude showed his usefulness to the Pride, and he was nervous about such things.

The old country had not been kind to him. Or to his mate Amelia.

Trevor's Voice rumbled into life, adding another layer to the sonic blanket over one exhausted Kith girl. *I'm not ready for this*, she said mournfully, but still went along, obedient until the moment her legs failed.

Either she'd been beaten into submission, or she was so desperate even this strangeness seemed better than what she'd endured so far. Both prospects were maddening, and Jack had to take yet another deep breath. Hermann would give a report on his reac-tions in the car, of course; any member of the Pride was Trevor's eyes and ears when it came to his unpredictable, half-crippled heir.

Except now, between one moment and the next, the dragging weight had vanished. Jackson Rouje was fully functional for the first time in seventeen-plus years. This girl—her mouth finally relaxed and a shadow of what she might look like when she wasn't stiff with terror peering through—would make him the heir in truth. An unse-cured *demi* was untrustworthy; with her next to him, Jack could finally, at long fucking last, take his proper place in the Pride.

He was more than ready. And it looked like she had no skin friends or false "family" to get in the way; if Angelina was still alive, they might still be looking all over the globe for Trevor's escaped wife and getting exactly nowhere.

Nebraska, for God's sake. And the records showed involvement in that silly little cultlike church with its scamming pastor, because of course Jack and Zoe's mother had been a *religious* woman.

He tried to imagine growing up a Kith surrounded by fanatic-bigot skins, confused and utterly alone, and for once, his imagination failed him.

"You're angry too." Trevor unfolded, and his bright blue glance was very much like his daughter's. "What does she know?"

"Almost nothing. And if a situation ever called for anger, Dad, finding your *demie* in rags working a shitty little supermarket job and afraid of every passing shadow does." He exhaled sharply, tossing back the second brandy and relishing the sting. A Kith-fast metabolism meant goodbye to drunkenness, but the momentary bite was pleasant and the habit lubricated all sorts of social interactions. "She ran for three years once Mommy Dearest was gone, staying under the radar, and came with me because she's got nowhere else to go. I mean, just look at her."

"At least she's safe now, and that's one worry shelved. Because they've—" Trevor cocked his head, and a moment later the intercom gave a pleasant chime.

"*We'll be ready for takeoff soon, sir. Please buckle in and make sure everything is properly stowed.*" Markham was always uncomfortable giving orders to higher-ranked Pride, but there was no help for it in this particular situation. At least stratification wasn't as severe as it had been even fifty years ago.

There simply wasn't room, in modern times. *Adapt or perish* was the cardinal rule.

With a Pride leader and her *demi* rumbling, there wasn't a chance of the returned prodigal waking up. Jack made sure she was well secured before settling himself on the couch near her head, wrapping one hand in her long dark braid. The contact sent waves of warmth up his arm, taking a break in his shoulder and spreading in a haze through his chest. Dad saw it, of course, but said nothing, and takeoff was accomplished with a minimum of fuss.

It should have been a relief, but Jack was uneasy.

At least she's safe now, and that's one worry shelved. Because they've...

He didn't want to think about what Trevor had been about to say.

11
WEIRD ENOUGH

THERE WAS A TRICK TO WAKING UP BUT NOT LETTING YOUR BREATHING change, and it was one she'd practiced for a long, long time. Mama was easy enough to fool, Bea slightly more difficult, and Royal, of course, had considered all women stupid and cunning at once.

The dumbshittery of claiming to believe both things at the same time never occurred to Roy. It might have interfered with his absolute conviction that he was the smartest man on God's green earth, and *that*, of course, could not be borne.

Zoe wondered if he'd been able to get to the hospital in time, or if he'd called 911 and paramedics had stopped the bleeding. Maybe these people could tell her—they'd tracked her, which meant they *had* to know about him.

And about Bea. Right?

She lay on her side, deep waves of unfamiliar relaxation spilling through her. It was relatively comfortable, except for the deep mechanical thrumming married to a drilling whine. There was a strange floating sensation, too; they were moving.

Plane. I'm on a plane.

It was her first flight, and she hadn't even been awake for takeoff. Had she passed out on the stairs? *Typical*, Roy would sneer.

She hated thinking about him. How long had she been out? What were they doing at the Greenfield right now? Poor Steve, he'd warned her and she'd been caught anyway.

Whether or not being caught was a good thing remained to be seen.

Voices. *Male* voices. Her hearing was sharp, and they weren't making any attempt to be quiet.

"...cleaned up in Miami." A smooth, resonant voice, clipped and cultured, what Bea would have called *big city*. "Good work, by the way."

"Thank you." This one was Jack; how could she recognize him so quickly? Still, they'd spent a whole hour-plus car ride together, even if most of it had been silent. "She'll want to see the paperwork. Didn't even know her own middle name."

"Surely Angelina told her something?" It wasn't the driver, either; this voice had to be...him. The father. *Her* father, if they were telling the truth. Her nose untangled several layers of scent—Jack's, the driver's, and another male, big and blond and forceful, bright and vivid like normal people weren't unless temporarily in the grip of high emotion.

Her nose was busy, returning impressions of leather upholstery, the slightly oily whiff of maleness, a tang of alcohol—someone was drinking, maybe they'd get angry soon—and faint tangs of after-shave, a certain staleness of recycled air.

How hard was it to get out of a plane? Zoe didn't know. The fall didn't worry her, but the sudden stop at the end was an entirely different story.

"That you were dead. And me too." Jack, again. Sound of shifting cloth, paper moving. "Car accident."

"Well, the woman never was very creative." The older man sighed. "My poor little girl. She tried to run?"

Jack sounded like he was smiling. "As if I was a bill collector."

"Must've been your tie." Amusement colored the older man's

tone, too. "So, she thought she was an orphan, and survived on her own. Smart, and brave. I couldn't be prouder."

Was he talking about *her*? The mangy little brat who couldn't do anything right according to Bea, the cross her mother had to bear? *Amber, you little bitch*, Royal would fume. Zoe hadn't ever felt smart, or particularly courageous.

It wasn't *brave* to be scared to death, hiding in corners and garbage-filled squats. A smart girl would have figured something else out by now, something better, and not been caught.

And what if these people had made a mistake? But Jack knew her first name, her *real* name, and Mama's too. Apparently there were papers, though those could be forged.

Who would bother to fake papers for her? She was a nobody. And she'd probably made a bad impression by passing out like a junkie on a nod.

Very slowly, very cautiously, Zoe let her eyelids drift up. The world was a bright smear, sunshine falling through funny windows with rounded corners. There was the impression of space, and she was on something soft—well, soft-ish, and what had to be real leather stuck to her flushed cheek.

The fake stuff was sweatier, and she should know. Royal's apartment had been full of it.

God, I hate thinking about him. Cut it out. She let her eyelids fall mostly closed again, a tiny careful subterfuge. The seatbelts on this couch were unbuckled; one lay over her hip, loose and easy.

The carpet was deep wine-red; there were white and cream blobs that resolved into seats, a chrome-trimmed shape that looked like a counter, two darkish blots with wide shoulders and golden smears at the top. Two blond men, then, at what looked like a bar. A slight liquid sound—someone pouring a drink.

"Of course," Jack said, quietly. "Brave enough to go right through a fence and across a freeway if I hadn't managed to catch her. Strong-willed. And yes, highly intelligent—she was asking all the right questions, looking at all the right things."

They can't be talking about me. But there was no brassy edge to the scents that would mean a lie.

"When she wakes up..." The older man now sounded a little wistful. "Do you think she'll be disappointed? We didn't find her soon enough. I won't forgive Angelina, and I might not ever forgive myself either. *Nebraska*, of all places. And wherever she went after that."

"If she's disappointed, we'll work on making it up to her." One of the grey-suited shapes made a swift, sharp motion, instantly controlled. Zoe peered through her lashes, keeping her breathing slow and even. Could they hear her pulse, the way she could often hear the heartbeats of others? "Lot of birthdays and Christmases to catch up on; I was thinking about that earlier. I'll move back into the main house. Maybe she'll want to go to school." Jack paused. "I don't even know what she likes."

I like not being beaten. I'm pretty fond of not being yelled at, too. Anything else is just a cherry on top. She didn't stir, listening intently.

She had a brother. A real live one. And a father too. And they had a private jet, of all things.

Maybe it was a rental? But why would anyone go to this kind of trouble for her? And they were going to New York, or so the younger man said.

"There's time to find out," her father said, quietly. More paper moved, sly little whispers. "She's safe now."

God, Zo hoped *that* was true. Maybe all she had to worry about was the inevitable disappointment when they realized how small, scared, and stupid she really was.

Not like that was any better, but still. The need to move tingled in her arms and legs, and she really had to find a bathroom soon.

"We'll land in about an hour," her father continued. "Maybe we should wake her up?" It wasn't often Zo heard a guy, especially an older one, sound outright tentative. "But she looks so tired."

Zoe let her eyelids close completely, escaping into darkness. Her clothes were all rumpled, and her boots were gone. Her feet were defenseless, just one filthy sock on the left and a relatively clean one on the right. Starting from nothing meant the only direction to go was up, right?

Pastor Bea always said that, right before he set out to grind someone deeper than bedrock.

One of the men was approaching. Zoe produced a hopefully creditable impression of waking, pushing herself upright and trying not to stare wildly at the looming shape.

"Hey." It was Jack, and he sank into a graceful, nonthreatening crouch, blond head tilted and dark eyes warm. "Hi, Zoe. You're safe. We're in the air, about an hour from New York. We might have to circle before landing, though. How are you feeling?"

Hungry. Tired. Fucked-up in the head. "F-fine." It was her other mantra, right next to *I'm sorry.* "I'm fine." Zoe couldn't help it; she looked past him.

The slick-haired driver was behind the chrome-edged wooden bar, rubbing a wineglass with a snow-white cloth. On the near side, though, there *he* was.

Her father. Tall, like Jack; his suit was dark grey, and sharply creased in all the right places. He wore wingtips instead of Jack's boots; they were mirror-shining and had thicker soles than the ones she'd seen on rich businessmen while bringing drinks to customers at Royal's club. The older blond man set down a squat glass with a trace of amber liquid clinging to its interior—rum, she thought, catching a hint of spice in the alcohol-tang—and regarded her with bright, paralyzing blue eyes.

Eyes like hers, just a shade or two darker.

A long patrician nose, high cheekbones, a trace of gold-edged stubble. He was older but hadn't run to fat; the high-gloss finish of money hung on every inch of him. His heavy gold-and-silver watch looked antique; Royal might have known the brand. And that gold ring with its dark, red-tinted stone should have looked like a mobster's crackerjack prize, but it didn't.

On his broad, tanned hand, it seemed completely natural. He

looked like he spent a lot of time outside; he wasn't orange from a UV booth.

You should be glad he's dead, Mama had said over and over again. *He was a beast; I saved you from Satan. Don't ever forget that.*

But Mama had also let Bea do...what he'd done, and when she was on her medicine she said even stranger things. Morphine *was* a medicine, Zo knew as much, but shooting up for years before the cancer ever appeared was more a junkie's move. Still, it was Bea who got the vials and works for Mama before hospice care, probably because he wanted her to stick around.

Mama was good for the church since the old ladies loved her; she stuck around because she was getting older and besides, he had the medicine. All addicts, whether they were on morphine or power, liked easy access to their score. Even Royal tried the same thing on his prize girls, or at least the one or two who looked likely to get away.

He hadn't tried that shit with the girl he knew as 'Amber', but Zoe had realized it was only a matter of time.

She studied the man somberly, hoping he wasn't going to get irritated at her scrutiny. He returned the favor, holding her gaze— not aggressively, though now she knew why Mama was always saying *don't look at me like that, you've got the devil's eyes.*

A deep inexplicable instinct—the thing that saved her in the church cellar and that last terrible night in Royal's apartment, not to mention kept her moving restlessly, avoiding notice—suddenly relaxed inside her, a rubber band stretched so hard and for so long the sudden slack was almost painful.

"Oh," she said, as if he'd spoken. "I know you."

"You do," he agreed gravely. He didn't move, though. "You recognized my voice before you were born, you know. When you learned to walk, you were always dancing. And always laughing, too."

I don't remember. It felt like forever since there had been anything to laugh about. "Trevor," she said, testing the word. "Trevor Rouje, right?"

"Yes. And you're Zoe Arcadia Rouje, my daughter." He'd gone eerily still, and so had Jack, though the driver kept polishing glasses. It didn't look like they needed it, but maybe he was nervous. "Your mother took you when you were three years old. She fled while I was at the pediatrician's with Jack; she said she was afraid he had an ear infection. She planned your abduction for a while."

I rescued you from Satan. Remember that.

Zoe was pretty sure she shouldn't repeat what Mama said about this man, and especially not the more outlandish things. This was already weird enough. So she swallowed hard, and tried to find something reasonable to say.

"I, uh, I don't want to be rude, but are you sure? Because honestly, I'm nobody. My mother was Angelina Simmons, but that's a pretty common name, right? I just..." She shot a quick glance at Jack, but he just stayed there, like it was super normal to hang out in a crouch on a plane hurtling through the atmosphere. "I don't want you to be disappointed," she finished, lamely.

"I'm very sure, and I am not disappointed. Here." He reached for the bar, and gathered up a sheaf of papers. There were two manila folders, a thick expanding file, and some fluttering-loose sheets. "You can look through these, it's all here. Once some man in Nebraska filed for her death benefits, we began tracking and tracing."

"Bea," she said. "Pastor Richard Beaton, right?"

"That's what he was calling himself. It appears that originally he was plain old Leroy McFisk from Boothe, Nebraska." He said it like it was no big deal, too. "The IRS is quite interested in him, especially after it also appears he burned his own church down."

Leroy? Oh, man. No wonder he changed his name. "The IRS?" The tax police were the only thing Bea really seemed to fear. It was official, Zoe *was* feeling the desire to laugh now.

They were blaming him for the fire, too? That was kind of close to the truth, but...oh, if there was a God, Zoe was going to hell both for whatever she'd done and for finding some part of this funny as shit.

Maybe this golden-haired man really was the devil, and at the other end of this flight she'd find out what brimstone really smelled like.

"He's been running the church scam for a long time," Jack said. "Church of the Righteous Savior was just the latest iteration, and Angelina was pretty clearly his accomplice at some point. They—are you sure you want to hear about all this now?" His dark eyebrows raised, slightly, and Zoe was suddenly aware that if she didn't find a bathroom soon, she was going to be even more embarrassed than a pair of falling-apart boots and a lack of ID could ever make her.

"Uh, okay. Can I...is there a restroom?" *I think I'm going to scream.*

"Right there." Jack pointed down the tube of the plane to a door that looked like actual wood, instead of the closet-type plastic deals you saw in movies. "Take your time. We'll have new shoes for you when we land."

Oh, gee, really? The urge to be sarcastic, to poke and prod and find out just how bad it would be when these men lost their tempers, was overwhelming. It was the same impulse that had driven her to set Royal off, but it didn't come from the same place.

Roy had deserved disdain, or outright contempt. These people were *scary*. But the truly terrifying thing was that instinctive, deep feeling of safety.

She didn't trust it. At all.

"Thank you," she managed, rocketed to her feet, almost overbalanced, and scrambled for the bathroom, avoiding Jack's outstretched hand.

12

A FAIRYTALE

HIS *DEMIE* PERCHED ON A SPINNING STOOL AT THE BAR LIKE AN EXOTIC BIRD, her nose pink and her cheeks damp. Splashing cold water on your face was supposed to cover traces of weeping, but all it did was make hers more visible. At least she didn't flinch when Jack started taking out papers—certified copies, cover letters, inquiries and bank statements, Xeroxed utility bills and school records from districts Angelina had dragged her through as they wandered the Midwest, finally settling in Nebraska—and arranging them, attempting to treat it like a report for legal counsels who needed to be brought up to speed on a particularly complex case.

She'd also rebraided her hair, though he would have preferred it down. The blue-black strands were pure silk, and the feel of them under his palm during takeoff wouldn't go away.

Zoe politely refused any drink, even water. She had to be hungry, but wouldn't even take a packet of peanuts. Her reticence was understandable, but also maddening.

Still, he had his *demie* in front of him. In the entrancing, soothing, magnetic flesh.

It was the school records which seemed to finally convince her. "Mrs. Barton," she said, touching a bright yellow report card with a fingertip. Her fingernails were still short but not chew-ragged now; the change was just under the surface, working subconsciously. "I remember her."

It was dangerous for a Kith to tap into their beast the first few times without help and the collective pressure of a Pride to keep the guard rails on. "She gave you an 'excellent' in behavior." Jack had a hip hitched on another stool, and Dad had retreated down the bar a bit, speaking quietly to Hermann. Zoe kept glancing at him.

The resemblance between father and daughter was marked, especially around the eyes. Still, she took after Angelina more; their mother must have had something special indeed.

For all the good it did.

"She used to let me color during recess." A somber smile finally brushed his *demie's* mouth, fading swiftly. "I didn't get along with other kids then, and Mama was...well, she was on her medicine by then."

"Medicine, huh?" Jack kept his tone carefully neutral. "After that you guys moved to Montana for about six months. Right?"

"It all adds up. Everything." Zoe's gaze returned to Dad. Did he feel its weight? Every time she glanced at Jack, his nerves gave an electric zing. "And the pictures."

There was the wedding photo, Angelina in a cloud of white lace with a whisper-thin veil over her long ravenwing hair and Trevor in a sharply creased tuxedo next to her; there was a leftover invitation to the ceremony on heavy cream-linen paper. The birth announcements, the pictures of both infants securely swaddled. An old photo of Zoe learning to walk, her arms outstretched as she grinned and Jack toddling in her wake with a fierce frown of determination. Then there was the last photo taken on the clipped, pristine green lawn of the main house, Zoe's dress trimmed with yellow eyelet lace, Jack in tiny trousers and a bright red rugby shirt glowering over her shoulder.

"We have school photos," he said. "Kindergarten in Cedar Falls, here."

It was obviously the same child, but Zoe was no longer smiling. Wide, haunted blue eyes stared from yellowing photo-paper, and she exhaled sharply, as if it hurt. "Yeah, that's where we were. I don't remember it, but Mama sometimes talked about how we had to leave in the middle of the night. She never said why, though."

The intercom chimed; she jumped, letting out a thin, wounded cry.

"*Sir.*" Markham's voice floated from the speakers. "*We're approaching Albany now; please buckle in and make sure everything is properly stowed.*"

Which meant they wouldn't have to circle forever. The pilot was just doing his job, but Jack's urge to tear through a couple bulkheads and rip the throat out of someone who had frightened his *demie* was almost overwhelming.

Zoe stared at him, those blue eyes huge, and she could probably smell the sudden spike of bloodlust.

"That's Markham," he said. "He and Gibbs are good fliers. But it's kind of startling, the voice from nowhere."

"Yeah." She relaxed again, attempting to help him sort the papers. "So. Private jet."

"Yeah." Jackson's hands moved without his direction, collating and straightening. She handed him the exact piece he needed to put the school photos in order, and didn't seem to notice. Trevor drifted closer, and Hermann began checking the drink cabinets, the first step in his landing routine. "Beats flying commercial. I mean, I don't think you'd want to have this conversation with a lot of strangers around, even in first class."

"I guess." Zoe kept handing over the exact papers he needed, and a slight chill walked down Jack's spine. "It just seems...expensive."

Sorcerer's Gene. I'd bet hard money on it. She was already exquisitely sensitive, and any wrong move on his part would probably trigger another wild flight. Given where she'd been living, this must seem like a fairytale.

So. He simply had to make sure it was the right one, play to her expectations. "Don't let that bother you." She was a princess, after all, and what little girl didn't love Cinderella? "Not to be crude, but Dad's got it to spend."

Her unease returned, a thread of sharp acrid yellow in her gorgeous, softly vivid scent. Still, she kept selecting the right papers, handing them over without looking. Of course Dad would notice.

Not much escaped the old man's attention.

"It's well worth it, if it brings my little girl home." Trevor was now at her shoulder, his smile turning almost-diffident. The change from his usual cold, brisk self-possession would probably shock any of the Pride, unless they had daughters of their own.

None of them had a *demie*, except for Bella and Dimitri's mother. Zoe was going to be an object of curiosity for a good long while. It might even drive her into the shelter her *demi* represented.

He'd like that.

"I..." Zoe's gaze flickered to Jack, and he had a moment or two to feel grateful he already meant some kind of safety. "I guess you don't know why she left, do you."

"You might be able to tell us." Trevor was doing his best to sound soothing, and to see the distant, forbidding god of Jack's youth attempting such a tentative approach was stunning in and of itself. "But she was your mother, and I'll try not to speak ill of her. I want to be happy you're returned to us, and focus on learning about you."

Jack of course had his own thoughts on the matter, but now wasn't the time. "That's right," he chimed in. Soft and easy. "Let's get everyone settled so we can land."

She reached out, slowly, and laid her fingertips in Dad's extended hand. "I'm not very interesting."

"I disagree, little dancer. Come, sit down. You've had quite a day."

Jack finished arranging the evidence, and squashed his own unease. His *demie* was safe, and no hint of possessiveness was allowed.

At least, not at the moment.

13
BEST ROOMS IN THE HOUSE

IT WAS LIKE A MOVIE. A FANTASY, OR MAYBE ONE OF THE OLD ROMANTIC comedies Jenny Scarsdale loved to watch on the classics channel. Jenny was back in Hall City with her grandmother, a terrifying leather-voiced woman smoking endless packets of Virginia Slims and displaying an absolute refusal to watch any film made past 1965. Auntie Scarsdale, as everyone called her, was one of Bea's favorites in the congregation, because her donations were regular as clockwork. Zoe couldn't even hold it against the old lady.

Auntie was just lonely, like everyone else.

Jenny had a fetching overbite, a raucous laugh when her grand-mama couldn't hear, and she had agreed with Zoe that Pastor Bea was an oily jackass. She might even have been a friend if Zoe had been able to trust anyone at all, but the night of the fire it was best to disappear without a trace, so Zo had.

Now she almost wished Jenny was able to see this.

Well, not the snowy wasteland around a scraped-clean runway, hangars crouching in the distance, or the idling black limousine—a twin to the one in Marquette, but this vehicle had two seats in the back instead of one, and Zoe's father sat in front of the smoked-glass partition even though it meant he was essentially traveling backward. And of course she didn't think Jenny would want to see the brand-new pair of black Nikes in Zoe's exact size that was somehow brought up the stairs to the airplane's hatch after the stomach-clenching landing was accomplished, every internal organ Zo possessed turning over two or three times and hunger making her head light as a balloon. Not to see yet another freeway on a winter afternoon, the signs different, the light failing, and the bitter cold held outside privacy-tinted windows—it wasn't New York the city, but New York the *state*.

The pretty countryside as the freeway was left behind turned out to be nice, though, and a two-lane country road unreeled under the long black car. Jenny would have certainly enjoyed *that* bit.

The driver—Hermann—was obviously not feeling jet-lagged. The time difference was only an hour, and he seemed to know where he was going.

She couldn't decide whether to call Trevor *Dad* like Jack did, or *sir*, or *Mister Rouje*. So she tried for her best job-interview politeness, listening to stories about what she'd done as a toddler, what Jack had done at various times, how they'd looked for her. *We thought Angelina had left the country*, Trevor said, and Zo could have told them that wasn't an option.

Mama would never have left the States; she thought foreigners were dangerous. Of course, *everything* was dangerous according to Angelina Simmons, especially after she met Bea. Mama's entire life was fear, and it only got worse when Bea didn't give her one of the little vials of medicine.

Of course, once the cancer really took hold there wasn't a shortage. The hospice even called it *palliative*.

Jenny would have liked some of the stories, too. Zoe did her best to pay attention, to laugh in the right spots, to act like she believed all this despite the roaring in her head and the gnawing in her stomach. Then the limousine slowed, and bands of snowy forest on either side pressed close.

The thought that maybe she was being taken into the woods for something like a horror movie occurred to her, but just as her nervousness reached its peak the car crested a slight hill, the trees drew away, and there was a massive house with white columns along its face, a flight of shallow granite stairs leading to giant red front doors covered with a detailed, geometric carving, floodlights twinkling amid shrubbery, gold shining in windows and the house's wings sweeping back like a bird's. The driveway, a pristine black ribbon, circled a dry, glittering icicle-hung fountain and its attendant featureless shrubs buried under white blankets; all around, smooth hillocks of snow showed what had to be more clumps of ornamental shrubbery sleeping for winter.

The house had carvings scattered in its granite facing too, and those columns were something else. Christmas lights glowed, cheerful colors dancing in the warm golden windows as well as along the roofline, and Zoe couldn't help letting out a sigh of wonder.

"Amelia had them put the lights up," Jack said. "Haven't done that since you were taken. I'll bet she sent Lev out for a tree, too."

"Probably more than one," Trevor agreed. He looked pleased, peering out the window. Both he and Jack were singularly unrumpled by the plane ride, their suits still creased in all the right spots; Zoe was the only thing out of place here.

And she knew it, but the house was *beautiful*. Maybe she'd dreamed about it, or maybe she was beginning to believe because the place *felt* familiar, the same way Jack did.

The same way her father did.

"Jack's been living in the carriage house for a while, but maybe you can both stay in the main house?" Their father didn't quite sound tentative, but he looked at Zoe with his golden eyebrows raised, and it never occurred to her to say *no* or even *slow down, I can't handle this*. She nodded, as if it was old hat to be whisked across several states and plonked down here.

The sky was a pall of snowclouds just aching to dump their cargo, and the wind cut right through Zoe's flannel and T-shirt. The steps were scattered with crunchy deicer pellets; she forgot the cold the moment the doors opened and the great foyer appeared, sweeping steps rising along one side like a belle in a huge frothy dress was going to descend them at any moment. The house smelled like beeswax rubbed into old wood, lemon polish, and a mouthwatering tinge of cinnamon from something good just pulled from a hot oven. Zoe's nose untangled more scents—old threads of Trevor, fainter traces of Jack, a few hints of Hermann and others she didn't know yet. It was all impossibly *real*; there was new sap and cedar in the air too, a faint breath of smoke from burning applewood.

The assault was overwhelming, but what caught Zoe's attention was the newel post at the bottom of the stairs, a sleeping caryatid carved in glowing mellow hardwood.

I've seen her before. Zoe stopped dead, staring, and the sense of being in a dream roared over her with terrifying intensity.

"I know you," she murmured, and hunched defensively.

"She probably remembers you, too." Jack didn't tell her she was crazy. He didn't bump against Zo to get her out of the way either, just stood and waited, half out in the cold.

She hurried to step aside. Black and white marble squares glowed underfoot; she hoped she'd wiped the new sneakers enough.

There were other people in the house; she could sense them moving around. But Jack led her up the stairs, Trevor following, and there were entire hallways half-smiling like old friends. Jack kept pointing things out, a running commentary of history she hoped there wouldn't be a test on later. *Right there was where I skinned my knee once, roller-skating. Dad about had my head.*

Down that way is the solarium, it's nice for breakfast. Maybe tomorrow.

That was acquired by our great-grandfather in the old country, hung there ever since the house was built.

The annex is that way; Dad's office is in the other wing.

Getting lost in this place would be easy. How on earth did they heat the whole thing? Snow was kept safely outside crystal-clear

windows shielded by velvet drapes, parquet floors gleamed, paintings in heavy baroque frames watched, and even an abstract sculp-
ture or two in glowing pale marble witnessed her arrival.

*Those are Jolie's. You'll meet her later, she hangs out with McKenna.
Keeps him out of trouble.*

The art was kind of weird, but at least it wasn't naked Greco-
Roman. She might have started blushing.

Finally, halfway down a long hall with wide windows looking
out on a snowy vista she didn't have time to examine, Jack turned to
the right, and swept open a pair of white-painted doors with ornate
silver handles. "And here we are," he said. "Best rooms in the house,
and if I know Amelia, she's had some clothes delivered."

That was the moment most like a movie.

Because it wasn't just a bedroom. It was a what they called a full-
on suite—a sitting room with pale blue velvet upholstery on pretty
baroque-carved birch furniture, a fire in a small cozy granite fireplace, and vanilla-scented candles burning in plain glass holders. For
all the curlicue carving, it was curiously spacious, and the pale fleur-
de-lis wallpaper wasn't overdone at all. There were blank spaces for
more art, but maybe they didn't use this part of the house much.

The actual bedroom held itself hushed and private past another
set of white double doors, a birch four-poster bed with a royal-blue
coverlet and a mound of blue pillows, subtle blue varnish worked
into the hardwood floor, and the bookcases, all neatly dusted,
standing empty sentinel. No fireplace in the bedroom, but a velvet
seat in a huge bay window looked over a snowbound garden
completely enclosed by the house, and there was a French door to an
ice-frosted balcony behind a heavy indigo curtain patterned with yet
more fleur-de-lis in contrasting thread. A walk-in closet big enough
for its own zip code was carpeted in thick cream. Plain white boxes
sat quietly on white-painted shelves, hanging things swathed with
white tissue paper huddled nearby, and there were five candy-
striped shoe-boxes arranged neatly underneath. A white vanity with
a water-clear mirror showed a rumpled, mussed Zoe as she turned

full circle, staring first at the window, then at the massive white armoire. An antique white wooden clock kept analog time on a pretty white-and-silver nightstand, next to a small white cardboard box placed precisely in a circle of golden glow from an ornate Tiffany-style lamp, its bright blue dragonfly pattern in heavy stained glass.

The bathroom was white tile and antique silver fixtures, a big enameled cast-iron tub in one corner and a glassed-in shower—very modern, and likely a recent addition—tucked opposite. The towels were sky-blue or cream—there were even decorative blue soap rosettes in crystal dishes; the liquid handwash was vanilla-scented. Full bottles—expensive shampoo, conditioner, face wash, toner, a whole battery of personal care containers—stood to attention on the white tile counter near the sink; the front of the mirrored cabinet was ajar, showing pristine, unopened toothpaste and a toothbrush still in the packaging, all the ephemera of grooming ready and waiting. Everything was very clean, and while it didn't smell bad there was still a faint breath of disuse lingering under the bright smoky scent of the fire in the sitting room.

"We've guessed at your sizes," Trevor said, glancing in the closet as if he was going to grade an assignment. "But if anything doesn't fit, that's easy enough to fix. The phone on the nightstand should be ready to go, but if it isn't, just let Jack or me know. Your brother's home office is next door and there's a desk for you there too; we'll have a computer for you tomorrow, as well as ID and, well..."

Did he sound, of all things, *nervous*? Zoe hugged herself, her elbows cupped in her hands, and tried to figure out what to say.

"It's been a big day." Jack stood at her shoulder, the edge of his warmth touching hers. "Maybe you'd like to clean up a bit, get changed? There should be sweats in the closet, and when you're ready we can have something to eat. You're probably hungry."

She was starving, but what looked best of all was the big blue bed. It had a slice of inviting shadow beneath, and she was ridiculously tempted to slither under, curl up, and just wait for the whirling in her head to stop.

This was the part of the movie where a montage began, showing the winsome heroine getting accustomed to sudden luxury. But all Zoe could think of was her tiny dark room at the squat. The small pile of books, a scanty stack of neatly folded clothes, and a few other abandoned items standing guard—had someone torn the locks off yet?

They probably didn't know she was gone yet. It hadn't even been a full day.

She had nothing but eleven dollars and Martha Smith's blurred fake ID. Zoe realized the silence had gone on for far too long and hunched defensively. "I'm sorry." Those two stupid, useless words again. "I should...I don't know what to do."

"All right." Jack's palm touched her shoulder. His fingers curled loosely, a kind touch, absurdly comforting. "How about this? You get washed up, and look in the closet for some sweats. I'll be back in about twenty minutes, and we can go down to the kitchen. Amelia will make us something easy, and we can pretend you've been here all along."

But I haven't. She stared at Tre—at her *father*, and if he'd looked anything other than encouraging, his eyebrows up and his smile warm and forgiving, she might have collapsed right there, attempting to sink through the handmade navy throw rugs.

At least the room's not pink. Pink would have been too much. "Okay." She had to clear her throat. Her father nodded slightly, encouragingly. "Okay," Zoe repeated, a little louder. "That sounds like a good plan."

"Jack's excellent at planning." Her father's bright blue gaze—almost exactly like hers, except Zoe could never look so confident, so composed—swung past her to Jack, and he nodded sharply. "We'll have a light dinner; Amelia will be glad you're finally home. You didn't develop any food allergies, did you?"

Mama never believed in those. "No. I just...I don't like onions." Was it the wrong thing to say? *You'll eat what I give you* was the rule at Bea's, and Mama always concurred. And who was this Amelia?

Had her father remarried? Stepmothers were supposed to be dangerous.

"Who does, unless they're grilled over a steak?" Jack let go of her shoulder, a careful loosening. "I know it's overwhelming. Things will seem a little better after some food, you'll see."

They withdrew, the hall doors closing quietly as if on an invalid, and she was left with silence except for the breathing of the fire.

Jenny would have loved this. Mama would've—but Mama had been here, hadn't she? And she'd left, with baby Zoe. She'd never said precisely why, and Zoe had always suspected it had something to do with the nebulous "car accident" that was supposed to have killed her father and brother.

Angelina was always afraid. No, she was *terrified*. But who would ever want to run away from *this*?

There probably wasn't a way to escape. Zo didn't know if she needed to, so she turned in a full circle, taking in the bedroom and waiting for the montage music to start.

It didn't, but that was all right too.

"Closet," she said, and flinched at the sound of her own voice. "First step's the closet. Then you can wash your face."

14

LEASHED

AMELIA SZEGEDY WAS IN HER USUAL SEVERE WASP-WAISTED BLACK, SLEEK auburn hair pulled back and her nails bright crimson. It wasn't polish, it was showing control of the change, especially since she was jäger. Anyone attempting a raid on the Rouje manor might be forgiven for thinking Trevor or Jack the largest danger, but a jäger female was almost unstoppable while defending her chosen territory.

The manor was Amelia's home ground, and she treated it as such. She was, like her mate, from the old country; the two were a package deal.

The vast farmhouse kitchen with its unfinished oak, rough rustic stonework, and sleek silver appliances was warm and cheerful, the breakfast bar polished to a mirror gleam. Perhaps Amelia was nervous, because she sounded almost tentative as she placed a plate of strawberry crêpes before Trevor Rouje's returned girlchild, a snow-white towel draped over her arm as if serving a visiting dignitary. "It is very light," she said, the trace of an accent growing more pronounced with each word. "But I do not know what you prefer, eh? And there is plenty. Eat, eat."

"That's how she says she likes you." Jack settled on the stool to

Zoe's right."She's our housekeeper." *Retainer* was more accurate, but somewhat old-fashioned.

His *demie* had found a grey sweatshirt with a wide ballet neck and a pair of matching pants cinched hard at the waist; both were a little too large. Once she had a few good meals, though, that problem would solve itself. A pair of thick white socks and the black Nikes—of course she'd want something halfway familiar—finished the outfit, and her hair was neatly braided again, though not nearly as tightly as before. A breath of jasmine soap clung to her intoxicating scent, and the trace of warm dampness at her nape spoke of a hurried shower with that gorgeous hair piled high and dry. The little girl would be sleepy-eyed soon, and food would only accelerate the slide toward natural rest.

"Thank you." She was very polite; of course, Angelina had probably trained her to be mannerly. Respectful, obedient little girls were far easier to take advantage of. "I'm sorry, I didn't quite catch your—"

"I am Amelia." The housekeeper glanced at Jack, a swift look to gauge his reaction. "And *you* are so very welcome here, little one. Your father, he is always speaking *when we find my little girl.* And your brother, he is very big mischief, but a good boy. You'll see."

"He seems all right." Zoe touched her heavy silver fork, but didn't make another move toward consumption. "Your accent's very pretty. Where are you from?"

"Oh, the old country. Very bad there, better here. We come to work for Mr. Rouje long ago, let's see, fifteen years? Very quiet house. Always looking for little girl." Amelia clicked her tongue, a familiar sound. "Eat, eat, it will get cold. And *you*, Jackson. I know that hungry look. You start with crêpes too, but peach."

"You know best, Meel." The childhood mispronunciation of her name rolled off his tongue; he couldn't help it, and he elbowed his twin—but very lightly, a single whisper-tap. "Better eat. She gets fierce when you don't."

Amelia rolled her large dark eyes before retreating to the double range—gas and electric, both halves sparkling clean, and strangely that was what seemed to put Zoe at ease.

At least, his *demie* gave a small, forlorn, but real laugh. "It looks so nice. I'm almost afraid to ruin it."

"Best consumed warm," Trevor said from the door, and at least Zoe didn't flinch. "I'm famished, Amelia. Is there any chance of a steak?"

"But of course." The housekeeper all but beamed, pouring crêpe batter. "In just a moment, though. Children are very hungry, and perhaps *fata mica* would like something savory too? Oh, and hot chocolate. Very good for tonight, it will be cold."

"Not all at once." Dad took the stool on Zoe's other side, and she finally picked up her fork. "Jack, I just heard from Caruthers."

Peter Caruthers was temporarily taking point on negotiations with the Plainswalkers while the Pride waited to find out if the stray Kith in Texas was indeed the missing Rouje daughter. Jack suspected the case would now be kicked upward, possibly even to the Amerlanes.

Dad would spare no expense or influence on this matter.

"That's good. How's Pete doing?" Talking business was probably the best way to get Zoe used to hearing things she might not quite understand. Pretending she'd always been here was seductive, and it might even work to ease her over the transition.

"They're being cagey. He says it makes his nose itch; diplomatically speaking, they don't have a lot of room for maneuver." Trevor didn't have to state the obvious—Fantome's people had already offered a formal apology as if they hadn't known Angelina and a Rouje *demie* were on their turf, and yet it was fishy as all hell. The only reason they would have refrained from sending a commission to return such a precious package posthaste was if Angelina had been involved with one of their number on a more-than-casual level. "There's no reason for them to behave like this..."

"...unless they were sloppy, or involved." *And Fantome's not care-*

less. Jack nodded as Amelia flipped a crêpe. "Which rather changes things."

Zoe watched the process of cooking with interest, but her shoulders were tense.

"Not the important things." The leader of a Pride, injured to this degree, was well within his rights to demand reparations. Still, his precious daughter was safely between them, reaching cautiously for the glass of milk Amelia had set out.

For a moment Jack was six years old again, an aching, struggling ball of fury denied his twin. *Strong bones,* Amelia always said, glaring balefully. *You drink that, and no more fussing.*

"So, Zoe," Trevor continued, turning slightly and resting his elbow on the counter. "May I ask you a few questions about your mother? If you'd prefer not to speak, it can wait."

She swallowed hastily, set her glass down, and there was very little of that yellowish fear in her scent—which was good. She also leaned subtly toward Jack, probably unaware of just why she found his presence so comforting on such short acquaintance. "I figured you'd be curious." At least she didn't stop eating, with those exquisite, though starveling, manners. "And...well, it's not like anything can hurt her now. I just wish I knew why she left. It's beautiful here."

So Cinderella likes her new palace. Good. "Wait until spring. You'll like the roses, and the woods. There's the carriage house too—at the end of the back drive, near the creek." How many times had he roamed the manor, burning with need? Showing her every hill and hollow would be a pleasant way to blot out those terrible memories, his beast attempting to slip free of its chain and eat him alive.

He probably wouldn't hunt a Broken again for a long while—not while she was being carefully, gently brought to full knowledge of her status. Ironic, though, that he was now absolutely immune to their fury.

His beast was fully leashed, and he no longer needed an analyst's cold to insulate him. All the energy spent keeping its ire controlled without his twin's soothing comfort could now be redirected.

"It'll probably take me months not to get lost in here." Zoe studied her plate, smiling shyly, and the powerful surge of relaxation spreading from her made even Amelia's steady motion pause.

Little girl *definitely* had the Sorcerer's Gene. Was that why the Plainswalkers wanted to keep her? Not that it would do them any good without her *demi*. A Kith packleader simply couldn't be that stupid; George Fantome was rumored to be both intelligent and vicious.

"You have time." Trevor went still as Amelia slid a plate in front of Jack and returned to her work, moving with swift grace through her undisputed domain. A tumbler also appeared before the Pride's ruler, spiced rum glowing amber. "Your mother was very ill, before you moved to Nebraska?"

"No, we moved, and then..." Zoe paused, clearly choosing her words with care. "She was fine for a few months. But then she collapsed during a service and they took blood at the hospital. I could have told them she was sick; she'd...she'd smelled wrong for a little while." She laid her fork down and looked anxiously at their father, a student wanting to please a possibly harsh teacher. "And she got tired while cleaning. Righteous Savior needed a lot of cleaning."

A burnt-caramel edge of deeper fear invaded her scent. She had little to no control over radiating. What had she suffered without her *demi*, at the mercy of the skins?

"You don't have to talk about it now," Jack said. Softly, but with a touch of Voice behind the words.

"It's a relief." Her hands knotted together in her lap, squeezing brutally hard. "I was never able to talk to anyone before, ever. And after a while, you know, nobody cares. They just want whatever they can get out of you."

She was far too young to know that particular truth. Still, she'd survived on her own—without, apparently, knowing she was Kith, without even knowing what the word *meant*. Of course the Sorcerer's Gene could help her avoid trouble—but it could also invite worse.

Much, much worse.

"Mh." Trevor's soft sound said he agreed. This was a new side to Dad, and one Jack had to factor into any future analysis. "You must have seen dreadful things, living on your own. I'm sorry."

She froze, her slim back under the grey sweatshirt presented all too trustingly to her *demi*. He applied himself to peach crêpes; Amelia's slight approving smile was another novelty.

"I still can't believe this is real," Zoe said, quietly. "This morning —or when I woke up, I guess—I didn't even have electricity."

She had to be exhausted. Amelia had decided Jack needed orange juice; he liked the sting against the peaches.

"There's so much to make up for." Trevor gazed down at her. Amelia turned back to the stove, and there was a hiss. The good smell of seared meat rose—grass-fed, pasture-raised, the flesh wasn't flooded with terror and chemical crap. "Do you like the suite? Is there anything you need? You have only to say it."

"Oh, no." Very cautious, a stray kitten delicately testing a room with one eye to an open door. Her hair glowed, bright-glossy as a crow's wing, in the kitchen's golden light. "It's beautiful. It's more than I've ever had."

If she felt that way about a half-empty suite, she was about to drown in a flood of gifts. Jack was already wondering what she'd stack the bookshelves with, the clothes she'd want, the music she'd like. There were restaurants to take her to, museums to explore, concerts and shows, classes if she wanted college, the garden to wander through on summer evenings, birthday cakes to present, long discussions about growing up, about serious subjects, about nothing in particular...

It was enough to make a *demi* sweat. Dragging her off the seat and demanding she tell him everything, *everything*, wasn't even close to the best strategy.

But he was tempted.

Dad's quiet attention was doing the trick, because she continued speaking, with frequent tiny, graceful movements—glancing up to check Trevor's expression, of course, and the habit led Jack's analysis of Angelina's parenting in a dark direction indeed.

"We were in Hall City about a week before she met Bea—he was the pastor, you know? He invited her to church and made a big deal out of it. Mama liked that the congregation was so nice. I don't think she saw...I think he thought she had money. Is he..." Her tension was palpable now. "The tax people are really after him?"

Oh, they're about to be the least of his problems. Reading between the lines was easy, now. Jack caught the flicker of his father's scorch-blue gaze over her bowed head, and Trevor probably read his son's expression with no difficulty at all. It wasn't the first time, but it had grown to be a less regular occurrence over the years.

"They are indeed," Dad said. "But I promise you, Zoe, you never have to think about that man ever again."

"Not even to testify?" Her thin shoulders hunched afresh; she was used to making herself smaller. "Because of the...because I was there?"

Ah. Is that what you're running from? "If they ask, we'll tell them no." *And set a few lawyers on them.* Jack returned to his plate. "Come on, eat some more. Meel gets cranky if you don't do crêpes justice."

"What if..." Even under heavy fatigue, plucked from everything familiar, and under a double rumble of Voice from a Pride leader and her *demi*, she still resisted. She was strong.

And that was *very* good news.

"Rare." Amelia had a plate for Dad, and in a trice there was silverware and linen too. "Fresh slipper-bread, just baked today? The potatoes will take a short while longer, if you want them. But you, young miss, must have some hot cocoa. There is perhaps pasta I could make, if you do not like the strawberries?"

In other words, the housekeeper thought questioning his *demie* could wait, and while Jack bristled at a retainer's daring, it didn't outweigh the fact that she was in this case undoubtedly right.

"You made *ciabatta*? Oh, Amelia." Trevor's attention seemingly swung to his own food, though he was certainly aware of Zoe's every slight shift, weighing her responses. "You spoil us. I don't suppose—"

"Horseradish." She had the small glass jar and its matching silver spreader ready. "But of course. Eat, eat."

"See?" Jack didn't have to hide his amusement. "Food is serious business around here." *Along with everything else.* "I advise you to just do as she says, Zo. Then we can make sure your phone's working, and you can get some real sleep."

"All right." And the little girl did her best, of course. The smartphone would reassure her—it was, after all, a window to the outside world.

Jackson didn't think she'd want to look out for a while, though. And by the time she did, it would be too late.

15
ANONYMITY

A WINTER WONDERLAND PRESSED AGAINST THE WINDOWS. THIS NEW BED was just soft enough, and she didn't have to keep an ear peeled for strangers in the squat's cold brooding pile. There were no sirens, no traffic, just a sough of ice-laden wind while she was warm and snug. Zoe wasn't even hungry; Amelia had insisted on making plate after plate of crêpes. It had been a long time since fresh fruit was an option, and even more since she'd had a full stomach.

Yet Zo couldn't relax, even though she was so fatigued her right eyelid was twitching. It was, she decided, *too* quiet.

The sleek silver phone was absolutely brand-new, the first one she'd ever had—Royal's burners for his girls didn't count. Jack walked her through changing the passcode and thumb-lock, even. They didn't say anything about making her pay for it yet. It was much faster than public computers at the library, and already loaded with Jack's numbers—work, private, office, and with Trevor's as well.

Dad, she reminded herself. The word was weird; Pastor Bea always wanted to be called Father. Some of Royal's girls called him Daddy, but 'Amber' had resolutely stuck to just plain old Roy.

Now she had a father who might even answer the phone. *All our numbers so you can always get hold of us, and Amelia's and Hermann's too,* Jack said.

So far her brother was the best thing about this. The deep sense of comfort, of familiarity in his presence, was well-nigh irresistible. Neither he nor Trevor seemed prone to anger, though of course plenty of men were nice enough in the beginning. Amelia was all right too—apparently she wasn't a stepmother, but married to the chauffeur.

Which solved one worry. There didn't seem to even *be* a step-mother; Trevor hadn't mentioned remarrying or dating.

Zoe stared at the phone's glowing screen. It connected to the house's wi-fi just fine. Maybe there was a keylogger on it, but they couldn't be mad if she was curious, could they?

At least she didn't have to ask how to spell her new--or old, depending on how you looked at it—last name; *Rouje* had been on the birth certificate. Searching for their father brought up interesting stuff.

The term *multimillionaire* was used, and *reclusive*, too. Despite that, there were stories about charitable foundations and donations —mostly to wildlife and conservation groups, it looked like. Jack was mentioned a few times too, and there were pictures of both of them at gala functions, surrounded by people in expensive clothes. Assorted companies and corporations were listed—a little bit of everything. Clearly they were doing just fine.

Angelina had always told Zo business was filthy and money the root of all evil. Both could be true, but as far as Zoe could tell cash was also indispensable, and if you didn't have it people who *did* could do whatever they wanted to you. Filthy lucre was, as far as she could figure, necessary for self-defense.

For all that, Angelina wasn't mentioned except once as an "estranged wife" in a very old article scanned from some archive's microfiche. Mom had used other last names before going back to her maiden one, as if daring Trevor to catch her. All the names, all their secrecy and striving, were on the papers Trevor and Jack had. Zoe could look at the files any time she liked, they said. If they were forgeries, they were expensive ones—they even had her report cards, for God's sake.

Nobody would go to this kind of trouble unless it was true. Especially rich people.

According to the internet, Mama had almost not existed. Zoe herself was invisible, for that matter. But seventeen years was a long time—practically a geologic age online—and you didn't have to be careful if you were rich. Money could buy some kinds of anonymity.

Which, frankly, sounded like a good deal.

Zoe bit her lip, glancing from the phone's glow across the beautiful blue and white bedroom. Doors she could close or leave open, a bathroom all her own—the tub in particular looked like a great time. She'd rarely been able to have a long soak even as a child.

It was a movie. Or a fairytale, though those always had teeth and claws lurking under the surface.

She typed in Pastor Bea's name, and *Hall City, NE.*

There were almost more news stories about *him* than about the Roujes, and apparently the arson investigation had been ongoing since that terrible night almost three years ago. Leroy McFisk, a petty criminal bailed out on more than one charge during a misspent youth as he moved around Nebraska. He finally settled in Hall City's Church of the Righteous Savior, using it for all sorts of financial hijinks. There were stories about all the elderly he'd cheated out of retirement funds and more—Zoe could add to those, but nobody would ever ask her—and the authorities all said he'd started the fire in the church for insurance money and to cover his tracks.

There was, the news said, no way the entire structure of Righteous Savior could have been aflame so quickly and thoroughly if McFisk hadn't set it.

Zoe's entire body turned cold while she read those articles. She didn't want to think about that building ever again, her wrists in agony and the cuffs rattling before they sprang open with tiny metallic clicks, that strange sense of pressure bleeding off and Bea's scream of surprise when he opened the cellar door and smoke billowed free, Zoe snarling as she leapt...

Don't. It won't happen again.

Except she didn't even really know *what* had happened. Things were...hazy. It was the only word that applied. There was no way *she* could have started the fire, right? Flames didn't just appear out of thin air.

She wasn't a demon and she didn't really have superpowers despite Mama's insistence on deviltry. About all Zo could claim were some weird physical talents and an unreliable memory. Bea had probably tried to burn the place down with her inside; maybe he'd thought he could get death benefits for her as well as Mama and vanish to start another church in another state.

But Zoe's hands tingled. Her fingernails could be sharp, she knew. And they could lengthen in a moment, despite her habit of chewing on them under stress.

Mama wasn't mentioned in any of the articles about Bea, though other "victims" were listed. A missing foster daughter wasn't mentioned either.

Finally Zoe thumb-typed Royal's name into the search bar, adding *Akron, OH.*

Nothing in the news about him, thank God. But there were some social media profiles, and eventually she found him, though only when she took Akron out of the search bar.

He'd moved. Well, people did that all the time.

The important thing was, Royal Petterson was still alive. Zoe felt a brief flash of disappointment before a wave of relief made her gasp. She looked around the room guiltily, the contrast between bright screen and dimness stinging as her eyes swiftly adapted.

Looked like Roy had not only moved but had a real job now, though most of his profile was locked down. The scars down one side of his face were livid; he wasn't the sneering-handsome young tough he'd been two years ago. And it also looked like he'd found religion, all his public posts were about God and church.

Maybe he was a Bea-in-training. It was so fucking Midwest she almost laughed. Stuffing her face in the pillow and screaming was an option, too. Would anyone hear her in this vast house?

Jack's room—or maybe it was a suite even more luxurious than hers—was two doors down, past his 'home office'. *I moved into the carriage house a few years ago, but I'll stay here for a while.*

She wondered how long.

It was...good, she supposed, to know Bea had survived whatever she'd done, and Royal too. Maybe she hadn't needed to run so far so fast, and stay so far below the radar. It had sure seemed like a good idea at the time, though, and that deep instinct had never failed her.

Now, however, it was silent. Everything was.

The phone had its map and GPS functions turned on; it showed her location as an arrow held in a wide green space north of New York City, a few roads curving nearby. Hiking through the snow to get to the next town or suburb didn't sound like a good time, but at least now she knew where it was. And they were closer to the actual city than she thought.

It was all too good to be true. If this went sour Zoe could always escape. After all, she'd done it before.

But, she realized as she set the phone aside, its charging cord snaking neatly off the nightstand, she *wanted* it to be true.

A lot.

16
TIGHT-KNIT

THE SOLARIUM, ITS GREENERY RUSTLING WHILE SNOW DRIFTED AGAINST MILK-glassy panes segmented with wrought iron, was a pleasant place to have breakfast. In summer it was cool and bright; in winter it was warm and cheery even when ice made baroque traceries on the outside of its semi-opaque walls. A white wicker table covered with bright green cloth stood companionably with matching wicker chairs; Dad was already up, his suit immaculate but tie absent and the first two buttons of his shirt undone. He was buried in the newspaper; a white china coffee mug steamed gently before him.

By long agreement, neither of them spoke before breakfast was finished. Jack took his own chair, glancing at the empty one; Zoe's door had been firmly closed when he passed just a few minutes earlier.

Maybe she'd sleep in. He'd paused with one palm spread against the wood, trying to sense her moving or breathing behind its barrier.

He'd go back in a little bit, just to see if she was awake. Or if she needed anything.

Jack's own coffee was piping hot and set right where it should be; Amelia had a genius for knowing when anyone would arrive at the table. The third chair, empty, was set at an inviting angle, and its ivy-painted cushion was plump and ready.

Jack set his phone down at its allotted spot, and his keys went neatly next door. He settled in his familiar chair, stretched his legs out, rested his elbows on the arms, and prepared himself for deep thought, his fingers tented before him and his gaze unfocused.

Normally, pre-breakfast time was reserved for a short analysis of any current case requiring his attention, from a business matter to a less-than-legal concern. Hunting a Broken rarely intruded on this time; those called for thinking while running. If there was something Dad wanted him to take a look at, a file with any particulars would be at his place for quiet consumption.

Today something else filled his skull, details demanding to be processed. When his coffee cooled to a drinkable temperature he reached for it, but he was still no closer to a solution.

She was an enjoyable quandary, certainly. And it would take time. His own impatience had to be accounted for, accorded proper weight.

Amelia appeared again. This time she carried a wooden tray, and in her wake, Zoe tiptoed down three white-painted wooden stairs.

His *demie* moved tentatively, her unbound hair damp and glowing in the snowy light, last night's sweats loose enough to drive home how thin she was. At least she'd opened one of the shoeboxes; she wore a pair of grey canvas Keds. Solid rest had done her a world of good; the shadows under her eyes had lessened and her skin was lambent.

Trevor laid aside his paper and rose; Jack surged upright. Zoe halted, confusion crossing her gaunt, pretty face; Amelia nodded, bracing the tray in one slim hand and setting a heavy white cappuccino cup down before the third chair. "I told you," the housekeeper said over her shoulder, then beamed at Dad. "Look who found me in the kitchen. I bring breakfast soon."

"Good morning, and thank you." Trevor all but beamed as well.

"Don't worry, we simply rise when a lady arrives. Did you sleep well?"

Zoe glanced at Jack, probably for reassurance; he hoped he looked comforting. *Now* he could breathe a sigh of relief. She was right in front of him, whole and well.

"It's very quiet," she said, and lowered herself gingerly into the chair. "I was out like a light. Did...did you sleep okay?"

"For the first time in years." Trevor kept smiling as he settled in his own seat again. The paper was pushed aside with an elbow, and he applied himself to coffee. "We thought it best to let you wake in your own time."

"We're normally quiet before caffeine," Jack added, so she wouldn't be unnerved next time. "The solarium's one of my favorites."

"A lot of plants," she agreed, touching the cappuccino cup with a fingertip. "This place is huge. I mean, it's beautiful." A worried line between her dark, finely drawn eyebrows as if she suspected they might take offense. "I managed to find the kitchen again. Amelia's nice."

She should be. Offering any sort of insult to Jack's *demie* would garner a swift, painful result. "She'll want to know all your favorites. We can go shopping today, if you want."

"Shopping?" Zoe visibly decided the cup wouldn't bite her, and wrapped her hands around it as if she was cold.

"Clothes. Books. Music. Anything you want." *Just let us do something.*

"Oh." Her eyes were round, and very blue.

"Lev should be bringing the new desktop today," Dad weighed in. "Salerno's visiting midmorning; he'll have a packet with everything you need to start ordering online, too. I'll be working from the office here for a while."

Salerno would also have an update on diplomatic negotiations with both the Howler and Fantome. "You'll like Lev." *Shut up, Jack.* He couldn't help himself. "There's Sarah and Gessel, too; you'll meet them eventually. Some other staff on a rotating basis. The house might seem empty at first, but sometimes it's a hive. There's also the monthly parties out at the estate, and Allison will be out soon. She's one of Dad's right hands." The shaman would confirm his *demie* had the Sorcerer's Gene, and would know how to start training her. Subtly at first, of course—and Jack would have to be present for any interaction between Zoe and the Pride, at least to begin with.

For the foreseeable future, really. Her first Moonfall was going to be one helluva event.

That was a worry. She was ripe for the change, it was all over her. Had she already accomplished it, without any sort of help? *Demie* couldn't be Broken.

At least, he'd never heard of any. They always had their twin as insulation from the bloodlust, and vice versa—though once or twice, a *demi* had gone down when mischance or misadventure had taken their twin.

Usanaugh weren't separated, ever. Yet he and his counterweight had been.

"Sounds like a lot of people." Zoe's thin shoulders hunched; she stared into the cup.

"You don't have to see a single one of them." Dad's tone brooked no argument. "Not until you want to, and if that's never, little dancer, then it's never. You won't be rushed into anything."

"They'll be curious," Jack hastened to add. If she truly decided to retreat from the world, he was more than willing to bring her anything required. Or wanted. "Only because you're so important. But Dad's right, you won't have to see anyone but us if that's how you want it. I'll bring you anything you need." *Like a princess in a tower.*

For some reason, that made her smile, and she straightened. "Like the Man in the Iron Mask. Won't all these people be surprised? I mean, I'm not exactly...there wasn't anything in the news about Mama taking me."

So she'd been researching. Jack banished a smile; so far, his *demie* was surpassing any expectation. "None of the Pri—ah, none of us would speak to reporters. We're a pretty tight-knit group. Like a clan."

Outside, the wind picked up, rattling tiny bits of falling ice against the solarium's panes. If McKenna visited he'd probably stay rather than drive back in this weather. So would Allison, though the shaman might slip out at midnight and roam the icy hills, speaking to whatever took her interest.

Shamans were strange. And soon his *demie* would be one of them, listening to voices regular Kith couldn't hear, sensing things too subtle for a patterner or an analyst.

Whatever Jack didn't see, she would. It was the best possible combination, icy logic paired with deep, warm intuition.

Dad picked up his cup, took a long drink. Maybe he was even wishing there was an alcoholic booster present. Caffeine's effect was pleasant, though just as evanescent as liquor's. "Perhaps it might be easier if we asked what *you'd* prefer, Zoe. You've probably noticed we kept your room very simple; it can be changed to suit you at any time."

"It's beautiful too." The shy smile she bestowed on Dad soothed every inch of Jack's nerves. "I like it a lot. I wonder..."

Amelia reappeared, and behind her curly-haired, quick-footed Lev, scrubbed and wide-eyed in his best jeans and a well-ironed red flannel shirt. The kid—strictly speaking, he was a little older than Jack, but lacking any dominance except a Kith's natural share over skins—had his best denim jacket on too, and carried a massive wooden tray.

"Breakfast!" Amelia announced. "This is Lev; he works for me. Good with his hands, fixes things. I had him bring Christmas trees. After this, we decorate."

Jack might have bristled, but Zoe looked pleased. "Mama didn't really celebrate Christmas much. You've got a tree?"

"Ah, my little kitten." Amelia began unloading plates onto the table with practiced ease; maybe Zoe wouldn't notice how easily snub-nosed Lev handled his load, or how quickly, utterly gracefully the housekeeper moved. Lev smelled a bit nervous, but who wouldn't be? "We have *three*. You pick one for first, and choose colors for lights. And your father, he will need many ideas for presents."

Trevor opened his mouth as if to remind Amelia she certainly did not order his daughter around, but Zoe brightened. "Maybe I can help decorate? If you wouldn't mind?"

So that's what we'll be doing all day. Now that she'd expressed a preference, Jack's tension evaporated. "I'd like that. Meel will be thrilled to have me reach the top branches. Maybe we'll even put Lev on a ladder."

"Was on one all yesterday," the kid said, cheerfully. "With the lights. It was fun."

"They're great." His *demie* beamed at Lev, and Jack had to take a deep breath, squashing his beast's faint growl. "That does sound nice. I'd love to—I mean, if nobody minds."

"Mind?" Dad laughed, settling a napkin in his lap. "Taking a day away from reading P&L statements and going over dry corporate legalese? My dear, it would be a positive vacation. Perhaps you could even force Jack into having some fun too. He used to be a bit of a layabout, but these days he's a workaholic."

Because the only thing that kept me from running amok was work, but now my control mechanism is sitting right here, about to have blueberry pancakes. "Dad's being charitable." Jack watched her profile. "I was a holy terror."

Amelia bustled away; Zoe eyed her plate. "Mama always told me I was too. I guess I was a little hyperactive. I was in dance for a while, though, and that helped even though it was expensive. We had to stop classes."

You mean Angelina took it away as a punishment. The deduction was swift, unwelcome, and undeniable. Jack's hackles were well on their way to raising again. "There's a studio in town, if you want to go back to it. Not in-city, although there's more than a few there too."

She sobered, waiting for Dad to pick up his fork before sampling her own breakfast. Amelia had done favorites today—blintzes with raspberries for Jack, Dad's steak and hash browns with wheat toast. Crispy bacon on a plate, glowing glass jewels of syrup, whipped butter in a tiny stoneware crock, every small civilized thing to soothe the returned princess, to make her happy. And the ever-present glass of milk; Amelia was determined to baby her.

Making up for lost time. He longed to know more. "You like blueberries?" *Tell me something, anything.*

"They're my favorite." Zoe's smile was small, but definite. "I'd ask how she knows, but I think it's magic."

"Then it is," Dad said. The silence that fell was companionable.

Almost, Jack dared think, familial.

17
HAZY BUT DEFINITE

THERE WERE INDEED THREE CHRISTMAS TREES, AND ZOE CHOSE THE smallest because if she messed it up nobody would be too upset. Maybe she shouldn't have worried, because there were big color-coded Rubbermaid bins full of miles of tinsel, spun-glass or round ornaments in a variety of shades, and other decorations wrapped in tissue paper, plenty of them homemade and all with stories.

This was your grandmother Rachael's; she loved deer...you made this the last Christmas we had together, see the handprint?...This is from the old country, they put candles on the boughs there...oh, I remember that, wasn't that McKenna's first formal visit? Allison gave us that the Christmas after you two were born...

It was a far cry from Mama's insistence that the holiday season had to be spent in prayer, begging Baby Jesus to forgive you while low-key sneering at people who thought money or presents could buy anything other than hellfire. Still, Zoe liked Midnight Mass, with all the candles, incense, and chanting; the winter she was twelve and they had to move from Montana, Mama had decided Catholicism was bad because some of it was beautiful.

They'd arrived in Hall City just after New Year's. She'd left Zoe in the flophouse and didn't come back for three days. Zo had been just about ready to venture outside and find something, *anything* else the night Mama came back with glazed eyes and the sweetish burning rot of some drug on her breath.

Even that young Zo had figured that after a certain point, you just had to take your chances elsewhere.

Those three days were terrible, though—hoping her mother would return, hiding wherever she could in the crumbling building that had once been apartments, sometimes sobbing when there was nobody to hear, wondering what she'd do if Mama *didn't* remember her and come back. At the same time, it was almost...liberating, though she hadn't had the word to describe it then.

It was that strange sense of panicked freedom Zoe had thought of just after she'd staggered away from the burning church and Bea's cheated, gurgling howls.

But Mama'd met Pastor Beaton during those three days, too, and from then on it was all about the Church of the Righteous Savior. No matter what else Bea did, he was also Protestant and thundered about hell and sinning, and that was right up Mama's alley.

Zo didn't have to think about all that while the smallest tree was pronounced finished and tinsel strands were hung on the second-biggest one. Her father—she could think of him that way, she decided, at least for the moment—somberly asked her opinion about the placement of almost every ornament. At least it wasn't like a test he expected her to fail. Every once in a while Jack piped up, but he seemed otherwise content to unwrap the different decorations, telling her what they were. But in a nice way, like of course she'd remember, they were just making conversation.

As if she'd been with them all along.

Halfway through the morning the front door opened and Trevor disappeared, returning after about an hour as an engine purred outside. So that was the visitor, and maybe they were telling the truth—maybe she didn't have to talk to anyone else just yet.

It was an unexpected, welcome relief. And after that, they ended up decorating the largest tree as well. There was no shortage of ornaments *or* lights. Was this what having enough money was always like?

Lunch was a small mountain of crispy golden grilled-cheese sandwiches and mugs of homemade-tasting tomato soup. It was perfect for a snowy afternoon, and by that time even the biggest tree was looking distinctly overloaded, Jack had a tinsel crown, and Trevor—*Dad*—had two long silver ornaments looped over his ears, bobbing every time he turned his head.

For the first time in years, Zoe caught herself laughing outright, her sides aching not from hunger but from merriment.

When the trees could hold no more, Jack suggested they take a tour of the house and pulled her away, leaving the leftover ornament-and-tinsel mess for someone else to clean up despite the worm of guilt under Zoe's breastbone. Hard pellets of almost-snow rattled against the windows; she pitied anyone driving or working in this messy weather.

They stopped in the kitchen; Amelia pressed a fresh mug of coffee on Zoe. Then hallway after hallway unreeled around them while her new brother kept pointing things out. Some of the stories were halfway familiar, others made no sense at all, and Zoe was hoping once more there wouldn't be a quiz on any of this when they found a spiral staircase going down.

The walls were wood-paneled; the banister wrought iron. Jack was still wearing the loop of tinsel, tilted at a roguish angle on mussed golden hair. "—so I thought, of course, if I put a sheet on for a cape I could probably fly, right? Right."

Zoe's head whirled. She tried to keep her mug steady, but liquid sloshed and he stopped dead two steps below her, turning to peer up through a fringe of bright hair. The tinsel crown slipped, falling with a soft flutter.

Oh, shit. He's going to think I wasn't listening. But everything was catching up to her at once, and there was a tomato-soup burp rising behind her breastbone. She searched for something to say that didn't sound idiotic or dismissive, and couldn't scrape together a single word.

"Hey. Oh, hey." His hands flashed out, palms meeting her skin. He cupped her hands, both wrapped around her own thick white porcelain mug. "You're overwhelmed. It's okay. Look at me."

Usually she'd induce some kind of pain when her head got this muzzy, biting her lip or driving her fingernails into her palms, a bright spike to nail her back into her body. The mug wasn't hot enough to hurt, but the warm pleasant contact of his skin against hers brought the internal whirling to a halt so abrupt her knees almost buckled.

The house was alive around them, tiny creaks and stealthy sounds as building materials expanded or contracted, caught between heat inside and devouring cold without. There were footsteps—Lev somewhere, calling a question; Amelia answering between snatches of humming in the kitchen; their father was still in the room with the largest Christmas tree, very still but with his breathing rapid and deep as if he was upset. A faint creak was Hermann closing a side door and stamping his feet briskly to rid them of snow. The front door, what felt like miles away, had opened, letting in a gush of chill air.

Someone else had arrived. A normal person wouldn't know that; they heard practically nothing. Zoe had always known what she wasn't supposed to; it drove Mama to distraction.

More like a demon than a child. Don't look at me like that, you've got the devil's own eyes.

"Look at me," Jack repeated. His eyes were like Mama's, but much kinder, and they held tiny upside-down reflections of her own pale face. "Very good. Just breathe. It's fine, you're just sensitive. Inhale, Zo. That's it."

A rush of blessed oxygen filled her lungs, whooshed out. Again. *Sensitive,* he said, like it wasn't an insult. Like he didn't mind her weirdness.

"Good." Calm and matter-of-fact, as if he dealt with this sort of thing all the time. "You're radiating again. It's not a problem, because I'm here. Just look at me."

The new arrival closed the front door, quietly. But Zoe was drawn back, retracting inside her own skin, and the thump of returning to her fleshly home was so loud it might have spilled her down the stairs if her brother hadn't been holding her hands.

She *remembered* him. The memory was hazy but definite, a crib with a brightly colored mobile hanging overhead, a faint tinkling tune that had played in her dreams more than once, and her twin's dark eyes wide open, staring at her. There was no pain, simply a sense of connection—one consciousness in two bodies.

"There you are," he murmured, and exhaled. A shiver went through him, communicating up her own arms and sliding down her back like tinkling ice cubes in a crystalline glass. "Christ, how many years..."

...since we were able to do this? The sentence finished inside her head. She didn't have to say it; the thought leapt between them like a spark.

Which was terrifying. But the sense of contact receded like the sea she'd never seen, waves rushing along a pebbled beach. "I do know you." She sounded as dazed as Mama on her medicine. Was there something in the coffee? Not likely, Zoe would have smelled it.

Besides, the one time she'd stolen some of Mama's medicine to try, it did nothing but make her skin tingle for a little bit. The worst part was preparing the needle, but she'd seen her mother do it so many times there was no mystery in the process, just a bright hot loathing when it pierced her skin.

"Always," Jack said. There was nothing in his tone but honesty. "I'm not going to let anything hurt you, Zo."

You can't promise that.

Maybe he read it on her face; she wasn't doing too well at keeping her expression neutral.

"Oh, yes I can." He straightened slightly, pushing his shoulders back, and for the first time he looked...young. That calm, confident self-possession cracked just the slightest bit, and underneath he felt just like she did.

He just hid it better.

"That'll be Allison at the front door," he continued, and the wall between them was back up. Still, his hands were warm, and he didn't let go. "You'll like her. She tends to show up just when she's needed."

Is she the stepmother? And you can hear things too? Zoe couldn't make herself ask, but at least her thoughts were all her own again. He pulled on her hands, gently, and the coffee in her mug trembled.

"What if I don't want..." The words died in her throat, and she waited for the anger. There would be a price for this new paradise, and she had to pay it sooner or later if she wanted to stay.

She hadn't had to make small talk with the other visitor, but this one was obviously different.

"Don't want to see her? Then you don't have to. Easy." One of his broad shoulders lifted, dropped in a casual shrug. The two of them really didn't look very similar, Zoe thought.

Still, she *knew* him. Or that deep, unavoidable instinct did. "But you want me to."

"I think you'll like it. And it'll help. She's kind of...a therapist." Jack went still, watching her expression. "But if you don't want to, I'll just tell Dad so."

And have him get mad at me the first day. Yeah. That'll be great. "It's all right." Her words fell like the tinsel crown had, weightless, discarded. Therapists were easy, like school counselors. You simply lied, and they agreed with you because they were overworked and didn't really care anyway. "I'll meet her."

"You really don't have to. I didn't think she'd be here so quickly."

"I'll do it." To prove it, Zoe leaned back, and though he clearly didn't want to let go, he had to, or else slop hot coffee over them both. "I will."

"Brave girl," her brother said, gravely, and she wished it were true.

18

SECRETS

Dad wasn't wearing Christmas ornaments over his ears anymore, but his hair wasn't as ruthlessly controlled as usual and he wore the very slightest of smiles when Jack pushed open the study door, taking in the terrain with a brief glance before allowing his *demie* to come into view.

It was, after all, traditional.

Trevor Rouje's study was a wonderland of shelves lined with leatherbound spines, ranks of books broken every so often by an antique curio—an ivory statue of a snarling jungle cat, a gilded cedar box, a globe of rock crystal with a single vertical crimson flaw in its heart, and others. Dad sometimes returned from business trips with yet another small, priceless thing, and it went into a handy space with no trouble at all.

The furniture was chunky and likewise antique, dark wood and red leather, comfortable and marked with long use. His desk was mahogany, a real monster, and cluttered with paper—file folders, ephemera, invitations. No computer here; this was where Trevor spent time largely without electronic interruption.

The vast heavy oak mantel, beeswax-polished, held family photos in heavy, tarnished silver frames. There was one of toddler-

Zoe in the middle with a small glass votive set before it. Nights when a candle burned there, everyone in the house knew to move quietly and not to address the Pride leader unless it was with news of a death, or of his missing daughter.

A merry blaze crackled in the cavernous stone fireplace, breathing softly as frozen wind swept across the chimney-mouth. And there, her long dark mane holding one stripe of silver at the left temple, the Pride's most powerful shaman turned her hazel gaze upon Jackson and his *demie*. Allison wore a dark silk Chinese-collared shirt, faded jeans, and boots with heavy silver buckles bearing traces of damp; tiny drops of melted snow clung to her hair. Someone must have taken her jacket—probably Hermann, since Amelia was busy and Lev deathly nervous of all shamans.

As anyone with any sense should be, Jack thought.

Trevor handed the shaman a martini glass. The leader of the Pride was power visible, leonine stride and muscle married to force of will. Allison was...otherwise.

She accepted the cosmo with a nod, her hair moving slightly as her own personal breeze touched it. It was even funny after a while, like the old joke. *Did you feel that? Must be a shaman.*

"Zoe." Dad spoke first. "This is Allison, a friend of ours. She met you right after you were born, but you wouldn't remember that. Allison, this is my daughter, returned to us at last."

Zoe took a half-step aside, obviously meaning to go around her brother. Jack, though, paralleled the movement, keeping himself between his *demie* and the shaman. She had to peer around him, still clutching her coffee cup like it was an anchor.

"How do you do," his sister said, politely, and of course neither Allison nor Dad would miss his unspoken point.

Dad would further guess his daughter had sensed the new arrival, and might even be coming to the same conclusion Jack had—the Sorcerer's Gene, and all its attendant sensitivity.

It would make him even prouder, if that were possible.

"How do you do." Allison's voice was a restful stroke along soft fur, quiet and controlled. "My goodness, you grew up beautifully. Your eyes are just the same as when you were little."

It was, of course, the right thing to say. Zoe relaxed slightly and freed one hand, her fingers brushing Jack's arm. It was the first time she'd deliberately touched him, and he wasn't prepared for the spike of heat straight through his bones. "They told me about some of the Christmas ornaments you gave them." Was that a shy smile in her voice? "I'm sorry I don't remember you. It's been a long time."

"No apology necessary, kitten." Allison's laugh was just as soft, just as calming as ever. "I wanted to welcome you, but if this isn't a good time I'll simply stay for a drink and hop back home." She was emitting relaxation with a vengeance; a less dominant Kith would be a puddle on the floor.

His *demie*, though, was made of much sterner stuff. "It's nice of you to stop by." Zoe's fingers were still on Jack's sleeve as she edged past. Was she trying to keep *him* calm? Maybe it was instinctive. "Jack tells me you're like a therapist."

"That's one way to put it." Allison didn't glance at Dad; instead, her gaze settled on Jack as if she suspected his temper might slip.

It wasn't likely, with his *demie* right next to him. Zoe surprised him again, stepping fully into view, her chin lifted. She smiled like a queen bestowing favor on a foreign ambassador, and Dad's satisfaction was visible.

Jack decided nothing would go too badly wrong in the next few moments, and turned to pull the heavy study door closed. He didn't like losing contact with her, but...

When he turned back, Zoe stared at Allison. It wasn't a dominance challenge; there was no edge of hot intransigence to her gaze or body language. In fact, she looked thoughtful, slightly surprised—and interested.

The shaman stared back, her pupils swelling, and another soft breeze circled the study, brushing every surface.

"Well done," Allison said, softly. "Trevor, your daughter bears the Gene. And it's awake." Her tone didn't change, dreamy and slow, but

Jack had seen her shift from utter immobility to blinking through space, finishing by wrapping her fingers almost casually around an angry Pride member's throat—no claws, but an indestructible iron band forcing a fellow Kith to stillness. "Oh, my little kitten." The words shifted to a croon, Allison's eyes now bearing a bright blue spark in dark pupil-wells. "You have secrets."

Zoe shuddered, her hand loosening; Jack moved, catching the coffee mug on its way to the floor. Not a drop spilled. "I think you want to sit down." Nice and easy was the way to play this, he decided. Allison would do her best to figure out if his little sister had changed already, and if she was at risk of losing control. She could also tell them the best way to help Zoe adjust to her new status.

But if the shaman did anything that truly disturbed his *demie*, he was going to take issue.

Zoe didn't answer. She stared at the shaman, that same blue spark struggling in her own pupils, her irises simply a thin glowing thread. She was so thin cords on her neck stood out as she surged against Allison's hold, but even a *demie* was little match for a fully trained shaman. Finally his twin stepped forward, still visibly fighting unfamiliar sensations.

"I think that's best." Allison lifted her glass, took a long hit off the Cosmo. "Come, sit down. Fear nothing."

Tension fled Zoe's slim frame. She moved with fluid Kith grace now; Jack set their coffee cups on the sideboard. He considered the brandy decanter, poured himself a measure. The sound of splashing liquid was very loud, married to the fire's soughing and the spatter of ice pellets against the window.

"Rum, Dad?" His back ran with gooseflesh; his instincts howled.

No. Allison won't hurt her; you know that. You serve her best by showing your own control.

"A fine idea." Trevor would not normally sound so hushed. Even a Pride leader with extraordinary dominance could feel a little awe at the power of the unseen. "What do you think she'll prefer?"

"I don't think my *demie* drinks. When she starts, she'll let me know." He brought a tumbler of spiced rum to Trevor, every inch of his skin aware of Zoe sinking down upon an old, scarred oxblood leather couch, the upholstery barely making a sound as it accepted her slight weight. She still stared at Allison; the line of their linked gazes hummed with force.

"So many secrets," Allison crooned. "Don't worry, you can keep them, little kitten. You helped your mother hide, didn't you."

Zoe shivered.

That would explain a lot. Jack settled next to her, cradling his brandy, just close enough to feel her heat. Which meant she would feel his, on some level.

He hoped it was comforting.

"She was so frightened," Zoe whispered. "I didn't mean to."

"A little girl loves her mother," Allison soothed, immediately. "You did what you should, Zoe. Of course you did." And a *demie* with the Sorcerer's Gene, even dormant, was capable of misdirecting a jäger's keen nose or a patterner's anticipation.

"So that's why." Trevor turned away, bolting half his rum in a single shot. After all, he'd married Angelina; he should have been able to predict the behavior of a simple skin.

Even one who could throw a pair of *usanaugh*.

Zoe flinched, but Jack had her hand, his warm fingers lacing with her slim cool ones. "It's all right." He pitched the words low and soft, Voice thrumming through them. Allison still held her gaze, an eternity measured in slow ticks from the grandfather clock in the hall.

Finally, Allison raised her drink, finishing the martini with a long swallow. The blue sparks in her eyes burned steadily. Her hand drifted down and aside; Trevor, sensing the motion, took the discarded glass with a slight, unseen bow.

The white stripe in the shaman's hair glowed as she took one step, another, her now-dry boots silent. She bore down upon Zoe, feeling her way with fluid authority, every motion controlled.

Zoe's hand slowly warmed in his. Jackson held still despite the growl rising along his spine, threading through his ribs. The biggest danger to her calm was his own easily triggered protectiveness.

Well, it could also be called *fury*, but that was beside the point.

Allison's boots settled a short distance from Zoe's canvas shoes. The shaman bent as Zoe's chin tipped further up. She looked so small, and so heartbreakingly vulnerable—Jack had to exhale sharply, a lifetime of control without his *demie* clamping down hard as Trevor's fingers.

"You're going to be all right," the shaman said, quietly but with deep force behind every word. "You're going to trust your brother, your *demi*. Do you know what that word means?"

The faintest suggestion of shaking her head. Zoe's hair rippled, black silk running with blue highlights. "N-no," she whispered. "I'm sorry."

"It means he's your twin, your other half," Allison said, ruthlessly calm. "And you will trust him, Zoe Arcadia Rouje. That's your true name, and you will accept it. You will not fear him or your father." Her tone sharpened as Zoe made a restless movement. "Answer me, little kitten. You will trust, and will not fear."

"Yes." The word ended with a hot sibilant.

A flush slipped through Jack's body, fading reluctantly. Her scent shifted, losing that constant sharp, yellowish edge of trepidation. He hadn't realized how integral the fear was to her smell, and how maddening. His grasp on his own temper firmed, and the relief of finding her alive was a puddle next to the ocean of calm swallowing him now.

Allison straightened. "Put her to bed," she said, suddenly businesslike, the contact between her and Zoe snapping cleanly in two. "Let her sleep until tomorrow. She needs it; it's a wonder she's still conscious."

"Will she..." Trevor glanced at his son and heir, weighing the question against the likelihood of Jackson's control slipping, as usual.

"Oh, she'll change. If she has trouble, her *demi* will take over and do it *for* her. The bond's indissoluble." Allison glanced at Jack too, but hers was a quick, pleased smile, a teacher with a slow but thorough student. "He's already holding her still, I barely had to do anything. But a word of warning, she suffered things that will...upset you." The pause held all the caution in the world. "If she does feel like talking about it, any show of anger or disgust will be taken as a judgment on her. I'd avoid that, if I were you."

"Duly noted." Trevor nodded briskly. The fire popped, but none of them moved. Even Zoe didn't flinch. Her eyelids drifted half-shut, long dark lashes veiling blue as her pupils shrank. "She'll need training."

"Right now what she needs is her *demi*, and some rest. We'll approach training in a short while." Allison stepped back, stretching gracefully; she paced to the fire. "We have a few other items to address once you've settled her, Jackson."

"They've raised their heads again." It was a depressingly simple guess; Jack had been waiting for Dad to broach the subject since Houston. He dispelled the urge to draw Zoe closer, slip an arm over her shoulders. The closeness might be comforting for him, but it might also disturb her sedation. "An actual kill, or just an attempt?"

"An attempt, overseas. Lucile, the Golden's mate. She's fine, all defenses are working as intended."

"At least that." But it might not last. "How did Michel take it?"

"He's livid, of course." Allison sighed. "But at least now he understands that Swiss group is an actual danger. He was somewhat dismissive, before."

"Of course he was." Most Kith leaders considered skins nothing more than an annoyance, though one deserving cautious treatment by virtue of sheer numbers. Jack quelled a restless movement, watching Zoe's somnolent profile. He was somewhat glad she wasn't truly hearing this, lost in the peculiar rest a shaman could induce, granting a wounded Kith surcease. "They've graduated to open attempts. This is a problem."

"Which we're well equipped to handle," Trevor reminded them both. "Another cosmo, Allison?"

"I'd love one, thanks." The shaman paced to the fireplace, bracing a graceful hand on the mantel and looking into the flames. She was unmated so far, though there was no shortage of interested parties. The lady believed in taking her time. "Go ahead and put her to bed, Jack. Then if you could manage it, I'd like you here for the discussion. It won't take more than an hour."

Attending to his *demie* was paramount, and this was yet another test—could he step away, knowing she was safe? Did his control stretch that far? "I'll be back as soon as she's settled, then." He rose, cautiously; Zoe unfolded with clockwork grace, her hand caught in his. "I'll want to see the particulars of the attempt on the Golden's mate. I don't like that the time between European incidents is getting shorter."

The incidents were also mounting in seriousness. They hadn't managed to get much usable data on the new Swiss skin hunters yet, either. Perhaps it was only a function of their utter failure to cause any damage so far.

"Exactly." Trevor stalked for the heavy oak sideboard. "I'll pour you another brandy. Good work, Jackson."

He hadn't done much, but the approbation was still welcome. "Thank you, sir. Come on, *demie*. You need some rest."

She nodded, slowly, a trustful sleepwalker. The profound relaxation would ease her into healing slumber as soon as he had her recumbent in the blue bedroom; the only difficult part would be tearing himself away to attend what promised to be a highly unpleasant strategy meeting.

He led Zoe for the door, carefully steering her around furniture.

"Are you certain she's all right?" Trevor, for once, sounded almost wistful.

"Bent but not broken." Allison pitched the answer loud enough to qualify as a response for both the Pride leader *and* his son. "Who wouldn't be frightened, in her shoes? Poor girl."

It wasn't perfect. But it was a damn sight better than Jack had expected, and he almost staggered with relief once they were in the hall. His *demie*'s hand lay trustingly in his, and he steered her through warm safety to her suite, just a few steps away from his own.

He already couldn't wait to return to her side.

PART TWO
KITH AND KIN

19
DARK WATER

Her first week in the huge house was a blur. The next was a little less so but still refused to come into focus, and at times outright dreamlike.

Oh, it was pleasant enough—waking in the blue bedroom each snowy morning, a breakfast that was always just what she was craving, and wandering the house until a lunch that was, more often than not, childlike as well. There was a comfort in peanut-butter-and-jelly or more grilled cheese, especially when there were three whole sandwiches accompanied by cut-up apples with a bath of lemon juice to keep them from browning, as much milk as Zoe wanted, and seconds if she was still hungry. And the hot chocolate —*real* hot chocolate, not the grainy mix kind. Amelia melted tiny medallions of bittersweet in heavy cream, adding fine sugar and whisking in a copper saucepan.

The house seemed to understand Zoe, too. It *felt* friendly, just like some places were watchful or actively nasty. There was no need to go out in the cold when there was the solarium full of green rustling, the library with its couches and heavy red velvet drapes, the ballroom with its acres of hardwood and its faintly dusty, delicious song of long-ago gatherings still vibrating in the floor. Stairways and hall-ways, forgotten corners—there was so much to explore.

Her brother, for all they mentioned his "work", seemed to have plenty of time for doing almost nothing. He pointed out little details —an angel carved into a corner, a painting half-hidden behind drap-ery, a door leading somewhere you wouldn't expect. He never seemed hurried, but he never quite let her out of sight unless she retreated to the blue suite and closed the door.

There was enough in the suite to keep her occupied, too. Even sitting in the window seat watching the weather was a deeply deca-dent luxury. No hurrying to catch a bus, no waking from a fitful doze and dragging herself through a double shift of stocking shelves. No shivering, no screaming of child or woman in a squat's cavernous echoes, no sirens to listen for, no need to stay so constantly, hurtfully aware of every small nearby sound just in case.

She missed things, of course, even about Marquette. Like a coworker's smile when Zo did something small to ease a fellow retail-soldier's burden, like the dawn rising bright gold over skyscrapers, like sipping overboiled coffee from the free truck on Boylon Avenue while homeless people traded jokes and gossip. Or the parks and public libraries in each city—the libraries especially, hushed and serene.

She hadn't checked any of her old email accounts yet with the phone or the shiny new second computer in Jack's office. His desk was sleek chrome and black glass, the entire room almost painfully modern, but another had been moved in—a traditional oak affair with carved legs and locking drawers, and he said it was hers.

The cushioned ergonomic chair was comfortable and there was a manila folder sitting right next to the keyboard holding a real social security card, a real birth certificate, real New York driver's license even though she hadn't taken the test.

Jack simply asked *you can drive, right?* And the next day the license showed up, with a photo she didn't remember taking.

It was either magical or terrifying; she couldn't decide.

Also in the folder were three credit cards and a bank card—the PIN attached to the latter on a sticky note with instructions on how to change it—along with shiny brochures about their benefits and a statement for each showing ungodly balances and credit limits.

She didn't touch those just yet, since there was no telling what she'd have to do for them. Sure, Jack said things like *that account's got a feed from the main, it'll never go dry* and *just order something, look, here's the delivery address for the house.*

But Zoe didn't.

Still, the first few times she mentioned a book she liked, it showed up on the desk a little later—mostly brand-new editions, but others had dog-earing and underlining, a friendly fellow mind at work on the pages. She liked the latter better; some of the margin notes were in a strong clear handwriting she'd never seen before yet faintly familiar at the same time.

There were other small things, too, like the pretty glittering earrings or bracelets, maybe real silver, in a small black velvet boxes left on her nightstand. A pair of black boots like the ones she'd had in Marquette except of vastly higher quality, a stack of brightly colored dancewear catalogs and brochures from studios "in town" or "in the city", both of which meant different things—the city, of course, was New York proper, just a short train or car ride away. A long black woolen coat, a little too large for her but still wonderfully thick and sturdy. A leather messenger bag and a smaller, matching purse, both with nickel rings and buckles. A trio of high-quality notebooks and an assortment of brand-new pencils both plain and colored the day she remarked that she used to like drawing. A long, soft, red cashmere scarf. Two pairs of knit gloves that fit perfectly. Expensive cherry lip balm when the temperature dropped, the snow halted, and the air turned dry-frigid. A silver keychain with house keys on it, and two car keys, both with different buttons on their broad plastic heads.

She didn't ask where the cars belonging to the keys were.

Photo albums in the library showed Mama and Trevor—she tried calling him *Dad* like Jackson did, but half the time she was uneasy, and once even said *Mr. Rouje* and flinched when he looked a little pained—together. There were ones where Angelina seemed happy, especially the wedding photos. She looked like an angel in all that white lace, and there was a large glossy picture of them dancing, Trevor's hand against the small of her back and Mama gazing up at him.

If that look on Mama's face wasn't open adoration, it was certainly close.

There were pictures of Jack as he grew, wearing a sullen expression when he wasn't simply thoughtful. In most he was a little blurred, as if he couldn't quite hold still; she remembered the feeling. But now, it was different. He glided along, sometimes with his hands in his pockets, full of easy conversation or companionable silence, and his patience seemed infinite.

It was enough to make her want to provoke him or Trevor, just to get the inevitable over with. Each time she got nervous, though, a wave of drugging calm swamped her and she couldn't quite remember the end of Allison's visit.

You were pretty tired, was all Jack said. *If you want to see her, Zo, I can make a call. I'm sure she'd love to visit again.*

The blue suite's shelves looked a little less forlorn with new books scattered on them. Still, the rooms were like a stage set. Her old jeans and flannel arrived back from the laundry smelling of expensive fabric softener, and she hid her old socks deep in a wardrobe drawer just in case.

She kept the Martha Smith ID, too.

Roaming the house was interesting enough, but after lunch she either retreated to the suite or the library, curling up on the window seat—if she was in the blue rooms—or on a wide leather couch that seemed friendly enough. She could read for as long as she wanted without Mama's aggrieved sigh or Bea's *get your nose out of that and go do something Christian*, without worrying about a candle's fitful flickering or having to work in a few hours.

Maybe that was why time grew so slippery; Zoe wasn't used to not having a schedule. They worked you until you were too tired to think outside, but in this house there were hours like dark water slipping under a bridge, quiet and endless.

If she settled in the library Jack chose a book and dropped into a wingback leather chair, reading as well. Or he stretched his legs out, tented his fingertips, and stared over them at nothing in particular. Still, thoughts moved in his dark gaze, and when there was a quiet subtle buzz from his phone he dug it out and glanced without seeming very bothered or even interested.

Eventually, though, it would be time to eat again. The dining room, with its long table and intricate place settings, was...well, she couldn't quite call it *frightening*, but it was definitely uncomfortable. She liked the breakfast bar in the kitchen better, but Amelia seemed to think it was almost scandalous to have supper there regularly.

Maybe the housekeeper just didn't want them watching her cook. When Zoe once offered to help with the dishes, Amelia's lower lip quivered like she'd been caught doing something wrong.

That was concerning, but also comforting in a strange way. Because it was Jack who touched Amelia's elbow and murmured in her ear, and the older woman's expression eased as if by magic. She actually looked *grateful*, and smiled—not the grimace of putting on a show, either. The tension fled, and Zoe's halting apology was accepted with a plate of fresh sugar cookies and a glass of cold milk.

Ice creaked and dripped as the weather warmed slightly, though the meteorologists said more snow was on the way. When she didn't retreat to the blue suite after dinner, the evening was spent in their father's study or the small parlor on the second floor, both with a fireplace and Trevor's careful, measured tones as he talked about family history. Or he and Jack would discuss "business"—not quite cryptic, but nothing Zoe could really pin down.

They certainly weren't in Royal's line of work, or any other she'd come across living below the radar. Which worried her—what would they do if they found out about Roy?

It didn't bear thinking about.

The Saturday of her second week, Jack was at the fireplace, holding a broad-bellied glass of brandy; Trevor had his rum. Zoe toyed with a bottle of mineral water—tap wasn't good enough for these folks, no sir—while she stood at the window. The dark outside was filigreed, clouds racing over the night sky and muffling a swelling, growing moon.

A shiver slid down her spine. She rolled the bottle between her palms.

"I told you Greg couldn't be trusted." Jack stared at the flames. "He was always a little toad. Practically a misbegotten."

"I listened, didn't I?" Trevor shifted slightly in his massive chair. He didn't need its weight; he took up all the attention in the room just by *existing*. "I think you should handle it, though."

The sudden silence made her back prickle. Zoe's reflection hung in window-glass, the snow's pale gleam like static behind it. Her hair, caught in a loose braid, swung as she turned.

Trevor's blue gaze was on Jack, but her brother's rested on Zoe. Was she supposed to say something? She had no idea who 'Greg' was, and even less idea what the hell they were talking about.

The quiet continued, and the sense of having to pass a pop quiz in a class she'd never taken was disturbing. "Do you need me to do something?"

Of course there was a price to all this. It was a relief to finally have a chance at discovering how high it was going to be.

20

BOTH TO WORK

"You could order some books, those shelves look a little lonely." Half Jack's mouth tilted up, a charming enough smile. "Dad and I work together—family business, learning the ropes, that kind of thing. He's asking if I'm ready to come back yet, and I'm saying no."

It was reflexive to stiffen slightly and look at Trevor, gauging the emotional weather. But the expected, normal spike of fear never materialized. Zoe had only felt dim, dozing alarm for weeks now, and each time it faded swiftly.

Which was...odd.

"And all's well." Trevor lifted his rum, a lazy salute. "I was merely stating a preference, *if* you and Zoe wanted to go into the city."

"Just interview Greg on the way in, and have brunch after?" Jack's smile broadened as he ambled for a second couch set at an angle from their father's chair; the question sounded like a family joke. "What do you think, Zo? We can do a day trip. Get some shopping in."

What am I going to have to do? "Okay." There was no place to set the green glass water bottle, so she let it dangle from her right hand. She'd seen a few fights at Royal's club—it was rare for bottles to break the way they did in movies. Still, they made pretty effective blunt weapons. "When? Tomorrow?"

"Slow down." Jack took a hit off his drink, dropping down onto the couch. Both of them consumed a fair amount of booze, but it never seemed to make them sloppy or angry. At least, it hadn't yet. "It's only if you want to."

But I should want the right things, shouldn't I? "I'll do it." It wouldn't matter if what she *wanted* was to hide in this quiet, friendly house forever; Zoe was going to have to earn her keep. Wherever she and Mama moved, that was the rule, and it proved absolutely correct later when she was on her own. "I should...I should find a job, too."

They exchanged a significant look, Trevor's eyebrows lifting and Jack shaking his head a little, ruefully. Zoe winced internally; she'd put her foot in it, misreading *something* in the situation.

The sense of alarm struggled against an iron weight. *You will not fear*, a woman's voice said softly, and there was a wall between Zoe and her best, oldest friend.

Terror kept you awake, not to mention thinking. She needed both clarity and brainpower to navigate this strange new world.

"Not before college, little dancer," their father said. "But there's no hurry. We've only just found you again."

"You already have a job." Jack's eyelids had dropped to half-mast, as if he was tired of her not catching the hint. "More than one. But the biggest is to just...exist."

That's a tall order. "I'm sorry." It was time for apologies, to hopefully stave off the worst. Some bosses were forgiving, at least at first. "I don't understand."

"Come sit down." Her brother patted the leather cushion next to him. It sounded like a good idea—he even *felt* safe, which was a novelty.

But she stayed where she was, aware of the potential for a trap. Mama was safe until she wasn't, switching back and forth according to some schedule Zoe never quite figured out; Bea and Royal had never been *safe* but they were, at least, reasonably predictable.

When it became obvious she wasn't moving, Jack didn't sigh or shake his head. He simply returned his attention to Trevor. "McKenna can do it. As long as Jolie's with him to keep him from going overboard—or Sam Coughlin might be able to, come to think of it."

"Mac would prefer the lady, I'm sure." Trevor nodded, studying his glass. "And there's no need to go into the city if you don't want to, Zoe. As for a job, absolutely not. I forbid it."

Is this some kind of reverse psychology? Zoe didn't glance toward the window. The idea of hopping through it the way she'd broken the Greenfield's doors was brief, but also seductive. "This is the longest I've been without one since I was twelve. It makes me nervous."

"Let me guess. Angelina's habit got a lot worse that year." Jack made a brief, graceful gesture when she stared at him, an apology in motion. "I'm sorry, Zo. But I'm not wrong."

"No," Zoe had to admit. "You're not." The instinct to protect Mama was still alive and well, though it no longer mattered. "But I like working." It was a lie—nobody liked it, for God's sake. You still had to do *something* every day, and at least you could retain some small measure of independence no matter how bad the job was. Holding back a few dollars from her under-the-table stints before Mama found Bea had been survival, not stealing; she'd already been making hazy plans to save, to get out, to be free.

She still felt the old bite of shame and guilt under her breastbone, and the worry. Now she was an adult, she knew freedom was a lie.

You always had to do something for someone.

"You're Trevor Rouje's daughter, my dear." There was no trace of irritation in their father's words; it was almost eerie how calm both he and Jack were. An odd thrumming hum lingered under his voice, probably the forced-air heating even though they kept the fireplaces going in several rooms. "Maybe after college you can take a job, if you're absolutely determined. But for right now, no, and that's final."

"There it is." Jack didn't look disturbed in the least. He pushed his bright hair back with stiff fingers, and took a small sip of brandy.

"You have any idea how many times I've heard *that's final?* Means it's no good arguing."

"Not that it ever stopped you." Trevor took a shot of rum, lowered the tumbler thoughtfully. The fire popped, adding its two cents' worth. "My apologies. I simply miss my heir and right hand."

"You'll make me blush." Jack's dark gaze hadn't left Zoe, an almost-physical weight. "Zo? You all right?"

"Fine." She glanced out the window again—nothing but ice over snowdrifts, re-freezing now that it was dark. The clouds had thickened, hiding the moon.

"The Christmas party's coming up," Trevor said. "And Moonfall's at the estate in January."

"I think Zo and I might sit that one out," Jack said, as if it was normal to have an 'estate' just lying around. "February's early enough, if she agrees."

Oh, Lord. "I'm okay." Zoe fought the urge to cross her arms. She barely knew what day it was, even with the phone to glance at whenever she went into the blue bedroom. "Really. If you want me to go to a thing, I'll go." *Everyone will take one look at me and laugh, but okay.*

Maybe they wanted to embarrass her. Sometimes people liked that—pretending to be kind before pulling the rug out from underfoot.

"*I* don't want to go." Jack's nose wrinkled, briefly. "So I'm using you as an excuse, Zo. Don't blow my cover."

"Oh, now we get to the real reason." Trevor's laugh was warm and forgiving, and there was no angry edge to his scent or tightening around his eyes.

The rumbling from the heat registers was soothing, and Zoe's shoulders relaxed. Falling out of the habit of constant vigilance just drove home how exhausting it was in the first place. "Is that one of my jobs?"

"It absolutely is. Come on and sit down." Jack waited until she took a tentative step in his direction to grin encouragingly. "See, now that you're back, I can slack off a bit. Dad *had* to put me to work before. School was boring."

"Juvenile delinquent," Trevor supplied. "But once you were adequately challenged, the bad behavior was ameliorated."

"Every kid's got a rebellious phase." Jack's expression could best be described as *mischievous*, his dark eyes glinting and his hair a messy thatch of gold. When she settled gingerly next to him, his arm rested atop the couch back, a wing she could shelter under if she wanted to. "Mine was just an overachiever. Anyway, once I was off the stupid treadmill and in interesting classes, as well as learning Dad's business, I didn't have time to misbehave. By then we were searching for you in France; Angelina had some very distant family in Marseilles. *That* was interesting. Anyway, I spent a lot of time on transatlantic flights crunching numbers, reading files, and writing policy recommendations."

"Some of which have become standard procedure." Trevor smiled, relaxing into his chair. The subsonic rumbling plucked at Zoe's unease, smoothing ragged edges. "But *your* job, little dancer, is to enjoy what we've made. Soon it'll seem natural."

France. Marseilles. Another quasi-memory tugged at her. *You helped your mother hide, didn't you.*

Was she going crazy? Had the pressure of survival been the only thing keeping her on Mama's straight-and-narrow path? Angelina had basically abandoned Jack; should Zoe feel jealous or relieved?

"What is it?" Jack leaned slightly toward her, his other hand balancing the brandy glass on his knee. "You've got that wondering look. Just ask."

He kept saying that. *Just ask me. You can't make me mad, I promise.*

But she knew better. Still, he hadn't popped off yet. "I just was wondering why Mama took me instead of you."

"Could've been opportunity." Jack didn't miss a beat, simply considering the question with his head slightly tilted and his eyebrows drawn together. "Could be she liked a girl better. Could even have been her knowing Dad would never do anything to jeopardize a daughter, so he wouldn't look for her in...certain ways." The steady warmth of him didn't alter. Maybe the axe wasn't going to fall tonight. "Probably a combination."

"I'm sorry." Were there any two more useless words in English? The damage was already done; Mama was dead, and Bea was going to be in jail for a long time.

A good girl wouldn't feel so relieved at either thought. You weren't supposed to be happy your own mother was in heaven, for God's sake, and you weren't supposed to be overjoyed at her slippery religious con-man boyfriend spending time behind bars.

"I almost wish she'd taken me instead. What she did to you..." Her brother trailed off, his lips pulling back briefly in a grimace, and took another fraction of booze.

Zoe's fingers were cold. The bottle creaked under her fingers so she eased up, hoping neither of them noticed the tiny sound. "She was just scared." Mama's fear, that giant overwhelming invisible beast, had died when she did. Except its ghost lingered, often pressing against Zoe's own skin, making her pulse pound. "Of everything. Maybe it was a mental illness."

Another long pause. "It could have been," Trevor allowed, softly. "I don't think I'll ever forgive her, though."

"She's beyond forgiveness." Jack's tone was icy enough Zoe shivered, and he dropped his hand onto her shoulder, drawing her into his side.

It felt oddly natural. Zoe let herself relax into the safety, a tentative thaw. It wasn't like a handsy guy on the bus, or one of Royal's "friends." Or the dates she had to go on after working at the club. He was her *brother*, for God's sake.

"She's gone now." Maybe Zoe was supposed to be the peacemaker? But they got along fine without her, more like friends than father-and-son.

All her knowledge of functioning families came from sitcoms and school gossip. Neither were exactly reliable sources.

"Mh." Trevor hadn't moved; he stared at the shelves across the room, clearly seeing memories instead. The fire returned to its hushed consumption of dry wood. "We'll probably have many more conversations about Angelina's motives. The important thing is that you've been found, little dancer. Jack's right, you should order some books. Does your suite need anything?"

It was the most she'd ever had in her life, but it didn't look like these guys grasped as much. Zoe shook her head, and finally decided to risk cracking the seal on the mineral water. "It's fine just the way it is. I like it."

"One of these days you'll decide on a full revamp." Jack looked down at her, his smile turned lazy. He looked half-asleep, but the gleam in what could be seen of his dark eyes was sharp interest. "Probably redecorate the whole house while you're at it."

"I like everything about the house. It's confusing, but friendly." *Like the rest of you,* she realized, and a great wave of relief hammered her again, passing from her scalp to her toes in a tingling wave. "Lots of places feel bad, or like they're watching you. But not here."

"You sense things other people don't." Jack sounded like it was no big deal. "I'm more the analytical type."

"You'll perform well together." Trevor lifted his glass. "My sensitive little dancer and my heir. I can't wait to see you in action."

"See?" Jack murmured in her ear. "He'll put us both to work soon enough. Just go with it, Zo-baby."

She was hard put not to laugh, and Trevor didn't seem upset with a joke at his expense. Bea would have said *if there's something so funny, share it with us, please,* and proceeded to embarrass his target almost to death.

So far she liked this much better. Even if she did have to lift the green glass bottle to hide her smile.

21

CONVERSATIONAL PROGRESS

JACK COULD HAVE TOLD DAD SHE WASN'T READY FOR A TRIP INTO THE CITY, much less seeing her *demi* deal with a potential Pride traitor, but the old man had his own methods for testing such things. At least Zoe was relaxing; she didn't look ready to bolt more than twice a day. The great communal Moonfall celebrations could wait; right now she was a quivering mass of raw nerves, a shy doe just barely coaxed from the forest's edge and more than ready to vanish into undergrowth at the slightest provocation.

Fortunately, Jackson Rouje had a great deal of patience, and his own form of sensitivity. The intuition of the Sorcerer's Gene was far beyond his reach, but an analyst's talent—what they used to call the Strategist's Mind, accorded high honor among all Kith—was sufficient to watch his *demie*'s expressions and reactions, even the most fleeting, and make deductions.

The entire world was a puzzle, some areas complex, others simple. Collecting data was enjoyable, solving various riddles satisfying, and watching the interaction and meshing of each particular quandary kept his restless mind occupied. Especially on long, insomniac nights during his *demie*'s absence.

Lying on his back, clad only in a pair of black pajama pants and staring at the familiar ceiling of his old room, Jack exhaled softly, his fingers laced behind his head, impatience sharpening its claws inside his bones. He was no stranger to sleeplessness, and the thought that his *demie* was just a few walls away was more frustration than comfort at this point. It took much of his control to stay still, considering his next few moves, instead of rising to pace like a caged animal.

He'd called it a curse more than once, but the cold, unblinking, bloodless detail-orientation of his talent had kept his beast chained and now gave him the strongest weapon possible to defend his *demie* —and the Pride, by extension, since she was safest inside their shelter.

Black and chrome, glass and sleek lines, his suite was just as he preferred it. A blank canvas, nothing to distract. It was his refuge, but now it felt more like a trap that hadn't quite closed yet.

For almost two decades he'd been telling himself *when we find her, when I find her*. Now, with the breathing reality either before him or just a room away, he was almost painfully calm. After the constant struggle to keep his beast in check, the striving to pass every test for a Pride heir with half his soul missing and the resultant bleed from the wound weakening and distracting at every moment, the sudden loss of pressure stood a distinct chance of doing what no real enemy could.

In other words, he was deathly afraid of committing a misstep. She was achingly lonely, her intuitive sensitivity terribly battered but still shining through the damage. Not to mention she was a smart girl, with far more going on behind those baby blues than the skins she'd been in contact with—including Angelina—probably ever dreamed.

The more Zoe trusted her *demi*, the safer she was. To ease her ever-so-gently in the proper direction wasn't robbing her of choice; he kept reminding himself as much. Her talents had probably been a handicap while she was trapped among skins, and maybe the glimmers of the Gene even frightened her. He was the best placed to help her control them—and as dangerous as his own beast was, a scared, wholly untrained shaman was much, much deadlier.

The only problem was how to broach the subject without terrifying her. His stories of childhood antics were probably growing thin, but she was beginning to open up and share a few of her own. They filled him with icy, clinical rage.

It was a good thing Angelina was dead and past all punishment. The woman was no kind of mother, and he couldn't decide if it was worse or better that she had no doubt known or guessed some of her husband's secrets. Maybe she thought she was rescuing Zoe in some twisted way, but there was a good chance she actively intended to punish a child she knew was not quite...well, not quite *normal*.

Not quite human.

His ears twitched. His beast was restless and the change ran just under his skin; his senses, normally acute, were even more heightened now. He heard it again—the faint sound of hinges.

He was off the low bed with its snowy sheets and black comforter in a moment, and he made no sound as he strode through the sitting room, every shape clean and sharp-edged. There was little light through the windows; the overcast had thickened and snow would start in the next hour.

Jack's hand curled around the hall door's smooth brushed-nickel knob. He tilted his golden head, listening intently.

A soft, sliding footstep. His face felt odd—he was smiling. He'd been waiting for her to get curious.

He stepped barefoot into the hall, yawning and scratching at his head. "Oh, hey." That was the right tone, he decided—mild, believable pleasure at an unforeseen circumstance. *I was waiting for you* might be...disconcerting. "Can't sleep either, huh?"

Zoe whirled and stared at him, her heavy braid swinging and her eyes huge with shock. She swallowed visibly, her pulse a high wild tattoo in her slim throat, and an edge of anxiety crept through her scent.

She was throwing off Allison's feartaking. It was a sign of

strength, but also a warning to tread carefully. "Shit," he muttered, ruefully. "Didn't mean to scare you. Were you heading for the kitchen?"

At least his *demie* was in a grey sweatshirt and fleece pants, barefoot and obviously not intending to bolt. He had no intention of letting her get further than a door to the outside unescorted, much less off the estate. If they'd grown up together she'd take his presence for granted, understand her role and her rights within the Pride.

And he would never have committed a quarter of the wild bullshit he did when puberty hit.

"Oh. Hi." Her slim, pretty hands dropped to her sides; her fingernails weren't ragged or bitten down anymore. "I'm sorry. I don't know where I was going. I just can't...yeah."

"Happen a lot?" He'd done a lot of staring into the dark, praying for a clear path to finding her, some kind of break, any clue at all.

It made sense now. A terrified, untrained *demie* with the Gene could tangle Kith pursuit, albeit unconsciously. Even the most skilled and committed jäger would have a difficult time chasing a shaman who didn't want to be found.

"Sometimes." Zoe shifted uneasily, studying him in the gloom. The hallway had no nightlights, but snowglow filtered through skylights and windows well enough. "You too?"

"Used to lie in bed looking at the ceiling, trying to think about you hard enough to reach." *Usanaugh* had a deep bond, but they'd only been toddlers. Had Angelina known about the Gene? It wasn't out of the question. "I kept thinking, *show me where you are, just give me a sign.*"

"Really?" For some reason, that made her sway; his hand tingled with the need to steady her.

But he stayed where he was, sensing some knife-edge of decision was approaching. "Yeah. You ever hear me?"

"I..." Zoe took a step back, soft and willowy. She'd probably taken to ballet with a vengeance—Kith were graceful as a rule, but she was in a class all her own. "Maybe I did," she continued, quietly. She halted, and now regarded him with those big, solemn baby blues. "You hear things too, don't you."

My sweet demie, *you have no idea.* "Hear things, smell things—yeah. I'm fast, too. Faster than normal." *So are you, and you must have noticed.* He was betting very heavily that this was what she needed to hear, and Allison's warning that any show of anger would be taken as judgment flashed through him. "And stronger."

"God." Another small movement, but instead of retreating she simply swayed again. "You...you know. You're like me."

"I'm your twin." It didn't get any simpler. "We call it *usanaugh.* If you'd been here all along you'd know it's natural and you wouldn't be afraid."

"I've always been afraid," she whispered. Maybe it was the darkness providing boldness, maybe it was the absence of any other confidant and the unfamiliarity of her situation, or maybe he'd simply made the right move.

Maybe it was all three. He wasn't going to overlook good luck. "It's all right. I'm here now."

"But for how long?" Her hand flew to her mouth, sealing her lips as if it could call the words back.

"You'll have a hard time getting rid of me." His *demie* shouldn't look so heartbroken, or so shocked. Jackson's beast didn't like that at all, and neither did the cold calculator inside his head; he forced down a growl threatening to thread through the slightest edge of soothing Voice. "I'm warning you now, Zo-baby."

It must have been—a miracle—another right thing to say, because she no longer looked so lost. She took her time watching him before responding, seconds ticking by smoothly, relentlessly.

He didn't care. She could stand and think all she wanted, as long as he could see her. As long as she was close, he didn't care *what* she did.

Just the mere fact of her continued existence was enough.

"It's not that I don't like it," she said, finally. "It's just a bit... much. I keep waiting for the other shoe to drop."

"That's reasonable." It was also a traumatized child's coping mechanism, but he didn't want to voice *that* little observation. Being raised as a skin would fuck a Kith right up, between their strange prey taboos and the fear of insanity when a young Kith knew, saw, or *did* things skins couldn't. "You had seventeen years with Angelina. All I'm asking is a chance to show you she was wrong. We want you here. You can't imagine how much."

"I guess." She rubbed at her upper arms, probably very close to hugging herself for comfort. Learning to self-soothe without your twin left a mark. "What's that word? *Uzza*-what?"

"*Usanaugh*. Family term, for boy-girl twins." Regular Kith didn't have fraternal multiples, merely identical; it was only when a dominant Kith found a human mate with a certain indefinable quality— maybe a recessive of the Sorcerer's Gene, maybe something else nonphysical—that *demi* and *demie* were thrown, and then only rarely. Most Kith-human couplings were sterile, though never loveless.

Skins had a hard time with Kith mates, though. Their fragility was heartbreaking, and often ended badly. It wasn't quite frowned upon for a Kith to take a skin mate, but it was considered somewhat unfortunate.

Whatever Dad's true feelings on Angelina had been, they remained unspoken.

"Family term." She nodded. "Okay. And the other stuff? Hearing things, and...and seeing things?"

"Your senses are a lot sharper than the norm. I've got that too." The important thing was to give just enough information, but not overwhelm. "You want some tea? Hot chocolate? Glass of milk?"

"Won't Amelia be mad? The kitchen's, you know. *Hers*."

She'd be surprised to hear you say that. Property among the Kith was largely and thoroughly communal. "She might be down there stirring a saucepan already." But he hoped not. He wanted to be the one soothing his *demie*. "She often knew when I couldn't sleep; she'd make me something warm."

"Did you ever miss Mama?"

"No." Or if he had, he hadn't noticed it. Trevor, for all his forbidding, overwhelming dominance, was also a Kith father, and that meant safety. The leader of the Pride had done his best to see to his heir's every need, even though they both felt the lack of Zoe's presence, and of course the rest of the Pride stepped in at any moment to help. A *demi*'s loneliness could only be truly assuaged by one thing, but they had tried—and he had known they were trying. "Only you."

"Is it bad that I don't miss..." She bit her lip, and Jack realized he was closing the distance between them. He couldn't help it, drawn as irresistibly as a magnetized needle pointing north.

"Doesn't sound like there was much to miss." *It's probably a good thing we didn't find her alive. Dad might have had to do something he'd regret.* "I just wish we'd rescued you sooner."

"It does feel like a rescue." Her head tilted back slightly as she gazed up at him. "I keep thinking I'm going to wake up back in Marquette."

"I'm real." His skin was alive with her nearness. If she felt the same, she hid it well. "You can pinch me." Jackson wished he had McKenna's way with women—the bastard could charm almost any female, except a certain shaman. Jolie had given him short shrift for years, but it looked like Mac had figured out what he wanted and was just as focused on that as he had been on having fun before the realization struck.

Jack wished them both luck. And he hoped, while he was thinking about it, that Mac would have little to no effect on his *demie*.

"I wouldn't." But Zoe relaxed still further, and there was a gleam —she was smiling, and it looked like a broad, happy one, too. The sight threatened to take his breath away, even in the dark. "Do you really have to go back to work? For Tre—I mean, for Dad?"

"Eventually." *And you'll be with me. But that's not for a while.* "The most important thing is taking care of you. Reassuring you that we're not going to vanish, that we don't want you to pay for anything." He didn't miss her slight flinch—a girl raised poor and traveling under the radar knew very well what men offering money might demand in return. All things considered, they were lucky she was taking this so well. "I'm pretty sure you've seen a few unpleasant things." This was more conversational progress than they'd made in weeks, and he was once again taught that patience was the best policy.

"More than a few." An edge to her scent—she was very aware of his closeness, now.

Good. "If you ever want to talk about it, I'm here. And if anyone did anything to you, *demie*, all you have to do is tell me."

"And then what?" She didn't ask what *demie* meant, but he didn't think she hadn't heard. Maybe, if Angelina hadn't stolen her, he would have been able to predict his twin. As it stood, though, she was an exceedingly pleasant mystery.

If he could relax. If he could be sure she wouldn't vanish again. "What do you think? All you have to do is say the word." It was too soon for such bare honesty, but he had what amounted to a death-grip on the situation. A Kith girl raised to believe herself a skin had no way of fighting a fully trained analyst comfortable with his own talent and aware of his strengths.

Even if she did have the Gene.

"Great. Now I just have to figure out *which* word."

It took him a moment to catch the laughter in her tone. She was actually *joking* with him.

Definite progress. And all it took was a midnight rendezvous, both of them sleepless without the other's comforting closeness. Not to mention the weeks of diligent work, the equivalent of sitting motionless outside a mousehole with a morsel of something tasty, waiting for a tiny flicker of motion.

So Jack let himself smile, and offered his arm. "You'll find one or two eventually. What are you reading now?" Books were a sure way to draw her out.

"I finished a collection of short stories." Her hand rested inside his elbow. "That's probably why I can't sleep. Algernon Blackwood's not relaxing."

Well, that's a clue. "We should go into town." The contact sent singing awareness through him, enough to make his own steady pulse skip a beat. "They have a couple bookstores."

She didn't shoot the idea down immediately, nor did she withdraw. Instead, she ambled, letting him set their pace and guide her steps. "I like libraries. They're free."

If that's what you want. "We have libraries here, too. We're not completely uncivilized."

"Not completely, no." More laughter under the words. "You've got to admit it's kind of gothic. Snowbound in an old house, a sudden heiress."

With beasts all around. We should get you a red hood. "No monsters in the attic. Or mad wives, either."

"No, she kidnapped a princess and went on the run." Zoe stopped, examining his profile.

"But they can't hold the princess forever." He was careful to keep his tone light and amused. "Eventually she's rescued."

"Or rescues herself."

Maybe she thought she'd been doing all right. "And doing a good job of it, too," Jack said. Certainly she'd survived, but Jack was cold all over at the thought of a thin, tired *demie* shivering while she worked a dead-end supermarket job. There were dangers other than the physical for a Kith left stranded among skins. "But I'm here now, so I might as well pitch in. I'll make you something nice, the way Amelia used to for me."

"All right." She let him draw her along again, and he was hoping the kitchen was empty.

It was, so Jack made her hot chocolate, their companionable silence broken only by the silent static of falling snow. And when she returned to her suite she paused in the doorway, as if she was reluctant to leave him.

It was enough.

22

TRUTH, STING

Four days before Christmas, the nightmares returned.

Normally Zoe jolted out of bad dreams with a silent lunge, stiff and sweaty-shaking, her knuckles jammed against her mouth and the scream safely trapped inside her ribcage. She should have known any relaxation at all was dangerous.

But...Jack's voice, soft and reflective. *Just show me where you are, just give me a sign.* Had it been him all those years, speaking across thousands of miles? Would they have found her despite Mama's frantic insistence on running and hiding, if Zoe hadn't been...strange?

She wasn't quite sure if she'd cried out or not, sitting bolt-upright in the bed, her skin greasy-cold and the pretty blue suite a sudden, unfamiliar trap.

"Zo? *Zoe!*" Someone was upset. There was a bang, a crackle, and footsteps more sensed than heard; even the air here was strange, soft and pleasant instead of sticky with menace—Zoe was just about to let out a choked, relieved sound when a heavy shadow landed on her bed and warm, very strong arms closed around her. "Dream, it's just a dream, I'm here, okay? I'm here. Calm down."

Her body didn't listen, clawing and thrashing until she realized who it was. Zoe went limp, blinking in the darkness; the bed was a soft cloud. Her brother had all but tackled her, driving her flat, and his weight atop her was either a comfort or a cage.

She couldn't decide. Her throat was dry, all her breath gone, and the trembling going through her in waves threatened to chatter her teeth to fragments.

"Calm down," he repeated, and there was no shred of anger or irritation in the words. Jack sounded, all things considered, very mellow indeed. "Just a dream, Zo. I'm right here, nothing can get you."

Where were you when I needed to hear that? She swallowed the words; they jammed up in her esophagus, and what came out was a soft, strangled sound.

"Am I crushing you? Whoops." Jack's weight shifted, but he was still *over* her, his elbows on either side of her shoulders, the taller bulk of him atop the covers. "Better? Easy, Zo-baby. It's me, it's your *demi*. I'm here."

She expected a slap, a kick, something painful. What Zoe did *not* expect was the flood of instant relaxation or the sudden, vertiginous absence of terror. *What the hell?*

"Jack?" she managed, a despairing whisper. The window was full of quiet snowy night, and she had no idea what time it was.

"Yep. I heard you." As if this was a normal occurrence, to be expected. Jack went still, balanced catlike, graceful even when still. "I don't think I broke your door, though. That's good."

Oh, God. "I'm sor—"

"Don't be." Again, there was no shadow of anger. His bare skin was very warm, his arms brushing her shoulders. Lost in deep shadow, his face held only a glitter of dark eyes. "If you heard me having a bad dream, you'd do the same thing. Here."

She had no time to tell him maybe she wouldn't, because he shifted and spilled to the side. A few brisk, efficient movements later her head was on his shoulder and he was sprawled next to her, still on top of the covers. They pulled tight because he was so much taller and bulkier, turning into a cradling cocoon.

"Better," her brother said. "My heart's racing. It's nice to actually have you here."

What the hell does that mean? The words stuck in her throat. The shaking was going down, though—that was, in Mama's terms, a blessing and a half.

Of course, Mama hated Zoe's nightmares. *Stop being dramatic,* she'd hiss, usually with a brutal pinch on her daughter's arm or leg. *Just go to sleep.*

"You get bad dreams a lot?" Jack continued. He didn't sound quite as controlled as usual, a betraying huskiness at the bottom of the words. "Because I used to hear what I thought was you and I'd turn the house upside down in the middle of the night, looking. But you were gone."

"All the time," Zoe whispered. It was a relief to finally have her words working. "But n-not since I c-came here." *Really? Stuttering? For God's sake, Zo.*

"Good. Wait, that's good, right?" Did he actually sound *anxious?* Unbelievable, he was always so calm.

Zoe nodded, her flushed, damp cheek moving against his bare shoulder. "Yeah." Thankfully, her throat was deciding it could ease up a little. "I'm all right. I didn't mean to wake you up."

Even Royal had never liked her nightmares. *What, again? Go sleep on the couch, bitch.*

"I was up already," Jack said, softly, and maybe it was true. "Thinking about chemicals."

"Chemicals?" About the only thing Zoe was thinking about was breakfast, but that was probably hours away. She could move to grab her phone and check the time—the bedside clock was analog and lost in darkness—but it didn't seem worth the effort. The last of the fear drained away, leaving pure exhaustion in its wake.

"Yeah, there's a...you'd probably find it boring." Jack shifted as if he had an itch, then went still again. "Certain additives to materials for automobile tires and how they affect the manufacturing process."

It sounded complicated, not to mention math-related like all chemistry. "You were thinking about that?"

"There's all sorts of stuff on the internet for when you can't sleep."

"I guess." She was used to books instead, or simple insomnia after terrible dreams tore through any attempt to rest. At least her boxers and tank top weren't impossibly rucked-up and tangled, another blessing. "I'm okay now."

"Want to talk about it?" He tucked his chin a little, breathing into her hair. "They say if you do, the nightmares have a harder time coming back."

"Really?" It didn't seem possible.

"Try it. Tell me."

"Mostly it's just...things that happened." It wasn't the church cellar this time, or a cheap hotel waiting for Mama to return, swinging between agonizing hope and pure terror. No, the dream had been Royal's apartment in Akron, and that terrible last night spent with him. *Get it through your fucking head, Amber.* "I was living with this guy and it didn't end well."

"He hurt you?" Oh, *now* there was a faint thread of menace in Jack's calm, even voice.

Not as much as I hurt him. But what would he—or Trevor—think of sending some guy to the emergency room because her fingernails could lengthen, sharpening to curved stiletto points? Jack knew about the speed and strength, about hearing things other people couldn't, but if he found out she'd attacked and could have killed someone...

But Roy was still alive, and so was Bea. "I got away." That was the important thing.

"Not an answer, but okay." Her twin stirred, settling himself like he intended to stay for a while. His arm was going to go numb if she kept resting her head on it, but she couldn't move just yet. It was too warm, too comfortable. "So you were dreaming about it?"

"Sort of." Zoe froze when he shifted once more, but he just stroked her arm with his free fingertips, a light forgiving brush. Did he have claws too, or was that only her? "Did you ever lose your temper? When you were young?" It was scary to think of someone so big and so controlled finally snapping.

"Sometimes. We often do when we're still kids, that's why Dad was always on me about control. The Ki—the entire family helps young ones stay calm, stay on track. It's also part of why we worried about you so much; Angelina wasn't equipped to raise one of us."

One of us. Zoe stored that intriguing statement away for further thought. "One of the *uzza*-thingies? Or one of the...the family?" it felt weird; for so long 'family' meant only her and Mama, period, the end.

Jack and Trevor were always very careful to say *the family*, like it was the Mob. Or like there was another name for it, in that strange language. Maybe it was from the 'old country' Hermann and Amelia talked about.

"Both." Thankfully, her brother clearly didn't consider the question outlandish.

Slick fear-sweat had dried all over her, a faint irritation. The cold silence outside said it wasn't snowing but the weather was thinking about it again, and thinking hard. "Are winters here always like this?"

"Yeah. Didn't you get snow in Montana? And Nebraska?"

"Of course." Winter meant miserable shivering hunger for days on end, since Mama could rarely afford to turn the heat on. Zoe had thought Texas would be warmer in the winter, and it was—only incrementally, though. She'd been considering moving a bit further south than the Panhandle. "But this is different."

"Well, New England. You don't have to worry about anything, you know. I'm right here," Jack continued, almost as if talking to himself. "If I start to lose my temper, you'll calm me right down. And vice versa. It's natural."

Mama said nothing about me was natural. But Angelina hadn't been the expert, it looked like. The sense of being caught in a fairy-tale, or a movie, was stronger than ever. This was a nice dream, and she was afraid to move too quickly and break it. "Are you sure?"

"I am." He sounded so certain, she could almost believe it. "I'm also the resident expert, since I've been here the whole time. Just trust me."

You make it sound simple. "All right."

"You mean you will?" Slightly baffled, or surprised. He took a deep breath, like he was smelling her hair, and she was glad she could take all the showers she wanted. Being clean was one of the greatest luxuries of all, and even the soap here was expensive.

Maybe I will trust you. Who else do I have? "You haven't done anything bad yet."

"But you're still waiting. You know, for a shoe to drop."

"Maybe." The truth didn't sting, which was a first in Zoe Simmons's—now Zoe Rouje's—experience. "Does that bother you?"

"Figure it's normal. That woman did a real number on you, Zo."

He called her *that woman*, like she wasn't even related to him. But if a mother left you behind like unclaimed luggage...they weren't supposed to *do* that, right? He'd had it just as rough as she did, even if the setting was more luxurious.

Zoe's eyelids were very heavy. Normally, anyone this close while she was trying to sleep would mean an uncomfortable night half-dozing, ready and alert. "She was scared," she mumbled. "People do weird things when they're scared."

"She didn't have to be, though. Dad would've...never mind." Jack had relaxed now, and it was nice to whisper in the dark. "Do some deep breathing, that's better. For both of us."

Her entire body was heavy now, right down to her fingertips. The same strange deep almost-heard thrumming radiated from his chest, very soothing.

Normal people can't do that. Well, who wanted to be normal, anyway? All it had ever gotten Zoe was kicked in the teeth. "You have to go back to work soon." Would they leave her alone in the house eventually? Or did they think she'd steal the silver and disappear?

"You'll come with me. It'll be fun." He kept brushing her arm, light butterfly strokes. "You're tired, *demie*. Rest."

She wanted to say something else, but her body decided differently and she fell into deep black velvet unconsciousness.

23
GOOD PRACTICE

HARD NOT TO BE IN A GOOD MOOD WHEN THE ENTIRE WORLD WAS GOING your way; that was one of McKenna's little proverbs. Jack caught himself whistling while he shaved—a good morning habit, even if the change made it practically unnecessary—and smiling as he chose a shirt. There was even the temptation to dance a few steps before he left his bedroom, because not only was his *demie* found and alive, but she had well and truly thawed.

Maybe it was the late-night talk, maybe it was waking in his arms, or maybe it was just that his pheromones were naturally appealing and comforting. Or maybe it was all of the above. The point of a miracle remained, its mere existence more than enough. She relaxed around him, looked to him for guidance, and soon enough he could move to the next stage, easing her through the restrictions of a skin upbringing.

Jackson could barely wait.

He was just reaching for today's watch when there was a shy, tentative tap on the hall door; his entire body snapped into singing alertness. "You don't need to knock," he said. "Come on in, Zo."

His *demie* peered through, her hesitant smile strengthening under a wild glory of black curls. Confining that hair was a sin, really; each lock was so vitally beautiful. She didn't even have to bat those charcoal eyelashes over her baby blues—a single somber glance, and he was more than ready to do whatever she required.

This was an occasion, though, because the princess had consented to an outing.

"You said nine-thirty, I'm early." She even came a few steps into his domain, examining the sitting room with interest, as usual. Jeans, a black V-neck sweater, her new boots—oh, she was a vision, even if he couldn't get her to order anything online.

Today would help, though. All her survival instincts were geared toward dealing with skin poverty; she was adrift in this new world and he was more than happy to provide a compass.

"And always welcome." He didn't have the words to tell her *how* welcome. "Have a seat. Want a drink? Best thing for nerves."

"At this hour?" But she did edge into the room a little further, obviously curious about the view from his window. "You have a bottle in here?"

"Maybe some Scotch somewhere. I'd have to look." Jack decided he could do without if she didn't like it, though. "If it bothers you—"

"Not really. Always good to know where the closest stash is." Laughter ran under her words, and she tucked a curl behind her ear. Her earrings were long twisted silver drops—a gift from Dad, and it was good to see her wearing them. "Just in case I want to raid it."

Now he had to lay in a supply, just in case. "Try the closet first. If I haven't hidden something in there Mac—that's McKenna, you'll meet him eventually—probably has."

"You mention him a lot. Is that where we're going?"

Christ, no. If he tries to flirt with you I'll have to eviscerate him. It was an irrational response, but knowing as much didn't help. "Nope. It's almost Christmas, and I talked Dad out of doing the whole Advent calendar. So we're going shopping." He glanced sidelong at her, buckling the selected watch with thoughtless, habitual speed. "Don't worry, I've already handled your present for him." *As promised. Ask me for something difficult.*

She nodded, and the easing of her expression was another gift, in and of itself. "He probably has a million cufflinks."

"But none from *you*," Jack repeated. They were traditional, silver with the family crest, and getting them engraved at short notice was well worth the hassle. Seeing her relief when he agreed to handle something as a *demi* should was at once gratifying and maddening. "And today you might see something else to get him."

"That would be nice." She peeked out the window, her hands clasped politely behind her back. It wasn't as aesthetic as her garden view, but the geometric shape of the paved walk and the bulk of the west wing rising on the other side was comforting and there was enough sun for a plant, if he'd ever felt like taking care of any living creature other than his missing *demie*. "I still feel weird about it. The, you know. The cards."

The next step was to get her comfortable with using Pride resources, including funds. "All the more reason to get it over with." He slipped his wallet in the proper pocket, and though he didn't like the prospect, it was best to go unarmed for a little while. She was extraordinarily sensitive, and might draw an errant conclusion or two if he was carrying; a Kith analyst didn't need much in the way of firepower anyway. "Dad'll worry if you don't. He'll start adding more, thinking it isn't enough."

"Sounds gruesome," she agreed, cheerfully. "Maybe I should hold off a little longer."

Not only was she relaxing, but also testing him with small jokes. "If you do, let me know." Jack thought it very likely her sense of humor was far sharper than she'd ever let on, and couldn't wait to hear its real contours. Sooner or later, when she trusted him, the edges would show. "I'll provoke him."

Her eyes all but sparkled. "Is that wise?"

"Trust me. I'm a professional." One last glance to make sure every button was properly done, as Amelia would say, and he was ready except for his black knee-length wool coat. "You're going to need a jacket, Zo." *And a hat, not to mention gloves.* The custom ones to fit over her signet were due any time now. "It's cold."

"I have the one Amelia gave me." She paused, standing next to the bright rectangle of the window; the bench seat there was hard polished wood, bare of any ornamentation. Not like hers. Jack didn't like cushioning; he wanted every edge and plane right where he could see it. "Are you sure about this?"

I could let you stay here forever, but... "Of course. We'll visit Traleski's, then go to a couple stores, have lunch at Pannore. It'll be *fun*, even." Janine Traleski was jäger, her control almost as absolute as a shaman's; she and her lieutenants would keep their cool even with an untrained bearer of the Gene at close quarters. "I'll be right with you the entire time."

"I know." But Zoe's smile said she liked to hear it anyway. On the one hand, handling her so well was great. On the other, he was keyed-up, wondering when he was going to put a foot wrong and have to coax her out again—or, Moon and God both forbid, frighten her. "After all, I might decide to book a flight to London and stay at the Ritz."

"Huh." He didn't *think* she was serious, but his beast didn't like any hint of her withdrawal or fear. Jack concurred; it took plenty of control to keep his tone light. "Maybe we should? If Dad's the only one here for Christmas Amelia will stuff him like a goose."

Zoe dissolved into giggles, cupping her hand over her mouth as if she expected someone to scold her. Her eyes sparkled, and Jack almost lost his breath. He was content to stand still, letting her amusement wash over him in warm waves. Each time their gazes met his another cascade of laughter shook her and he knew he was smiling like a complete dolt.

"Maybe the Savoy instead," he continued, when her merriment faded. "We can spend a few days in the museums, too. Visit the Royal Ballet."

"One thing at a time." She straightened self-consciously; with her cheeks flushed and her eyes bright she was a completely different girl than the skinny, terrified waif fleeing a second-rate grocery store. She'd gained some weight, now vividly and visibly Kith from lucid skin to fluid grace. "You're all dressed up. Should I wear a skirt or something?"

It was only a day suit, but he was still pleased that she liked it. And the thought of her in a pencil skirt, or schoolgirl plaid, was incredibly intriguing. "If you want to change, go ahead. I think you're fine the way you are." *Not to mention Janine likes to see you comfortable before she starts buying.* "If you're ready, grab your coat." He'd been hoping she'd leave her hair down, and was rewarded now; it just begged for fingertips to untangle heavy rippling silk.

Another reward was her almost-dash for the door, a marvel of coordinated Kith motion. She was forgetting to impersonate a skin; by the time he stepped into the hall she had nipped into her own suite, reappearing with the smaller leather bag Hermann had made and the coat Amelia had fretted over—*what if it doesn't fit?*

The housekeeper expected a pampered Pride princess, not an anxious, polite girl who took every offering with dutiful enthusiasm. Fortunately, Jack could break or bend etiquette as necessary to smooth any incident, and he'd be doing a lot of that as his *demie* integrated with the Pride.

It was a pleasant prospect.

"Perfect timing." He'd missed the pleasure of holding her coat, but she didn't have the habit of letting him perform the small courtesies yet. She fell into step beside him as if they'd never been separated. "Got your gloves? Good. You should have a hat—fine." He caved, of course, when she made a face. "Now, rules." *Begin as you mean to go on* was almost always the best strategy. "I'm going to drive because I'm a control freak, and you're going to let me."

"I am?" She all but bounced, forgetting her usual watchfulness for a few precious moments.

"In this weather, and especially since we're going somewhere you've never been? Yes." Besides, he wanted her used to being chauffeured. It was the absolute least she deserved.

"Point taken."

Having his *demie* agree with something, no matter how small, was *extremely* satisfying. Did she feel the same comfort? "You're going to work on the letting-me-open-doors thing. It's expected."

"It's medieval." She thrust her hands in the coat's pockets; it was slightly too large, the hem all the way at her ankles. Still, his *demie* made it charming, a kid playing dress-up, and it was a smaller copy of his own overcoat. The boots fit her perfectly, thank God; his eye for sizes was still good.

"More Renaissance, since I'm leaving the chainmail and spiked mace at home." Now came the important bit, as they hit the stairs at the end of the hall. She knew enough to let him precede her here, and hopefully would handle elevators well too. "Let me take care of introductions. You don't shake hands, unless you absolutely want to. All right?"

"Why not?" She sobered, visibly regretting the question. She'd relaxed so much, but the waters were by no means clear. Any shred of irritation or impatience made her withdraw in a hurry, hiding behind a shield of reticence and genteel etiquette Angelina had schooled her in, probably harshly.

So Jack took care not to display a single whiff of anything resembling pique or vexation. It was good practice. "It's just not what we do, Zoe." Shamans, let alone *demie*, were too precious to be handled willy-nilly. And while he was fairly certain his control would hold if a dumb skin or a Pride male touched his twin without her consent, he didn't want the crucial test happening during their very first foray outside the house. "Will you try, at least?"

"It's actually what I prefer." Her sunshine returned, muted at first. If the flinches were maddening, the glimpses of vulnerable sweetness between were doubly so, in a wholly different way. She was starved for any approval at all, and grateful for much less than would satisfy many others—what might she have been, if Angelina hadn't stolen her? "I hate handshakes."

"I don't doubt it." With her sensitivity, the contact was probably excruciating. "So no worries, you never have to do it again."

"But you do?"

"I don't mind." An analyst could gain valuable feedback from the contact along with a much finer pheromonal picture of an opponent. Plus, getting close enough to shake was close enough to take a throat out with little ado. "Makes me feel useful."

She hesitated only once, passing the kitchen. Amelia hummed an old lullaby and something sizzled; the Christmas baking and candy-making were proceeding at a furious pace. "Should we tell her we're leaving?"

"Pretend we're sneaking out," Jack mock-whispered, caught her hand, and pulled her along. The jolt of skin contact up his arm, the sudden relaxation of his beast, her delighted, muffled laugh—he'd fantasized about his *demie*'s return, and he had to say, he was a little disappointed in his own imagination.

There was simply no comparison. His wildest wishes were handily outstripped by the bright, overwhelming reality. She glanced over the smaller garage, her eyes going round, and he could have laughed at her surprise. The black SUV, her chariot for the day, wasn't flashy at all despite its under-hood modifications. It was heavy, and safe, and dependable—just the thing for a town trip. And she let him handle her door, carefully shutting something precious in a metal cocoon.

He had to hurry on his way to the driver's side, fighting the irrational fear that she might vanish. Maybe the panic would fade, in time—but the relief when he found her buckling up, the leather purse cradled in her lap, was intense enough to blot out every anxiety once again.

"You're going to like Janine," he predicted.

And if she didn't, he would whisk her away.

24

UNCHARITABLE
THOUGHTS

THE ROADS WERE SCRAPED, SANDED, AND SALTED; THE FRESH SNOW WAS dazzling. There was an extra pair of sunglasses in the central console, but they were comically big on her.

"You look like a movie star," Jack said, and even though he couldn't have meant it she still laughed, secretly pleased, and kept them on. Hiding behind shades seemed an excellent idea now that they were out of the house's warm nestlike embrace.

You couldn't stay in a paradise forever, after all. Zoe didn't really think Jack would drive her out into the countryside and leave her in the cold wasteland, laughing while he sped away—but still, she hugged the purse on her lap and paid attention to every turning and landmark.

Such as they were, under all the snow.

The SUV's radio was tuned to a classical station; whoever was in this car last probably liked it. So did she. Every damn retail place she'd ever worked in played Muzak or anemic oldies, the thumping bass at Royal's club hurt her ears, Bea's evangelical pop grated the same four chords over and over. But when Zoe was young Mama liked classical music and public radio while driving, and the announcers' slow, soothing voices were friendly. Jack didn't even mess with the volume. He just drove, a faint line between his golden-dark eyebrows and his mouth set.

Fences thickened to walls before both vanished entirely; the houses lost their protective fields, drawing closer together and swelling with self-importance. A scattering of smaller, less pristinely maintained domiciles trundled by, and all of a sudden there was a town snuggled amid wooded hills.

It was the sort of small, polished place Mama would sigh at, knowing there would be nothing a faded single mother exiled from her rightful queendom could afford to rent. And Zoe would shrink in the car seat each time, knowing she was the anchor her mother couldn't loosen.

This type of town had anti-littering signs without graffiti responses as well as quaint, freshly painted trash receptacles all up and down Main Street. The shops were tiny, full of bright, overpriced luxuries, and the supermarket at one end of the main shopping strip was the kind of high-end organic wholeness place they didn't let you work at if you didn't fit the aesthetic, so Zo had never bothered.

A Kroger, Piggly Wiggly, or Greenfield was more her speed. But with the clothes they'd given her, not to mention Amelia's skincare regimen, maybe she'd be able to get a job here.

It sounded intriguing, though she suspected working at high-end places was just as bad as anywhere else. But maybe, just maybe, she could even get an apartment of her own?

It was dizzying to have an actual shot at not just survival, but something actively better. Her downward spiral had been arrested, but the vertigo kept turning her stomach over at random moments.

Antique stores, two bookstores, an art gallery, assorted small tourist shops, an old City Hall-type building with a local museum on one floor and various offices on others, a well-clipped isosceles of a fir tree on its quadrangle of public park decorated for the season with weatherproof lights and tinsel—it was beautiful as only a stage set could be.

The fir tree might even be offended at the thought that a homeless person might need shelter under its boughs. There was nary a manger nor an unhoused person in sight. The residential section crowding on the shopping area was full of cheerful, slightly seedy pseudo-Victorians and colonials, all aggressively quirky, their gingerbread painted contrasting colors and their postage-stamp yards full of decorative bric-a-brac mounding the snow in strange shapes.

There had to be a smaller, poorer townlet nearby to do all the landscaping and janitorial service for its rich neighbor. Zoe eyed the bundled-up pedestrians and was deeply, miserably aware of her own foreignness. Everyone here had money, except for whoever emptied the trashcans.

The big beautiful house and her new luxurious life were soap bubbles. If she even breathed wrong, everything could vanish.

"You're worrying again." Jack eased the car into yet another right turn, tires grinding on screamed and salted pavement. He was circling, as far as she could tell. "It'll get easier, I swear. And that's why we're doing this first."

I could just hide under the bed. "So this Janine's what, exactly? A teacher?" You had to be careful to blend in with rich people; Mama's manners were clearly from this strata and she'd raised Zo to not be an embarrassment.

Well, at least not *more* of one. Even in exile Angelina was regal, and very conscious of her fallen state. Her daughter couldn't hope to be otherwise, especially since she'd never measure up.

You had to be born into this, and raised with it too.

"Sort of." Jack checked traffic, his thumb moving slightly with the rhythm of a Schumann piece. At least, the radio's display said it was good ol' Schu, and that was confirmation enough. "*Lifestyle consultant* is what she calls it. You're undergoing a transition, you're in a new world. Of course you'll need a little help adjusting."

"Yeah." It would be the same as everywhere else, but with money you could avoid a few of the worst parts of life. It would be even better if Zo could find a more-than-minimum job—she didn't for a moment think the prohibition on working was real, just something polite to say—but using her new ID felt strange and illegal in a way the fake ones never had. "So she's kind of like charm school? Tutoring?"

"Charm school." Laughter bubbled under the words. "That's a good one, I'll have to tell her. Think of Janine like a cross between a personal shopper and a dotty old aunt who knows all the gossip. Here we are." He cut the wheel, and the SUV slipped neatly into a just-vacated parking spot. "Good to see my instincts are still sharp. Don't touch the door, all right?"

Yes sir, white knight. "I might forget in the time it takes you to walk around the car." Teasing him was fast becoming second nature, and he seemed to like it.

"Try not to," Jack mock-growled in return, and opened his door.

It was easy to forget he was bigger than her, had been here all along, and knew everything. He was more like one of the nonthreatening boys at school or a good coworker, one with steady hands and no management sympathies. The small, still voice of her survival instincts kept insisting he was safe.

The feeling had never led her wrong before, and if it stopped working she was dead in the water. But it was so strange not to fear a male, not to flinch when he offered a hand to help her out of the car or stepped into her personal space—and very, *very* strange to wake from a nightmare to his calm.

It's fine, she repeated for the umpteenth time, her own personal mantra right next to apologies. *This will all be okay. I'll do whatever I have to, just let me stay.*

At least the coat was the right kind to help her blend in here, and so were the boots. The skin stuff and haircare Amelia stocked were incredibly expensive, and by golly did they work wonders. She might get away with this, if she didn't talk. Or touch anything. Or—

Jack's hand closed around her elbow as she stepped up on the curb, an efficient steadying. "Where are your gloves?"

"Oh. Yeah." She dug in her pockets, and as soon as she produced

them he whisked them away, motioned her to one side of the pavement, and tugged the heavy grey knitted fabric over her hands like
she was a little kid. "I can—"

"Sure, you can. But it makes me feel useful, remember?" One
corner of his mouth rose, and he shot her a quick, flickering glance,
dark eyes warm and depthless. "I've got years of catching up
to do."

"Years of being a glove-wrangler?" Still, it was nice to be helped,
for once; had Mama ever done this for child-Zoe? She couldn't
remember. A man in wingtips and a camel coat hurried by,
crunching on deicer pellets.

"Glove-wrangler, door-opener, drink-bringer, handshake-giver,
problem-solver, fixit-man, coffee-stirrer, and all-around fun time." It
had all the rhythm and speed of a long-standing joke. Jack squeezed
her gloved hands, a brief, affectionate mini-hug. "I'm a whole Swiss
Army knife."

Pocket knives were something she knew a little bit about. "All
anyone ever uses are the corkscrews, though. Or the blade to cut tape
on boxes."

Get it through your head, Amber. Royal had displayed a switchblade once or twice, when a girl got mouthy or a club customer
attempted to leave without paying. Those were bad memories, and
she hurriedly stuffed them in the tiny box where everything nasty
lived during the day.

At night the bad things came out and partied, but she couldn't
afford to concentrate on them now.

"Shush." Jack's smile was all easy forgiveness. "It's a secret, don't
tell anyone."

"You have a million secrets." His weren't anything like *hers*,
though. Of course he'd never had to do anything bad to survive.
Money was great insulation.

It was weird, though, because he didn't seem...weak, like rich
people often did. Maybe the emotional trauma of a missing mother
had toughened him right up. Neither Mama nor Trevor seemed very

touchy-feely, though Dad had taken to offering grave, careful hugs as if he was afraid Zoe would break.

"Man of mystery. That's the corkscrew." Jack looked satisfied when she laughed, offering his arm. "See? I also moonlight as a court jester."

He kept saying *pretend you've always been here*, but she didn't quite have the hang of it yet. Waiting for the inevitable crash was nerve-wracking. She wished she were back in the blue suite, the door closed and comfortable silence wrapping around her.

Yet she was anxious there, too, especially late at night.

The nervousness only retreated when Jack was nearby, and she didn't quite know how he did it or what she should think. On the one hand, he was her brother. The proof was in black and white, on papers that couldn't be forged—or if they were, it was by masters who had to be expensive, and nobody would spend that kind of trouble on *her*.

On the other hand, he seemed content to spend every waking moment with her, and she wasn't sure when that would stop—and what she would do when it did.

"There it is again. You're worrying." Jack didn't set off, just stood in the cold looking down at her, a high blush touching his shaven cheeks. The wind teased at her hair—it would be a mess before long —and carried a dry metallic tang of more ice soon. The Puritans had landed somewhere around here, and Zoe was pretty sure this weather was part of what made them so weird.

It was nice when you had a warm window to look out of, though. She couldn't deny that. "I'm thinking about the Puritans. And people who have to sleep outside."

"Puritans and sleeping outside." He nodded thoughtfully, and took a single step, as if testing her willingness to move. She let him steer; there was no point in doing otherwise. "I'm listening."

He always listened. It was a bit eerie. Zoe watched her boots, crunching on tiny pellets scattered to keep wealthy people from slip- ping. The world was dangerous but safety could be had, if the cash was available. "Are any of these places hiring, do you think?" In other words, could she get applications? Putting a real Social Security number in a tiny box was going to be strange; she already had the new one memorized, but anxiety would probably force her to refer to the card again and again.

"Dad'll have my head if you keep talking about it." He turned them for the park in front of the big brick City-Hall-looking building, and he didn't make her run to keep up with his longer strides. He just...glided along. "Your job is to spend, Zo-baby, not collect. It's a Pri—ah, a family thing."

Yeah, that part's not going to sink in anytime soon. None of this made any damn sense. Mama came from money and she knew the manners; why had she run away from all this? *I married Satan himself,* she used to say, but Trevor was endlessly patient, never even raising his voice.

The tension of waiting for him to show whatever had made Mama leave was turning Zo's nerves into hamburger. "Why do you think she left? Angelina, I mean." *Don't be mad, Mama. It's what they call you.*

Of course begging was useless. Even if her mother wasn't gone, she would never forgive Zoe for even *listening* to these guys, let alone sleeping in the same house and thinking uncharitable thoughts.

"If she was still around I'd ask." Soft and thoughtful, Jack's tone was also faintly chilly. He was steering them directly for the big brick building, his strides shorter than usual so she could keep up. "Now that we've pieced together some more of it, though, I think it was the drugs. She was heavy on postnatal painkillers; Dad says he suggested medical intervention and she got better for a little bit. Might've already been planning to disappear then."

Zoe, startled, almost tripped. Mama's medicine had been such a constant, it never occurred to her to wonder just where or when the habit had started. It made a certain amount of sense, though, especially with the way Angelina got when the needle—or its equivalent —was unavailable.

"But we might never know," Jack continued. "I don't care so much. Just wish we'd found you sooner."

What would have happened if they had? "Yeah." She tried to imagine Trevor or Jack showing up at one of her schools, or coming home to find them in whatever rundown apartment she and Mama were renting. What would her mother have done, seeing her husband again?

Would Zoe have stayed with her? Would Trevor have taken Angelina to court and gained custody?

Was it bad to wish he had, and that she'd grown up here instead of in shabby apartments or cheap hotels, keeping an anxious eye on Mama's moods, and finally enduring Pastor Bea, not to mention Royal?

If it was, she was guilty. It was a certainty after many years of wonder; Zoe was a greedy, ungrateful daughter, and she was going to hell.

She couldn't even find it in herself to halt the ride.

The big brick building swallowed them with a faint sigh of heated air through well-used vents, wood polish, and a tangled mess of people-scents. There were some much more vivid scent-threads, and her nose almost twitched. Maybe it was the weather, or maybe her senses were getting even more hurtfully sharp. Or maybe some Yankees simply smelled better, more *there* and real, for some other reason.

Old-fashioned black and white linoleum, lovingly cared for, melted into hardwood floor at office doors. The tiny local museum took up half the first floor, another slice was a bright appealing gift shop with tchotchkes ranged on shelves and Muzak carols playing at a well-bred whisper instead of a crass commercial shout.

The elevator was an old wooden lift instead of a sleek steel box, and it rose slowly to the fourth floor. Jack even reached past to make sure the door wouldn't close before she was through, a brief, thoughtless courtesy. "So why were you thinking about sleeping outside?"

"Because it looks like there's no homeless people around here."

"Yeah, it's a bedroom community. Still, it's convenient and Janine likes having her home office a little upstate. She's got one in-city, of course, but she likes to make people come to her. It drives up the price."

This job sounded intriguing. Maybe Zoe could get some sort of apprenticeship, if she didn't embarrass herself at this first meeting. "Is business good?"

"For us, business is always good." His profile just missed being severe by a millimeter or two around his mouth, a slight hint of softness. "She's probably going to redecorate both her offices after New Year's, just to keep everyone on their toes."

The lift door opened slowly, revealing a hallway ending at a single frosted-glass door. A niche on the left was lit with a recessed spotlight, a flower arrangement nestling on a carved, black wooden table directly in its beam. The door had a single arc of gold lettering —*Traleski's*. Just the one word.

Zoe pasted on what she hoped was her most accommodating and apologetic smile. The hall seemed to take forever, and Jack reached for the door like he did this every day of the week. It opened smoothly, and a flood of grey sunlight burst over them both.

25
RUSH PERFECTION

"Punctual as always, Jackson." Tall, slim, sheathed in a black turtleneck and long black skirt, her black stilettos tapping, copper-skinned Janine Traleski beamed over the receptionist's shoulder, her ruddy hair piled artlessly high in somewhat-planned disarray to balance the severity of her outfit. Tiny silver hoops glittered at her ears, and her nails were matte crimson—it was Amelia's trick, showing control of the change.

The receptionist was the same blond tennis star she'd had last summer; the boy was athletic as well as discreet and thoroughly capable—for a skin, at least. He seemed in no hurry to move on just yet, which suited his employer almost perfectly. Good help that knew when to keep its mouth shut was precious indeed, and even though this fellow had no idea his boss wasn't strictly normal he could still do her business some damage by a breach of confidentiality *or* a bad client interaction.

That he hadn't so far, or even approached doing so, was a good sign. Of course, he was paid well for his tact and carefulness.

Very well indeed.

Janine hurried around the reception desk. The skylights were wide and beautifully spaced, transforming the top floor of an old grange into a cathedral dedicated to fashion and graciousness.

There were offices and two dressing rooms, of course, tucked along the left-hand wall. But most of the space was open-plan, full of brilliantly healthy potted plants, couches arranged just so on muted rugs, wooden sample cases with bright crystalline glass, a large gas-insert fireplace on the west wall, and a few well-chosen sculptures. It looked like an old-fashioned salon waiting for an evening full of wit and sipped alcohol.

"And you must be young Miss Rouje." Janine halted, cocking her coppery head; dull black iron chopsticks held her hair captive. "Oh, Jack. You always bring me such *beautiful* things."

"Always a pleasure." Jack tried to gauge his *demie*'s discomfort, decided some nervousness was unavoidable, and stayed well inside her personal space. "This is Janine Traleski, Zo. And Janine, this is my beloved baby sister Zoe."

"How do you do." Janine's smile was megawatt-warm and deployed to crushing effect. "Your hair is magnificent, darling. And those eyes. We've simply got to get you into some Chanel."

"So it begins," Jack muttered, and busied himself taking Zoe's coat.

Zoe surprised him once more, not only allowing the tiny polite-ness but also bobbing a shy curtsey. "How do you do?" Her hair lifted on a warm, stray shaman's breeze. "I love your office. The plants are happy."

"That's all Evgenia; she waters *and* talks to them. You'll meet her in a few moments." Janine folded her arms, appraising his *demie* afresh. Even in jeans and a plain black jumper, Zoe shone—or maybe only he would see her that way. "Good bones, good material, this is going to be fun. We go on vacation this afternoon, but before then, miracles can and will be worked. Are you ready, Brad?"

"Born that way," the receptionist answered, cheerfully. He skirted the desk to take a double cargo of coats, the tiny diamond chip in his stainless-steel earring glittering. "I'm Brad, Miss Rouje. We'll get everything sorted out."

"A complete wardrobe, accessories, tutorials. A schedule. So many pretty things to select." Janine almost bounced on her toes, her excitement infectious. "How much time do we have, Jack?"

Only as much as she gives us. "We've some other shopping to do, and I want to take my *demie* to lunch at Pannore."

"I should say so." Traleski beamed at the mention of a good meal. "Is Bertram holding a table?"

"He will." The Kith chef would be the first outside the main house to serve Trevor's precious daughter a meal, and was likely already fretting in anticipation. "So an hour, hour and a half max, unless Zoe gets tired of being measured." As if Janine didn't have her sized already—but this visit was serving more than one purpose.

The rest of the Pride was hungry for news. A missing daughter was serious enough, but a missing *demie*, and for so long? They would be eager to witness such a blessing returned, and Janine would be deluged with invitations and requests for gossip.

"We'll be very gentle." Janine's tone softened, Voice giving a smooth note of comfort. "Don't worry, Miss Rouje, you are in very good hands."

"Please, it's just Zoe." This new side of his *demie* was gracious as a duchess, the few subtle signs of her discomfort quashed almost as swiftly as they appeared. Still, she didn't offer her hand for a shake.

Which was all to the good.

"And I'm Janine. We're going to be great friends. Come this way." And they were off, Zoe a slender yacht escorted by battleship. "Now, I'm on call for a few very special clients like you, so we'll get my private number into your phone in a few minutes; Jack can do it if he's in a useful mood. I am *always* available for you, my dear, no matter the day or hour. Before you leave Brad will have a tiny binder for perusal at your leisure. How's your father, by the way?"

"Very well indeed," Jack supplied, sensing Zoe's discomfort;

small talk was dreadful but unavoidable, and he could at least take that burden for her. "Looking forward to the Christmas party."

"And the young lady will need a dress for that, too. Not just any dress, but then again…" In short order, Janine had them in the vicinity of a long red couch with a baroque-scrolled back, the table crouching before it an old, well-loved Shaker varnished to a mirror gloss. "You aren't just any young lady, now are you?"

"It's a secret," Zoe returned, deadpan, as she perched on the very edge of the couch. "Don't tell anyone."

Jackson couldn't help it. His mouth twitched; he smothered a laugh, settling easily next to her.

Janine's eyebrows shot up. "Now I *have* seen everything." She half-turned, beckoning, and her lieutenants were already appearing from the offices, brisk and efficient, exchanging amused glances. "Ah, there you are. Shanice is my right hand, Evgenia here is our sensitive artist, and Ji Ah is our coach. We're doing a full reset, ladies, starting from scratch."

"Another one." Ji Ah grinned, clasping the clipboard to her navy blazer. "There was a fire in my flat last year. It was awful, but everyone got together and we did a complete reset. That house-warming party was the *best*."

"Nothing a Pride can't do," willowy Evgenia added, tucking a long straight lock of dark hair behind one shapely ear. "Do you have a town apartment of your own yet, Miss Rouje? I love picking out dishes."

Good God. "Uh," Jack said. If his *demie* decided she wanted a solitary residence, he would have to do some very quick thinking. *Usanaugh* didn't live separately; it just wasn't done. "Actually, that's not—"

"I'd hold out for a condo like Bella's, frankly." Shanice settled her ever-present attaché case against her straight-backed chair across from the couch. "Right in Manhattan. Sleepovers with the girls, wild parties, and a rooftop garden? Now *that's* living."

"Let's not get too excited." Janine beamed mistily at her three apprentices, each a skilled jäger in her own right. "Miss Rouje is from out west, and they do things a little differently there. That's why we're starting from the ground up. Ji Ah, we need a complete schedule starting in March; Evgenia, I want her colors and very classic, very understated as a theme. Shanice, my dear..."

"Cedar. Sandalwood. Spice. Nothing cutesy, nothing floral." Shanice eyed Zoe speculatively, and her dark gaze was also kind. "Pearls and silver only. The requisitions for the family heirlooms to transfer to the manor are on my desk."

"Oh, good job, anticipating me as always. Well, Miss Zoe, if we can borrow you for the teensiest minute to get your measurements?" Janine's hazel gaze rested on Jack, who very carefully did not tense.

Another test, and Traleski had all three of her lieutenants here both to show the proper amount of respect to a Pride ruler's daughter and to keep Jack on his best behavior.

Old habits died hard.

"Oh. Yeah." Zoe rose reluctantly; both Ji Ah and Evgenia watched her move before returning to their tasks—one with the clipboard, and the other with a sleek, whisper-thin silver laptop. Jack's *demie* looked in his direction, uneasily. "I guess I go with them?"

The proof of her trust—or even her simply considering him a safe refuge—warmed him clear through. "Don't worry, it's painless."

"You should've seen the first time your father took Jackson to a tailor." Janine's laugh held no sharp edge of dominance; Zoe's unease, though quiet, was plainly visible. "He used to fidget something awful. Now, this is our fitting room, it will be just the three of us. We'll take measurements for all sorts of things, and do tell me, what's your favorite color? Or colors?"

"I never..." Zoe glanced over her shoulder, a flash of bright blue. She was counting on Jack for reassurance, and he met her gaze, pouring strength into the contact. "I like grey. And green."

A smile, a quick flicker, and she was gone behind the swinging wooden door. Of course Jack's ears were sharp enough to monitor the situation, and the slight sound of cloth moving meant she was stripping to her underthings behind a curtain.

The thought was desperately enticing. But Evgenia looked at him, sweeping her bangs aside with a graceful, habitual movement. She had the dreamy gaze of a shaman but not the Gene; still, she was very sensitive for a jäger, almost treading into patterner territory. "What does she like, Jack?"

Books, and quiet afternoons. But they were after something different. "She did ballet for a while, loved it. Don't know about films or concerts yet, but I don't think she'd mind the symphony and a few museum tours." He had to make sure he wasn't projecting; getting her to express a preference was difficult. Still, there was all the time in the world, now. "We can try piano, she might like that. She had some French in high school."

I liked it, she'd remarked, shyly. *Mama wouldn't hear of me taking Spanish.*

Ji Ah nodded, her black bangs shining. "I'll look at arts-and-culture boards and charities. What with your father in conservation, it will round out nicely with whatever you choose." The jäger made notes on her clipboard paper, exhaling sharply as she underlined a single word. "School?"

"Next year, probably legacy, and late. We'll start small." Without his *demie* Jack wasn't able to take over charitable board positions or do nonprofit work, but now he could find a niche and begin service. He could almost sense the jägers' fiercely reined curiosity. Not many Kith were completely orphaned and raised outside prides, packs, or sleuths these days—at least, not on this continent; the wars skins were addicted to caused havoc elsewhere among many a species. "More concerned about her settling in. She'll be at the Christmas party, but probably no Moonfall yet."

She was simply too anxious to take the great monthly celebration right now. Dad concurred, but he was uneasy about it.

"That's a shame." Ji Ah nodded thoughtfully. Her hands kept moving. "Can always use another shaman."

"Soon enough." Of course, since Zoe was relaxing and most of Allison's feartaking still held, the fact of the Gene was plainly visible, especially to jäger. "We're just happy she's back."

"Oh, absolutely," Evgenia hurried to agree, pushing a chestnut-dark strand behind her shapely ear. Her marcasite-and-silver earrings glittered. "The entire Pride's...is it true she doesn't know?"

Calm, Jack. He wanted to snarl that his *demie* was nobody's business, but that was inaccurate. She was, in the very deepest sense, *Pride* business. An uncontrolled Kith, even without a talent, was a danger to skins *and* the Pride; how much more damage could a bearer of the Gene do?

Just like that, a sudden illuminating flash filled his head. The key had to be Angelina's tax-dodging pastor boyfriend, who the Plain-swalkers hadn't made an official offering of just yet. In fact, Leroy McFisk was still rotting in jail on arson and fraud charges, with an overworked public defender gumming up the legal works to an amazing degree.

Jackson pulled his phone out, his hands itching. "It's true," he said, quiet but not curt, and dialed Amerlane the elder, rising and pacing to a handy window while the phone rang.

Zoe laughed—Janine had made a joke about the measuring tape. His *demie*'s pleasure was very soothing indeed; he didn't have to spend half his energy keeping his rageful beast contained.

"Amerlane," the phone barked in his ear, a definite snap of of Voice to every word. "What can I do you for, Jackson?"

"A loaded question." Jack's faint smile would be echoed in his tone. "Can you get someone to poke into the financials for that public defender on the big thing out Okie way? That matter's dragging, and I'm curious."

"Funny you should ask." The head of the legal division's whiskey drawl was particularly effective on judges, and he was capable of both down-home aw-shucks and icy professional precision, which-ever would get a court to fall the way he wanted. "One of the assis-tants got curious and looked. Hutchins—that's the PD's name—just paid off a significant part of his student loans. Fantome's taking a hand, but not in the usual way."

"That's interesting." It meant there was a direct connection between the packleader and McFisk. Fantome *had* to know they would find out; why was he being so overt? "Who's handling the negotiations?"

"My daughter." Amerlane's pride was audible. "She and your father have a conference scheduled this afternoon. Sam Coughlin's flying out there today too."

"Good choice." Sondra Amerlane was smart, tough, dominant enough to stand up even to Fantome; Coughlin was a full shaman in his own right. "If the defendant is one of theirs, Dad'll have to make the call on responding." Frankly, Jackson would recommend erasing every single Plainswalker from existence for the crime of keeping a Rouje *demie*, especially given the state he'd found her in. But Dad could play the good cop in this scenario, and by the time it was finished the Pride would have an opportunity not just to expand financial influence but also a substantial chunk of territory. Any Kith taking a part in the kidnapping of a *demie* would be considered part of the disgrace, and a blood atonement might even be possible. "Should have known one of yours would flag it. Give that assistant a raise."

"I intend to; that boy will go far." Amerlane demanded much from his clan within the Pride, but he also drove himself twice as hard and took care to give even the lowliest of his employees significant vacation time. He was, in short, a model Kith elder, and knew it. "How is your dad, by the way? And the young miss?"

"Both in very fine health. How's Maria?" Truth be told, Jack found Amerlane's mate far more frightening than the old man. Maria was a senior analyst in the requisitions and mergers department, and could strip a business to bare bones in forty-eight hours while smiling and calling everyone *honey*.

"The same, the same." Every time he spoke about her, Amerlane's tone softened. He was probably smiling.

"Good to hear. Tell Sondra we appreciate her, and we'll see you at Christmas?"

The old steel-haired Kith chuckled. "With bells on. Anything else?"

"Just your good mood, sir." He'd hate to be the skin caught in Amerlane's claws—the father *or* the daughter, frankly. Sondra was utterly merciless.

"That you can have for free, my friend." It would have been a mere social pleasantry if Amerlane had been talking to a skin, but to a fellow member of the Pride it was a bare statement of fact. "Don't hesitate if something else crops up, and please pass my respects along."

"Will do." Jack cut the connection and stared out the window, watching the shopping strip below as it went about its business. Why was his *demie* thinking about people sleeping outside?

McFisk has to be connected to Fantome. Maybe just distant kin, though? And Fantome either didn't know what had fallen into McFisk's lap or he was planning to trade my demie *for something, if it could be handled discreetly enough. Might have even attempted a breeding.* Loathing prickled up Jack's back, and another answer arrived, an analyst's mind unable to stop until it answered a question with sufficient precision. *And my sweet* demie's *thinking about being poor, because she was. Of course a place like this makes her nervous.*

Maybe she'd never grow used to living reasonably well-off, but he was going to do his best to flood her with comfort. The day she didn't give a thought to such things would be a happy one.

His attention returned to the Plainswalkers. If Fantome, by some uncharacteristic oversight, hadn't known a cousin had somehow stumbled across a *demie*, he would be attempting to keep the connection well-covered. The slightest hint that the Roujes had figured it out would mean tying off every loose end, hopefully before a territorial confiscation could be enforced, and there would go some of the leverage. So far, the packleader could still claim complete ignorance, playing it as if he'd been caught flat-footed, which was insulting but better than the alternative.

Far, far better, especially if Fantome's position at home was shaky in any way. Sondra would report on the solidity of his rule, but he had a pretty good idea of what she'd say. None of this made sense *unless* Fantome was being challenged within his pack in some fashion.

And the challenge had to be ongoing, a long-term thing. Which was interesting, because no breath of trouble had escaped Plainswalker territory in a long while.

"Jack?" Zoe peered from the swinging wooden door. Her sweater had been hurriedly pulled on, and her hair was disarranged. Her boots dangled from one graceful hand. Even her sock toes were delicate. "Everything all right?"

"Business." He slipped the phone back into its home. "Don't worry, and don't hurry. Can't rush perfection."

"If you stand still it doesn't take as long," Janine piped up from behind her. "Tell him *that*. He used to practically vibrate in place, but you're a dream, young lady. I think kitten heels at most—Shanice, those tortoiseshell ones?"

"The ones we saw yesterday?" Shanice's voice was muffled; she would be attending to the measuring tapes and making yet more notes. She was mildly famous as a hunter of Broken, often working with Bell and Dimitri. "I thought so too. We'll go classic. Prep school princess meets SoHo hippie, I'm thinking."

"I'm inclined to agree." Traleski was in rare form today. "I've got the moodboards, let's settle for a few minutes, Miss Zoe, and then you can be on your way."

"That's it?" Zoe sounded baffled, moving out into the bright light with cautious doelike steps, still watching Jack. Now he knew what plants felt when the sun deigned to notice their existence.

"Darling, we are *professionals*, and we're here so you don't have to think about a single thing. We'll take care of it all. Give your brother your phone for a moment—Jack, put my number in, will you?" Janine sailed into view, her smile wide and utterly genuine. Her nails had lengthened a fraction as well, their bright matte crimson deepening a shade or two.

Jack found himself ambling to obey, drawn irresistibly toward his *demie*. Even that short while out of sight was too long.

It wouldn't occur to Traleski that a *demie* might not want her twin pawing at her phone. In the eyes of the Pride, *usanaugh* were a singular unit. Still, Zoe unlocked the sleek silver rectangle and handed it over, watching almost anxiously while he thumbed in the number of Janine's private line, made sure it was clearly labeled, and handed it back in short order, keeping the face tilted so she could see he wasn't prying.

Not that she would have many secrets from him in the long run, or vice versa. He was looking forward to being known.

And he was very much looking forward to anticipating her next need, however small.

26

FOLLOW THE PULL

It was exhausting to make so many decisions, to give preferences. Mama had never really worried about Zoe's clothes unless her daughter was growing again, and that was always high-stress.

Zo couldn't stop her body lengthening and costing money for fresh cloth covers. Still, sometimes she'd tried, concentrating fiercely while lying in bed, attempting to will herself into shrinking while her bones stretched without her consent, arms and legs grinding with the deep, desperate pains only young creatures know.

Pretty impossible, and obviously irrational—kids grew, it was what they *did*—but Zoe still felt the same old bite of shame, and was relieved when they left the building, hurriedly remembering her gloves and tugging them on so hard she was afraid she'd tear them. At least Jack didn't have to remind her about anything more than once.

Any reminder was generally one too many, but he was a lot easier to please than Royal, that was for damn sure.

Zoe's nerves were, in Mama's immortal phrase, almost shot. The "moodboards" were pretty—collections of different outfits and accessories displayed on Janine's tablet, while the woman pointed out small details and waited for Zoe to say what she liked. There were a lot of nice clothes, but she couldn't stop calculating what they probably cost.

The constant, reflexive addition inside her head was exhausting, and even more shameful.

Jack didn't take them back to the SUV. Instead, breath puffing white in the frigid air, he tucked her hand into his elbow and set off down Main Street—it was *literally* named that, proudly, on all the signs. It was a nice downtown, even if Zoe kept a sharp lookout for the cops and cameras.

"That wasn't so bad, was it?" Her brother's golden head was a torch in the bright snowy glare; he steered her around a patch of ice. Their boots made friendly sounds together. "You looked like you were beginning to have fun near the end."

Not exactly what I'd call it. "I expected it to take longer."

"We could go back." His grin was equal parts mischief and amusement, and the cold wind played with his golden hair. "If you want."

Oh, God. "Shouldn't we go home?"

"No, we're shopping, remember? You have to buy at least one thing today. Let's try there." He indicated an antiques mall, the bell over its door ringing merrily as an obviously married or dating couple in dark coats and cashmere scarves, all wrapped up for Christmas weather, swung through. "I should have brought you a scarf. And another jumper, it's cold."

"I'm fine." Some internal switch had flipped, too, and her body had enough fuel to keep warm. It was amazing what a few good meals would do; Mama had always been after Zoe not to get fat unless there was something hideous for dinner, in which case she had to eat everything on her plate. "*You* should have a scarf. Your hair's shorter."

"You'll have to buy me one for Christmas. Just one of the many things a *demie* does for her dear brother."

"*Demie.*" Now was a good time to ask, since she hadn't embarrassed him at Janine's. Or at least, she hoped like hell she hadn't.

Sooner or later she'd adapt to all this. "That's just another word for a twin, right?"

"Sort of." Jack's expression didn't change. "*Usanaugh* like us, that's what we're called. *Demi* and *demie*, two halves. It can be an endearment, too."

Zoe couldn't find a hint of irritation or contempt in his tone, so it was safe to ask a few more questions. "Janine's 'family', right? And the other ladies, too. But not the man there, the receptionist." The women were more *there*, more vivid, and the blond guy wasn't.

He just smelled washed-out, like regular people.

"Yes. You're very perceptive." Jack shepherded her up a wheelchair ramp and held the door for her; they plunged into a comfortable dimness. Old furniture, ancient newsprint, things valuable because they had survived, now polished and put on display for people who likely had no idea what they were buying. Mama didn't like old things unless they were *truly* exclusive, like real china or jewelry. D*on't pay for age, pay for quality.*

Still, it was...pleasant, and quiet. Classic rock ballads instead of carols were piped through expensive speakers, and the entire space was artfully cluttered, an imitation of an old house. The floor was hardwood, and everything was arranged for you to touch or hold.

If you were shopping around here, you obviously had enough to pay for any breakage.

"Easy to tell who's family and who isn't," Jack continued, as if it were the most normal subject ever. "Smells different. You ever run across anyone else like that?"

"A few," she admitted. "Mostly I stayed away from them." *Except Bea. Couldn't figure him out.* Mama's 'special friend' was stronger than regular people, but not nearly as present and *real* as Jack or even the young woman with the dark chestnut bob, Janine's 'sensitive' one.

"Clever girl." Jack gave the employee at the counter—a balding fellow in a cheerful striped cardigan and very sharply pressed khakis, the register at his elbow—a courteous nod. The man sized them both up, noted the quality of their coats and Jack's high gloss, and examined Zoe with far more interest before being distracted by a woman in a hat that looked like a frightened bird caught atop her sleek brown hair, a gently glowing piece of milk glass in her beringed hand. "Must've given you a turn when I showed up."

"Mama would call it a real joy." She watched, alert for any sign of impatience with her mentioning Angelina, moving obediently after him down an aisle with old, well-dusted display cases on either side. "I thought you were a cop."

"Really?" He seemed to find that funny. In any case, he laughed. "Look around, *demie*. See anything you like?"

Now she had to inspect everything. Baseball cards in plastic sleeves, cedar boxes full of commemorative silver spoons—some with the patina that meant real metal—and old, creepy dolls on tiny refurbished rocking chairs, ancient magazines from dates of mild historical interest, an actual Chippendale sideboard under a snowdrift of random items its original owner would've been horrified at. It looked like several dealers in the area rented out display space; each item had a small ticket tucked discreetly out of sight with a control number and the price's bad news. Two very old mirrors in highly carved wooden frames, a collection of hats, open wooden cigar boxes in the display cases holding refurbished straight razors, polished cutlery, and gleaming keys fitting no surviving lock. Old mixing bowls and egg-shaped wooden sock darners, a rack of antique guns safely behind glass, shelves of ancient-looking books nobody had ever read, accounting for their fine condition—she saw what Mama meant.

There was nothing in the place worth buying, even with the credit and bank cards weighing down her small leather purse. The bag was expensively handmade, and a silent signal that she was supposed to be here.

Still, she carefully kept her gloves on and her hands well away from anything even remotely fragile. And Jack didn't press, just ushered her back out into the cold.

The bookstores were nicer, full of paper-scented hush. One had nothing but new titles, but there was a bigger one which took used books for store credit and Zoe found a stack of potentials there, including a Saki collection and two Murakamis she had only seen in libraries. Her left arm cradled six volumes as she halted in the history section and tried to figure out which one would give her the most reading time for the least amount of cash.

"No putting anything back," Jack said softly. The blonde girl behind the register, perched on a high wooden three-legged stool, was absorbed in a thick newspaper, only glancing up every now and again to make sure her domain was still at peace. "Ever read any Bolaño?"

"Not yet." Zoe eyed the red-and-black volume he offered for perusal. "Just some of his translated poetry."

"Good." Jack's hair was wind-mussed, and his dark gaze was warmer than Mama's had ever been. He had a Collected Grimm's, too, and two Zane Grey paperbacks. Fairy tales and Westerns, a good combination—it didn't matter what you read, only *that* you read, like her English teacher Mrs. Halliburton used to say. "What about one more antique shop, then lunch? Or we can skip it if you want to stay here for a while, then go to Pannore."

"It's all right." She tried to figure out what he would prefer, breathing in the good safe scent of vanilla and binding glue. "I should see everything."

"Whatever you like. But you are *not* going to put anything back." His mock-glare wasn't even forbidding now, just hilarious, and she suppressed a guilty giggle. "I expected you to load up a box."

"Start small," she murmured, and was rewarded with another one of his slow, electric smiles. He never seemed to use them on anyone else. "Besides, I've got to carry it."

"Oh, I don't think so." He shook his head, *tch-tch*ing like an old granny. "Carrying packages is another of my Swiss Army duties."

The total came to a ridiculous number, but the bank card worked perfectly. She would probably never get used to it, and her heart pounded when she signed the slip. *Zoe Rouje*, her new name.

She'd practiced writing it in the blank art journals, and now it came naturally. No flashing red lights descended from the ceiling, no sirens sounded, Jack didn't snatch anything away and laugh at her, and the blonde girl behind the counter just grinned like all three of them had made excellent choices today.

"Happy holidays," the girl called as they headed out into the cold again, Jack carrying a paper bag loaded with their companionably mingled purchases.

The other antique shop was hushed as a temple. The proprietor was a woman with steel-colored hair trapped in a tight bun, wearing a black designer dress Janine would have approved of, the wide belt bearing an asymmetric silver buckle. She didn't greet them, merely smiled and nodded as if Jack and Zoe were old friends returning from a walk.

Space and quiet ruled here, giving each item room to breathe. A thrill ran down Zoe's back.

This place was *real*. She was drawn, almost magnetically, along plain wooden flooring—the boards still remembered the chainsaw's bite, despite being nailed down and polished until not a single splinter remained. A particular case held a secretive gleam in its depths, and Jack was at her shoulder, moving with her as if they were on one of the staircases in the big friendly house.

The sensation of dreaming, unable to wake though she knew none of this was real, returned with riptide force. "There," she heard herself say, a breathy little hum. "Jack? Right there."

It was a collection of antique watches, bright and refurbished. Tiny placards with brand names and dates—nothing younger than 1929—in calligraphic fountain pen sat next to each one. No prices visible here, because if you had to ask you couldn't afford it anyway.

"Which one?" Jack leaned close on her other side, and the heat of his nearness was a comforting bulwark against the drowning sensation. It was like standing under a weight of very clear water, watching the world blur and ripple; Mama hated it when Zoe had these episodes.

That's Satan's work, Zoe. Don't you dare.

She couldn't help herself. Zoe's gloved fingertips hovered over glass, a mere breath away since it was rude to smudge a case *or* point. "The one with the blue face. For him. Trevor, I mean." She took a deep breath; the pocket watch glowed on royal-blue velvet. "Dad."

It even felt natural to say.

"A Buhré." Jack nodded. "Nice. You're right, just the thing."

At least you know what it is. "Do you think he'd...I mean, for Christmas?"

Of course Jack had already taken care of getting Trevor a present ostensibly from Zoe because she was anxious about it, wanting to make a good impression. But this was something different, and the fear that her brother might be somehow offended faded as she looked up, finding him leaning over the case to inspect the watch. "I think he'll love it. You want to pay, or should I? Either way you can wrap it, make it personal."

The owner, sensing a sale, drifted close on padded slipper-flats. "Would you like to see anything more closely?"

"The Buhré, there." Jack took over, the way he always seemed to. It wasn't like Royal's dipshit aggression or Pastor Bea's oily, unctuous control; instead, her twin simply *handled* things, with quiet efficiency. "Boxed, but not wrapped—unless you don't have time, Zoe?"

"I'll wrap it." She even knew where the right paper was, buried in color-coded plastic bins full of decorations and other craft supplies in a storeroom tucked under a staircase on the second floor. There were boxes of ribbons and bows there too, all new. No re-using here. *I can't believe I'm saying this.* "But we can look more. There's something..." *Something else.*

"Lead on, then." He nodded at the owner, whose faded brown eyes lit with pleasure.

"Feel free." The woman's voice was warm caramel, and though

she smelled washed-out and normal, there was still a hint of incense to her.

Zoe was suddenly much more comfortable. Nothing in this place would harm her.

"Over here." She even dared to take Jack's coat-sleeve between two gloved fingers. The pull was strong, undeniable, and if she'd been alone...well, she would never have come in here no matter how powerful that internal pressure. Not when it was too easy to trip and break something she'd never be able to pay off. "That case, right there. Look."

He did, and stopped short. For a moment she was afraid she'd done something wrong, but when he looked at her, there was no anger or impatience.

In fact, Jack stared at her with a mixture of surprise and pleasure, that smile nobody else received from him intensifying. "You're a miracle, you know that?"

I don't even know what's in there. She took a closer look. Small containers of wood, brass, or other metals; the calligraphy on a small, heavy piece of cardstock said *Snuff Boxes*. The one she was drawn to had its own card: *1790, combination lock, refurbished.* "Snuff?" Zoe tried not to sound perplexed. "Really?"

"Started out as a joke. McKenna got me an old silver one a few years back. Now I pick them up sometimes. You're absolutely right, I've never seen one with a lock like that before. Tell you what, you grab it and wrap it for me, and on Christmas I'll be surprised."

Was he serious? Zoe weighed his expression. "Is that even legal?"

"What, surprising me? I hope so."

"But it's not a present if you know." It was a pale, paltry objection, but she couldn't think of anything better. Besides, good luck getting down here again before Christmas—although she had car keys, didn't she? They had to fit one of the vehicles in the garage. The route was simple, especially if she looked up the store's name and used her phone's GPS.

So this was what it was like to be rich. You had *options*. Now she just had to figure out which ones she could use.

"It most certainly is a present. You found it, that qualifies." Jack turned away from the display case, catching the proprietor's eye. "Anything else in here?"

Zoe shook her head, biting her lower lip gently. The deep, irresistible internal pressure had vanished; the world was its usual self again. "You really collect these?"

"Scout's honor." He even held three fingers up, cocking his golden head and turning somber.

"You were a Boy Scout?" *Along with everything else?*

"With a few other Pride kids, yeah. Hated every minute. Camping's a drag, but knowing how to start fires is pretty priceless." He greeted the approaching owner with a nod. "We've got to get to lunch. Get out your American Express, Zo-baby, unless you want me to pay."

The total was astronomical, ridiculous. It was more than Zoe could make in a month, or even three. But the credit card was accepted and the owner didn't even ask for the new ID. Zo merely signed the slip and—hey presto—two much-smaller packages were nestled safely atop the books almost before she knew what was happening. And again there were no flashing lights, no alarms, just the black-clad woman smiling and inviting them to come back anytime.

Jack had witnessed her doing something strange, and acted like it wasn't any big deal. Mama would have been livid. *Don't you do that witchery*, she would hiss in Zoe's ear, grabbing her daughter's arm. *That's Satan's work.*

For a moment, the world went away—antique stores, bright winter day just past noon with the clouds breaking and the snow glittering vengefully, bookstores and hurrying pedestrians, shining cars moving decorously down the road. *You will not fear*, Allison's voice said, almost sternly, and Zoe found herself walking next to Jack, her gloved hand caught in his. He swung the paper book bag slightly, and hadn't even blinked at the total for the watch and snuff box.

Super-senses. Strange pulls toward presents. Her fingernails, and the eerie speed, not to mention the unnatural strength Jack shared. What other weird things could 'family' do?

It seemed to be an open secret. Maybe they wanted to see if she'd say something stupid instead of keeping her mouth shut the way Mama always insisted on. Some things just weren't talked about, ever.

Getting older meant you didn't trip over that invisible line as much, thank God, but when you did it was always a doozy.

"You all right?" Jack still didn't hurry, their steps perfectly matched, and instead of continuing down the street he pointed them toward the parking strip in front of Janine's building. "Hungry?"

Starving. "A little." Now she had to get through a restaurant meal. At least Mama had taught her proper etiquette for nice places, so she wouldn't embarrass Angelina in front of a boyfriend who could pay rent for a couple months. Mama's sophistication could be flipped like a switch, and a lot of her habits made sense once you found out Angelina Simmons—or whatever she was called herself in a new town, though she often let Zoe keep her first name—came from 'good family' and couldn't ever quite believe she was reduced to the life of a rootless single mother with a hungry child dragging her down.

"We can go home." The sun turned Jack's hair into a bright blaze, and he was comfortingly solid. Her coat looked just like a version of his, in fact, and it was nice to think a passerby might assume them a matched set instead of a quality article with a cheaper one bundled in. "Pannore's amazing, though. It's Provençal. The bread's really good, and Bertram—the chef, he owns it—is one of Dad's old friends."

"I'm fine." Her stomach was a knot. It would be far better to just go home and take a chance on raiding the kitchen.

"It's a short hop from here, the other side of town." Did her brother sound anxious? "But if you're tired—"

"I'm *fine*," she repeated, and watched him in her peripheral vision just in case her insistence was somehow unwelcome. Royal would have told her to shut up, to do what she was told.

So would Bea.

Jack just nodded. "There's some ice. Be careful."

Relieved, she watched the pavement. She was getting through this, bit by bit, and as long as she kept it up, she'd be all right.

Or so she hoped.

27
PEPPERING PRANKS

BY THE TIME THEY ARRIVED HOME ON A DARKENING WINTER AFTERNOON THE first boxes were arriving. Janine and her staff were, true to their promises and their nature, working minor miracles. Amelia's choices were fine as an emergency measure, but now Zoe would have a proper wardrobe and the closet in the blue suite would no longer look so forlorn-empty.

The daily wear—jeans, casual slacks, T-shirts both plain and silkscreened, sweaters and underthings, socks, certain off-the-rack blouses—came first; anything needing alteration would arrive late tomorrow, just in time for the season between Christmas and New Year's. Shoeboxes with flats, heels, trainers, slippers, and boots arrived by the stack. Amelia looked genuinely thrilled over each item as she helped with the unpacking. The fragrances, the new luggage, a vintage silk shawl with hand-knotted fringe, two fluffy bathrobes— every item was something a girl who had lost everything, or never had it to begin with, would need or want.

And his *demie* knew quality when she saw it. Angelina's impover- ished gentility had been good for something; her daughter's manners were also exquisitely calibrated. Tall, plumpish Bertram Pannore had been beside himself, almost expiring with glee at having Trevor Rouje's returned daughter at one of his tables, emerging from the kitchen's bustle to personally pay court. Jack's *demie* smiled and did not offer her hand, but complimented the entire meal with the proper amount of reserve.

All in all, the first foray into her new life had gone as well as possible—including a display of just how strong the Gene was in her. Of course she was *demie*, but still...the fine hairs all over Jack's body prickled when he thought of those few moments, Zoe's baby blues wide and softly luminous as she followed a call even he couldn't hear, making beelines for two perfect gifts.

She was even close to voluble at dinner, telling Dad all about their day, effusive in her praise for Janine and for Bertram's salmon. "I tried the wine he recommended," Zoe confided, while Trevor looked slightly bemused, his golden head cocked and all his attention resting upon his returned prodigal.

"Was it good?" Dad reached for his water glass. "Bertram has a fine nose."

"It was okay. I'm not much of a booze person." Her nose wrinkled slightly; maybe his *demie* would never acquire the Kith habit of easy drinking. Perhaps she'd seen the havoc it wrought among skins who had no pride or control. "Then Jack let me drive home."

"I should hope you took something with snow tires." Dad's mock-severity was greeted with an actual laugh from their grave, nervous girl, her happiness filling the entire dining room up to the gently glowing chandelier.

"We took the CRV." Jack was occupied with his steak; Amelia did something to the rub he'd never been able to figure out. Honestly, he hadn't intended to let Zoe drive in anything less than dry and clement weather, but she'd looked so intrigued by the notion he'd been unable to resist.

A sucker for sure. A sudden spike of uneasiness punctured the day's good feeling. *Huh. What is that?*

"I bought books," Zoe continued. Something in the day had relaxed her, and Jack liked the result. Her eyes shone and a shaman's calm spread in ripples, soothing any ruffled fur. But the faint trepidation crawling up his spine had started at dusk, and just wouldn't go away. "And tonight I'm going to curl up with two Murakamis and have strange dreams."

"That sounds like either a good time or very dangerous." Few in the Pride would recognize the expansive, smiling Trevor at the head of the highly polished mahogany table, attacking his own steak Continental-style with fork and serrated knife. Dad looked down-right relaxed, not to mention that chimerical attribute, *happy*. "Murakami? Do I know the name?"

"You might if you like surrealism or Japanese literature, although he writes in English and..." Zoe's mood faltered for a bare moment; she checked Dad's expression anxiously and must have found reas-surance, because she forged onward. "Mama didn't like talking about books at dinner. She said meals were for light conversation and nothing boring. Anyway, Murakami just sort of burrows into your head and won't come out. Other writers, it's like they're talking in crowded rooms, but *he's* whispering in your ear at midnight and everything's a dream. I felt that way a lot, growing up."

Caught in a nightmare. Jack could well imagine. "I've always heard that literature at dinner is civilized. You're going to love the Bolaño." He liked handing over his own cherished books; the thought that their eyes would pass over the same pages sent a pleasant shiver over him. "I put it on your shelf, by the way."

As usual, a flash of trepidation crossed her face when a gift was mentioned. "I thought you bought it for yourself."

"I've already got a copy." Soon, he hoped, she'd learn to accept a present without worrying about a cost extracted later. "Consider this one an early Christmas present." Jack glanced at the dining room's mullioned windows, a faint reflection of snow glittering even in the dark. There were mounds of brightly wrapped boxes under each Christmas tree; Trevor had indeed gone a little crazy with relief this year. "If you ask Dad nicely he'll probably let you open a few others."

"Weren't you the one lobbying against Advent? A very civilized custom." Dad looked relaxed, certainly, but he was watching the windows on other side of the long parquet-floored room.

So he felt it too. Well, at least Jack's instincts weren't rusty.

"I can't open them early." Zoe sounded faintly scandalized by the notion, and perhaps a little indignant as well. "Besides, they're not all for me. There's some for everyone."

"Santa's working overtime." Dad cut a thin ribbon of steak. "Which isn't allowed."

"*You're more productive when you take proper rest,*" Jack quoted. "Someone used to say that to me a lot."

Trevor snorted. "Along with *we don't solve problems with punching* and *what is that on your face?*"

"To be fair, that last one was Amelia's." Jack leaned forward slightly. The chair across from his, empty at dinner and any Pride function for years, now held his *demie*.

"I can't imagine you dirty," she said, blinking owlishly. "You're always so...collected."

Well, she hadn't seen a hunt for a Broken yet, and it would be a long time before he'd risk her safety. There were a few other filthy little duties he would be glad to set aside as well, if only they weren't part of his job as the Rouje heir. "Control, control, control," Jack chanted, lifting his wineglass. The deep, constant reassurance of her presence showed no sign of abating. "Rules one, two, and three for Trevor Rouje's son."

"And for Jackson Rouje's father, don't forget." Trevor's ring glinted and his tie was only slightly loosened; he was headed back to his office after dinner. He was going to be utterly bowled over by the pocket watch—of course she had no idea he collected them—and Jack couldn't wait for the unwrapping.

Having a secret to share with his *demie* gave Jack a deep, entirely gratifying frisson each time he thought about it.

"So what are my rules?" Zoe used a light, laughing lilt to deliver the question, but her eyebrows had drawn together and her shoulders tightened. Just a fraction, but a visible one. "I have the same ones?"

"Yours are different, little dancer." Dad pinned her with a bright blue gaze. At this angle, the similarity between father and daughter was unmistakable. "Trust your brother, and come to me with anything, at any moment. Oh, and would you pass me the pepper?"

"Certainly." The sweet curve of her wrist as she reached for the wooden mill was better than a Botticelli. "Pepper's a rule?"

And Jack was granted another miracle, because she looked positively mischievous. The glimpse of what she might eventually be when she discovered her true place in the Pride—a *demie* who trusted her twin, who accepted the warm blanket of comfort and cooperation, who was carefree as a Kith daughter should be—threatened to knock the breath clean out of him.

"Dear God," Trevor said through a chuckle. "You're going to pepper everything I eat from now on. I can almost hear you enticing Amelia into a prank or two, like your wheedling brother."

"Wheedling?" Jack's eyebrows shot up. He suspected he'd never be ready for the spectacle of a Kith daughter teasing his serious, unbending father into laughter. "I believe you call it *dealmaking*, Dad, and you're quite proud of my negotiating ability. Especially the time I got Amelia to bring home hair dye." He enjoyed how round Zoe's eyes were, surprised by his daring or Trevor's gentleness. Or both. "He was furious."

"I wasn't angry, merely perplexed," Trevor corrected. "I could understand dyeing your hair, but *tie*-dyeing is something else. Don't try to distract me, Jackson." He tried to look serious, but his mouth kept twitching and his eyes danced. "You're both planning to pepper your old man."

"I think we'd have to braise you." Jack tipped Zoe a cheerful wink over the table, and was rewarded with a wide, disbelieving grin. "That's how you tenderize tough old meat, right? Amelia would know."

His *demie*, like any kitten, was eager to play. "Braising your father sounds very Greek-tragedy, though. Oedipus Roast."

"First peppering, now cannibalism. It's dangerous around here at dinnertime." Dad's gaze traveled down the windows again. His beast was restless; Jack's was too. At least Zoe was distracted, or she might catch their unease.

Not yet. Let her have some time. "In any case, you did it to yourself." Jack's nape itched. Whatever lurked out in the night hadn't quite approached the house yet...but it was close. "You asked for peppering, you can't deny that."

"An excellent argument, as usual." Trevor eyed him balefully. "Why didn't you go into law, again?"

"Because you said I might actually enjoy it?" The hunger to make his father proud could ask for no greater proof of Trevor's regard than a lightly sarcastic fencing match. "Can you imagine, Zo? Me, a lawyer?"

"Don't look at me," she said, raising her hands and spreading her slim fingers. "I told you, when you showed up in Marquette I thought you were a cop."

It was the first time he'd ever heard his father outright guffaw, and the sight tipped Jack into unrestrained laughter for the first time in years as well. Zoe watched them both, for once completely at ease. He was getting more and more glimpses behind her careful, cautious curtain, and each one made him more curious.

"I'm going to tell everyone she said that," Dad finally all but wheezed. "Can you imagine?"

"Please." Jack knew very well he wouldn't, but the thought was still hilarious. "Mac'll start calling me *Officer* like it's a dirty word. Tommy and Sam will start making handcuff jokes. Jolie will make sure everyone knows within a day. Amerlane'll ask me about parking tickets."

"Janine." Trevor's sides shook. "After that time you got arrested."

"You got arrested?" His *demie* perked up visibly at this revelation. "What for?"

Which time? "Long story," Jack muttered, and was rewarded by a cascade of *her* laughter. "Janine gave me the most furious dressing-down you can imagine through the holding cell door, and the officer on duty asked if she was my mother. She said *no, he's lucky I'm not, because I'm going to kill him* and the cop says *just don't do it here*—look, it made sense at the time, right? I was a wild child. No *demie* to keep me on the straight and narrow."

"Oh, that's my job? I'm your..." For a moment, she couldn't come up with the right word, but her baby blues sparkled and she brushed a jet-black curl from her face, smiling at him so sweetly he almost forgot his own name. "Your minder? Babysitter?"

Ha. "Holder of my leash, Zo-baby, and don't forget it." Sooner or later he was going to have to play the angry beast restrained only by her will, which sounded not only fun but also instructive. There was nothing more dangerous than a Kith analyst who had suddenly had *enough*.

Unless it was a fallen Kith, but someone else could hunt the Broken for a good long while. Jackson found, upon further consideration, that he never wanted his *demie* near a juggernaut of baffled rage and hunger.

Even if he was confident of his own abilities *and* her eventual mastery of the Gene.

"Sir?" Amelia appeared with two well-loaded plates, Lev right behind her with a glass water carafe and a slightly anxious smile. Hermann was out at the shamans' estate conferring with Allison this evening, as well as putting some of the junior myrmidons through their paces, and wouldn't be home until morning. "Did you call?"

In other words, she was aware of something not quite right outside the house, too.

"Not so much." Trevor greeted them with a smile. "It's only your impeccable instincts. I believe the children are attempting to pepper me, and want to make you an accomplice."

"Pepper you?" Amelia shook her head, leaning over the table to set Lev's plate at the place next to Jack. She sat next to Zoe, a high honor; Lev, scrubbed and shining, folded himself down gingerly and scanned the windows. "No, you would need a red wine sauce, sir. After a very long braising."

"What did I say?" Jack, triumphant, saluted the housekeeper with his wineglass. Zoe dissolved into helpless giggles, one hand over her mouth and tears standing in her gorgeous eyes. "Thank you, Amelia. You've managed to completely vindicate me."

"He'll be insufferable for weeks now," Trevor grumbled, but his gaze on Zoe was soft and pleased. "You'll have to puncture his ego regularly, little dancer. We're counting on you."

"Looking forward to it." Jack couldn't ignore the looming danger, but he could be grateful his *demie* was right where he could see her, as safe as possible with a jäger on one side and a Pride leader on the other, not to mention her twin right across the polished wooden river of the table. "You two arrived at just the right time, Lev."

The gangly Kith youth grinned, his teeth gleaming; his restlessness could be mistaken for natural ebullience. The prospect of a good scrap always cheered him up. "Mr. Rouje is always saying punctuality is the mark of a man."

"How very wise." Amelia turned to the princess of the house. "The lemon in the pasta, is it enough?"

"Perfect." Zoe beamed at her. "I wish you'd teach me. Or let me help."

"Tomorrow." The housekeeper ducked slightly, almost overwhelmed with the praise. "Sugar cookies. You will help then?"

"I'd *love* to."

Jack, watching his *demie* light up at the prospect, lost all his breath once more. The fact of her presence kept hitting him, padded sledgehammer blows, and a faint trace of sweat touched his lower back.

It was going to be an interesting night.

28
WAKE UP

Every evening, it was the same. *Sleep well,* Jack said, hands in his pockets and his bright head cocked, regarding her with peculiar intensity. *I'm just down the hall.*

A strange feeling spilled through Zoe then, incrementally more intense with each recurrence. The right thing to do was nod, close the door to the blue suite, and heave a sigh of relief at another day's performance carried off without a disaster, so that's what she did.

But it was hard. Sometimes, the irrational fear that Jack—and her father, and the entire house—would disappear if she looked away for even a moment mounted as she roamed the blue suite, touching furniture and hoping it stayed solid. Nothing good ever stayed, and...well, she had to admit she liked it here.

She liked it a *lot*.

Dinner was the first time she'd really felt like she belonged. In fact, it was hard not to smile as she settled in the blue-cushioned window bench, looking out on what had become a familiar winter vista. Down in the garden, snow was packed to a hard crust where it wasn't cleared away from stone paths—Lev said he liked the shoveling. *Keeps me in shape,* he confided with a grin, and actually seemed to mean it.

It sounded like a particular circle of hell to Zoe, but so did raking and most other forms of yard maintenance. She'd had a summer working landscaping after leaving Akron, and the constant harassment from male employees, not to mention the scorching, unrelenting heat, had almost been bad enough to force her back to Nebraska to see if Bea was still alive and maybe in a forgiving mood.

The operative word there being *almost*.

Now, of course, she was glad she hadn't caved. But it had been a close call. Moving to Marquette seemed like a blessing at the time, what with finding the squat as well as a job in a gas station before hearing the Greenfield was hiring.

There was a lot of think about, the entire day swirling around inside her, refusing to settle. So many clothes had been delivered, and all of them fit. Still, she liked the sweats Amelia had brought best, and the ancient green and yellow plaid shirt she'd been wearing when Jack found her was an old friend. Barefoot even though it was well below freezing outside, Zo could pull up her knees and rest her chin on them, breathing deeply, occasionally glancing at the suite to make sure it was still stable.

Still *real*.

For someone Mama called a beast or even Satan himself, Trevor was nice enough. He could easily become scary, Zoe supposed, but there was a curious, undeniable feeling of safety around him as far as she was concerned. And he didn't say a word about the shopping trip other than *I hope you found something nice for yourself, little dancer*.

No sign of anger or even displeasure, though she'd been here long enough to start seeing below the mask of politeness used for guests. The instant she overstayed her welcome, she'd know—and then she could start making plans, if necessary.

If she had to leave. But there was Jack.

She'd miss him the most. After all, he was her twin, and everything about him just seemed to...fit. It was powerfully comforting to simply stand next to him, another safety so deep and undeniable it was, if she was being strictly honest, a little scary.

No. A whole *lot* scary.

Zoe stared at the ice-glittering garden, wriggling her bare toes. So many people took heat for granted even on nights like this; she hoped she never would. No mildew, no screaming or thumping on the walls, no fear of frostbite, no shivering under a manky old blanket, attempting to sleep and unable to because of piercing cold.

Her room at the squat was probably picked clean by now. She missed some of the books, but honestly, that was a small price to pay. For once.

What the hell? Zoe stiffened, her eyes narrowing.

Misshapen shadows moved along the garden paths, deep black against the snow.

The light in her bathroom was on, but none of the others were; her window wouldn't show a silhouette. Zoe was deeply glad of that fact a moment later, when she realized what the shapes were.

People. At night, in the garden, with funny helmets on.

At first she thought it was a practical joke, or Jack and her father were bundled up and taking an almost-midnight walk in the middle of winter. But that was ridiculous, and besides, there were *five* shapes moving swiftly, clasping long metallic-gleaming things.

The shadows were bulky because they were in some kind of body armor, the helmets bug-eyed because they had night-vision goggles, and the shapes in those gloved hands were actual-factual *guns*.

Zoe's mouth turned dry as burnt toast, and she tasted copper. She could hear the shapes now, a faint scratching of footsteps.

Were they cops? What the hell were they *doing*?

The armored men disappeared under the bottom of her window as they approached the house. Zoe found herself staring fruitlessly, her forehead against icy glass. Her fingers and toes, toasty just a few seconds ago, were now cold and clumsy.

She spilled off the window seat and bolted across both bedroom and sitting room, skidding to a stop before the hall door and listening intently.

Somewhere close by, there was a muffled crunch—glass, breaking.

Move. Panicked certainty filled her. *Move now.*

Zoe slipped into the hall, swiftly padding past her brother's office. The door to his suite was ajar, and she paused for a moment, dreadfully unsure if she should knock. "Jack?" she whispered, and the house's quiet, once profound, was alive with tiny scrapes and slithering, her ears working overtime and adrenaline turning every faint whisper into a tall man with a blank-visored helmet, the very personification of violent authority.

The only thing Mama feared more than Satan or poverty was cops, and whoever was in the garden looked an awful lot like law enforcement.

Maybe Royal had sent them? Or Bea? Ridiculous, Bea was in jail and Roy had been strictly small-time. He was on social media bleating about religion, after all—but that could be camouflage. And besides, how could either of them have found her? Roy didn't even know her real name, and Bea had only known her as Zoe Simmons.

"Jack?" she repeated, tapping at the door. "Are you there?"

Nothing, not even the invisible sense of breathing presence every person, 'family' or not, carried around. Zoe pushed the door open a little more, peering in—sleek chrome, polished glass, black upholstery. He didn't like curves or decoration; there was probably a lot of comfort in straight lines and sharp corners. The blue suite no doubt drove him batty, even if it suited her right down to the ground.

She closed her eyes, listening intently. Maybe her father and Jack were discussing something in a study or the main library? They did that a lot, all 'business' and mentions of people she didn't have any desire to meet just yet. Or ever.

Would they think she was stupid if she said she'd seen—

Crash. Thud.

The sudden ruckus was in a completely different part of the house, and if her senses were normal she wouldn't have heard it so clearly. Zoe stood, frozen and irresolute, listening to banging and muffled pops. More glass shivered into pieces, and there was the faroff thunder of a growl she recognized without knowing quite how.

It was her father, and he sounded *pissed*. A regular person wouldn't make that noise.

OhGod. Do something. Anything.

Her biggest urge was to hide under her bed, but the most sane reaction would be to grab what she could and get the hell out of here. Fleeing into the snow wouldn't be comfortable, but it sure sounded like a good idea if a SWAT team was breaking in.

More soft stealthy movements, and the footsteps weren't Jack's or her father's. Nor were they Amelia's light brisk sounds, Hermann's quiet glide, or Lev's cheerful thumping. Jack said after Christmas there would be more house staff, plus others returning in spring, and maybe they'd all eat in the huge dining room too. A big family dinner, everyone talking and laughing like a church picnic...

You might not be around for spring, let alone Christmas. Wake up.

Oh, now she was *entirely* awake. The fear stung, deep red, and swept the clutter of the past few weeks away like a broom on smooth level concrete. Because the new footsteps were coming from the *other* end of the hall, far away from the crashing and banging.

When normal people tried to move silently, they made almost as much noise as usual, just in different ways. And now she realized that had bothered her about Bea—sometimes he just appeared, seemingly out of nowhere.

Jack could do that. And their father probably could too. Maybe the entire 'family' could? Mama wasn't like that, so...

Zoe shook the thought away. She could brood about implications later. Right now, she had to do something, anything.

You dumbass. Hide.

She whirled, her hair swinging heavily, and whisper-footed down the hall past her own suite, soundless as a flying owl. A closet, half-hidden behind a plinth bearing a scarred, discolored marble bust—Jack said it was Victorian instead of classical, despite its condition and patina—accepted her with little trouble, and she pulled the door closed slowly, easing the hinges past any small squeak.

Now she was in complete darkness. It felt safe, like pretending to sleep in the backseat of a jalopy while Mama drove to find the next town. Her ears sharpened yet again, and the footsteps paused.

They're outside Jack's room. She was trembling, Zoe realized, and her hand fell away from the closet's doorknob.

Now she could hear hoarse whispers as well.

Clear...Clear...Clear, there's nobody, let's go. A long pause. They passed the office, and halted outside the blue suite.

Males, all of them. Her nostrils flared slightly as the scent reached her. She could imagine them, their big crushing boots still bearing traces of snow, their pulses thundering with excitement. The sour sweat of authority just looking for something to beat down or destroy drifted around them, invisible anemones.

"*Well,*" someone whispered in her bedroom, "*where the fuck is she?*"

Were they looking for her? Were they from Roy, or Bea? *God, please.* The old, familiar prayer rose unbidden. *I know I'm bad, I'm probably even evil, but don't let them find me. Please don't let anyone find me.*

There was no doubt the intruders thought they were being very quiet indeed; she counted four sets of footsteps leaving her suite and trooping past, leapfrogging like they did in movies about the cops or the military, providing cover. Hopefully none of them would even notice the closet door; she hadn't until Jack had pointed out the bust.

Her hands shook, her knees were gooshy, and her breath came in soundless shuddering gasps. She sank into a crouch—if they *did* find her, she would spring just as she had at Bea. Her palms ached, her wrists throbbing, and she knew without looking her fingernails were lengthening, turning razor-sharp.

Is this some kind of test? A practical joke? If so, it was a shitty one, and despite the luxury and warmth, she would take everything she could carry and get the fuck out of here.

There was another consideration—Trevor was rich. Maybe this was the price of being able to buy all the books you wanted and a nice house, too; people would want to break in and take something. But whoever this was knew Zoe was here—unless they thought it was Amelia's room?

That was the problem with hiding. It turned you into a shaking animal, your brain eating itself alive because fear demanded you *do* something while also paradoxically nailing you helplessly in place.

Hunched on the bare wooden floor of an empty closet, breathing the thick sneeze-inducing smell of dust, Zoe waited. Her fingernails tingled as they sharpened into claws, her eyes dry and grainy as they lit with a faint but definite blue glow.

And she blessed the devouring terror, because it was familiar.

29
IMPLICATIONS

"Amateurs," Trevor said softly, gazing at their prisoner. If not for the obvious disdain, his tone might even have qualified as amused. "Breaking a picture window? Really?"

Amelia finished the last knot and straightened, ignoring the mewling from behind a cruelly tight gag. This heavyset blond skin, the sole survivor of the squad which had penetrated the east wing, was tied to a straight-backed wooden chair from what had been the servants' dining room long before this house had been added to Pride properties. Now, the space was only used for an overflow of party guests.

The jäger's eyes glowed like hot coals, and she cocked her sleek ruddy head. The change burned in her, tiny ripples passing under her skin as her beast moved restlessly. "Shall I question him now, or...?"

The skin made another desperate sound, straining against brown rope. Nylon had too much plastic stink, especially when new, and zip ties only took you so far; hemp was a lot better. The slight amount of stretch in natural material could even be used for interrogation, as well as the fibers swelling when damp.

Endless possibilities. Sometimes the old ways were indeed best.

The invaders had good gear, at least; they looked like well-paid mercenaries. Further analysis could wait; Jack had other concerns at the moment. "How many more?"

Amelia straightened, listening intently—a jäger's ears were sharper than a patterner's, and sometimes even better than a shaman's when tracking prey was involved.

Lev was outside, circling the house, ready to catch any fleeing skins. Dad paced to the library door, ignoring the draft from the shattered floor-to-ceiling window—it was the most tactically sound place to effect entry, but only if you wanted to make a big production out of it.

And that bothered Jack.

"At least one more group." Amelia, tense and ready, closed a hand over the prisoner's shoulder and squeezed, halting the skin's frantic writhing. "Sir...they're in the west wing, and up. Near the young miss's rooms."

Of course. A loud break-in to cover a quiet one. Jack was already heading for the door, and the growl bursting free of his chest threatened to rattle the room into splinters.

It was the sound of a *demi* whose twin was threatened, promising swift retribution.

Dad wisely didn't attempt to dissuade his heir. "We'll handle it," Trevor snapped in Amelia's direction, and was already at the door. He didn't use his full speed often, but that didn't mean it was inoperable.

Jack didn't care. The only thing that mattered was his *demie*, left safe in her bower under an hour ago. If she was asleep, they could have this sorted out without her noticing, by far the best option.

If she wasn't, and a collection of armed skins got anywhere *near* her, he would show no mercy.

They blurred through the halls, father and son both Kith-silent; it was hard work to keep the growl from throbbing in his ribs again.

Jack leapt six stairs and took the first skin with a short strike to the solar plexus, robbing the bastard of breath and knocking him aside for later questioning. That was the only restraint he'd show, since the staircase they were on could only be reached from a particular hall—the one leading to paired suites for *demi* and *demie*. The second skin fell under Trevor's swift onslaught, a neck cracking like dry, well-seasoned wood; Jack's fist met the ribcage of the third, the force battering through armor plates to stave in every bone on that side. He hooked two fingers under a handy helmet-strap and wrenched the skin's chin aside as an afterthought, probably shearing a cervical vertebra or two as well.

Only chance saved him from tearing the entire bowling-ball of the head free. That would cause arterial spray, and there would be enough cleanup tonight. More staff would arrive early in the morning, getting ready for the Christmas party—the next Moonfall was late next month out at the shamans' estate, especially since the Rouje manor held a precious, recovering *demie*.

The last skin in the squad had time to lift his rifle, and fury boiled deep and ragged through Jack's belly. The shape of the gun wasn't precisely right, because it held tranquilizer darts.

Son of a bitch. Jack punched the skin in the stomach, rupturing a great many internal organs, then gave a short, strong jab to the face. Nightvision goggles shattered and the skin dropped like a forgotten toy, half his skull crushed. *Did they go right past her door? I swear, if she's been so much as scratched...*

He left the prisoner and skin corpses to Dad's not-so-tender mercies, rocketing up the stairs at full speed.

It took an eternity to reach his *demie*'s rooms, and the half-open door turned his heart to ice. He plunged through, smelling sweat and rancid stress hormones boiling through the four skins.

So they *had* come in here.

Her bed was neatly made, and thoroughly empty. Zoe's scent was a drench of calm failing to sink into his flesh because its source wasn't here, not even in the bright white bathroom. She wasn't in the closet, either, its empty spaces mocking him while they waited for Amelia to launder the clothes Janine sent.

Jack was suddenly certain his twin had vanished into thin air, and this time he wouldn't find her. The rage rose, his beast suddenly, venomously quiet, and if he couldn't hold on, next would come the grateful descent into crimson-tinged insanity. Only one or two *demi* in Kith history had ever become Broken, when their *demies* were taken by war or misadventure.

Even an analyst's cold logic wasn't helping him now. To have his *demie* returned and snatched away shortly afterward might well break him. It would be ironic to become what he had hunted so long and so successfully. Purging the Broken was an outlet for the baffled fury of a *demi* denied his other half, and each cannibalistic monster he had given peace was a sign that *he* was still controlled, still sane.

Still fully Kith.

But the attackers had tranquilizer guns. He had to *think*. Jackson Rouje stood, his head down, violent shivers coursing through him as his beast fought to slip its fetters and begin tearing the house, the town, the city, the entire *world* to pieces searching for—

"Jack?" A thin, painful whisper. "Oh, God, is it you?"

He was suddenly in her sitting room, with no memory of the intervening space. His arms closed around a warm, welcome slenderness, and his nose was full of her glorious narcotic scent because his face was buried in her silken, messy hair. He all but crushed her, his lips pressed against inky curls, and the relief threatened to unstring every muscle he owned and send both of them to the floor.

She didn't hug him back. For one thing, his *demie* probably couldn't move, but his grasp wouldn't loosen. Jack's body simply wouldn't let go. Tremors raced through her, and the sawblade edge of yellow fear to her scent would have enraged him if he'd been capable of further fury.

But she was near, and if she was in his arms she was *safe*. "Thank you," he whispered raggedly. "*Thank* you."

"There are…" She gasped in a breath, probably uncomfortably constricted. "Jack, there are people in the house. There are—listen to me." She wriggled, and the slight movement almost, *almost* pushed him off a different cliff.

Control. For your demie*'s sake, and for your own.* "I know." A harsh growl underlaid the words. "It's all right, it's handled. Did they hurt you? *Did* they?"

Because if one of the skins had even *breathed* on her, he was going to kill the ones saved for questioning and savage the bodies beyond recognition before tracking down whoever had been so foolish as to send these assholes to extend the favor in their direction as well.

He might even put their heads on sticks in the old fashion, a medieval warning.

"I hid," she whispered. "You weren't in your room, I...so I hid in the hall closet."

Smart girl. Smart, beautiful girl. "Good." He inhaled her again, the shudders turning pleasant as her nearness burned like a star in the dark. How did others live without a twin? He downright pitied them, even the Kith. "Everything's all right." *As long as you are, that is.*

"Does...does this..." She moved again, restlessly, but he still couldn't let go. "Um, is this normal?" The jaundice-gasoline tang of fear was receding under the double assault of her *demi*'s nearness and a welter of Voice spreading from his bones, but she was probably incredibly confused.

If these bastards had cost him even an inch of progress with her, Dad would have a hard if not impossible time arguing Jack out of truly barbaric behavior.

"Not really? But..." How much should he tell her? "We have enemies. Sometimes it happens."

And she neatly solved the problem, in her own inimitable way. "Because he's rich. I figured."

"That's part of it, yeah." *How am I so lucky? Christ.* The shaking in his limbs would not abate, not yet. "And because of the things the family can do. They should never have been allowed to come near you. I'm sorry." Now his arms would obey him, but only so he could clasp her shoulders, holding her at arm's length and peering at her face in the dimness.

His *demie* was pale, and her blue eyes were enormous. Her half-buttoned plaid shirt showed the fragile arches of her collarbones and a slice of one soft shoulder, and the deep painkilling comfort of her presence was only rivaled by a piercing ache in his chest at her fragility. Shorter, slighter, and far more sensitive than her *demi*, she could probably have handled all four skins instinctively on her own.

But it would terrify her, and one of them could have gotten lucky with a stray shot or ricochet. And the tranquilizer—he didn't like the implications of that, at all.

The ever-present skin hunters were changing their game, or a new group of them had entered the fray.

"Trev—Dad. And Amelia. And Lev." Of course she was worried about others. It was natural for a *demie*, let alone a shaman. "Are they—"

He pulled her close again. "Everyone's all right, don't worry." *Just stay still. I need a minute.* He needed more than that, but she wasn't ready, not by a long shot. Still, the axis the planet rotated around was pressed against him, probably feeling every single twitch and muscle, and if he let his grasp falter for even a moment he might be flung into empty space. "Are you sure you're not hurt?"

"Just..." A galvanic movement slid through her, crown to soles, and it echoed in his own body. "Just scared," she whispered, as if it were somehow shameful to be terrified when armed skins burst into your bedroom.

"I'm here." It was the only answer he could give. "You don't have to be frightened."

"I know." She shuddered again, but less violently. "What do we do now?"

He pressed his lips against her hair once more. All his own fury drained away, leaving him cold and waiting, an analyst's readiness like a viper under a rock. "Hold onto me. Breathe. That's it, good."

A soft unsound in the hallway was Dad, moving from shadow to shadow. "Zoe? Jack?"

"We're fine." A normal tone instead of a whisper was probably best, though Jack's voice tore the expectant hush and his *demie* flinched. "Any more hostiles?"

"House is clear." Dad took the hint; a touch of growl edged the vowels. "Is she—"

"She's all right. Wasn't even touched." *Thank God, and the Sun and Moon as well.* "Zoe, tell him."

"I'm okay." Her voice quivered a little, but the fear was fading. "I h-hid in the hall c-closet."

"Very smart." Trevor was merely a darker blot in the hall's gloom, keeping a careful distance. His beast thrummed under the words, his control was absolute—but Jack could sense the rage in him, a coal seam burning underground. "We'll attend to this. You two stay here."

There was no arguing with a Pride leader in this situation, and Jack knew it. Still, the order wasn't given for his benefit, but for hers; now he had an excuse to stay with his *demie*. "We will."

"Good lad." Then Dad was gone, and Jack drew Zoe close again. She relaxed, abruptly and completely, and her arms stole around his waist.

"Is he going to call the cops?" Zoe whispered.

Not likely. Amelia would question the survivors in the library, Lev would find their transport; the two would handle the cleanup afterward. Dad was probably already calling Allison. By morning Hermann would be back from the shamans' estate and the house would be humming. "If it's warranted."

"They had guns." She leaned into him, and surprisingly, laid her cheek against his chest. An instinctive movement, and all the more precious because she was so tentative.

"I know." Normally he'd be questioning the intruders himself, drawing inferences and sifting through intelligence. His *demie* was more important, though, and her calm could break at any moment.

Anyone, raised skin *or* Kith, would find this distressing. "You're safe. Dad will take care of it. In the morning it'll be like it never happened."

"They'll want to question us," she whispered.

Oh, my sweet demie, *nobody will interrogate you, ever. Except me, and even then not very much.* "I don't think so. And in any case, that's what lawyers are for. We've got a few of those, don't worry." Whoever had sent these fools was about to have a very bad year, if not decade.

"Are they after me?" The sadness in her question threatened to crack his own heart.

Now why would you think that? "Of course not, Zo-baby." But his arms tightened, and a quiet, unerring part of his analytic talent told him she might be close to the truth. First he would calm her down, and calm himself in the process.

Then he would stay, watching over her rest, while he used all the cold clarity his own talent could give to contemplate a danger to his *demie*.

And how he would destroy it, as soon as the Pride found its source.

30
TOP FIVE

I<small>T SEEMED IMPOSSIBLE TO SLEEP AFTER ARMED, ARMORED MEN HAD BURST</small> into your bedroom, but once the shakes went down and some warmth stole back into her extremities Zoe crashed almost between one breath and the next.

She'd slept like that before, most notably in an abandoned gas station out on Route 385 the night after fleeing Bea and Hall City, and once more on a Greyhound bus going south after leaving Royal. Then there was the first squat in Marquette getting raided by the cops; she'd just barely escaped that sweep and passed out that night in a homeless shelter off Galatea Avenue.

It helped that Jack had insisted they both *just lie down for a moment, if Dad needs us he'll call.* The question of just how Trevor would do that hadn't occurred to her at the time, nor had she wondered why they were so *calm.* Even Mama was a little shaky after, say, an eviction in the middle of the night, when all her charm and grace couldn't fend off a sheriff's deputy or two. Curling up and passing out was a sign that the danger was finished for the moment, and when Zoe woke to a bright crisp winter morning, a pillow on the other half of her bed held a dent and someone was in her bathroom, humming slightly as water ran.

The blue bedroom wasn't nearly so forlorn-empty now. A stack of novels sat companionably on the nightstand, ready to take her through another evening. The closet door was ajar, a new, fluffy, striped indigo bathrobe lay across the foot of the bed, and the slippers Jack had insisted she set out last night sat ready for her feet. The curtains were only halfway closed over the big bay window with its seat, letting in a bar of thin gold, and the shelves had many empty spaces, true—but those gaps looked decorative now, instead of aching, open toothsockets. A pair of long silver-drop earrings in an open black velvet box perched atop the books on her nightstand, and she couldn't smell the men from last night at all. Instead, there was merely a tang of icy freshness, as if Jack had opened the window or French door for a short while.

Fear nothing, a woman's voice echoed deep inside her head. *Trust...*

The internal sound faded, carried down a long empty hall. Had she been dreaming?

Zoe sat up, wrapped her arms around her knees, and yawned, shaking her hair back. It would tangle relentlessly, but she liked its warm weight.

And, to tell the truth, she also liked that her mother would hate all of this. Wild-haired and living with her father, spending money and thinking ungodly thoughts—oh, Mama would be horrified. She would grab Zoe's arms, her fingernails digging in hard, and give a vicious little shake.

I raised you better, Angelina would spit, and the familiar slipstream of panic would fill her daughter's ears.

The water shut off, the shower door made its whispering sound, and Zoe rested her chin on her knees.

Maybe Trevor is the devil, but I like it here. It's better than Hall City. Not to mention it was *loads* better than Royal, or Marquette, or anything else she'd ever had. Sure, she'd probably go to hell—but that was a long way away, and if she figured out the rules it couldn't be worse than the Church of the Righteous Savior.

But if this wasn't hell—and she couldn't be sure yet—it apparently came with armed break-ins. Did she really want to stay? It was a problem even her wanderings after Mama's passing hadn't quite qualified her to handle—and she'd thought she could roll with just about anything.

Some of the girls at Royal's club had stories about dates pulling guns or knives, and there had been more than one alcohol-fueled melee in that throbbing neon-lit cave. Not to mention the casual violence at some of the squats, or in other places where the desperate gathered. Poor people mostly tried like hell to take care of each other, but they were easy prey and that meant risk.

Her instincts weren't screaming at her to get out, to run. They also hadn't warned her about intruders with the usual clarity, but then again, she was nervous as a matter of course these days, praying she wouldn't somehow shatter this soft, beautiful dream.

It was like the song said, should she stay or should she go now?

There was a clatter, a muttered curse as a dropped item was picked up and replaced, then Jack strolled out of her bathroom, scrubbing at water-darkened hair with a blue towel. Barefoot and bare-chested, he was otherwise in a pair of jeans, and damp gleamed on his broad shoulders. Muscle flickered under his skin, and he made a short, gruff *good morning* noise.

When she first arrived, it would have frightened her. Now she knew it just meant he hadn't had any coffee yet, so she regarded him somberly as he moved to the French door, pulling aside the curtains after glancing her way to make sure she had no objection.

The sudden flood of sunlight turned him into a gilded statue. He glared at the day outside like it had done him some personal wrong, and Zoe swallowed a laugh.

He glanced over his shoulder, dark eyes glittering. "Everything's fine." Morning was caught in his throat, turning the words to gravel. "Hurry up, I want breakfast."

Last night receded into the haziness of a bad nightmare, waiting for further brooding once she could shut her suite's door and retreat into solitude. Zoe bounced out of bed, tugging at her flannel shirt; it was just like racing to get ready for school.

Still, after she grabbed a fistful of clothing from the closet and bolted for the bathroom she could stand in the shower for a few moments, thinking furiously while she worked expensive jasmine-scented shampoo into her hair. Jack and Trevor didn't seem to consider the whole thing any big deal, but what seemed strangest was...

Well, their *concern*. Mama might have run for the hills and left Zo behind after an event like this. Indeed, old childhood fears that one day Angelina might do just that rose bitter and dark in Zoe's chest, only dispelled when she thrust her head under a steady stream of hot water and exhaled hard, willing them away.

Fear nothing, the voice whispered again, a faraway train-horn crying at midnight. *Trust your brother.* Jack had burst into her room looking for her, for all the world as if he really cared. And Trevor, too.

Dad, Zoe reminded herself. *You might as well call him that for real.* At least she didn't get soap in her eyes; she hurried through dressing and fairly leapt back into her bedroom with her hair caught in a sloppy towel-wrapped pile.

"Slow down." Jack, sitting on the edge of her bed, looked up from tying his boots. A black T-shirt strained at his shoulders. "I'm not going anywhere without you."

"Mama never liked waiting." *Especially not for a stupid little kid.* Zoe had a tank top on already, and would be ready once she grabbed one of the sweaters Janine had sent.

The luxury of having preferences—this top, that skirt, this lunch, that book—was a powerful inducement to staying. She just didn't know yet whether it was powerful enough to outweigh...well, a group of armed invaders.

"She was wrong." Jack's glower deepened. "About everything."

Not everything. It was hopeless to defend Mama, but the old reflex was still there. Sometimes Angelina was kind, hugging Zoe and saying *us girls against the world, right?* She was the most beautiful mother in any town, that numinous air of royalty and slight well-bred smile forcing teachers to admire her—and men too, until she got too thin with the cancer.

But Mama was dead and besides, Jack knew things Zoe didn't about their strange senses and her weird talents. Staying to gather every bit of information she could until her instincts told her to jump was probably the best course, but of course it was also the easiest.

Was she just being lazy?

Zoe scrambled for a pair of canvas shoes and the sweater she wanted, indigo merino with a ballet neck and three-quarter sleeves. When she settled on the vanity bench, he rose from his perch on the bed, ambling toward her.

"You don't like it when I talk about her." He reached for the towel holding her hair, and she let him scrub a bit at the wet mass before unwrapping. "Turn around, and hand me a comb."

"It's not that," she began, but he leaned past her, easily swiping a heavy silver wide-tooth comb from the vanity's top.

Maybe he was angry. Zoe shifted and turned, facing the mirror like a good girl, lacing her fingers together and squeezing *hard*, a small bite of pain to help her focus. Her stomach flipflopped like it didn't want any breakfast, just a Styrofoam cup of cheap coffee before hurrying to catch the bus for another long, thankless shift at a backbreaking job.

If leisure came with things like last night, did she want it?

Jack smiled into the mirror, and began working at her hair like it was the most natural thing in the world.

It would save some time, so she didn't duck away. "You can talk about her all you want," Zoe continued. "It's just that—"

"You don't have to explain, *demie*." The edge of irritation was gone, and he didn't tug sharply at her curls like Mama would have.

Should cut all this mess off, Angelina would mutter, and Zoe would stiffen, close to clapping her hands over her ears and screaming. Kids had no power, really, unless it was pure sonic embarrassment.

Tantrums were always paid for later, but sometimes the price was worth it.

Especially when Mama wanted her to go on 'Bible retreats' with Bea. Zoe froze, the comb sliding through wet curls tentatively, then with more authority. Jack wasn't very efficient, probably too afraid of pulling her hair.

It was a nice change. "Did Mama leave because of things like last night?"

"So that's what's bothering you." At least good conditioner meant there weren't many tangles to yank at. Jack was getting more confident the longer he worked. His touch firmed, and he wore a slight frown of concentration. "It happens sometimes, that's all. If she was worried about it she should've stayed where the safety was."

Is it really safe here, though? Zoe stared at her hands.

What, precisely, *was* this 'family' of theirs? "I wonder..." She was about to ask *what happened to them, the people yesterday*—but it didn't seem like a healthy question. Royal would give her a halfhearted slap and a wholehearted encouragement to mind her own business.

Get it through your head, Amber. At least she never had to use that name ever again. She had that much power, small though it was.

"Well? What is it you wonder, *demie*?" Now her twin sounded amused instead of grumpy.

"Nothing." She froze again—Mama was always on her to stop fidgeting. Were there already police in the house, asking questions, poking into corners? She didn't hear them. "We can go to breakfast. It's just going to tangle anyway."

"Then I'll do this again." He picked up the towel again, pressing gently on dripping ends. "Maybe I should grow mine out."

"Lots of upkeep."

"That's true. I'll just live vicariously through you." He was almost done, so she tilted her head, shivering slightly as he worked at the ends. It had been a long, long time since anyone else touched her hair. "If you're worried about those bastards from last night, Zo-baby, don't be. It's part of Amelia's job to take care of things like that."

Amelia? "But she's..."

"Dad's personal bodyguard when he's home. Lev's not bad himself; he's training with her." Jack paused, then ran his fingers through her hair, testing. "I should have been up here last night, but I thought you were asleep and Dad needed...anyway, I'm sorry."

He apologized like he meant it. It was one more drop in the *stay* bucket, and the *leave* one was emptying fast.

"You can't plan for a home invasion," Zoe said. Of all the sentences she'd ever used in her life, that one had to be in the top five weirdest—and that was saying something.

Jack laughed as if it was a good joke, and finished combing her hair.

31
CERTAIN ADVANTAGES

THE SOLARIUM WAS ITS USUAL QUIET GREEN MORNING SELF, AND THE HOUSE was now humming with a full complement of staff. Of course the Christmas party was approaching, but in reality the Pride was about to arrange itself around a newly returned *demie* with a protective vengeance.

Last night had been entirely too close, and the tranqs obviously bothered Dad as much as Jack. Trevor was at his usual place, setting his newspaper aside and rising with a warm smile for Zoe, who sank into her now-habitual seat with enviable grace.

She was pale, and nervous. Fortunately her scent held no edge of outright fear, just faint nose-stinging anxiety. Stretching out next to his sleeping *demie* had granted Jack a measure of calm even if he was too keyed-up for real rest, but the need to touch her, physically or otherwise, was near-constant. It was a *demi*'s urge to soothe both himself and his twin with contact, and it was a blessing she didn't seem to mind.

His fingers still tingled with the feel of her hair. There was so much going on inside her pretty head he wanted to hear, but she was back to silence and noncommittal replies, deftly turning any conversation in his direction and staying camouflaged behind politeness.

Treating him, in short, just like everyone else. It was unexpectedly frustrating, especially juxtaposed with her shy trust—she hadn't said a word about him sharing the bed, and it didn't seem like she was getting ready to bolt after last night's unpleasantness.

Progress was made, but not nearly enough.

Amelia must have just been in, because a wide red cappuccino cup sat at Zoe's place, and the usual mug of coffee waited at Jack's. Trevor waited until she was settled, sank into his chair, and refolded the paper.

"Did you get any rest?" he finally inquired, softly. "I'm sorry, Zoe. You should never have had to put up with that."

"I didn't even see what happened, not really." At least she looked to Jack for reassurance, her baby blues wide and dark. "I wouldn't have known anything was wrong if..." Another tiny glance at him, and her chin rose slightly. "If I hadn't still been awake."

Unexpectedly sweet, that she would take strength from his encouraging expression. Jack lifted his coffee, letting his eyelids drop to half mast.

He'd spent a lot of last night thinking, flat on his back and listening to his *demie* breathe while his entire body burned with frustrated, leftover aggression. Focusing to sort through analysis and impressions provided some relief, and manufacturing reasons to brush against her today would grant more.

"At least that." Trevor reached for his own caffeine. "There are new people in the house today, not least for security; I'm sure you've noticed. I know you like the quiet, but better safe than sorry. And the party's tomorrow."

"Amelia said I could help with sugar cookies." Zoe took a deep breath. "Am I going to have to talk to the cops? About last night?"

"Of course not." To his credit, Dad didn't look more than mildly baffled. "We have lawyers for that, my dear. It's being taken care of, and you don't need to worry about a single thing." He paused. "There's another question, I can tell. Ask."

Zoe bit her lip, studying Dad's face. Finally, she nodded slightly, some internal balance shifting. "Is it true that Amelia's your bodyguard?"

"While I'm at home, yes." Dad didn't miss a beat. "I'm perfectly capable, but the family feels better if we're all protected. Naturally there are quite a...well, there are a few people who bear me some ill will. Some of them have the money to pay for little displays like last night's. It's nothing you need worry about."

"Because the 'family' will take care of it?" Zoe regarded him steadily, and a thin cold fingertip of unease brushed Jack's nape. The silence stretched, and Trevor set his cup down.

He didn't pin his daughter with a bright, paralyzing stare, of course, but he did meet her gaze and tilt his golden head slightly. "You make it sound like we're the mafia."

"I know I shouldn't ask." A shadow crossed her expression, a drifting cloud Jack longed to chase. "But..."

"No, little dancer. You, of all people, may ask anything you wish." Dad kept his tone very soft, very level. No whisper of irritation, no hint of aggression or impatience. "I should point out we're *not* the Mob, though. We just have certain...advantages."

She watched him closely, and the vibrating worry Allison's feartaking should have erased struggled to break free. His *demie* was indeed throwing off the shaman's touch, and that was both good *and* bad. On the one hand, she would make an incredibly strong shaman.

On the other, the fear might make it difficult for her to accept a few things, not least her *demi*'s natural closeness. "Zoe's already noticed a few of those." Jack took care to make his tone level as well, as neutral as possible. She probably had no idea there had been two teams last night, and her reaction said she wasn't quite a stranger to violence intruding upon a night's rest. Which led to some interesting, albeit maddening, deductions about just what she'd suffered, either with Angelina or otherwise. "Must've been confusing, growing up."

"I can only imagine," Trevor agreed, soberly. "Having to figure all that out on your own, dealing with high emotion and the more, ah, *physical* gifts—it takes strength and intelligence to navigate that alone. You're a bright young lady, Zoe."

"I told her, but I don't think she believes me." Jack now had the exquisite pleasure of seeing his *demie*, her lips slightly parted with obvious shock, look to him for reassurance once more.

"It will take time." Dad reached for his coffee again; Jack's *demie* echoed the movement, her slim graceful fingers pale against red ceramic. "And I would very much like it if the process wasn't interrupted by petty displays like last night's. So, we'll have a full complement of staff here for the foreseeable future, double security, and I'm sorry, Zoe, but I'm going to ask you to take Jack along if you leave the house. He knows the dangers, and will help you avoid them."

"Besides, it will keep me from having to work," Jack muttered, and was rewarded by a slight smile tilting his *demie*'s lips.

"Your guiding star." Dad mock-glared at him, a thunderous line between dark-blond eyebrows, carefully not including Zoe. "Just wait until your sister gives you back to me, young man."

Fortunately, she didn't seem about to. "I think maybe I should keep him for a little while." The unease in her scent didn't disappear, but she tried to sound light and amused, lifting her coffee and half-hiding behind the large cup. "He can get things off high shelves, after all."

"See? I'm useful." Jack had to hand it to the old man, neatly solving a potential problem with a direct attack. Now Zoe was encouraged to view last night as a mere annoyance, and introduced to the idea of the family's essential difference as well as her own. She was more likely to accept the presence of Kith security, and become further accustomed to her *demi*'s constant presence. "Keep me safe, Zo-baby. I'm counting on you."

That earned him a very startled, very blue glance before she stared back into her latte. "All right," she said, softly, and Jack realized his beautiful, nervous, uncertain *demie* had beyond a doubt been weighing the thought of vanishing from the manor as she'd disappeared from Hall City or any number of towns afterward.

She wouldn't get far, but his own reaction to the attempt might well frighten a girl raised as a skin. And he didn't like the idea that she was used to hiding from groups of armed men, either.

Amelia, with her usual impeccable timing, appeared in the doorway bearing a heavy wooden tray. "Breakfast," the jäger chirped, and Jack watched the doors behind his *demie*'s eyes slam shut. "And how is your coffee, *fata mica*?"

"You put honey in it?" The contrast between Zoe's calm, closed expression and the note of anxious-to-please in her voice was jarring, but perhaps only to a closely watching *demi*. "And...salt?"

"Very good! Sea salt and lavender honey. Tasty, no?" Amelia beamed, and Lev appeared over her shoulder with another tray. A faint whiff of snow and healthy outside exertion hung on the lad; he must have been running the perimeter this morning. Their calm, and the fact that *they* didn't seem to view last night as anything out of the ordinary, would mitigate his *demie*'s reactions. "Today, we make cookies. So much to do, you must eat."

"Am I still allowed to help?" Zoe glanced again at Jack, her slim shoulders relaxing.

At least there was that.

"Allowed? My dear, I am *counting* on it." The jäger was all business, her black trousers sharply creased and her heavy wine-red sweater providing a festive note. "Sesame waffles for you; try the pomegranate syrup. Jackson, you have breakfast burrito; I toasted the chipotles this morning. Lev, set the butter there."

Zoe studied Amelia closely, but didn't flinch. And Jack, turning his attention to his own breakfast—protein-heavy, the jäger obviously thought he needed the fuel for upcoming festivities—also decided he'd better keep an even closer watch on his *demie*.

32

CHANGE OVERNIGHT

INSTEAD OF FAMILIAR, NUMBING QUIET, THE HOUSE WAS FULL OF HALF-HEARD footsteps, soft voices, and humming activity. Doors opened and closed, the stairs quivered like plucked strings, and Zoe's nose untangled vivid threads of unfamiliar people-scent.

So, there were more of the 'family' here today. It was a whole new language—'family', 'security', and 'advantages' all taking on different meanings, like 'gifts' and 'Christian' changed shape when Mama met Bea, or 'dates' and 'work' once Royal knew he had a girl he thought was named Amber on a hook. Each time Zo landed in another school or town, she had to learn the lingo.

Most words were solid, but you couldn't count on them staying that way.

Zoe peeked out her suite door at the now-familiar hall. She'd excused herself to get hair ties, since she'd be in the kitchen—passing any food handler's test meant you didn't embarrass yourself or give anyone E. coli, at least if your head was screwed on straight.

The now-familiar hall with its wide, velvet-curtained windows was deserted. All the activity was elsewhere, leaving her rooms—and Jack's—in a bubble of quiet. Maybe that was intentional, but either way it was welcome. Zoe slipped three ponytail elastics into her pocket and gave the hall another long stare.

Finally, she tiptoed out and turned toward her brother's suite, moving quick and soft as possible. The house had absorbed most of the evidence of last night's intruders, but not *all* of it. She could still trace a very faint trail of sour male sweat and high adrenaline excitement, especially if she kept her eyes half-lidded and let her other senses do their work.

It was just like finding a dead-end, ill-paying job in a new town, or avoiding truly bad trouble—follow the nose, stay on your toes. To the end of the hall, a hard right turn, and a staircase she hadn't explored yet swallowed her. While she glided down, her fingertips resting lightly on a satiny wooden banister, she had to keep her ears peeled for anyone close by as well.

Would Dad be angry at her sneaking around? Would Jack? She'd been here long enough she couldn't just say she got turned around or lost—and besides, unlike Mama, both of them could probably smell a direct lie.

They were different, and so was she. Mama's rambling about demons and ungodly powers made a lot more sense now. Not only that, but both her father and Jack were very, very careful when mentioning those 'gifts'.

Maybe they suspected she didn't share them—or they knew she did, and were keeping quiet for an entirely different reason.

The big question was if that reason was something Zo could go along with, or not. She tiptoed, following an invisible trail, thinking furiously and hoping nobody would come looking for her. What would be a good excuse for being in this part of the house?

I don't care. I'm staying. Then, a few moments later, she weighed the idea of flight. Nothing this good was ever free, or even cheap— but where would she go?

And would they follow, especially if she took anything with her?

The scent-track ended at a small utility room with an outside door—the door was new, fitting into its socket comfortably, and its latticed glass window in the top half was sparkling clean, for all the world as if freshly replaced. Despite that, marks on the frame showed a pry attempt lately; it was just like coming back to a squat to find your lock had been tampered with.

Zoe sniffed again, untangling the fading traces of last night's intruders and the far fresher overlay of Lev's scent. He'd spent quite a bit of time here.

No sign of broken glass, no footprints, nothing but a spotless, quiet utility room with a wide granite counter and a thoroughly scrubbed double sink under a larger window looking out onto a snowy expanse, the white blanket broken only by neatly shoveled paved paths scattered with deicer pellets. Wooden cabinets stood sentinel opposite the sink, holding nothing more exotic than cleaning supplies, rock salt, a couple brooms, and a high-end vacuum cleaner as well as several dusters—cloth, lambswool, plastic static-charged ones.

Breaking in here gave the intruders almost a straight shot to her suite and Jack's. Zoe peered out the window over the sinks, trying to decide if it was worth sneaking out to see if she could find tracks in the snow.

What would you do then? Chase them like a bloodhound? This wasn't a place you got to by walking; where were the attackers' cars? Had Lev and Amelia taken care of *that*? Hermann was supposed to be back this morning too.

Wait. I don't smell any cops. Just the guys from last night and Lev.

So had they called the police, or just...what? Covered everything up, made it disappear? Well, with this kind of money you could pay people to ignore a few things. Royal was always talking about how everyone was on the take, especially badge-carrying pork.

Zoe tried to imagine Roy tracking her down here. Jack would take one look at him and...do what, precisely? Maybe he'd protect Zo, or maybe he'd be disgusted at what she'd done to survive. And then there were the scars down Roy's face—and to think, she'd once been utterly convinced she was in love with him, and that he was doing what he could to take care of her in return.

Live and learn was one of Mama's maxims, but Zoe didn't like most of the lessons one bit. Figuring out Roy was just a younger, slightly handsomer version of Bea without the religious bullshit had been plain awful. Of course, to judge by his social media right now, he'd gone and picked up Bible-thumping, so maybe it had only been a matter of time.

Not like it mattered. Zoe had more immediate problems.

The only prospect scarier than leaving this comfortable nest was being thrown out because she'd done something unforgivable while scrambling to stay alive. Maybe she could make herself useful in some way, but *how?* They already had everything they could ever want.

Zoe's nape tingled; she turned away from the door, eyes wide and searching. The sense of being watched was unmistakable.

She retraced her steps, peeking into the hall, this one lit with old glass fixtures instead of daylight through windows. Obviously the invaders had been looking for someone, they'd whispered *where is she?* Royal didn't have this kind of pull—or he hadn't when she knew him, and it was a jolt to realize that was almost two whole years ago.

If her life could change overnight, his probably could too. What if Jack and Trevor hadn't been the only ones looking for her?

But who would want Zoe Simmons? She was nobody.

Maybe it was just Zoe Rouje they were after? It was scary to think total strangers had known more about who she was than she ever had; the idea made her feel funny and slippery inside.

In any case, she had to get to the kitchen. Amelia was waiting. Zoe gathered her hair for a quick braid while she retraced her steps, her brain working overtime, practicing reasonable explanations if she was caught.

Maybe she was paranoid, but who wouldn't be? And now she had a relatively easy escape route from her beautiful blue rooms memorized.

Just in case.

"Here. For protection, the flour goes everywhere." Amelia was all business, settling an unbleached cotton apron over Zoe's clothes, tying it at her waist. The vast rustic kitchen was full of good smells, and there was a new arrival.

A young woman with long, straight sandalwood hair was at one counter using a rolling pin; her braid moved slightly as she glanced over her shoulder. Her eyes were deep and dark, amused by everything, and positively enormous; she had a perfect nose, high cheekbones, and a small, well-satisfied smile on naturally beestung lips.

In other words, the new arrival was drop-dead model gorgeous like Janine and her helpers, with the same humming vitality as everyone else here.

So she was 'family', then.

"Hi there." The young woman shook her head slightly, though her precision-cut bangs would never dare to hang in those huge eyes. "I see Meel's roped you into the baking, too. I'm Jolie, *enchanté*."

"I'm Zoe." Her mouth was suddenly dry. Next to this girl she was a gawky mess, and knew it. "How do you do?"

"Oh, I do, and I *do*." Jolie had a lovely contralto; she was in jeans and a casual sweater just like Zoe, not to mention a matching apron. "We're going to be great friends, you and me. I can just feel it, you know?"

I'm not so sure. You're too pretty. Still, the other girl's smile held no hint of anything other than amusement, welcome, and warm good nature. "I hope so," Zo agreed, cautiously. This was probably a test, and the trembling sensation of *you're about to fail* filled her stomach, jostling with sesame waffle and crispy bacon. "What should I...uh, where do you want me to start?"

"Come on over here," Jolie said. "Don't worry, I'm very easy-tempered. After all, I put up with McKenna following me around, so—"

"Pfft." Amelia rolled her eyes, and gently pushed Zoe toward the counter and its well-floured cutting boards. "Big mischief, that boy, just like Jack. Here are the cutters, *fata mica*, and you will choose the shapes." Three huge craft boxes with neatly sectioned trays held a stunning assortment of cookie cutters.

Zo's throat threatened to close up with panic. Working food service had not prepared her for this. "Maybe I should..." Where was Jack? She hadn't realized just how much she'd been relying on him for direction, and that was scary too. "There's a lot of them."

"I suggest starting with the trees. They're easier than the reindeer." Jolie grinned, reaching deftly for a shallow metal bowl full of flour and tossing a little across the circle of rolled dough with a practiced movement. "And we need some music. Come on, Amelia. It's Christmas, let's have some carols."

Oh, Christ, did they expect her to sing? Zoe almost panicked, but Amelia bumped her again, gently, aiming her at the boxes.

"I turn on stereo," the housekeeper said. "But *no words*, all instrument. The words confuse the food."

"And we can't have that," Jolie cheerfully agreed. A deep, indefinable calm pervaded her scent, teasing at Zoe's memory. "I've got some flour to dip the cutters in this dish here; grab that tree one on top...perfect, come on over." She moved aside, indicating a place on the rolled dough. "Start wherever. I like to nibble the raw stuff, but Amelia—"

"Filthy child, we do not eat like that." Amelia bustled away. A shadow at the kitchen's back door was Lev, stamping snow off his boots on the other side of yet another airlock-like utility room. "We shall listen to Tchaikovsky. Good for you."

"I've never done this before." Zoe settled the cookie cutter, hopefully in the right place, and snatched her hand away as the other girl reached for it.

"Easy as pie." Jolie's shoulder pressed against hers, but the contact wasn't a scrape against her nerve endings. Instead, that strange half-familiar calm flooded outward. The other girl pushed the metal cutter down gently. "See? Give it a little wiggle, exactly like that. Good. Now the trick is to dip the cutter each time, and turn it so you get the most out of each rolling. Like a puzzle. Oh, see, you've got it. Maybe Amelia will let us make the gingersnaps."

"I will not," the housekeeper huffed from another part of the kitchen. She was certainly forbidding enough to be a bodyguard, and she moved with swift graceful economy Jack and Trevor shared. Were her senses heightened too? How fast was she? "Those are mine to do."

"I try every year," Jolie mock-whispered, her eyes dancing. It was easy to tentatively like her; in fact, she reminded Zoe of Jenny Scarsdale, or of a blonde girl in Montana—what was her name?

Laurel. It took a few moments to remember. *Laurel Graines.* A nice, relatively popular fourth-grader, who didn't laugh at the new student with her beautiful mother and weird ways.

A sudden piercing very much like homesickness flooded Zoe, and she had to pause, taking a deep breath. What was Jenny doing now? Or Laurel, who probably didn't even remember her because it had, after all, only been a few months? It was probably best to not wonder.

"The best part is when they come out of the oven." Jolie's fingers settled over Zoe's and she pressed gently down, a subtle twist of her slim wrist freeing a cookie-shaped bit of dough from what had been a seamless whole. Even that skin contact wasn't an irritating rasp; the touch sent another flood of calm racing through nerves and bones. "Nice and fresh, and then Amelia doesn't mind us stealing a few. See? We're going to get along *swimmingly,* you and me."

Zoe hoped it was true, and turned the cookie cutter a few degrees, trying not to waste any dough.

33
INTERESTING
RAMIFICATIONS

HE WANTED TO BE SHEPHERDING HIS *DEMIE*, BUT DUTY CALLED. AT LEAST SHE hadn't tried to step outside, just worked the intruders' backtrail to point of entry and examined the door for a short while, thinking...what?

Jack longed to know, but the *usanaugh* bond, while unbreakable, was far more tenuous than it should be. In any case, she'd turned away, pulling her hair back and braiding with swift fingers as she moved, graceful and nervous as a stray cat testing a new home's hidden dangers. She went straight downstairs to join Amelia and Jolie; maybe she even felt his shadowing.

It was no great trick to move unseen by skins, but a *demie* was something else entirely.

She was safe enough with a jäger and a shaman in attendance; Allison's protégé was broadcasting waves of warm goodwill and deep relaxation but using no Voice. Jack retreated, heading for Dad's home office, and was surprised to find nobody but Trevor there.

He'd expected McKenna and Hermann, but maybe the cheerful bastard and the retainer were both busy. "She's in the kitchen," he said by way of greeting, closing the door with a soft snick. "I'm not sure, Dad, but I think my *demie* might want to bolt."

"I hope not." Trevor's lip lifted, a half-snarl. His suit today was dark grey, crisp as cold fresh lettuce and not daring to wrinkle one iota. He stood by the window, iron-colored winterlight burning in golden hair, and his leashed fury, spreading in a heat-haze, might have frightened his daughter. Or, indeed, any Kith who could sense it. "Analysis, Jack."

"Of her current state, or of last night's unpleasantness?" He headed for the massive oak sideboard, the beast inside his skin uneasy but willing to remain chained for now. "And do you want rum?"

"All of the above, and double measure, please."

The regular, habitual act of pouring steadied Jack; so did the cold clarity of his gift. "She's relaxing, but still waiting. Angelina alternated clinging and harshness, probably almost at random. Has Amerlane checked in about McFisk yet?"

"Her father called this morning. He's gone."

What the hell? Jack returned the decanter to its home. "Gone?"

"Found dead in the shower. Took three fellow prisoners with him. They were all from a certain white supremacist gang; it is, according to prison officials, a deep mystery." A mix of amusement and irony lingered in the phrase. "Fantome's giving a good impression of baffled innocence, but Sondra Amerlane's paralegal is a patterner and went back to the public records. McFisk's birth certificate was altered. I'll let you guess."

Jack's brain raced as he poured his own drink. Three on one? The surprising thing was the amount of damage a so-called 'pastor' was able to do in self-defense. He reshuffled the data, including everything Zoe could be induced to say about McFisk, and the solution was depressingly simple. "Angelina's little religious friend was a misbegotten, and related to Fantome in some way." The Plainswalker wasn't mated, but he had a sister—and cousins, not to mention an uncle.

"Give the man a prize." Trevor's snarl eased as he accepted a tumbler of rum; he and his heir stood shoulder to shoulder, looking out over the snowbound west gardens. A blanket of fresh predawn snow covered all traces of last night's events. "We don't know how closely related, but it doesn't matter. If Angelina wasn't dead I'd strangle her myself, exposing my daughter to *that*."

A great deal of Fantome's behavior, not to mention Zoe's, fell into place. It was good to know his instincts were still working as they should; Jack took a burning sip of brandy, letting the alcohol's fume mix with the fire's scent. Unease crawled through his guts, poked at his heart.

She's safe where she is. Do this quietly and do it right, so she's even safer.

"It makes sense, especially if Fantome's position has been weak for a time." The conclusion was inescapable. "He probably knew about McFisk's little con, but didn't think it important enough to interfere with so they simply let him run as long as there was no real trouble. A misbegotten's almost a skin, after all, how much damage can they do?" With nothing like the power or control of a true Kith, the unfortunates stayed on the periphery of pride, pack, or sleuth— cared for, certainly, but not privy to real business. "He most likely didn't know his misbegotten kin had access to a *demie*, since I can't see him straying outside the codes that far, but now he does and he's protecting his own while also attempting to avoid blood atonement. We have full rights for that if my *demie* wants, but doing so might traumatize her further." With McFisk dead, his close-kin would be held accountable, especially since Fantome was not just an ordinary Kith but a ruler.

While Jack would welcome the chance to tear the Plainswalker or his chosen champion to pieces, it was tradition for the injured party, if not fighting themselves, to watch the vengeance being meted out. And Jack certainly didn't think Zo was ready, in any sense of the word, for that display of Kith law.

"I wouldn't want that. It's enough to break my heart, seeing what *that woman* did to her." Dad glowered at the window, Voice rumbling almost fit to rattle the panes. "What was last night, then?"

You already suspect, you're just asking for confirmation. Fortunately, Jack could give it. "Skin hunters. Attempted capture, and a pretty brazen one. We knew someone else was tracking her, and for a short while I thought it might be Fantome. But he's got his own problems, especially now. Amerlane's going to tear their pack's territorial heart out—tell me you sent enough backup."

"She doesn't need it. But Holley, Sam Coughlin, and DeSalva the elder are there. The shaman will restrain whoever needs it, Holley's not one to extract blood when money and prestige will do, and DeSalva's known for her command of jurisprudence. We'll have a significant territorial expansion before long."

"And there's no statute of limitations in a case like this." At least, not formally. Some of the Kith at large might look askance at a vendetta after too much time had passed, but that was a problem for another day. "It's last night's skins I'm interested in at the moment. Is the tranq analyzed yet?"

"Hermann woke up Hannah Belmario. McKenna hand-carried a sample over to her lab around four A.M." Trevor's snarl had faded, and he was every inch the calm, collected Pride ruler now. "He'll be back as soon as he can; he caught Jasperson last night too, before all the fun and games here."

That was good news. Greg Jasperson had escalated from merely wild to outright dangerous behavior. The dumbass had even attempted to hide, disobeying a summons from the Pride's ruler— McKenna had been sent to insist, found the little toad gone, and run him to ground.

"What did he do to Greg?" It was Mac's return Jack was really interested in; if he'd been run to exhaustion the man would be almost relaxed. He was dangerous when he had the fidgets, and Jack could test his own irrational response at the thought of his friend finally meeting his *demie*. "Do I even want to know?"

"I hear he behaved, for once. He and Pindar played good-cop-bad-cop; Allison is very proud of her protégé." Dad took another sip, consigning Jasperson the younger and his less-than-stellar life choices to temporary oblivion. "The tranquilizer's...concerning. Very strong. Nothing a Kith couldn't metabolize eventually, but it would take a short while. Hannah's untangling it so she can synthesize and come up with a counter. Says it's fine work—you know how she is."

I do indeed. Belmario was an analyst as well, but her talent focused on chemistry, organic and otherwise. She was, like most of her and Jack's kind, never happier than with a conundrum in her lap. "Could be another way to find these skin hunters. She probably already has the components sourced."

"You know, you're almost uncanny." Dad's satisfied half-smile was all the praise a son could want. "I shouldn't even ask, just let you tell me."

"It's fun to wait for the question, though." Jack's talent required pieces of data, no matter how minute or disparate, in order to function. Any thread would do, so he could begin unraveling. A shaman could grasp the whole picture with a leap of intuitive inward sight, but *he* needed something tangible.

What he didn't see, Zoe would.

The discomfort rose again, sharply controlled. Was she missing him as well, or happily oblivious? It was an unfamiliar—and unwelcome—torment, thinking she might have been so damaged by her upbringing she wouldn't even notice his absence. He bolted half the brandy like a stupid, swilling skin, and told himself of course his *demie* missed him.

She simply wouldn't know how to handle the feeling, maybe wouldn't even know how to articulate it. And now someone wanted to steal her away from the Pride.

Again.

They had known for about a year that someone else was attempting to track Angelina and her child. The searchers had relatively good resources, confined their efforts to the continental United States, and the inquiries were very quiet.

But they weren't Kith.

All of which meant McFisk filing for Angelina's death benefits had alerted more than one interested party. It was enough to chill Jack to the bone. If the Howler hadn't sent word north once a stray female Kith on his turf was noticed, would the other party have finally run her down?

Zoe might have escaped them with instinctive strength, speed, and savagery. But...a tranquilizer strong enough to knock a Kith down for any period of time was dangerous in its own right, and a confused *demie* raised as a skin would be further injured, psychologically and emotionally if not otherwise, by any capture attempt.

"Last night's players were mercs, well-funded and fairly professional with a good close rate." Trevor shifted slightly. His wingtips were polished to a mirror gloss, and he was wearing a tie Jack had given him last year, probably an intentional sartorial comment. "We took a look at the money. It went through more than a few washers, so it's practically anonymous unless we get the hackers on it and risk the other side knowing we're aware of their interest. What does that sound like to you?"

"A group of skin hunters functioning stateside, possibly new, certainly independent of the usual suspects. Could be the same people who were looking for Angelina and her daughter while we were, but there's not enough data to answer that particular question with any degree of accuracy yet." It irked Jack to leave any loose end, but whoever was searching for Trevor's vanished wife could have an entirely normal and prosaic reason for doing so; she had been the last of the blueblood Simmons clan, old aristocracy—or what passed for it in America—marrying into money to survive. "As long as they're sending hired hands to do the dirty work, it's nothing more than a minor annoyance if we observe some elementary precautions. But looking to *capture* instead of *kill* has some...interesting ramifications."

"That's what I was afraid of." Dad's eyes narrowed; he looked at the snowscape but probably didn't see any of it. A Kith ruler was ever-available to all those under their aegis for matters both small and large, and he was no doubt weighing several other pressing

Pride concerns at the moment as well. "Both prisoners were questioned thoroughly. They were to bring any female they could find and secure to a pickup point, but neither of the grunts knew the pickup—only the commander and lieutenant did, and they didn't survive to testify."

Any female they could find. Even more interesting. The idea of skin hunters attempting to drag Amelia away could even be described as hilarious. "Still, they had to have a rendezvous." No paramilitary group would overlook such a basic requirement.

"Which we checked at around six this morning." Dad's ring glinted as he rolled the tumbler between his palms, rum trembling amber in glass depths. "Nothing but a hotel reservation and two chop-shop cars. The survivors had little else to give, even under Allison's...attentions."

Allison was probably holed up at the shamans' estate with Aaron Januck and Susannah Smythe-Corrin, shaking off the stress and strain of looking through filthy skin minds. "The Christmas party will set her right." There was strength in community, and the Pride would close around Allison the same way it had wrapped around Zoe —though his *demie* didn't know it yet. "Not to mention Moonfall."

"About that." Trevor moved on to his next concern. "Jack, can your sister use the change?"

"Of course, she's *demie*." *I don't like that you're asking again, though.* "Allison said as much, too."

"And yet..." Dad finished the last of his rum in one fell swoop, baring his teeth briefly at the pleasant, momentary sting. "I worry."

"So do I." Saying otherwise, no matter how comforting the lie, was counterproductive at this point. "She's not ready for Moonfall yet, especially if half of what I suspect McFisk did to her is true. But she has the change."

That got Dad's full attention. "You think he—"

If Jack didn't interrupt, they might get mired in a discussion of McFisks's sins, which would be both enraging and pointless. "I think a misbegotten had access to my defenseless *demie* for the years she was in Nebraska, aided and abetted by her own mother. If we're lucky he only vented some frustration." If they weren't lucky, the misbegotten—enough strength to wound a fellow Kith and none of the control—had injured Zoe to a degree, physically or emotionally, which might possibly interfere with the change. Untangling *that* would take a long while. "I think she's still incredibly confused and ready to bolt the instant either of us makes a wrong move, and then I'm going to have to run her down and possibly frighten her more on top of it. We've made progress, though."

"At least that." Dad eyed him sidelong. "You should get back to her, then. Jolie's decided to stay until after the party; I think she's intending to do some preliminary training of our returned prodigal. Indirectly, of course."

"If Zoe likes her, she can stay as long as she wants." The only thing Jack didn't quite care for was the prospect of McKenna dropping by and possibly charming his *demie*. Which was ridiculous, Mac had set his sights in another direction—but the beast in Jack's skin wasn't rational, and there was only one thing to temper its possessiveness.

Ironically, it was something his sweet *demie*, raised as a skin and traumatized by a misbegotten, would have a great deal of trouble with.

"Of course." Trevor acknowledged the obvious with a wry smile. "Oh, and before you go, I've some good news."

"We could use some."

"Dimitri and Bella are back from their European tour. They'll be at the party."

That wasn't just good, but downright *fantastic* news. "Thank God." Uncharacteristic relief poured through Jack. Zoe would naturally be fascinated by another pair of *usanaugh*, and Bell would take it upon herself to explain *demie* things to her. "They know?"

"Yes. In fact, Dimitri called to say they'd come over early, and are looking forward to helping." Dad's amusement held no edge for once, and Jack's own relief was probably painfully evident as well.

"Now there's a happy thought." It was good to be Kith, but it was even better to be part of the Pride. Best of all was to be *usanaugh*, even if your *demie* had been stolen for a long while. He had time to repair the damage, time to teach her how to be fearless—and he would have all the help the Pride was capable of providing. "I'm bound for the kitchen, then. Amelia will press me into service, I'm sure."

"Better you than me. Enjoy yourself, Jack; I'll take care of every-thing else." Dad held out his hand for the empty brandy snifter. "You've done well. I couldn't be prouder."

"It's...good to know that, Dad." Jack turned abruptly away, striding for the door. It wouldn't do to get maudlin, but his eyes prickled. Without his twin he'd been a shadow, left on the periphery like a misbegotten himself—and as frustrating as the current situa-tion was, the fact remained that she was now here, and nothing would pry her loose again.

He would see to that.

34
FULL HOUSE

It started snowing again mid-afternoon. By then the entire house was full of movement, conversation, and the glorious aroma of baking sugar. The 'extra staff' showed up during the day for snacks or lunch—there was Sarah, who had an inky pixie cut and an engaging smile, big blond Gessel with sleepy blue eyes and a lumberjack's plaid shirt, Lev's sleek brunet cousin Josef carrying in a load of firewood and being scolded into pausing for a bite, and at least half a dozen others Zoe barely heard the names of as they passed through.

Jack ambled in while Zoe was arranging cookies on a baking sheet lined with parchment paper, peering over her shoulder. "Let me have a little."

"Amelia says not to," she whispered back, but couldn't help smiling. The relief of his presence was deep, instant—and frightening.

"You!" Jolie turned from the large wooden cutting board where she was rolling out fresh dough, pinning him with a fierce stare. "Don't get us in trouble, Jackson. I swear, it's just like having McKenna around."

"It is not," Jack retorted, hotly. "You actually like *him*."

"Lies." It was amazing to see someone so pretty actually blush a bit, a faint pink stain rising in Jolie's flawless cheeks as she pushed a tendril of dark hair away with the back of one floury hand. "Damn lies."

"And statistics," Jack finished, and bumped Zoe's shoulder like a cat wanting attention. "Come on, just a little bit of dough while Amelia's not looking."

Was he showing off for the other girl? They obviously knew each other pretty well. Zoe set the last cookie carefully on the pan, disliking the sudden rasping under her skin. She couldn't quite name the feeling, and that bothered her. "You're trying to get me into trouble."

"Me? Never." He leaned closer, his breath soft against her ear. "Just one. A nibble. I promise, I won't ask for more."

"If I had a nickel for every time I heard *that*." Jolie wiped her hands on a towel and whisked the baking sheet away. "Put him to work, Zoe. If you leave him unoccupied he'll cause mischief."

"So I've heard." Zoe stepped aside, toward the cutting board—or attempted to. Jack moved with her, oddly synchronized. "If you want to help, ask Amelia what—"

"She'll make me do something difficult." Jack's tone wasn't quite wheedling, but it was close. He wore a lopsided, very charming smile too. "You know how lazy I am."

Mama would have snapped at him and given Zoe a light stinging slap on the back of the head, hissing *get back to work*. She'd always been too tired for anything resembling family celebrations, and besides, according to Angelina cooking was something for the help to do.

It had never really sunk in that she and Zo *were* the help.

"Leave girls alone, Jack." Amelia swooped by, a clean wooden spoon on one capable, crimson-nailed hand; her manicure game, like Jolie's, was flawless. "Or I make you wash dishes instead of Lev."

"Oh no you don't, Meel," Lev called from the other end of the kitchen, half-turning from the sink. He wore a pair of large yellow rubber gloves and was scrubbing whatever didn't go in the huge dishwasher. "I *like* washing. Make him shovel snow."

"I thought you liked that too, though?" Zoe didn't even wonder how he'd heard them from so far away. The cheerful hubbub all through the house wasn't quite overwhelming, but it was close. "You said it kept you fit."

"Look at that, he's caught." Jack's laugh was warm and forgiving. "Hung by his own testimony. What shape are we doing here? Reindeer? Or the star?"

Maybe this was what the holidays were supposed to be. It was like a sitcom or a commercial, pretty people making witty comments while soft music played from hidden speakers. Amelia had the proper kitchen tools for *everything*, and she let Zoe watch while she rolled out paper-thin gingersnaps.

"All in wrist," the housekeeper said quietly, while Jack dried dishes for Lev and Jolie drank a mug of cinnamon-touched hot cocoa, teasing them both. "Soft, soft, like a whisper. See?"

There were no arguments, no deadly stares, no preaching. It seemed impossibly pleasant, and Zoe's nerves wound tighter and tighter, waiting for the inevitable. Even Jolie's deep, amused calm couldn't swallow her tension completely, though it blunted the ragged edges.

Rack after rack of cooled cookies needed decorating; Jolie had very definite ideas about color-coding and the proper amount of dye for each batch of frosting. Jack took over sprinkling sugar crystals, wearing a slight frown of concentration.

It was comforting to see something he *didn't* do easily.

Thankfully, once the gingersnaps started going into the two ovens Jack slipped an arm over Zoe's shoulders and announced she needed a break, drawing her out of the kitchen. "You look like you could use some quiet," he continued, as they climbed yet another flight of stairs. "I've been waiting to show you something."

Uh-oh. She'd washed her hands, but there was probably flour in her hair. Still, as the voices faded into a background hum and he navigated them through halls and doorways, her shoulders loosened a little, then a little more.

"Pretty intense, huh?" If he was angry at having to leave Jolie behind, it didn't show. "More will show up tonight. We'll have a full house until well after the party."

Great. "Jolie's nice," she offered, tentatively.

"Yeah, she even manages to keep McKenna from misbehaving *too* much, at least most of the time. It's a miracle." He let go of her shoulders to grab her hand, their fingers interlacing easily, naturally. "They'll end up a happy couple with a cub or two, and I'll tease him about going domestic."

She could detect no hint of jealousy in his tone, but that didn't mean much. Zoe followed in his wake, glad he was looking at where they were going instead of her. "You two sound like best friends."

"Mac and I go way back." They kept climbing, and she realized he was steering her around other people in different parts of the house, their route doubling back on itself or turning aside when they seemed likely to come across someone else. "He's always so easygoing, or it looks that way. I envy him that."

"You envy him?" How any of them could be jealous of each other was beyond her. They were all so...finished, so attractive.

"Oh, yeah. I was a ball of rage when I was younger. Mac and I got into a lot of trouble together, and he never left me in the lurch. He's probably glad you're holding my leash now, frees him up for other things." He glanced at her, one half his mouth turned up in a catlike smile.

Both he and Trevor kept saying things like that—holding Jack's leash, keeping him safe. "Did you really get into that much trouble?"

"Oh, you have *no* idea." He stopped for a moment, golden head cocked; his hair was mussed. "I was practically feral. Ask anyone."

Maybe Mama had thought a girl would be less trouble to raise. "Me too, I guess."

"I doubt you were out stealing cars and getting into fights, though." He was still listening intently, probably because Josef was nearby. Carrying something heavy too, by the sound of his footsteps.

"You stole cars?" Zoe had never dreamed of anything so daring; she'd had too many chores to do, and looking after Mama was a full-time job.

"Just ones the owners could afford to lose. I'm not a monster." He set off again, which meant she had to follow. "Besides, most of the time we brought them back. That's the goal, that they don't even know you took it. We had a whole scoring system. According to my math, I won. He disagrees."

"Well, of course." She couldn't help a little gentle sarcasm.

"We'll argue about it for years, I'm sure." Jack turned them down a narrow hall on the third floor—how did they keep this entire place so shipshape? Just the thought of the vacuuming alone made her exhausted. Mama had cleaned houses for a while, hating every minute of it; why had she left a place where someone did it for her?

Because they have these 'gifts' and she didn't. The realization was a splash of icy water. It wasn't a nice thing to think, but it *felt* right, or at least felt like the largest motivation. There were probably others, like Jack's theory about her medicine, but finding out she wasn't the most special thing around would drive Mama into *fits*.

Thinking about her mother like this would definitely send her to hell. Zoe wished she could slow down and enjoy the trip, at least.

"You all right?" Jack slowed. "Need a minute?"

She avoided saying *I'm sorry* with some effort, and had to choose the next best thing. "I'm fine." It would be nice to have some peace and quiet to really think about things, but life was all about running from one thing to the next, trying desperately to avoid tripping and falling on your face. "Just thinking."

"You ever gonna tell me what about?"

Can I? "About Mama. And why she left."

The windows in this hall were smaller, and there were no paintings on the walls. Jack's boots made soft sounds on hardwood as their pace slowed. "You wonder about that a lot."

Well, it wasn't every day you found out your entire life had been a nightmarish lie, of *course* she'd think about it. "Don't you?"

"Not really?" The words tilted up at the end, as if he wasn't quite sure. "I was too busy missing you. So why do you think?"

"It was a lot of things." She waited, but he didn't say anything, so she decided to risk a little more. "It might have been her medicine, like you said. She was also afraid, all the time, of everything. And I think she didn't like that...that Dad and you could do things she couldn't."

"And you, too." He nodded thoughtfully, and the end of this hall was coming up. There seemed nothing terribly special about it, just a small octagonal window set high up on the end wall over a small rosewood table holding a large, beautifully bright cloisonné vase. "Here we are. Hold on a second."

A small closet on one side opened up, and he rescued a hook with a long handle from its depths. It was the first time she'd seen anyone pull down attic stairs with one of those, and she watched while the wooden slats and struts unfolded with a creaking groan. At least he didn't scoff at her ideas, or tell her she was imagining things.

"There." Her brother shot her an anxious glance. "It's solid. If it'll hold me it'll definitely hold you."

"I'm not worried about that." Frankly, it cheered Zoe to see *any* uncertainty in him; her own was so constant it liked the occasional company. "We're going into the attic?"

"Unless you don't want to." Now he looked like a little boy expecting a scolding.

It was heady to think he wanted to impress her, even just a little bit. "No. I want to."

After all, she couldn't very well back out now. And maybe that was the whole point.

35

SECRETS

The attic was a vast hushed cathedral, relatively warm in winter since the house below let its heat rise. Shrouded monster-shapes of furniture lurked in ghostly rows—even here, Amelia's ruthless organization showed, except for the far northeastern corner. Maybe she'd deliberately left it alone, affection displayed through silence and restraint.

The familiar smell of dust and discarded lumber filled his nose; Jack took his *demie's* hand again, leading her through the maze. Having her here in the flesh was both unsettling and a powerful comfort; small shafts of grey winterlight from tiny shuttered windows gave just enough illumination for a Kith to avoid obstacles. "Those stairs are the easiest way up," he said, quietly. "I'll show you the others later; I used to do this all the time. Hide, and try to figure everything out. Even Dad couldn't find me. It's hard keeping a secret around here, but I managed."

"Yeah, seems like it would be difficult." Her fingers were tense, though not cold; he squeezed as gently and reassuringly as possible.

It was a shoddy kingdom for a dispossessed *demi*, a collection of canvas-wrapped shapes arranged to block sight of a small corner festooned with yellowing posters—a couple old rock bands, a Hokusawa print, a knight in battered armor on a black horse. An ancient futon was neatly rolled to one side, and old wine bottles filched from holiday parties crusted with dripping candle wax gathered in conspiratorial groups. A stack of old *National Geographic*s here, some forgotten textbooks there, a hassock with stuffing leaking from its shredded upholstery—all familiar as his own breath, and now the small space almost burst at the seams, because his *demie* took a few cautious steps over its border, her blue eyes alight.

"It's not much." Was he actually *nervous*? If Angelina hadn't stolen her, maybe they would have found a different place, a country of two to rule. Or for her to rule and him to simply watch over, ready to strike if a single foreigner stepped out of line. "I mean, I was a kid, so…"

"I like it." She squeezed his hand in return, welcome pressure, and because she'd been in the kitchen an enticing hint of sugar and caramel limned her scent. "I'd've done the same thing. You had candles up here?"

"Don't tell Dad, he'll start in about how I could have burned the whole house down. Make yourself at home. We don't have to talk, you've had a busy morning."

She slipped away, leaving him bereft, but he could watch her explore the tiny almost-room, stepping delicately, careful not to disturb a single item. Zoe sank into a graceful crouch, looking at the hassock.

He'd torn into the thing with his claws more than once. She traced the rips and gouges with slim fingers, and her eyes flashed blue for a moment as she looked up at him. "You did that with your nails," she breathed. "Right?"

"It's normal." The satisfaction of correctly gauging her readiness for this particular aspect of Kith life was only rivaled by the deep pleasure of her nascent trust. Regardless, Jack's throat was dry. He couldn't afford to fuck this up. "For us, that is."

Just by her left foot, four dusty parallel slices scored the floor. She traced them too, her fingers stretched wide because her hands were

smaller. Slight and delicate, doubly sensitive as shaman and *demie*—
the outside world would eat her alive.

Maybe it had. The thought of a misbegotten so close to this
gorgeous vulnerability could easily drive Jack into a rage.

But she needed him calm, so the ice of an analyst's talent closed
around him. Eventually the *usanaugh* bond would lay them both bare
to each other, but at the moment the appearance of tranquility was
enough.

"Hurts your wrists when the claws start developing," Jack
continued, evenly. "And sometimes you've got to be careful,
because they..." A bolt of adrenaline raced through her scent,
laying copper against his own palate, and his *demie* stiffened.
Bingo. Be very careful, Jack. "They come out in self-defense." He
hoped he had the right tone—easy, informative, no question and
no judgment.

"Self-defense." It was a bare whisper, her lips shaping the words,
and he couldn't look away.

"Happens to every one of us." He dared a few steps closer, sinking
down into a likewise crouch so he wasn't looming over her. "My first
time, I about knocked McKenna into the pond, and ripped his shirt
too." Only Hermann's presence had kept Jack from following, leaping
on the other boy, and tearing into flesh; the memory was still faintly
shameful, though he'd only been ten years old. "I was scared Dad
was going to hit the roof, but he just had me apologize and spent a
while afterward teaching me all about control. You didn't have that.
Must've been hard."

"Yeah." Fear and sensitivity made a powerful cocktail; she was
radiating again. The waves of feeling almost shimmered, just at the
edge of visibility. "Jack..."

Whatever it is, whatever you're afraid of, tell me. I'll fix it. The urge
to start babbling, attempting to comfort her, was overwhelming. *And
if it can't be fixed I will hunt it down and kill it, I promise. I swear I will.*

But he kept his mouth shut, waiting. His *demie*'s gaze was open
and raw, the blue paling until near-identical to Dad's. After last night

and almost an entire day spent in the middle of easy Kith companionship, she was about to break—and in the best way possible.

"Jack," she whispered, "what *are* we?"

At least he had an answer—all the answers she could ever want. The trick would be finding the ones she'd accept. "*Usanaugh.* Two halves of a whole. But what you're asking about is *Kith*—an old word for family. We're...different, that's all. I'll teach you everything, okay? Whatever you did before, it was because you didn't know any better."

"But what if I..." She touched the clawmarks again, soft fingertips against splintered wood. Her fingernails were pale and perfect, showing at least some unconscious control of the change. "What if it was something really bad?"

I hope you gave McFisk some scars; I hope you fucking eviscerated everyone who ever hurt you. And if you didn't, I will. "Then I'll blame Angelina. Not you. And if anyone has a problem with that, I'll handle it." Nice and easy was the way to play this, though eventually she'd see the beast in his skin. The thought was unexpectedly enticing. "You want to see my claws? I can show you."

"This is crazy." She shook her head, the long raven braid bumping her back. Stray curls framed her face, moving gently; had skins ever noticed the slight breeze she carried, the Gene stirring empty air? "Just...it's *crazy.*"

"Only because she stole you." Jack hoped he was getting through. Of course she wouldn't believe his encouragement the first few times, but this groundwork, if laid properly, would hold up everything else she had to learn. "If you'd grown up here, it would be normal."

"I guess." Zoe shifted; she sat down, hard, as if her legs had suddenly decided they wouldn't hold her up. "Are you...this isn't some kind of sick practical joke, is it?"

"No." To prove it, Jack held up his right hand. The change burned down his arm and his fingernails lengthened, sharpening into curved, translucent amber daggers. His wrist swelled with muscle as the bones shifted; the fierce joy of giving his beast a little room to play was matched only by the sharp consciousness that his *demie* was close and watching. "See?"

"My God." Though she'd gone pale, spots of bright red flush burned high on her cheeks, and if she changed now he had her nicely boxed in until her beast calmed down. Thankfully she didn't look ready to shift, just stunned, disbelieving, and comforted all at once— not to mention absolutely beautiful. "Mama...she kept talking about Satan. That she married the devil."

"Yeah, well." Another piece of the puzzle, only sensed before, slid into focus and place at the same time. "Dad always said she was religious."

"Are we going to hell?" Heartbreaking, the trembling in her voice.

Oh, please. Angelina, you bitch. "Been there, Zo." He kept his tone soft, reasonable, level. "What do you think growing up without you was?"

She stared at him. It was enjoyable to be his *demie*'s focus, but he wished she didn't look so...well, so *lost*. There was no reason for it, not when he was right next to her.

"Last night." Of course she surprised him, smart as a whip and turning on a dime. "Those men, with guns. Is this why they..." Her hands spread a little, as if she'd run out of words.

"Maybe." *Almost certainly, but you don't need to worry about that yet.* "The important thing is, you're safe here. I won't let anything hurt you. Neither will Dad," he added, hurriedly, "or the rest of the Pride. That's what we call our part of the Kith. It's kind of like a clan, or tribe. Think of it that way."

"Pride. Like...lions?"

Christ, she was quick. Of course, she had to have suspected some of this, and probably had absorbed some weird skin ideas about full moons and silver. "Almost." *We're better than skin or beast, though. And stronger.* "I'll teach you; I'll be right next to you the entire time. Don't worry, all right? This is my secret up here, and I'm giving it to you. I'll keep all yours, like you keep mine."

"I understand about secrets." Trembling visibly, his *demie* searched his expression in the dimness. "What if they're really big ones, though?"

"Doesn't matter." *Pretty sure ours will put yours to shame, little girl.* There was plenty of time to plumb every well between them. "And it's not going to change anything. You belong here."

"I've never belonged anywhere." There was no trace of bitterness in the words, just simple truth. The wind was up, brushing the sides of the house—a familiar, lonely sound, reminding him of days and nights spent praying to or outright demanding that whatever power moved the world bring back his *demie.*

"Give it a chance." His heart hurt, a swift piercing pain. "You might like it."

"All right." She didn't quite deflate; it was more of a graceful balletic drooping, all the tension suddenly draining away. She probably didn't know what it was like to truly relax, spending her entire life keyed-up on the thin edge of simple survival. "What...I mean, what do we do now?"

And just that quickly, that simply, the apple fell into his waiting hand. "I could light some candles?" He tilted his head, giving his best impression of McKenna's easy grin, and was rewarded with a shy, tremulous smile in return. "Haven't burned the house down yet."

"Yet," she agreed, and that tentative smile bloomed further when he laughed.

It was going to be an enjoyable afternoon.

36
MORNING ROUTINE

CHRISTMAS EVE DAWNED BRIGHT AND CHILL, A CLEAR, PAINFULLY BLUE SKY bearing deep smudges of approaching storm to the northeast. Waking in the blue bedroom was more than halfway familiar now; there was no moment of vertigo at the unusual quiet or softness, no jolt into consciousness with her heart hammering and her palms damp.

Here there was comfort, deep steady warmth, and a tang of golden scent that meant Jack.

We call ourselves Kith; it means family. We're stronger, faster, smarter, and we also have wicked tempers sometimes.

So she wasn't an alien or a freak. She was something else, and so was Jack, and Dad, and everyone else in the vast house. To go from being a pariah, a stranger, a secret foreigner impersonating normalcy, to *this* was intoxicating and terrifying all at once.

The deep relief of having a name for all the strangeness was tinted with bleak sorrow. Mama had been so endlessly frightened, and of what? Trevor never even raised his voice, but maybe he hadn't always been like that. Zoe could see how it would terrify someone, living next to his quiet intensity and knowing that your husband could grow claws at a moment's notice—and then having children, and seeing that strangeness in them from the cradle.

I rescued you from the devil. Don't ever forget that.

Well, Zoe wouldn't. Wherever Mama was now, Zo hoped she was happy.

As comforting as the mystery's solution was, it opened up a whole new realm of problems. Jack *said* her secrets were no big deal, but...well, she couldn't be sure. Especially her stint as one of Royal's girls.

Kith were never raised by skins nowadays, Jack said, though he allowed had happened a few times during historical wars and displacement. She was an exception even now, not quite fitting in.

It figured—you never could truly win. Zoe rolled over, pushed herself up on her elbows, and blinked at the bedroom. A soft, beautiful nest for a girl who had never eaten out of the trash, a girl who had never done what Royal wanted, a girl who had never burst out of a burning church cellar and clawed at a cheating, lying pastor—oh, she knew what she was now.

The knowledge was alternately comforting and scary as hell. Jack kept pressing her to ask questions, but good God, she barely knew where to start. At least his presence didn't overwhelm her; he was pretty much the only thing about this that didn't.

And yet...it was unsettling, how nervous she got when he was out of sight. She hadn't known what she was missing before he showed up in Marquette; now she did, and having some kind of refuge for even a short while would hurt so much more when it was inevitably snatched away.

Even her morning routine had become soothing. A bath instead of a shower since there was no hurry, choosing clothes—Janine's largesse was still being delivered daily, though Zoe hoped they wouldn't make anyone work on Christmas to haul another load over icy roads—and accessories while hoping she wouldn't inadvertently embarrass herself by wearing white after Labor Day or something, combing her hair as she gazed through a crystal-clear window at sparkling snow...she would miss this, all of it, when she made a mistake and the good fortune evaporated.

"Just waiting to fuck up," she muttered as she turned away from the window, her fingers tightening on a wide-tooth sandalwood comb.

There was a party tonight. The house hummed with activity. None of the Kith seemed unhappy with their work, they just *did* it. It wasn't the fake cheeriness of retail or service drudgery, either, they were simply...relaxed, and everyone pitched in with what they were good at. It was incredibly civilized, and she couldn't find a break or hole in the façade of goodwill and happiness. All her senses, sharpened by years of under-the-table and thankless dead-end jobs, were returning the same report. Nobody was yelled at, belittled, or pushed around here.

It was goddamn *eerie*.

And there was another thing. None of them looked poor, even though they were 'staff'. Was the entire extended clan rich? Did they share everything? Was it a sort of commune? Maybe she should write her questions down, though the list might reach Santa-length before long.

At last, clean and bright for a new day, Zoe cracked the sitting room door and peeked into the hall.

Deserted. If she wanted to, she could slip down the hall, to the utility door, and be outdoors in mere minutes. She could pack a bag, hightail it into the snow, and...

...where on earth would she go? Still, if she left of her own accord she wouldn't be worrying about when they were going to throw her out.

Even this far away from the kitchen she could smell baking bread, brewing coffee, and a rich good scent of roasting meat. Amelia was hard at work already. A housekeeper-bodyguard who could grow claws—maybe she could teach Zo a thing or two.

"Good morning," Jack said, and she flinched, the door opening a little wider. He came into view—blond mane impeccable and his dark eyes burning, but today he was in was jeans, boots, and a black sweater instead of a suit. He was carrying a bulky white box, too.

Jesus. How in the hell did he *know* when she was leaving her suite? Or did he just lean against the wall for hours, waiting? "M-morning." Her voice refused to work quite right; she had to clear her throat. "Am I late?"

"Of course not. I heard you moving around and figured you'd be ready for breakfast soon." He cradled the box like it was precious, and his smile widened slightly. "Excited for the party?"

More like dreading it. "Sure." It wasn't quite a lie; nervousness was close to excitement, right? "You?"

"Well, with my *demie* home, I get to stay up with the adults instead of being sent to bed early." His grin widened, teeth glinting. Even the gold watch clinging to his tanned wrist gave off a well-behaved gleam of expensive relaxation. "Maybe we'll get to see midnight."

It was ridiculous to think of anyone sending her brother to bed like a misbehaving child, and she couldn't help but smile. "You're thinking of New Year's."

"You're gonna love that too. But you're not late for anything. Oh, this came for you." He lifted the white box slightly; at least it didn't have a tinsel bow. "From Janine. I think it's for tonight."

"Oh." *Great. Fantastic.* The thought of running out into the snow was more and more attractive all the time. "Okay."

"It's all right to be nervous." He moved forward, easy and slow, and she barely realized she was backing up until he was suddenly inside her suite, nudging the hall door mostly closed with one boot and setting off for her bedroom. "It's going to be great. Really."

Anything she said would sound sarcastic, so Zoe just drifted anxiously after him, glad she'd made the big bed as soon as she rolled out of it.

He set the box on the wrinkle-free velvet coverlet and turned. "You want to open it, or breakfast first?"

God, they kept asking her for decisions, choices, preferences. She almost missed Mama's harsh rules and Bea's rigidity, almost missed knowing whatever choice she made would inevitably be the wrong one.

The certainty of failure was about the only thing she had left to call her own. "Breakfast?" The word spiraled up uncertainly at the end, and her stomach was a knot.

"Good choice." Jack offered his hand, like he expected them to go skipping down to the solarium. "Also, I've got a surprise for you."

Oh, God. "Another one?"

"They've all been nice so far, haven't they?" His smile wasn't secretive, or nasty. Just open, warm, and inviting her to share a little bit of his good mood. "You'll like it. Come on."

Nice is a pretty strong word. She laid her fingertips in his palm, warm skin slightly rougher than her own but familiar enough by now. A step, a tug, and their fingers were interlaced; he pulled her along as if it was completely natural to hold hands and stroll through a big old mansion.

All of this was magic, except she was too old to believe in *that*, wasn't she?

Devil-child, Mama's voice hissed inside her head. *Don't you do that witchery. You mind me now, Zoe.*

Zoe wasn't Mama's anchor anymore. She was Kith, and all of them were different too. The only problem with that was the sensation of being caught between two worlds, each dangerous. *Neither fish nor fowl*, Auntie Scarsdale might say.

And there was the scariest question of all—what, exactly, had the armed invaders been planning to do? How many people know about the Kith, and why had nobody told her?

Had Mama ever been tempted to...do something to her daughters, like the intruders obviously had planned? There was no way to ask either Jack or Trevor about that; her instincts shouted it wasn't a safe question at all.

It was a relief to find her weird inner senses were still capable of giving a clear signal.

"You're quiet this morning." Somehow Jack managed to stay just slightly ahead, opening the door and ushering her into the hall, setting off on the now-familiar path to the solarium, light on his feet and feline-graceful. "Sooner or later you'll relax, you know."

That just means I'll get hurt then instead of now, thanks. In a very real sense, she was as alone as she'd ever been.

Still, she'd seen—with her own damn eyes, like they said in Marquette—Jack's fingernails lengthening into hard, translucent amber claws with wicked-sharp points, his wrist swelling with tiny creak-crackling sounds. He didn't mind her other talents, and even seemed to consider them borderline cool instead of demonic.

"Is the party more family stuff?" She tried the other word on for size. "I mean, is it a Kith thing?"

"It is." His expression didn't change, all warm happiness—but it was one he didn't use on other people.

Just her. And she didn't quite know what to think about that. But her hand was caught in his, and though he was gentle, she knew he was strong. *Really* strong—even more than Bea.

All that carefully controlled force was terrifying, or comforting— a powerful protection, or a trap even worse than falling for Royal.

Zoe just couldn't figure out which.

37
ANOTHER PAIR

HE WAS SEEING THE KITH THROUGH NEW EYES, AND THEY WERE HERS.

The house was full of soft music, carols and orchestral classics threading through hidden speakers. The trees glittered with ornaments and each room held at least some tinsel; candles burned in glass hurricane lamps, little flames ready to stand vigil today, tonight, and into Christmas morning. The massive grandfather clock on the first floor was festooned with silver strands and tiny red glass decorations; the ballroom was already open and its floor was a mellow shining plain.

Amelia was everywhere in the kitchen at once, swift hummingbird motion, her reddish hair piled high. The extra tables were in the dining room, ready for dishes each local family would bring; Lev and Josef grinned and larked as they went from fireplace to fireplace attending well-seasoned blazes and trimming candle wicks. Hermann paused in the kitchen only long enough to take fresh orders from his mate, a slight but definite smile on his leathery face. Sarah sang as she danced from room to room, Gessel appearing and disappearing with loads of brightly wrapped boxes, last-minute decorations, or a thermal carafe of coffee whenever needed. Lena and Elizabeth and Marcus and Joey, not to mention all the others—

they didn't give Jack nervous glances or leave the room as soon as he entered, because his *demie* was right next to him, his temper safely tethered.

Every clan leader within the Rouje pride was hosting an event tonight, Kith families coming together in larger groups. Once they had celebrated the winter solstice instead of a few days afterward, but blending with the festivals of the time kept them safer and served the deep need for community.

The solarium was an oasis of calm and rustling green. But the table had two more chairs than usual and Dad rested his chin on one hand, listening as Dimitri leaned forward, holding a coffee cup and speaking rapidly in low tones.

Beside her lean dark-haired *demi*, auburn Bella glanced in their direction. Her smile was instant and charming-warm, though her hazel eyes held the bright calculation of an analyst. Dimitri was jäger, and the two were a marvel of coordinated motion on any hunt, large or small.

Zoe stopped dead, blue eyes wide as she examined the new arrivals. Her fingers tensed slightly in Jack's but she didn't pull away, and her quick glance in his direction was a sweet piercing pain.

"This is Dimitri and Bella," he said, quietly. "They're *usanaugh.* Like us."

Dimitri's left hand rested over his *demie*'s, thumb stroking idly. Their rings were gold and silver, smaller than the Rouje family signets, and held paired blue stones glowing almost as fiercely as Zoe's eyes. Dad nodded as the younger man finished making his point and rose when Jack took a few steps closer, easing his twin along.

She didn't quite resist...but she was reluctant, and Dimitri rose too, hurriedly.

"Oh, hey," Dima greeted them, his white buttondown's sleeves rolled up to expose coppery forearms. "Jack, old man, great to see you. And this must be Zoe. Hi."

"Hullo." Bella settled more firmly in her chair—a lady did not have to rise—and picked up her white china mug. A teabag's paper slip fluttered against its side. Looked like she was back to chamomile instead of caffeine, probably because Dima had been fussing about some kind of new health research that applied only to skins. "And wow, he's not scowling. I don't think I've ever seen you so relaxed, Junior."

Fuck you too, Bell. "Bell analyzes things, like me." Amusement curled through Jack and he held very still, waiting for some sign from his *demie*. "Except she has no manners."

"Hey now." Dimitri cocked his dark head, lifting an admonishing finger. "She's got plenty of manners, just no time for fools. Amelia blazed through and left your coffee. Come on, it'll get cold."

Zoe still hesitated.

"They just returned from Europe," Dad said. "I thought you might like to see another pair of *usanaugh*, Zoe."

"We understand things," Dimitri added, though Jack wished he'd shut up and give Jack's *demie* a moment to process. "Honestly, I can't imagine living without my twin for any amount of time. And whole entire years? Wow."

"Maybe we should wait until she's caffeinated, my darling." Bella shook her head. Tiny jet beads glittered at the bottom of two small braids framing her heart-shaped face, keeping the rest of her hair back. "Dima likes to rush in. Looks like you're the cautious one, though—which is good, Jack could use someone with a little sense holding his chain."

"Everyone says that," Zoe finally said, and her voice didn't tremble. Still, he thought it was close. "He says he was a holy terror when he was younger."

"Understatement of the *decade*." Bella made a small motion with her mug, exquisitely calibrated just short of slopping hot liquid onto the table. "If we're intruding, we can—"

"No." Zoe started for the table. "No, I'm sorry. It's just a lot to take in."

Jack followed, squeezing her hand gently. *I'm with you,* he wanted to say. Maybe she heard him, the spark of contact between them guttering under a cold wind. In any case, she settled in her usual seat, Dimitri and Dad dropping back into theirs, and Jack could address his own morning coffee. Maybe the rush of anxiety he felt was hers—it was a sign the link was settling in, growing by leaps and bounds.

"It must be." Bella rested her elbows on the table, her tailored blue corduroy jacket making a soft sound against the tablecloth. "I can't even imagine how confused I'd be. But you're here now, that's the important thing. And of course we'll help all we can. Kith is good, of course..."

"...but your twin is better," Dimitri finished, chapter and verse. His necklace was a single shark's tooth on a gold chain, its base also dipped in gold, nestling against his shirt with a secretive gleam. "Jack's a computer-brain like my sweet *demie*. Do you know where your talent is yet?"

Zoe shook her head, a blueblack ripple. "I, uh, probably don't have a talent."

"Zoe's pure magic," Jack said quietly. "But our mother was...well, religious. I think she probably didn't like the fact that my *demie* can do some amazing things."

A burst of panic drifted through his twin's scent. But she stayed stock-still, her blue gaze passing from Bella to Dimitri, maybe noting the way they leaned slightly toward each other, Bell's knee touching her *demi*'s under the table, the paired expressions flickering across their faces. The similarities in bone structure, evident among the Kith, were even more so between *usanaugh*, and when Dimitri looked at his *demie* Bella's fractional smile answered him.

"You're talking," Zoe breathed, wonderingly. "To each other. Inside."

"Oh, that?" Bella shook her head, her braids swaying. "It's normal. Takes some effort to block, after a while. But honestly, why would I want to? My *demi* knows almost everything going on inside my skull."

"And you still surprise me." Dimitri took her hand again, lifting it to press a kiss onto her knuckles. "Each and every day."

Zoe's gaze flickered to Dad. Trevor simply reached for his coffee. Tomorrow he too would forego suit-and-tie, but today he was impeccable as usual, and his signet glittered as he regarded his precious, tentative daughter. "We've thought it best to just let Zoe decompress for a little while." He smiled slightly, the expression reserved for company he found both polite and enjoyable. "One step at a time."

She still hadn't let go of Jack. Her fingers were cold now, and the trembling in her was just the same as it had been on a hillside overlooking a Texas freeway, caged in her *demi*'s arms. Another spark of contact bloomed between them, a tiny candleflame.

I'm here. He hoped it would echo into the link, washing up on her mental shores. *Right next to you. Don't worry.*

The only thing more heartbreaking than the hesitation was her bravery.

"I can't even figure out what questions to ask." She reached for her coffee and aimed a tentative smile in Bella's direction. "It's the competence gap thing, you don't know what you *don't* know."

"I read some articles on that last month." Bella leaned forward, her eyes sparking. "The most interesting thing was—"

"Coffee first," Jack objected. "Then we'll compare notes."

"You never used to be such a stickler." Laughter bubbled under Dimitri's tone; his mother said he'd been amused at the entire world since he was born. "Normally he and Bell start going on about data sets and inferences, and the rest of us are left to do the real work." He beamed at Zoe, who blinked owlishly at the amount of sheer charismatic goodwill the jäger exuded. He was the easygoing half of the pair, but a single breath of insult in Bella's direction and the veneer dropped with shattering speed. "Thank goodness you're back. Now they might start speaking English for whole minutes at a time."

"We could switch to Greek." Bell shook her head, settling more comfortably and lifting her tea. "Relieve you of *any* responsibility to respond."

"She threatens." Dimitri shrugged. "But she's really a big ol' marshmallow inside. Cries at pet food commercials."

"I do not," his *demie* retorted, cheerfully. "Anyway, you can ask me anything, Zoe. Nothing's off-limits, and we'll trade numbers, right? We *demie* have to stick together. And when your *demi*'s being a pigheaded irritant I'll take you shopping."

"That sounds nice," Zoe managed, faintly.

"It'll be so good to have another *demie* around." Bella was obviously in manager mode. "Your dad tells us you'll be in college soon. We'll have homework parties, I haven't had a good wrestle with calculus in—"

"You're going to plan her social calendar too, Bell? Give the girl a minute." Dimitri elbowed her—but gently.

Zoe smiled, and Jack's shoulders relaxed. The link hummed between them, contact established at last, as if she'd only needed to see it in another pair of *usanaugh* before she could let herself reach for him. She didn't speak much—frankly, there wasn't much need, Dima and Bell were off and running.

And her knee touched Jack's under the table, a soft slight pressure. Each time she shifted, the movement echoed in his own bones. He turned aside some of Bella's wilder ideas, kept up with Dimitri's jokes, and appealed to Dad just often enough to keep Trevor in the conversation. It was work, of course—but he didn't mind it.

Because his *demie*, at long last, was forgetting to be afraid.

38
FIRST DRINK

WINTER DUSK SETTLED EARLY OVER HOUSE, GARDEN, AND DRIVEWAY; THE doorbell rang at short intervals to announce arrivals. Zoe could barely hear the cascade of soft chimes from the blue suite, however, and preparing for her first real holiday party required all the attention—and bravery—she could scrape together.

Mama thought Christmas should be spent in church, and once Zoe left Hall City there was no time for anything but work and dodging trouble during the holiday season. Business didn't slow down at Royal's club during that time either—lonely men paid more for a bit of company or fantasy, that was all.

"Great. Now look up while you...that's it." Jolie watched, dark gaze level in the mirror's watery depths. Her calm cheerfulness never altered. It seemed possible she was simply that rarity, a genuinely nice person. "You've done this before."

Makeup wasn't hard; it just took practice once someone showed you the right way. The expensive stuff was definitely better than anything Zoe'd had access to before, though, and Janine had sent plenty of it. "I had a couple jobs..." She stopped, her lips parted slightly as she finished the eyeliner's smooth sweep. "Where you had to do stuff like this."

"Look at that, a lovely cat's eye." Bella nodded in approval. The suite wasn't nearly as crowded as the back room at Royal's club, even with three young women and all the associated ephemera of party preparation; Zoe was glad she'd made the bed and kept the rooms as neat as possible.

It was nice to be in a girls-only space again, though there was no throbbing music or surgical tape, no platform heels and definitely no skunk-reek of burning weed as working ladies took the edge off before another set or date. The good-natured laughter was the same, though, and so were the soft fingertips tweaking hair or cloth, wholly female mutual aid.

Still, her anxiety wouldn't recede. Both Jolie and Bella were gorgeous, and Zo felt like a deflated balloon—even, or maybe especially, considering the dress.

The box from Janine had given up a length of shimmering silver with spaghetti straps, an underlayer of smooth ivory silk resting lovingly against her skin. The dress had to have been altered on short notice, because it fit like a dream; it was almost flapper-style, just skimming her hips, tiny crystalline beads on short strings catching the light. A pair of diamanté kitten heels also fit perfectly, and a black velvet choker held a tiny silver flower charm. It was beautiful, and the long glittering silver earrings matching the charm were heavy enough to be real.

Zoe should have felt horribly exposed sitting on the vanity's padded bench with her arms and shoulders bare, but it was pleasantly warm inside the house, so all her shivers were pure nervousness. Jolie and Bella actually seemed to like her, too—or they were being magnificently kind. Neither of them wanted to sit, but fluttered around like hummingbirds having a grand old time.

So far the Kith were all sweet as pie, as Jenny Scarsdale would say, but without the raised eyebrows that meant she suspected the sugar was all a front.

"Here." Jolie reached for a comb, her shoulder brushing Zoe's. "Let me give you an updo, Zoe? Please?"

"If you want." It had been a long time since anyone played with her hair—except Jack, she realized, and there was no earthly reason for the flush rising to her cheeks at the thought.

Bella leaned over her shoulder to peer into the vanity's mirror, painting her lips with tiny brush from an expensive-looking tube. Crimson gloss suited her, and her dress was flapper-style like Zoe's, except a little shorter and bright red. Her jewelry was silver too, hoop earrings and a practically invisible filament at her throat holding a glittering chip too small and bright to be anything other than a real diamond. With her straight auburn hair piled artistically high, she was a vision, and the blue ring on her third left finger gleamed happily as she set off for the bathroom, sweeping the door closed like she lived here.

At least *someone* in the suite was comfortable.

Jolie had a black velvet pantsuit, tailored to a fare-thee-well, and stiletto heels sharp enough to qualify as weapons. Between them, nobody would be looking at Zo.

Which was just fine, she decided, capping the eyeliner, holding her head still for Jolie's attentions, and trying not to look in the mirror any more than absolutely necessary.

"Awesome." Jolie's grin was wide, white, and genuine. There was no breath of anything other than honest goodwill in either of them, and Jack was nearby. Or at least, he was in the same massive house, and that counted for something.

It was fine for the thought of him or Dad to be a comfort, Zoe decided. It was also nice to sit quietly, Jolie humming as she combed, pinned, and rummaged through the small plastic box Janine had sent with the dress, full of clips and other small hair fasteners, each in separate compartments.

Was all that going on Zoe's head? She'd either get an aching neck or suffer an embarrassing hairstyle failure at just the wrong moment.

"This is so great," Jolie said softly. "Not just for Jack, but for your father too. He's never forgiven himself."

What does that mean? Zoe stared at the vanity's white-painted top, her eyes unfocusing. Jolie didn't pull like Mama trying to deal with her daughter's recalcitrant curls, nor was she afraid of applying a little pressure to the knots like Jack. Hopefully the willowy brunette would slow Bella down a bit; the other girl-twin obviously moved at seventy per while the rest of the world was clocking along near twenty at best.

She and Dimitri were interesting to watch. And they could talk to each other *inside their heads*. Crazy—but not nearly as crazy as the fact that if Zoe concentrated, she could do just about the same thing with Jack.

She wasn't quite ready for him to go poking around inside *her* skull, though. Maybe he guessed about Bea and the fire, maybe not. But what if he found out about Royal, or the club, or what she'd done to survive and escape?

All the relief of finding out she wasn't a freak or an alien was drowned in the anxiety over what these people could do if she disappointed them somehow.

"Sorry." Jolie began gathering Zoe's hair into sections. "It's not my place to say anything, I know. But it's so good to see Trevor happy."

How can you tell? What was he like before? Zoe gathered her courage with both hands. "You don't think he's disappointed?"

Jolie's swift movements paused. "Disappointed?" She studied Zoe in the mirror, her dark gaze almost a physical weight; Zoe kept her eyelids half-down, avoiding the look. The powerful calm radiating from the older woman didn't alter. "Of course not. Now why would you think that?"

"Well, I just...I wasn't here." Zoe's fingers wanted to knot together, but she forced them to lay decorously in her lap. "Seventeen years is a long time, that's all."

"True." Jolie's smile was like sunshine. It wasn't fair—she was just so beautiful, and so was Bella. At least they weren't openly laughing at her. "But we never stopped looking, and now you're back. The entire Pride is relieved. Any daughter is precious, and a *demie*? Even more so."

"Even if the daughter..." Zoe swallowed the last half of the question.

"No matter what," Jolie said firmly. "Look up a little bit...good, right there. Let me know if I pull too hard."

Bella reappeared in the bathroom doorway. "Damn, we're beautiful." She was flat-out beaming. "Better than mortal man deserves, I say."

Jolie's laugh was warm, restful music. "Good thing we're meant for Kith. By the way, how was Spain?"

"Fab, of course." Bella didn't seem aware she was posing in the doorway; it looked entirely natural for her to lean hipshot as a fashion illustration. "Dima wanted to backpack and hostel. I told him he could, but his *demie* would be staying at a decent hotel. He accused me of lacking a sense of adventure."

"Nobody who's seen you on a hunt will believe *that*." Jolie lifted Zoe's hair, her fingers moving with swift dexterity. She was inordinately graceful—they all were.

"Mh. We swung through Copenhagen to visit Ruger and Hans on the way back, you should go next vacay." Bella examined her fingernails, though her crimson polish would never dare chip or flake. "The light's beautiful."

"Maybe. I had thoughts of Thailand, though." Jolie frowned slightly with concentration. "Make McKenna carry me through the jungle."

Real jet-setters. But Zoe decided they weren't showing off, it was obviously normal conversation around here. Did the entire extended family all hop around the world in private planes?

Or had she just not seen the poor Kith yet?

Maybe she could get a passport, do some traveling of her own? That took money, though, and who knew if they'd shut off the credit cards and everything else once she was overseas, stranding her?

They gave every indication of being for-real. But still, she could *not* relax. The thought of what they could do if they decided she wasn't worth this sort of trouble kept changing shape, creeping back into her head, turning her breath short and hiking her pulse.

"That boy always had an eye for you." Laughter ran under Bella's tone. "Admit it, I won and you owe me five bucks."

"He's not my mate yet." Jolie reached for a glittering corkscrew clip, and her cheeks pinkened. Jack teased her about this McKenna too; it was obvious she liked the guy. "He's got to earn something for once, instead of just kiping it."

"He hasn't gotten into trouble for a while." Bella wasn't ready to let the teasing go just yet. "When was the last time?"

"Oh, around a month ago, though nobody can prove it. Least of all me." Jolie moved Zoe's head again, delicate fingertips betraying no hidden ability to turn into claws.

It was enough to give you goosebumps, but instead a sharp, curious comfort loosened Zoe's shoulders. She took a deep breath, trying to hold her head perfectly still.

"Well, at least now Jack can join the living." Bella shifted, her heels tapping as she set off across the bedroom. "I've never seen him this relaxed, either. It's like magic—well, you *are* a shaman, you know. It's perfectly visible."

Shaman? Zoe didn't fidget, but it was close.

"Easy, Bell. That whole conversation can wait." Jolie fluffed a few curls and set the silver comb down. "What do you think of this, Zoe? I want to put another clip right here." She indicated the spot with a gentle fingertip.

Startled, Zo glanced into the mirror, taking in a pale face, her hair piled high and starred with glittering corkscrew-clips like fairies nestling in blue-black curls. "Yeah, that's fine." *Oh, that's polite and articulate, sure.* "I mean, whatever you think is best. It looks nice."

"Janine has you trained." Bella was amused by *everything*, it seemed. She bent over Zoe's shoulder, regarding her in the mirror for a few moments before nodding with approval and straightening, whirling away to set out for the bed. "I once tried to pick my own jacket on a shopping trip and she's never let me live it down. You have beautiful eyes, you know. Your *demi* won't know what hit him."

"Nor will yours." Jolie nestled one last clip among black curls. Thankfully, she didn't seem disposed to use the remainder—there were a lot still left in the box. "I love that lipgloss on you, by the way."

"Thanks. Well, Zo, what do you think?" Bella smoothed her hands over her hips, tilting her head. "Ready for the party?"

"Pretty much." Zoe stared into the mirror, caught by her own gaze. She looked a little like Mama in the wedding pictures, her hair caught in a simple but expert updo and secured so well even a small shake of her head produced no betraying unsteadiness. Maybe it *was* magic.

It was the first time she'd worn eyeliner since leaving Royal, and she'd forgotten how it made her eyes stand out. Not bad, she conceded inwardly. She might not be model-pretty as Jolie, but she wasn't a total embarrassment. "It looks great, Jolie," she said, shyly. "Thank you."

"Anytime." The brunette even seemed to mean it. "Thanks for letting us use your room, it's so much quieter. And this way we can be fashionably late."

"Not to mention already half-toasted." Bella dug in the pile of her and Jolie's day-clothes on the bed, neatly arranged next to the white box that had held the silver dress. She found her purse, a comfortably battered, handmade leather sling number that looked very similar to Zoe's own, and let out a happy chuckle. "You know what they say about the first drink on Christmas Eve."

"*Take it with people you like*," Jolie intoned, solemnly. "Should've known you'd sneak some in. It's like we're fourteen again."

"The difference between us and boys is that boys get *caught*, my dear." Bella held up a silver hip flask, the light hitting it with a mellow twinkle. "Come take a hit, Zoe, and let us welcome you to the Pride."

The other Kith drank as a matter of course, but Zoe preferred to keep a clear head. Still, this reminded her of sneaking quick hits from a bottle smuggled by one of Royal's other girls, or occasionally smuggling one in herself to hopefully provide a little relief.

Suddenly, everything about this seemed more familiar, and exponentially less dangerous. "Oh, God yes," Zoe said, with feeling, and Jolie returned the vanity to its former neatness with a few efficient movements.

"I told you," the brunette said, straightening and pushing her long hair back. Silken sandalwood strands made soft sounds against the velvet. "We're going to be great friends, Miss Rouje. We'll teach you everything."

"About being Kith?" *Let's see if they're shining me on.*

"And anything else," Bella replied, uncapping the flask. "You probably have some weird ideas, what with being raised skin and all."

"Skin." *Regular people, right?* She'd heard Jack use the term once or twice, explaining the differences between regular human beings and Kith. "Is that what you call it?"

"You're not supposed to," Jolie said, frowning slightly—but at the vanity, not in Zo's direction.

"It's not a bad word, or a slur. *Despite* what some of the academics might think." Bella waved away any objection, her necklace twinkling. "Come on, let's do this. I want to be the first to drink with both of you tonight."

The flask turned out to hold bourbon, and it burned all the way down. Each girl took a healthy swallow, and though Zoe had never been drunk—booze just didn't seem to affect her—she still felt a pleasant warmth for a few seconds.

"Happy Christmas," Jolie said quietly. "And welcome to the Pride, Zoe Rouje."

"Amen to that," Bella chimed in. "Blessed Yule, and welcome to the Pride. I'm so glad you're here."

You don't even know me. But Zoe ducked her head slightly, unable to stop a silly smile. "Happy holidays," she said, hoping that was fine. Mama had waxed indignant about it more than once—*Jesus is the Reason*, she would hiss—but Zo had always liked the idea of gathering varied winter rituals together like a bouquet. "And...what do I say?"

"You just smile and nod, that's all." Jolie's impish grin was impossible not to answer. "You look lovely, by the way."

Sure. But accepting compliments was good manners. "Thank you." Obviously they were going to go join the party now, and her throat was sour under the burn of bourbon. "Uh, don't suppose I could have another hit, could I?"

"My dear," Bella said, her dark eyes twinkling merrily, "I thought you'd never ask."

39
HISTORICAL TRUTH

"THERE YOU ARE," A FAMILIAR VOICE SAID. "LOOKING GOOD, DUMBASS. Clean up almost as nice as I do."

Jack turned, absorbing a mock-punch to one shoulder and letting his mouth curl into a half-smile. "Just considerably less pungent," he parried, and returned the blow with precisely calculated force.

McKenna's dark head cocked, and his hazel eyes all but glowed with cheerful mischief. He was the very picture of easy affability, from his faint raffish stubble—showing his control of the change, of course—to his loosened tie and collar, not to mention his ever-so-slightly-rumpled suit. On him every crease looked planned, even the off-kilter ones. "Flattery will get you nowhere. We're waiting for the girls, huh?" He glanced meaningfully at the ballroom's grand entrance, where a steady stream of Kith filtered through.

They were spreading through the house, many in rooms Jack had explored afresh with his *demie*. "A joy and a pleasure." He didn't even have a drink yet. Neither did Mac, which meant business was afoot. "What's up?" Jack continued, pitching the words very low indeed.

"I don't quite know." But McKenna's cheerfulness faltered for a moment. "I mean, it's *something*, I just can't tell what."

"Could you be any more cryptic? Get it out, dipshit." The casual roughness was almost a relief; Jack didn't have to hold himself so still and careful, hoping a stray movement wouldn't startle his *demie*. Jolie and Bella wouldn't let her bolt, and they would soothe her as much as possible.

She was so painfully nervous. He had to wait, and he didn't like it at all.

"Your dad's going to want to tell you first." McKenna grimaced, slipping his hands in his pockets and hunching slightly, the picture of easy, tousled elegance. Across the room there was a brief stir as Janine Traleski sailed in, smiling in every direction, shaking hands, air-kissing, and no doubt evaluating every outfit in sight.

Jack wondered, idly, what kind of dress she'd sent for Zoe. The anticipation was pleasant, even if maddening. "But you're going to tell me, and he must expect that. So give it up."

"Just be cool." McKenna glanced at the ballroom entrance again, and Jack realized he was waiting for any sign of Jack's *demie*.

Probably to keep the heir calm. "I'm not going to go off," he said, mildly. "Let me guess. You found out they were after my *demie* in specific."

"Well, I had an odd feeling. So after I took the tranqs to Belmario I went and visited my good pal Jasperson the younger again." McKenna's smile didn't change; an observer would think him merely engaged in the banter he was known for. "Some of the things he said before didn't quite make sense, even if my little kitten was satisfied."

"Always trust a shaman," Jack murmured. "How are things on that front? Progress being made?"

"I should be asking you." Mac's eyebrow lifted slightly, and his hand twitched as if he wished he had a tumbler of something alcoholic in it. "Look how relaxed you are."

"Get to the point." It wasn't quite a warning growl, and in any case, a steady thrum of Voice already ran under the holiday chatter, a comforting blanket of vibration. *She's fine. She's with a shaman and another* demie. *She's probably having a grand time, and she'll appear any moment now.*

"Well, some of little Greg's ramblings made me curious." McKenna's curiosity was legendary. He wasn't quite a patterner or a jäger, somewhere between the two and dominant almost to a fault. "So, like I said, I paid him a private visit, and once he saw there was no pretty shaman there to hold my leash, we had quite a productive little discussion."

There was only one logical conclusion, so Jack said it aloud. "He wasn't just milking old pension funds for drug money."

"Nope. He's been talking to the skins." In other words, Greg Jasperson wasn't just a junkie and embezzler but also a traitor. Now Mac looked faintly pained.

It was never good to give this kind of news.

Jack let the information settle inside his head, watching it ripple out through his assumptions about the skin attackers. "Did he give a reason?" Not that it mattered in the end—the Kith codes were strict about this sort of thing for a reason—but any details would help Jack predict.

And he had to, especially if the recent incursion wasn't simply a probe by one of the known hunting groups active in the States.

Some of the skins knew about Kith, of course. Most of the time they were ignored as crackpots, but a few of them inevitably decided to group up and grab weapons.

"Skate." McKenna grimaced, a swift flashing snarl. For a moment his beast shone in his eyes—his feelings on the one illegal drug capable of addicting a Kith were well-known, and not kind at all. "We knew he was a junkie, we just didn't know he was a traitor too."

"There has to be more." A simple skate addiction wasn't enough to induce a Kith to break one of the oldest rules—*thou shalt not betray thine own kind.*

It was right after *thou shalt not eat human flesh*, and though a traitor wasn't Broken, they could still be hunted like one.

"Right you are." McKenna nodded. "The dickweed thinks he's in love with a skin, had her set up in an apartment and everything. Turns out she was a little more than she appeared."

"A skin...operative?" *What the fuck?* Jack didn't like being—or sounding—startled. "Wait, you're telling me they have honeypots now? And he was dumb enough to—"

"That's how he held up under Jolie's questioning. He's got this whole fantasy of siring *usanaugh* and living happily ever after." McKenna shrugged, mystified by this as any reasonable Kith would be. "I can't tell whether he's delusional with withdrawal or just that fucking stupid. Anyway, for about eight months he's been feeding intel not just to your dad's business rivals but also a group we can't quite pin down. Including entry codes for some of the smaller trace programs monitoring for your mother and *demie*."

"Ah." Jack's guts turned cold, and it took all his control to simply stand still, absorbing the news. "We found her just in time."

"Yeah." There was a reason Mac was his best friend. It was evident in the way he gazed across the ballroom, giving Jack time to wrestle his temper down or just plain trusting him to keep his goddamn lid on. He never evinced any hint of fear at Jack's potential for explosive action, just almost-bored amusement and full willingness to join in.

Maybe that was the reason Jack's beast tolerated him so well. It took a certain amount of cool bravery to give a *demi* the news that his twin was targeted for kidnapping and other unpleasantness, especially when that *demi* had a reputation for hair-trigger ire anyway and had been missing said twin for almost two decades.

He was suddenly grateful for the man, even if he didn't like the thought of that easy charm turned on Zoe. "Where's the skin honeypot?"

"Dead." *Now* McKenna looked at him, broad shoulders stiffening for a moment. "Oh, not me, my friend. I dug around and found a police report. The day after we pulled Greg in to face the music she was sitting on a park bench when a man in a long dark coat sat down alongside, emptied a .22 into her, and walked away. Bullets bounced around inside a bit, like they do, and she was gone in minutes. Her apartment was cleaned out by big beefy skins with Jersey accents and a moving truck roughly half an hour later, and there's no next of kin listed. Her body's still waiting at the morgue." He exhaled sharply. "Merry fucking Christmas."

They would be wishing Zoe a happy holiday all night, and welcoming her to the Pride. "Snipping a loose end."

"Looks like it." McKenna didn't blink, his tone profoundly thoughtful. "Your father's triggered heightened security arrangements, and double guard on the shamans. Heard some gossip your *demie*'s got the Gene."

"That she does." *And in spades, too.* "Isn't asking many questions yet, though. She likes to think things over."

"Thank God," McKenna said, with something close to real feeling. "It's about time someone with some impulse control was in charge of you."

"Everyone keeps saying that." *Including me.* His mind raced with implications and deductions, pigeonholing and cross-referencing small bits of data. He didn't like the picture that was forming, and the sense of a nagging piece somewhere, a single instrument throwing off the whole orchestra, was acutely uncomfortable as well.

"Only because it's true." No wonder Mac wanted a drink. "You gonna get mad about this, or..."

"Why bother?" The cold all through him was welcome, his beast settled watchfully. "It won't serve my *demie*." He'd only lose his calm if she was threatened again, and some part of him might even welcome the chance to do battle in that situation—except, of course, for the certainty of frightening a skin-raised girl.

At least the recent visitors were completely unconnected to Fantome and his misbegotten kin. Two threats, one nearly neutralized and the other about to discover what happened when you troubled Jackson Rouje's *demie*.

"That's a relief." McKenna brightened as Dimitri approached. Lev was in a corner of the ballroom, buried behind a sound system he no doubt longed to turn all the way up and shiver the assembly to pieces with; thankfully, Hanna Grize was right next to him, and she would keep the volume manageable. "Hey, Dima. How was Europe?"

"Old, and beautiful in places." Dima grinned, and his handshake was as brutally hard as Mac's own. The two of them liked to play *who's the bigger bastard* almost as much as they enjoyed a good hunt. "My *demie* wouldn't let us backpack, though. Prefers four-star camping."

"The things we do for love." Mac glanced at the entrance again. "They're letting us wait, too."

"It'll be worth it." Dimitri gazed steadily at Jack. "You look grim. Something happen?"

"Skin hunters getting uppity," Mac summed up. "I hear you were looking into the ones across the pond."

"Yeah, the Golden was pretty upset." The dark-haired *demi's* mouth drew down. Part of his and Bella's trip had been investigating some of the slightly more professional skin hunters—especially that Swiss group—on the other side of the Atlantic. "They didn't get near his mate, but they *could* have. He was ready to tear down some walls."

What skins couldn't steal or control, they wanted to kill. Tale as old as time, really, even if most other skins considered any who believed in the Kith's existence as funny-farm material. Plus, the various groups rarely bothered working together, none of them wanting a seat at the table unless they could lord it over the others.

"As a man should when his mate's threatened." Mac stretched one side of his neck, then the other, a habitual loosening. He was going to ditch his tie soon, you could just tell. "You know what baffles me?"

"Literature?" Jack shrugged when Mac shot him a grimace. "Classical music? Tying your own shoes?"

"Fuck you, Jackson." McKenna's nose wrinkled briefly, and his smile said he appreciated the sarcasm. Play wasn't fun until it scored a direct hit. "I was going to say, these fucking skin hunters. Why are they even bothering? They can't win."

"Never stopped humanity before," Dimitri pointed out. "They like losing battles."

"They're frightened," Jack said; his *demie* was absolutely correct in that analysis. "Frightened people do stupid shit, yet another historical truth."

"I think that might be the most intelligent thing you've ever said." Mac's laugh held an edge. He caught sight of greying, iron-spined Caruthers in the crowd and grinned; the older Kith gave him a meaningful glare and held up a warning finger before turning back to exchange gossip with Janine Traleski. "I wish the girls would show up. I could use a drink."

"Couldn't we all." Dimitri eyed Jack. "How are you holding up?"

I'm frustrated as fuck and someone's used a traitor's intel to try snatching my twin. If she doesn't show up soon I might just casually run amok. Might even spit in a punch bowl or two. "Fine as frog's fur, thank you for asking." Jack kept his tone light, easy. "Just waiting on my sweet *demie*, and thankful for the chance."

"She's a delight. You'll like her, Mac. I wonder—" But whatever Dimitri wondered went unsaid, because there was a soft commotion at the ballroom's main entrance, a bright hint of crimson, Jolie's familiar storm-front sense of calm moving in ripples...and a flash of silver.

Zoe stood between shaman and *demie* analyst, sheathed in glimmering beaded silver, her slim shoulders bare. The heavy piled weight of her raven curls, starred with bright crystalline decorations, emphasized the graceful curve of her neck; kohl ringed her burning, beautiful baby blues. Jack's heart leapt into his throat and every nerve he owned tightened, strings singing in anticipation.

"Finally," McKenna said, with feeling, and swung into motion, making a beeline for Jolie. Dima followed, his gaze locked with Bella's and the connection between them vibrating almost-audibly.

For a moment Jack was frozen. Zoe's lips, gleaming with just the barest touch of clear gloss, were slightly parted, and she was tense. It probably took all her willpower not to turn and bolt, and if she did the chase instinct would swallow him whole. He wouldn't stop until he'd run her down in the most pleasant way possible, and she was nowhere near ready for *that* aspect of the *usanaugh* bond.

She might never be, but at least they had time to find out. Zoe lingered in the doorway, assembled Kith turning to witness the return of a prodigal, a hush spreading like Jolie's calm. Allison's apprentice was consciously radiating serenity with a vengeance, insulating and soothing an uncertain *demie*.

His *demie* wasn't just pretty. She was flat-out *stunning*, the magnetic pole the entire planet turned upon, and everything in him longed to fly toward her.

Instead, he found himself merely walking, Kith stepping out of his way with alacrity as he bore down on her. The pulse in her throat was a hummingbird's wings, but the link between them bloomed with fresh, almost painful intensity. Everything else—house, gathered family, the fireplaces full of crackling merriment and the good smells of food and community and belonging—went away. So did every consideration of Fantome, a junior Pride member's treachery, or the skin hunters.

There was only his *demie*, her head tilting back as she looked at him because he was somehow in front of her now, Mac saying something to Jolie, Dimitri catching Bella's hand in both of his.

Zoe's eyes were wide and drowning-deep. He fell into them for a long moment, and the relief was immeasurable. She was *here*, right in front of him, whole and breathing, the most magnificent, desirable gift in the world.

And all his. "Wow." He sounded poleaxed, Jack realized, and didn't care. "You look..."

She took a deep breath, one he felt in his own lungs. "Please don't say *ridiculous*," she muttered, but there was a soft, struggling spark of amusement in her eyes.

"Beautiful." He barely let her finish the sentence, offering his hand. "Enchanting. Delightful. Beguiling. Absolutely a thousand percent wonderful."

Her tentative smile firmed, blooming a little wider, and the anxiety lessened. Her fingers slid warm and delicate through his, and everything in the world was not just all right, but likewise wonderful. "What do we do now?" Her chin moved slightly, as if she wanted to glance at Jolie for direction, but Jack willed her not to look away.

No, my sweet demie. *Just focus on me, I'll get you through this.*

She nodded slightly as if she'd heard him, and one of her curls bobbed.

"Now you stay with me all evening. Or with Dad." He longed to plunge his hands into the silken mass of her hair, bring her close, taste her breath. "Everyone will welcome you to the Pride. Dad'll raise a toast before we start with the snacking, too." He caught a faint ghost of alcohol—so someone else had taken the first drink of the evening with her, probably Bella.

That was fine, he'd expected as much. But he would have the next.

"I don't know if I can eat." Zoe's shoulders tensed; she was exquisitely aware of being the center of attention. Jolie laughed at something McKenna said; the two of them would play rabbit-and-chaser all night, probably ending up in one of the south wing's bedrooms.

"I suggest a drink, then. What would you like?" *Ask me for something, anything. Let me please you.*

"Bourbon." Her anxiety spiked again, and she watched his expression carefully. "If that's all right?"

"Anything you want, Zo-baby. There's also dancing, if you like that. Dad will have you take a turn with him." The thought of moving through the ballroom with her in his arms was *definitely* enticing.

"Okay." She let him draw her out of the doorway, one small step at a time. "But not right now, I hope. My knees are a little weak."

"Mine too. You're stunning." Jack couldn't help himself; he stopped, raised her hand, and pressed his lips to her knuckles. She'd seen Dimitri and Bella do this, so she let him, and the sweet flush rising to her cheeks was a lovely change from the anxiety. Her scent changed a fraction, and his own responded, pheromones linking. It was nice to know she was far from immune to her *demi*.

He could use that.

"There you are." The crowd parted and Trevor Rouje stalked into view, his hair glowing gold under the chandelier's drench of electric light and his dark suit just avoiding full tuxedo by a few degrees. "Your timing is impeccable, little dancer. Everyone, gather 'round— and get a drink, so we can welcome my daughter properly."

40

READING MINDS

THE ENTIRE HOUSE THROBBED WITH LIGHT, HEAT, GOOD SMELLS, SOFT conversation, and laughter. The first toast was just her father lifting a tumbler with two fingers of spiced rum and saying *This season we have much to be grateful for, my beloved daughter has returned to us*, and everyone chiming in with *Hear, hear* or *Amen* or Jack's soft *At long last* before taking a swig. Then Lev bent to his work behind a bank of sound equipment, a girl with soft brown hair gently pushing his hand away from a certain dial. Other toasts were called out, and the snacking began as carols and holiday music began to play at just the right volume. Groups of Kith—bright eyes, glossy hair, skin in every shade glowing with vitality—formed, broke, and reformed with soft regularity. Zoe was greeted over and over, and the welcome seemed genuine.

Best of all, she didn't have to shake anyone's hand or be hugged. Jack's presence seemed to make it completely unnecessary, and with him hovering right next to her apparently nobody would dare to ask where she'd been or why it took seventeen years to show up.

Janine beamed, holding a champagne flute and gazing from Zoe's toes to top, a slow, appreciative inspection. "I told you," was her greeting. "A very special dress, for a very special young lady. You look lovely, my dear. Welcome to the Pride."

"Thank you." Zoe's stock of small talk wasn't exhausted just yet, but it was close. "And thank you for all the clothes, and everything. It's all beautiful."

"You'll have to tell me if you don't like a particular piece, though, or if it's uncomfortable to wear. I depend on that." Janine nodded at Jack. "I'll see you two again after the New Year, I'm sure. In the meantime, there's canapés, so I'm off in that direction. Happy Christmas."

"And also with you," Jack replied, his mouth twitching into a grin when she glared at him.

"You're not yet old enough to mouth off at me, pup." She dropped a wink in Zoe's direction and was gone into the crowd.

"Taking your life in both hands, Jackson," McKenna commented as he passed. Lean and brunet, he was also cheerfully rumpled, with an air of menace lurking just under the surface. He looked a little like Royal—or, more exactly, what Royal had been trying like hell to be. Still, every time his hazel gaze found Jolie it softened, and so did the rest of him. Incrementally, but the difference was plain.

He had a bad case for the tall brunette girl, and she absolutely knew it. Jolie fluttered through the crowd, socializing with ease, McKenna trailing her with one hand in his pocket and the other holding a squat, smoked-glass tumbler of amber Scotch. For all that, neither of them orbited very far from Jack; neither did Dimitri and Bella, who were greeted with much visible enthusiasm.

The kitchen was humming, Amelia had no time to talk and simply smiled in their direction before whirling away to snap a command at Hermann, who had lost his stony expression and outright grinned, hurrying to obey. People took turns helping out, carrying trays, or dealing with the nearest party disaster as a matter of course. Even the solarium was decorated with tinsel, though it was dim and rustling, a rest from the hubbub elsewhere. Zoe couldn't even guess how many extra miles of Christmas lights had been dragged out of storage for this event, but it was a considerable number.

In short, it was magic.

Best of all was the steady comfort of her brother's presence. And when the carols and holiday music shifted to Shostakovich's Second Waltz, Jack steered them back for the ballroom. "That's the signal for the ball to start." He snagged a fresh bourbon for her from a passing tray—the Kith girl carrying it smiled encouragingly in Zoe's direction, chirping a *Happy Holidays, Miss Rouje, and welcome home* —while keeping his own well-sipped brandy. "How are your knees?"

"Holding up." It was almost ridiculous, how much steadier she felt with him nearby. "But I'm not sure I—"

"You'll have to at least waltz with Dad, it's tradition. And don't worry, if you can't he'll just pick you up and carry you."

"I can manage a waltz and a foxtrot, I think. Just don't ask me to tango."

He brightened. "We should take tango lessons. That would be fun."

Costs a lot. The immediate objection drained some of the good feeling away; calculating every cent was great for survival but none of these people had ever done it.

On the other hand, the thought of being in a studio again, of standing tall at the barre and letting the elegant precision of ballet soothe her...it was seductive.

Very seductive.

"And we should get you some leotards," Jack continued, setting off again. She had to keep up, since her free hand was still tucked in his arm. "Pointe shoes. Right? that's what you'll need for ballet."

Is he reading my mind? Trying not to think about Bea or Royal, or any of a hundred other sins she'd had to commit, was exhausting. "I don't know." It was the most careful, noncommittal response possible. "Maybe."

"Will it make you happy?" He wasn't doing a lot of drinking, just inhaling the brandy's scent every once in a while with only the tiniest of accompanying sips. "That's the only consideration, really."

Zoe liked the idea, but she was woefully out of practice. The teachers would probably laugh at her, and any studio around here was likely to be stuffed full of rich girls. There were a thousand reasons not to do anything, and she could always discover at least half of them within mere seconds. "I'll think about it."

"You're busy arguing yourself out of it, more like." He shook his golden head slightly, steering them around a knot of older men, all in those quasi-tuxedo dark suits but one with a candy-cane striped tie, all laughing at one sally or another. All they needed were cigars and cummerbunds to be a picture-book illustration of capitalism, Mr. Moneybags from the Monopoly box. "And no, I'm not using the twinbond. I just know that look on your pretty face."

Twinbond. Okay. "Can you read my mind?"

"Not exactly?" The words spiraled up and his eyebrows drew together. He gave every question his complete attention, as if what she said was important. "It's more like empathy than telepathy. I just, you know, sense what you're feeling. We used to think inside each other's heads when we were little. It'll happen again."

That didn't sound too bad. Just not very private. "Are Dimitri and Bella always like that?"

"Well, yeah." He paused, glancing down at her. "*Usanaugh* can't be apart, you know. It's destabilizing, especially for the *demi*."

"But don't they ever want to be..." She took a bit of bourbon, enjoying the bite; she could see why the rest of them seemed to consider drinking a necessity. Having something to do with your hands was invaluable; it probably replaced smoking for them.

She hadn't seen a single Kith with a cancer-stick.

"Alone? I don't know. Never thought to ask." He didn't take offense at the implication, at least. "I know you like your space sometimes. Figure it's normal. You had to learn to cope on your own, you're not used to leaning on your twin."

That's one way of putting it. "You could lean on me," she said, shyly, and had to smile at a tall woman with wavy platinum hair, who chirped a *Happy Christmas, welcome* before swanning away, holding a flute full of some pinkish drink. "I don't mind it."

That earned her another of his slow, almost hypnotic smiles. "I do lean on you. See, I haven't been able to do this for seventeen years."

"Drink?" The bill for all the booze running through the rooms was bound to be considerable. What alcohol didn't do to her, the pressure of the crowd and alternating waves of anxiety and relief would. Zoe's head swam, and the quiet of the blue suite was more and more attractive the longer this went on.

"No, silly." Now there was a shadow in Jack's expression, dark eyes narrowing and his mouth turning down. "Attend a party like this. At least, not for more than an hour or so."

"Why?" Her heart hurt, a swift stabbing needle-pain. She'd learned how to pretend a certain amount of harshness after she fled Hall City—it was practically a requirement if you expected to survive in squats, shelters, or sleeping rough—but Zoe never liked anyone's distress.

And his was worse than strangers', her stupid empathy working overtime.

"Because my twin wasn't with me," Jack said, patiently. "You're my passport into the Pride."

Her ears had to be malfunctioning. "But you know everything." There was no way she was drunk on such a tiny amount of bourbon, even if her stomach had refused anything approaching food since breakfast. "You've been here the whole time."

"Yeah, but without my twin, I'm...unreliable. You know we have bad tempers. Mine's considered sharp even for Kith." Someone called his name across the room; he glanced up and gave a brief salute with his brandy, acknowledging a man with dark hair, a tinsel crown, and a beaming sloe-eyed toddler in his arms.

There weren't many children, but they were all excited in their holiday best and roamed the crowd at will, except for the very youngest. Every nearby adult acknowledged the small people in some way, keeping an eye on them, and when a blond boy in a bright red Christmas sweater—he looked about six, his cornsilk hair unwillingly plastered down except for a stubborn cowlick at his right temple—clattered by at high speed he was corralled by a group of businesslike elders.

But gently, and fondly, with paternal smiles and a quiet *it's not polite to run here, let's try walking.*

Nobody had raised their voice, thrown a punch, or started talking in tongues yet. It was worlds away from a church barbecue. Zoe's stomach settled all at once. "Is Bella Dimitri's passport?"

"They're not in our situation. Without my sweet *demie*, I'm a ghost in the Pride. I can see and hear, but not touch. It's lonely, and missing you made it worse." He turned them down a slightly less-crowded hall, drawing her aside as Janine and a small group of women left the library, a hum of conversation buzzing in their midst. "So, you know, I used to stay up in the attic or my room, listening to the party and thinking about how it would be when we found you."

When, not *if*. He was so sure, so certain all the time, but how much of that was a façade like Zoe's own? Still, finding out he actually needed her for something was a blessing.

"Did you ever think you wouldn't?" Her heart gave another swift deep pang at the thought of a little boy upstairs in the quiet, listening to everyone else having a good time.

She knew that feeling, especially when Mama was getting a new boyfriend and Zoe had to stay out of sight.

"I tried not to." Jack stopped dead, glanced over his shoulder, and tugged her out of the hallway traffic-flow. The doorway to the long narrow sitting room across from the library was unoccupied, and he drew her close so they could hear each other; the crowd was knotting up here for some reason. "I keep telling you, you're important. It'll take time to get used to it." He looked down at her, his eyebrows drawn together, dark eyes hot and intent.

I'm nobody. But that wasn't quite true, was it? She'd been born into this, and everyone in here had claws just like her—not to mention some of the other abilities, the ones Mama had been so frightened of. After a lifetime of watching from the outside, Zoe was suddenly *in* something, warm and complete.

What did they do to Kith who had done bad things? Jack said he wouldn't blame her, sure, that was nice, but what about the rest of them?

"And now you're worrying." Jack leaned closer, his familiar scent enfolding her and blocking out the rest of the world. The calm was instant, her body relaxing unwillingly. "The thought of being important just scares the daylights out of you. You'll get used to it. I promise."

What if I don't? Maybe she should get some kind of therapy. That was what rich people did, right? "I'm sorry."

"No need, Zo-baby. Come on, Dad'll want you for the first dance. He won't send me to bed early if I don't deliver, but he might get ironic at me or something."

How did he make her smile all the time? It was downright weird, but Zoe liked it. "Fate worse than death."

"There's my girl." Now he beamed down at her, as if she'd somehow done something right. "So, try to chill a little. I'm liking this *stay up past my bedtime* thing."

"As if you have a bedtime."

"It's whenever my *demie* tucks me in. Ready to dance?"

"I suppose." It probably wouldn't help, but she tossed the rest of the bourbon down. It burned, pleasantly, and vanished. Mama would be horrified at the breach of manners.

Here, among these beautiful, vital people, Angelina would have been the odd one out.

Jack checked traffic in the hall, a quick sharp glance. "Come on, then."

"I have a question." She refused to move, risking a little intransigence. "Did Mama—did Angelina come to these parties?"

"Well, yeah. Dad's wife and all."

"But there aren't any...there aren't any normal people here tonight." She hadn't seen a single one, and being surrounded by Kith made the similarities in bone structure and movement clearly visible. She had to fit in at least a little, right? At least, she *hoped* she did. "You know. Skins."

He didn't wince at the word, but he did study her somberly. "It's rare that one of us mates with one of them."

"What about Dimitri and Bella's...their normal parent?" *My God, I really am an alien. Are we a whole separate species?* Now there was an intriguing thought; she'd been an exile all her life, probably all the way down to the genetic level. "They had one, right?"

"Their dad? He died in a car accident." Another strange expression flickered across Jack's face.

That was a clear indication to drop the subject, and Zo took it. "Oh, God. I'm sorry."

"It was a long time ago. Their mom's probably in the kitchen with Amelia; the two of them get along like a house on fire." He glanced up as Jolie approached, gliding down the hallway with her head held high. McKenna ambled behind her, his eyes half-lidded and his stride quick but deceptively casual. "And we're about to be reminded it's time for dancing. Let's go."

41

FIRST DANCE

By the time they reached the ballroom Lev had switched to Strauss, and grinned from the far corner with a thumb's up as Jack and Zoe appeared. Dad made a beeline for them, and performed a very elegant, formal little bow upon arrival.

"It's traditional," Trevor said, and extended his right hand. "Would you honor me, little dancer?"

Jack's *demie* assented with a nervous, propitiating smile she must have used daily at the grocery store in Marquette. Dad whirled her onto the magically clearing ballroom floor; after a few bars other Kith made their bows and curtseys, and the usual revel began. Jolie consented to take a turn with McKenna, Dimitri led Bella onto the floor with barely repressed satisfaction, and old Amerlane went past with his mate Maria in his sturdy arms, the two of them gazing into each other's eyes like teenagers. Kim Anson and her mate Stephanie went past too, two redheaded jägers moving in perfect one-two-three unison.

"Happy Christmas, Jackson." Sondra Amerlane, back temporarily from Nebraska to receive personal diplomatic orders from her Pride's ruler, gave him a wide pearly grin. The others in the delegation would be celebrating with the Plainswalkers, a visible reminder amid the traditional merrymaking that something serious was being discussed.

And, not so incidentally, the shaman and patterner would be gathering information before it could be altered like McFisk's birth certificate had been. If Fantome's rank-and-file didn't know yet about their leader's sin—toward a *demie*, no less—the mercy was of short duration indeed.

Sondra's lumpy sweater bore a lopsided snowman in a Santa hat, leering as she raised her arm to take a sip of her mimosa. Every Thanksgiving a contest was held for the worst holiday sweater possible, and the winner's submission, along with runners-up, auctioned off with fierce bidding. The proceeds went to the Kith who had submitted said sweaters for their chosen charities, and the best part of the whole deal was the crowd commentary. This year Sondra had won, and Jack had to admit, the thing she was wearing was a goddamn horror.

"Hey, Sondra. Happy holidays, and have I told you lately how I hope to never piss you off?" It was strange to smile and actually mean it, rather than simply giving a good impression. With his *demie* present, he was approached just like anyone else.

It was a deep, unexpected balm, and his eyes prickled slightly.

"You and everyone else. Except McKenna." The lawyer tucked a strand of her bobbed chestnut mane behind one ear, her silver hoop earrings swinging gently. "I get to go back to Fantome after the holidays and peel off prime territory. Forgive me for asking at a party, but..."

Jack could very well guess her question. "There's no statute of limitations on atonement, but I don't think I'll go personally to collect. How close was Fantome to the misbegotten?"

"Funny thing, that. The birth records were altered and all our patterner can say is that he was delivered by a Kith doctor. Nobody there is really talking above a whisper; I can't blame them for closing ranks. I mean, a misbegotten is one thing, but getting tangled up with this kind of thing?" One shoulder lifted, dropped, a lazily elegant shrug. In the courtroom she displayed a bright, polite interest so soft-spoken, opposing counsel rarely realized they were dealing with predator instead of appetizer until it was far too late. "My money's on nephew, though. We weren't allowed to speak to Fantome's sister, the one they call crazy."

"I'd be crazy too, growing up with him." Jack offloaded his brandy and Zoe's empty glass onto a passing tray, thanking David St. Carchair with a nod. The kid was having a grand time stacking as many glasses as possible, teetering through the crowd with a frown of concentration.

If he tripped, Amelia would have him washing dishes all night.

"Wasn't there a scandal with her, some forty years ago? She's been in seclusion since, right?" Sondra gazed at the dancing, her eyebrows drawn together as if she saw a battlefield instead of a ballroom. "Dad and your father gave each other one of those looks when I mentioned it."

"I think so?" Jack trawled through memory, and didn't catch much in the net. "Nothing specific, just some talk about her retreating into seclusion. Timeline could be about right. Did we ever get all of the paperwork on the misbegotten's church?"

"Just your standard fire-and-brimstone, sucking up old lady pensions." Sondra rolled the glass's stem between her fingers, the fluid inside swirling. "Fantome was probably using it to wash a dollar or two as well. Angelina was one of McFisk's favorites." She eyed him, not quite nervously.

A misbegotten near a vulnerable, kidnapped *demie* was a blasphemy, and Sondra's caution was warranted. It was a very good thing this McFisk was safely dead and Zoe showed no interest in updates yet, so to speak. Jack looked over the ballroom, spotted his *demie* still safely in Dad's expert grasp, and even watching her across a crowded room was distracting.

She was just so fucking *perfect*. His twin ducked her head slightly and smiled at something Dad said; Trevor gazed fondly at her curls, steering her through whirling couples. The head of the Pride hadn't smiled so broadly in public for almost two decades, and instead of a respectful hush in his presence, laughter and merriment burst in scattered swirls.

A slight edge of breeze, a breath of icy moonlight, and Allison appeared on Sondra's other side. The streak in the shaman's hair glowed like the filigreed snow outside, and her eyes were bright. "Am I interrupting?"

"Never," Sondra said. "How's your head?"

"Still a little tender, but some of Amelia's gingersnaps should fix that." Allison was also radiating serenity, though not as hard as Jolie. Maybe her apprentice was taking the burden for her teacher, or maybe it was a training exercise. "Hullo, Jackson. Is your *demie* well?"

In other words, the head shaman expected a full report. "A little nervous," he said, carefully—it was the easiest, most polite way to say the feartaking might need another application. He enjoyed seeing Allison's eyes widen, her gaze swinging past him to search for an untutored bearer of the Gene who could shake off her work so quickly. "Jolie's been hanging out with her today."

"Good." But Allison still looked faintly troubled. "Did McKenna find you? He wouldn't say what it was about."

"Uh-oh." Sondra took a hit off her mimosa. "Is it my turn to ask if I should leave?"

"Oh no, you'll be wanted in the war room for this one," Jack said. "Mac went back to talk to Jasperson the younger." He laid it out in a few clipped sentences, watching Sondra's expression turn grim and Allison's shoulders tensing, ready to bear yet another burden.

"Poor Clementine," the shaman said, softly. "I haven't seen her yet tonight."

"She's at home with Mark," Sondra supplied. "What a mess."

"It's not her fault. She tried to raise him right." Allison looked very much like she wanted a drink, Jack cast around for someone on duty. Just in time, Gessel appeared, bearing a loaded tray. There were no cosmopolitans, but a good old vodka-and-cranberry would do; he subtracted one and handed it over. The shaman accepted with a graceful nod, the blond myrmidon hurried away, and she took down half the drink at once.

It was very unlike her.

"They did try," Jack said. "We'll do all we can for them." His reaction to the news of Greg's treason would be reported, and his deliberate, witnessed statement relieving the Jaspersons of responsibility for their son's bad choices would allow them to join Pack functions without anxiety or fear of a chill reception.

Well, at least, as soon as they wanted to. Clementine was no doubt beside herself, and her mate furious at their cub's betrayal.

"Indeed we will," Sondra agreed. "You don't think Fantome's connected to that too, do you?"

"He's not. We've established that much." Jack couldn't tear his gaze from Zoe, who swung free of Trevor, her dress glittering like wet fishscales, and spun neatly back with liquid grace. She even laughed, a glimmer of the fearless Kith daughter she would be in time peeking through. "Which is a relief."

"And a pity," Amerlane the younger said. "I'd love to take his entire territory."

"Acres of corn." Allison's smile was troubled, but wearily beautiful nonetheless. "Who would want it? Just strip out the mining rights and the financials."

Sondra toasted her with a chuckle. "And people call *me* bloodthirsty."

Strauss gave way to a lilting Philip Glass piece, and Trevor brought Zoe to a stop right before their small group. A smattering of polite applause went up, and yet more Kith crowded the ballroom's glowing expanse.

All was right with the Pride, for the first time in seventeen long years.

"Hello." Zoe, flushed and smiling, let her shoulder touch her brother's, stepping close. "It's Allison, isn't it?"

"You have a good memory." The shaman nodded to Dad, who would no doubt ask her for a dance as well. "Happy holidays, and welcome to the Pride. This is Sondra Amerlane, she's in the legal division."

"Christmas and welcome." Amerlane turned on the charm, as if Zoe was a harassed clerk needing ruffle-smoothing and sweet-talking. "That's the short version. It's good to have you back, Miss Rouje."

"It's good to be here." It sounded like Zoe meant it, too, and suddenly Jack couldn't wait a moment longer.

He snaked an arm around his *demie*'s waist, her warmth a pleasant scorch. "The next dance is mine, and I've been very patient. Excuse us."

His *demie* didn't demur, light as a feather in his arms, and the stream of dancers accepted them both with no trouble at all. Now all the tedious lessons with Janine and Evgenia were about to pay off, even if he doubted he'd be able to do anything showy on the floor.

"You can lead," she said, gazing up at him as if surprised. "You're actually not bad."

"I'll settle for not tripping." He kept an eye on their route, calculating the best angles to avoid collisions. "Dad hasn't danced since you left. It's great to see him loosening up."

"Jolie says he's happy now." Zoe's heels tapped gently; for another precious moment she was the carefree *demie* she could have been if not for Angelina. A few stray curls bounced, her hand in Jack's was warm and sure, and she tipped her chin up, mischief flashing in those adorable baby blues. "What was he like before?"

"Quiet." Jack kept counting inwardly; thank God this was an easy dance. "Intense. Serious. Me too, I guess. No reason to laugh with our Zo-baby gone."

She bit her lower lip, tilting her head slightly as the music changed. "Can I ask you something?"

A hot spear of satisfaction went through him. "Anything."

"Those...the people the other night." Searching his expression for any hint of displeasure, she handled the turn at the end of the ballroom adroitly. "What happened to their cars?"

Was that what she'd been wondering, working the intruders' backtrail? "Chopped into parts by now. Lev and Gessel would have made arrangements." Most likely with the Coughlin wrecking yards; they did good business, in every sense.

"Oh." She glanced to her right, her profile so beautiful another sharp pang went through him. The link between them was full of softness, with only a faint rasping thread of apprehension. A shimmer of Voice slid through the crowd, overlapping rumbles spreading a warm soothing blanket. The music changed again, but he paid no attention.

"Don't worry." Nobody else provoked the desire to over-explain; Jack's hand tensed against the small of her back. "You did exactly right, and they wouldn't have gotten out of the house anyway." *Much less carrying you, if they managed to get one of those tranqs in.* "You're safe."

"What if..." Another nervous glance. "What if they had? Gotten out of the house, I mean."

"Not possible." Was she going to make him tell her the ugly details? He would, certainly, if it would ease her mind.

But he didn't want to. Not during their first dance.

"You're sure?"

"Very." But he was also curious. Some sure instinct warned him not to ask what *she* thought they'd been after; when she was ready, she'd tell him.

And he would make that problem, like every other one she'd ever had, disappear. Jack smiled, handling the step change as the music shifted once more, and settled himself to wait.

42
CORRELATION, CAUSATION

THE ENTIRE HOUSE BECAME STILL AND BREATHLESS-QUIET AS MIDNIGHT approached. When the giant brass-and-oak grandfather clock in the vast foyer struck twelve, she almost expected the mansion and its occupants to disappear.

She was in a fairytale, after all. Zoe held her breath; everyone in the dining room was absolutely motionless.

A soft sound rose from the assembled Kith, growing in volume and eerie modulation as the tolling died. Zoe's nape tingled and goosebumps raced down her back, spreading through her arms and legs. Beside her, Jack was a statue, his chin set and his dark gaze thoughtful.

All night he'd handled the socializing whenever she was confused, smoothly stepping in with introductions, small talk, or a murmured *excuse us, I need my* demie.

When the chorus began, though, his arm slithered around her waist, drawing her into his side. Solid and comforting, he was a rock amid cold waves, so she didn't protest.

The sound grew, and grew, ringing in the upper registers like a crystal wineglass stroked with a wet fingertip. The shivers down

Zoe's back intensified—not unpleasant, but still a strange, sharp sensation.

Jack leaned down. His breath was hot against her ear. "It's just singing. Try humming first."

It reminded her of church. Of Midnight Mass in a cathedral, incense drenching the air and candleflames glittering against bright chalice and gilded paten. Her throat felt odd, because she was already humming. The noise all but demanded it.

The Kith were eerily still, their eyes burning like coals, shining hair stirred by stray breezes, their grace and strangeness over-whelming because it was repeated over and over through a crowd.

Do I look like that? Impossible to tell. Even Jack was glowing with that strange vitality.

Allison stood next to their father near the dining-room's formal, wide-open double doors. The pale stripe in the woman's hair gleamed, and she tipped her head back, her throat vibrating with a high unearthly trill. Jolie, next to McKenna, answered with another; the same crystalline note rose from the center of Zoe's bones. Only a few among the crowd produced that soprano blur, giving the entire throbbing hymn its melody.

All her life, she'd been missing this. For a few moments every vestige of fear vanished and Zoe simply *existed*, a warm safe pillar next to her and a comfortable blanket of peace laid over every nerve. Trevor's eyes were closed; Allison's arm was tucked in his. A voice nearby was Amelia's, blur-buzzing through the lower registers, Zoe didn't know quite how she recognized it.

The chorus faded in fits and starts, but the feeling of comfort and unity remained, pulsing in her marrow, a second heartbeat.

Jack's arm tightened, a brief hug. Was Dimitri holding Bella like this, somewhere else in the house?

"Make a wish," Jack whispered. "Don't say it out loud, though. Traditional."

There was only one thing she could want. *Don't let this go away,* she pleaded silently. *Please, just let me stay here.*

Motion began again, hushed goodbyes as if it were much later than midnight, handshakes and hugs and air kisses exchanged. The breakup of the party was handled with quiet efficiency, and there was remarkably little mess. After her brief stint working for a caterer in Oklahoma, Zoe could appreciate a houseful of guests who didn't leave crap scattered everywhere. A steady file of visitors even carried glasses and dishes to the kitchen, and she thought it very likely everyone had pitched in to help wash and dry all evening.

Maybe she should have, too. "Do we help Amelia clean up?" she whispered, afraid of breaking the ongoing, churchlike quiet.

"It's your first party," Jack said in an undertone. "So you don't lift a finger. I'll take a turn once the doors are safely closed, and you can go with me. But *no helping*."

"I like doing it." She had a transitory, hilarious urge to stick her tongue out at him.

"Not tonight, my sweet *demie*." He didn't move, his gaze passing over the swiftly emptying dining room. A few Kith waved in their direction, but there seemed to be a rule against yelling farewells tonight and besides, Jack's entire body shouted *no thank you, just go home*.

It was...nice, to have him as a shield. He certainly seemed to enjoy the duty.

The front door opened and closed, opened and closed, their father now in the foyer exchanging quiet words with every departing group. Zoe could hear the murmurs even from here.

Her senses were getting sharper—not that they needed much help. But the mutters were restful, and even the sound of people breathing and moving wasn't a rasping irritant. Deep, almost narcotic peace remained, unfamiliar but entirely welcome.

Very soon the ballroom was empty. So was the secondary dining room to one side; even the potluck table's oxblood cloth was neat and clean except for a few small crumbs. Jack tucked his chin slightly, smiling down at her. "Wasn't so bad, was it?"

"It was nice." *Especially the dancing.* For some reason, other words crowded her throat, low but urgent. "Is it really tradition to wish?"

"Yeah. And it comes true." His expression didn't change.

"Come on." She could have moved, pulled away. But she didn't. "Be serious."

"I didn't believe it for a long time." He didn't sound joking or insincere at all. Just thoughtful, again. "But mine did, so now I have to. Direct observation of an effect."

"Correlation might not be causation." The phrase was all over the internet, but it had the advantage of being true. She'd listened to more than one argument in the backroom at the Greenfield; Bubs had some kind of philosophy degree, and he was always full of weird aphorisms while running the forklift or working the hardware section. "Aren't you the math whiz?"

Where were all her various coworkers now? And all of Royal's girls? She hoped they were happy, or at least safe; her own good luck seemed shameful at the moment.

"That's statistics," Jack corrected, teasingly. "Do you want to dance?"

"There's no music." There wasn't even the hum of live speakers from the sound equipment; the party had well and truly shut down. Zoe might have crossed her arms and refused, but Jack already had her wrist, drawing her out into the ballroom's vast emptiness. "And everyone's gone."

"Best time for dancing, *demie*." His grin widened. "Come on."

There was no need for music, she discovered. Somehow she caught his rhythm with no trouble, even when he halted and she dipped, her weight securely held by a strong arm at her back, Jack's smile infectious and her own laugh echoing against the walls.

Christmas dawned pale grey and thin-snowing. Apparently it was one of the few days Amelia's iron grip on the kitchen relaxed and everyone was allowed to get their own breakfast. Zoe couldn't eat anything, her stomach a tight ball, but at least Jack could work the giant glittering espresso maker.

Everything went easier with coffee.

And at least there were a mountain of presents under the largest tree for her brother and Trevor—no, for *Dad*. Her own stacks and peaks of brightly wrapped boxes didn't seem so overwhelming in comparison, but the thought of how much cash they'd sunk into the glittering things wouldn't go away.

Their father chose a small, very familiar silver-wrapped box first, settling on a dove-grey couch across from the tree with every evidence of satisfaction. "I have been wondering about this for days," he said, cheerfully. Wearing black sweats and plush terrycloth robe, he was far more approachable than in his usual starch-suited crispness.

"I didn't say a word." Jack held up the small red box she'd wrapped for him, too, shaking it slightly for all the world like he truly didn't know what was inside. "Promise."

"It's fine." Zoe hugged her knees, her entire body tucked inside a very solid, very comfortable tan recliner. "You don't have to pretend."

"I said I'd be surprised, and I meant it." Jack, cross-legged on the floor near her chair, grinned under a tousled mat of gold hair. They were both in pajamas, but Zoe, up early and pacing the blue suite, wore jeans and a soft peach sweater as well as tightly laced sneakers.

It this went downhill, she could be gone in a hurry.

Their father peeled at tape, working at the paper cautiously. So he wasn't a rip-and-tear person; that was a hopeful sign.

When he opened the box, he stared at the pocket watch for what seemed an eon. "A Buhré," he finally said, softly, reverently. His blue eyes had grown glittering-bright. "Oh, my little dancer. It's beautiful."

"Told you." Jack all but wriggled with satisfaction, muscle flickering under his loose, faded black T-shirt. He tore open his own small not-really-a-gift with ruthless efficiency, and when he opened the plain white display box he inhaled deeply. "Snuff box with combination lock," he said. "I've been aching to really play with it. You know Zoe just walked right into the shop and up to your watch? Like she was on a fishing line."

Oh, God. Zoe hugged her legs tighter. She didn't think Trev—*Dad* was going to give her a lecture about *that deviltry, and don't you do it, you mind me now.*

A lifetime's worth of hiding was a hard habit to break.

"Well, she does have the Gene." Dad wiped at his cheek, scrubbing at a trace of dampness among gold-tinged stubble. "Thank you, Zoe. It's absolutely perfect. You can open the rest of my presents for me, you know."

"Look at him, trying to make you work on Christmas." Jack dug in the pile arranged near her chair, producing a small, narrow, rectangular box. "Here. This one's from Dad."

"Do you know what's in it?" She had to uncurl to accept the gift, wishing her weird talents included invisibility. That would have been *extremely* useful, and not just in current circumstances.

"I can't say." But her brother winked, and rested his hand against the chair's arm until she took the box.

"You really can keep a secret." Carefully working the paper free along taped edges, Zo tried to guess what it was. Very light, and it didn't rattle. In defiance of all caution and good sense, a spot of traitorous warmth bloomed inside her ribcage.

They didn't think she was demonic. They had words for her strangeness, and not only that, there were others like her in the...the Pride. The family.

Like Allison. And maybe Jolie, she thought.

The wrapping revealed a heavy bluegreen box, and when she opened it the glittering thread inside nearly blinded her. "A tennis bracelet," she breathed. *Tiffany's. Wow.* "Just like Mama's." Well, Mama had to pawn hers to pay for medicine in Kansas City, but before that, it had come out for special occasions, shining on Angelina's delicate wrist.

"I'm surprised she took it with her." Did her father sound anxious? "Do you like it? Jack said the size should be right. I thought...well, you weren't here for your thirteenth birthday, so..."

"It's an actual..." Zoe could barely believe it, holding the box with reverent fingertips. "It's so beautiful." *I can't accept this.* The panicked reflex forced a sour bubble up the back of her throat. "Are you sure? I mean, it's...they're really..." *These are expensive. Actual diamonds. My God.*

"Let's put it on. Either wrist, you don't wear a watch." Jack was suddenly beside her, handling the box gently. Last night they had danced in the empty ballroom, and for a few moments she'd even been able to rest her head on his shoulder, the Kith's humming resting in her bones, and pretend she belonged in this warm haven. "And yes, he's sure. Look at that, fits perfectly."

Cool metal warmed against her skin. The gems rested easily, a single burning strand saying she belonged here. The thought of what it cost made her dizzy. What if she lost it? "I'll be careful," she said numbly. "I'll be *very* careful with it."

"It's meant to be worn." But her father looked anxious, the corners of his mouth drawing down. "Is it the wrong color? Janine said silver, but I thought white gold more appropriate."

"It's *beautiful*." Zoe's heart hurt again, another swift stabbing pain. It wasn't right for him, of all people, to be so worried about whether *she* would like something. "I love it. I'll wear it."

"You'd better." Jack rooted around some more in her pile and rescued another tiny box, this one square and wrapped in red paper as well. "This one next."

"It's Dad's turn." It was out of her mouth before she had time to think, the first time she called him *Dad* without having to plan her sentence carefully.

Trevor beamed, his blue eyes almost brimming. "Ah. Well. We don't have to obey a strict order."

"Oh, now you say so?" Jack shook his head, setting the box on

Zoe's knee. "Good job, Zo. You're getting him to loosen up. Soon he'll even be dressing business casual on weekends."

"Bite your tongue, young man." The easy banter was back, though Trevor brushed at his cheek again. "Very well, we'll take turns."

It was the kind of Christmas morning she'd always dreamed of, right down to the snow and the sharp spicy smell of balsam from a decorated tree. And when she opened the box, Jack all but fidgeting next to her chair, it was to find a pale silvery ring with a brilliant blood-tinted gem sunk in its top, clearly antique.

"It's the princess signet," Jack said, and held up his left hand. "Changed the setting a bit to make it more like a traditional *demie*'s." His ring bore a distinct resemblance, though much heavier and in gold. "Go ahead, put it on. Left hand, like mine."

You could wear a cheap band on your left third finger to drive some persistent guys off; all Royal's girls had warned the new ones about the risks of doing so. Some dates got funny about it, and wouldn't pay. But that was another Zoe's knowledge from another life, and her cheeks were hot.

Dimitri and Bella wore rings like this, with blue stones. Dad had a signet too, its gem a baleful crimson glare, the flaw in its heart like a cat's vertical pupil.

The tennis bracelet was bad enough. What if she lost *this*?

Jack's hands were warm; he settled the ring on her finger and cocked his head, admiringly. "Sized just about right, thank goodness. Harold and Patsy are wonder-workers. They take care of some Rouje family treasures—well, technically it all belongs to the Pride, but centralizing some things works better."

"We're stewards, not owners." Dad reached for his coffee mug, perched nearby on an endtable of chunky dark wood, its legs carved like storks. "And now I can rest more easily, seeing my daughter wearing her ring."

Zoe stared at the glittering stone. She had never really learned how to be the good Christian girl Bea said she should, and failed dismally at being a help instead of an anchor dragging Angelina down. Still, she'd reinvented herself in every new town after fleeing Hall City, and *especially* after Royal.

She could do it here, too. She *had* to.

So she coughed, clearing her throat. "Thank you." Utterly inadequate, but it was the proper response. "Thank you so much."

"It was always yours, little dancer." Dad lifted another present, this one bulky but light and wrapped in blue paper, and peered at the tag. "This one's from Amelia. It's probably some kitchen implement."

"She does that every year. Buys Dad a few things she really wants for the kitchen, but won't use the house cards for." Jack's dark eyes danced.

"I can't believe there's something she doesn't already have down there," Zoe had to admit, which made both of them laugh as if she'd delivered the world's most hilarious *bon mot*, and the ritual of unwrapping was suddenly a lot easier to bear.

PART THREE
THE HUNTERS

43
BELONGING

New Year's Eve arrived quietly, the entire household and a few guests gathering in the second-floor game room to watch the ball-drop on huge flatscreen. Lev, in a suit and tie for once, hopped up and down with excitement, Hermann kissed Amelia under the mistletoe, Dimitri and Bella hugged each other for a long while, motionless and wrapped in their own private world. Sarah gave Gessel a resounding peck on the cheek, after which he blushed scarlet and shook everyone's hand. McKenna, of course, attempted to kiss Jolie, but she turned at the last moment so he only managed a likewise cheek-peck.

Zoe tried not to laugh. Her father hugged her fiercely, then Jack did, his breath a warm spot against her hair. "Happy New Year," her brother murmured, and there was no reason for her to flush so hotly.

Mama always celebrated New Year's Eve with her medicine; later, Zoe had picked up every extra holiday shift possible. Actually celebrating was just as much work as wrangling drunks and cleaning up, though her outfit was a lot more comfortable now.

Trevor air-kissed Amelia on both cheeks, shook Hermann's hand, and lifted Allison's knuckles to press his lips politely against them. Everyone else shook hands except Allison, Jolie, and Zoe, who said nothing when she noticed, too relieved at not having to touch anyone but her father and brother.

So far, she liked their way of celebrating.

"Jackson," McKenna ambled in their direction, hands stuffed deep in his pockets and a tiny party horn tucked above his right ear, its silver tinsel end brushing his cheek. "What do you say? Take a train into the city and find something to do?"

Jolie sighed, sweeping at her bangs with her fingertips. "Why?" Her skirt swung, and her knee-night boots were beautifully polished. "There's going to be loads of drunks out there."

Zoe heartily concurred, but nobody asked her opinion so she tried to slip away a few steps. Her black, shin-length dress was simple, but tailored—another one of Janine's finds, sent in three different colors so she could have a choice. The post-Christmas flow of clothes showed no sign of abating, and neither did anything else. It was unnerving.

Maybe she could get out of the room without anyone noticing, change into pajamas, and congratulate herself on surviving another day without a huge fuckup.

Jack, however, didn't move, his arm settling securely over her shoulders. "Dunno." He looked down at her, for all the world as if not noticing her attempted escape. "You tired, Zo? We generally go for a jaunt after the ball drops, but if you want to stay home—"

"Christ, you're no fun anymore," McKenna grumbled, loosening his tie with a finger.

"Not everyone wants to go partying at the drop of a hat, Mac." Jolie folded her arms, silver earrings swaying.

"Hey." Bella appeared, her auburn hair mussed and three thin silver bracelets on her left wrist chiming sweetly. "Are you guys going into the city? I'll make Dima hunt up some fun."

"We're doing what now?" Dimitri's face rose over his twin's shoulder; he blinked owlishly and scratched at his cheek. "Oh, no. Not another joyride."

"*You're* not driving," his twin informed him. Her skirt was shorter than Jolie's, but her boots were very similar—more of Janine's work, obviously. Traleski seemed to dress *everyone*. "You don't even meet the speed limit."

"It's the boundary under perfect conditions, not a baseline." Dimitri heaved a theatrical sigh, but a sly smile lurked at the corners of his mouth and he cast around for his suit jacket, which lay tamely over the back of a leather recliner. "Fine, I'll go get our coats."

"Come along," Jolie said, fixing Zoe with a pleading gaze, her great dark eyes impossibly wide. "You can help Dima and me keep these miscreants out of trouble."

"As if Jack isn't the biggest delinquent here." McKenna grinned in Zoe's general direction, plucking the paper horn from behind his ear and balling it in his fist. "What do you say, Miss Rouje? Can't start the new year right without my wingman."

"Don't let him pressure you." Jack's smile had cooled a few fractions, and the strange sensitivity—the twinbond—between them turned hot-raspy for a moment. Which was puzzling. "If you're tired..."

"Say you'll come." Bella bounced onto her toes, eyes sparkling and her skirt moving prettily. "We'll go for midnight milkshakes. Oh, and see the sun rise over the Atlantic. Best thing in the world on New Year's Day. Please?"

"Damn, Bell." McKenna half-turned to regard her. "I've never heard you this enthusiastic."

"It's another *demie*," she informed him, haughtily. "You wouldn't understand."

"There's so much to catch up on." It would have been better if Jolie had shown any pettiness at all, but her smile was kindness itself. "There's a place in Brooklyn we'll have to get breakfast at once the sun's up. Best waffles in the five boroughs."

It didn't sound like sleep was part of the equation. Zoe looked up, met her brother's gaze. *I don't know.*

We can stay home. His mouth firmed, like he was ready to say it out loud.

But getting out into the city, maybe learning her way around, wouldn't be a bad idea. And Bella was right, it felt natural to communicate silently with her brother; it was almost easy as breathing, and she wondered how she'd lived without the contact.

She also wondered why she'd been so afraid of it. "I want to," Zoe found herself saying. "Unless you're—"

"She said yes!" McKenna whirled, grabbing Jolie's hand. The flicker of motion was too quick for a normal person; Zoe suppressed a guilty glance around to see if anyone had noticed. "Come on, Pindar. You get to navigate."

"Oh, Lord," Bella said, but she was grinning. "Let me tell Sarah, she might want to come too."

"Are *you* tired, though?" Now that Zoe had agreed, a thin worm of unease slipped through her stomach; she studied her brother. "If you are—"

Jack's grin widened and his arm tightened on her shoulders, a brief hug. "Too tired to get a jump on my first New Year's Day with my returned *demie,* showing her the sights? I don't think so. We might have to grab a bottle of something good to accompany the trip, though."

"Shouldn't we tell Dad?" Trying to call him 'Trevor' now felt strange. She was learning the ropes, but the most dangerous time in any new environment was when you relaxed, thinking you could predict.

"He knows." Jack tipped his chin, glancing across the room. Trevor copied the motion, smiling slightly, before turning back to Allison, who was speaking softly, her expression set and serious. "Let's get you a coat. And your gloves. You'll need a hat too. We'll ride with McKenna, I don't want him out of my sight in this mood."

Going along to keep his bestie out of trouble was much better than just because she wanted to know what it was like to be invited, for once. "There really are a lot of drunks on the road tonight," she hazarded. "Even here."

"Mac's not going to get into an accident, not in front of Jolie.

She'd never let him live it down." Jack now had her hand, drawing her along. "And you have me, so don't worry."

I'm trying not to. She also tried to look excited, or at least pleased. It wasn't too hard.

McKenna handled the big cream-colored SUV with ease, its snow tires biting sanded, salted roadway. Jolie, riding shotgun, kept cautioning him to slow down. *We have Rouje's little girl in the car, Mac.*

We do, the young man replied, *and we're gonna show her a good time. You're not driving, Pindar, find us some music.*

Which Jolie did—jazz standards, the Rat Pack and their imitators. McKenna grinned wide and white when she turned the volume up. Behind them another SUV, this one cloud-grey, carried Dimitri, Bella and Lev, bundled in winter coats and all just as excited as Mac. Jack's hand lay on the seat between him and Zoe; her fingers curled tentatively through his, and the glitter of his ring found an echo in hers.

He didn't seem to mind the contact, even if she'd rolled her eyes and refused gloves or a hat. In fact, he squeezed gently and gave a few encouraging smiles, his dark eyes burning in the backseat gloom.

It was a short ride to the train station, even in this weather, and the commuter line was running into the city every half-hour. The group closed around Zoe like a blanket, and it was her first time on a train since buses were so much cheaper. Nobody seemed to notice she had no idea what she was doing.

Besides, the trip was free, part of an initiative to cut down on holiday accidents.

Zoe found she liked train-motion, the deep thrum of iron wheels on singing rails, and peering out the windows at a snowy landscape undulating gently before clots of buildings pressed close. The structures crowded and swelled, and suddenly the city swallowed them, buildings turning their backs on a heaving iron beast.

Jolie and Bella conferred in hushed voices, planning the itinerary. The seats weren't too crowded just yet; McKenna leaned over the back of his, keeping up a running banter with Dimitri; Jack kept his arm over Zoe's shoulders and occasionally spoke softly, names for neighborhoods and stops she didn't know yet. She didn't even try to memorize them, too busy watching the scattering of other people in the car.

Other passengers glanced at their group, but didn't seem to notice anything amiss. A few were clearly inebriated, some obviously envious of Jolie's beauty, Bella's to match it, or Mac's handsomeness. Not a single eye snagged on Zoe herself. She was invisible, a camouflaged pretender.

It was both a relief and something of a letdown. It would've been nice to *really* belong. And yet...she had claws, just like them. They were all *Kith*.

The ring on her left hand said she was too, didn't it? Maybe she belonged a little more than she thought.

"Penny for your thoughts?" Jack's breath brushed her ear. A shiver spilled down her back; he'd fussed at her to wear a hat, but Bella didn't have one on either. Besides, she wasn't cold.

Now she knew why she could hear things normal people couldn't, why she could run faster, and why she'd been so *hungry* every winter as a child. A Kith never had to worry about the weather, *if* they ate enough to fuel their metabolism. Jack said in summer it was the same, but you didn't need quite so many calories.

"Just nervous." At least if Zoe murmured it softly enough the others weren't likely to hear. Or if they did, they pretended not to, with faultless politeness. It wasn't the kind of 'manners' she was used to, the fake smiles and whispered backstabbing at barbecues and church socials; it wasn't even Mama's insistence on proper behavior, knowing which fork to use, and passive-aggressive verbal jabs.

"Hm." It was one of Jack's not-quite-a-word noises, familiar by now, meaning he was listening even if he didn't have an answer. How had she endured without the steady warmth next to her, the sense of him burning like a candle on a dark night? "Next year will be easier."

If I'm still here. A reflexive thought, twitching through her every time a school friend or a coworker said anything implying permanence. Jack squeezed her hand as if he understood, and the train was slowing again. Bella bounced in her seat, pushing at Dimitri, who rose with steady grace. He offered his hand to his twin just like Jack always did for Zoe, and Bell reached for it without looking, her woolen swing coat whispering as she moved.

"It's our stop." Jack rose, drawing Zoe upright as well. Lev glided for the door, walking as if the train wasn't shudder-braking. All of them were so easy, so graceful, so finished.

Maybe one day she'd look like that too.

The platform was crowded, champagne-cold air freighted with exhaust and the exhalation of concrete warrens. Jolie swept up to Zoe and took her free hand, tugging irresistibly. "Come on. Bell?"

"Girl time," the other girl-twin laughingly informed Dimitri, a twinkle in her dark gaze. Zoe had to let go of Jack, Bella took that hand, and the three young women were a single unit preceded by Mac and Dimitri, trailed by Lev and Jack. Everyone seemed to know their places, a dance she hadn't practiced for.

She could only hold on, and try not to stagger.

44

COLD FURNACE

ANOTHER PAIR OF *USANAUGH*, A SHAMAN, LEV, AND MCKENNA WERE GOOD protection for a *demie*'s first trip into the city. And of course, with her *demi* was close by she was safe enough. He would've preferred to keep her right under his wing, but Bella and Jolie had their own ideas —and girls knew what others of their kind required.

Besides, this was a test like any other. Zoe needed her twin, certainly—but she also needed others of the Pride, a warm shield of Voice and laughter, claw and hide. Bell kept whispering confidentially to her fellow *demie*, earning more than one smile; Zoe's lips turned down before rising, as if she couldn't believe her own amusement. Jolie simply ambled on Zo's other side, but the shaman was alert, her head up and her dark gaze moving smoothly over terrain.

Down into the rushing echoed vault of the subway, a flash of blue as Zoe glanced nervously in his direction warming him clear through, and their next train came to a halt with a feedback screech. It stank, but the smell was so usual he ignored it.

The crowd thickened, more people arriving at each stop, virtually every skin in some state of inebriation and ready for more to ring in the New Year. The subway walls, alive with bright graffiti, flickered by. Someone in another car was playing *Auld Lang Syne* on a tuba, another skin at the end of this one was in a full Darth Vader costume, and cheap glittering party hats and favors were strewn everywhere. The entire city was giddy at the prospect of a fresh start.

Including him, maybe. When he looked back at his *demie*—still safely sandwiched, Jolie's arm around a slim vertical metal pillar providing anchor for the trio—she was staring past him, though Bell was still excitedly downloading at a high rate in her ear.

A furrow had appeared between his *demie*'s winged eyebrows, and her eyes darkened. He turned, following the line of her gaze.

Near the opposite door, a coltish young woman in a fake-fur coat hunched thin shoulders while the man looming next to her—his suit dark as night-hunting shark and a gold chain glowing at his thick neck—firmed his grip on her upper arm. The man was scowling, but it didn't look like a lover's spat. His knuckles were white, and more than once the skin girl winced as his grasp shifted or he muttered something too low for even Kith ears to discern with all the drowning, rattling subway noise.

The girl's dark eyes were heavy with eyeliner, teal shadow, mascara, and false lashes, making them cartoonishly huge. Her mouth, bright and lush, was peach-glossy, and her long mesh-clad legs drew no shortage of appreciative glances. Under the coat she wore the briefest of tops and a plaid skirt, and while the man's necklace held the mellow shine of real metal, hers was a cheap zircon on an alloy chain. Bright, even gaudy—but not worth much, like her oversized earrings.

Jack shot a quizzical look at his *demie*; she was still staring. Bella didn't appear to notice. But Jolie had noticed Zoe's unease as well, and the shaman's expression changed slightly, a hint of sadness invading her calm.

Jack's talent for analysis grabbed this new piece of data, slotted it into place. The entire pattern changed, as happened so often when he found fresh evidence, and he knew he had the truth. Much more about his beautiful, nervous twin made sense now. A young orphaned girl escaping a misbegotten's rage and hitting the streets

—of course she had been preyed upon. To top it off, she'd been raised skin, with all the taboos and hateful, misogynistic double standards that implied.

It was a goddamn wonder she wasn't *more* damaged. And that she was so willing to trust him; thank God for the gravitational pull between *usanaugh*. He would have to move carefully indeed before they could bond in that most natural and elemental of ways, if ever.

He could wait the rest of his life if he had to. Still, Jack hoped it wouldn't be necessary.

The male noticed their observation. If he had done anything other than hurriedly look away, Jack might have painted the inside of a subway car with skin guts and probably wasted months of careful work—his sweet *demie* was nowhere near ready to see that sort of thing. As it was, the stupid bastard eased up on the skin girl's arm, and Mac moved smoothly between the pair and the Pride girls, effectively insulating them. A faint flush rose Zoe's cheeks; her gaze dropped. She spent the rest of the ride nodding and half-listening to Bell, who waxed merrily onward, thrilled at having found a captive audience.

But the other *demie*'s tone held a faint note of anxiety, too. Bella wanted to be engaging, and suspected she wasn't doing her job. Jolie stirred, joining the conversation. The shaman's restful purr, tinged with Voice under the subway's screech-thrumming, eased Jack's *demie* a fraction, then a fraction more, and by the time they reached their first stop all was well again.

But Jack had a lot to think about.

Dawn found a group of Kith upon a deserted boardwalk, gulls crying and the red thunder of winter sun rising from a limitless stretch of icy grey ocean. Lev whooped and played tag with the waves, gracefully avoiding tidespray; Dimitri and Bella ambled hand in hand past tightly closed seasonal buildings quietly rotting into oblivion. Jolie and Mac peered through barred doors, the shaman talking quietly about history and architecture, Mac listening as he hardly ever did to anyone else.

Zoe stood stock-still, watching the water warily. Her lips slightly parted, her hair moving on a stiff freezing breeze, she didn't flinch as Jack leaned close, hoping his warmth was at least welcome. The twinbond was alive between them, a taut humming line, but he couldn't name her emotion—was it fear, or awe? Whatever she was feeling, it was immense, and though she was right next to him his *demie* was as remote as if she were still with Angelina, suffering stupid skin bullshit without help or protection.

Finally, he could stand it no longer. "Penny for your thoughts." His hands stung, shoved deep in his coat pockets. If he unclenched them even an iota, he might do something inadvisable. "Again."

Her tension snapped and a soft, wondering smile spread over her face. "It's beautiful. I've never seen it before."

"The sea?" Jack tried to remember facing the immensity of salt water for the first time. "Huh. Texas has the Gulf, though."

"Never really got there. Besides, it's all oil rigs and refineries, at least anyplace I could've afforded to visit." Zoe's smile didn't alter, and she was so breathlessly beautiful not just his hands but the rest of him ached too. "But I suppose I could come out here again, if I wanted to. Right?"

"We've got a beach house." He was ready to offer her the entire seaboard as well as the West Coast, if she wanted it—and everything in between. It would be a challenge worthy of his talents. "Whenever you like, just say the word."

"God." She shivered, either from the chill or from the prospect of something she didn't have to wrest from an uncaring world. "Is it that easy?"

"It hasn't been, for you. But now? Yeah, it's that simple." Agonizingly pleasant, to hover at the edge of her personal space, waiting for a signal inviting him in. The hunter in him knew patience, but also sensed inevitability.

Where else did she have to go?

"I like it here." A small, searching glance, testing him for irritation or displeasure. "It's peaceful."

"And cold." But Jack couldn't help smiling. "But we don't really feel it. Just one more benefit."

"Yeah. Now I don't, at least." She went back to studying the sea. Shamans often heard voices in its steady rustling, always felt the Moon's tides in their veins more acutely than a regular Kith. "Jack, if I asked you..."

You can ask me anything. He waited. When she said nothing else, he found himself stepping over that invisible border, impelled by sure instinctive knowledge. With him looming behind her, the wind could howl all it wanted, but his *demie* was safely braced.

She didn't move. He slipped his arms around his other half, her back settling against his chest. Jack could rest his chin on her tumbled black hair, so he did, and breathed her in. The closeness was a balm, soothing every inch of him. In the distance Lev's cry of joy as he evaded another crashing wave, staying dry as a bone, was lost in the vast sweep of sand and sky.

"Whatever you ask," Jack said softly, "it doesn't change this. Nothing will."

"What if I did something and got kicked out? Of the...of the family?"

Was that what she was afraid of? Even traitors and skate addicts weren't shunned, merely held until they could be rehabilitated—if ever, because skate ate a Kith from the inside and regaining trust after you had betrayed your own kind was a hard, ever-upward road. "It'll never happen. You're a *demie*, Zo."

A few more details fell into place. His twin was deathly afraid of her own self-protective instincts, and had probably fought off the attentions of more than one skin male.

Her claws were just as sharp as his, and she had no doubt used them before. Dad was mildly worried about her being blocked from the change; sooner or later it would take her despite any psychological barrier, but when that happened Jack had enough control for both of them.

He had been trained for seventeen long years, after all.

Demie couldn't become Broken, but a fear-maddened shaman could cause quite a bit of damage—and trigger rage in every Kith who scented their distress. It was the only time he would be a brake on her behavior instead of the other way 'round.

Jack decided a little more clarity was in order. "Nothing you did would be bad enough for that. Ever." He put all the certainty he could into the words. "Not now, and not before we found you."

"But what if Dad doesn't...feel the same way?" She no longer stared at the sea, her head turned to listen to him. "Just...hypothetically."

At least she saw Jack as refuge enough to ask the question, which was a victory all its own. "There is nothing you could do that would make him lose his temper, Zo. Believe me, I've tried." Trevor was far more stringent with his heir than he would ever be with his precious, irreplaceable daughter.

She might have spoken again, but Jolie and Mac reappeared, the edge of McKenna's charcoal trenchcoat fluttering. So did Dimitri and Bella, their linked hands swinging easily between them. Lev, sensing the Pride gathering to move again, left the ocean to find its own fun without a playmate. The young Kith loped up to them grinning, only a few specks of salt on his jacket, his honey-tinted brown hair a wild mass. All of them were windblown, glowing with sheer sunny good health.

"I could go for breakfast," Lev announced, skidding to a stop on sand-crusted sneakers.

"You had three milkshakes and most of my fries." Bell grinned, leaning into her twin's shelter. "Good thing you've got a Kith metabolism."

"You're hungry too." Dima rubbed at his dark head, cheerfully rumpling his own curls even further. "Jolie? Your call, pick a cuisine."

"Maybe Zoe should choose." Jolie's smile held no shadow of

sadness, now. The shaman's shoulder touched Mac's—and he looked very pleased at the event. "What's the best thing you can think of eating at the moment?"

"You said something about waffles?" Zoe's voice lifted uncertainly. "I mean, it's breakfast time."

"Excellent idea. Start the new year right." Mac bumped Jolie slightly, a lingering brush. "I know just the place, unless you want to do your usual."

"Is anywhere still open?" Zoe stiffened slightly when both Jolie and Dimitri began to laugh. "It's New Year's Day, after all."

"Honey," Bella said, "no city never sleeps, and this one less than most. Clichés are like that, they always have a truth at the bottom. Come on, let's go."

Which meant Jack had to loosen his arms, setting his *demie* temporarily free. But he was rewarded almost immediately, because she reached for his hand as naturally as Bella for Dimitri's. Their fingers interlaced and the bond thrummed between them, a much hotter, brighter sun than the one hanging a handspan above a grey horizon.

45
OBSERVE, ANTICIPATE

She knew things would change as soon as the holidays were over; Zoe was even looking forward to the inevitable shift.

Well, almost.

Trevor still worked in his home office, but he often didn't show up for lunch and sometimes missed dinner. A steady stream of visitors began the day after New Year's as well. The front door was always opening and closing, and many of the voices—and scents—were washed out and pale.

Skins. Not Kith.

Jack also spent more time in his own office, and there was only so much aimless surfing she could handle on the computer on 'her' desk while he concentrated on whatever he was doing. She couldn't look up anything she really wanted to know on that sleek silver machine; she did that at night on her phone, huddled under the covers like she was reading with a flashlight and afraid of Mama catching her. It was harder and harder to close her door while Jack stood in the hall each night, but she had no idea what else she could do.

A week after Dad and Jack went formally back to work, Allison appeared on a clear cold midmorning, tapping at the door of Jack's office. "Zoe? Can I borrow you for a bit?" A blue cashmere sweater clung to her curves and her jeans were butter-soft, obviously designer but just as obviously old favorites. Her boots were innocent of any snow or melt, though their heavy soles could have handled a hike in the woods.

Uh-oh. Zoe closed her browser windows in a hurry and almost leapt upright, tugging at the hem of her black V-neck sweater. The chair's wheels squeaked, a little forlorn sound. Jack glanced up, his dark eyes narrowed, and began to rise as well.

He was back in suits, and was teaching her how to knot his tie in the mornings. *One more thing a* demie *does for her loving brother*, he said, lightly, and why did that make her blush?

"Just Zoe," Allison said, pleasantly. Her hair was down, long and glossy-loose, the pale streak at her temple glowing. "It's shaman-stuff."

Shaman. She'd looked the word up, but any definition online didn't seem to really apply. There was nothing real or true about the Kith anywhere, just old superstitions and horror movies. Neither seemed very reliable sources. Jack answered direct questions, sure, but she hardly knew where to start.

Or what was safe to ask.

"Nevertheless." Jack looked at Zoe, and she could, to her ridiculously intense relief, decipher his expression with that silent, secret inner sense. He was perfectly willing to drop what he was doing and go along, if he had to.

If she was scared.

Sooner or later she was going to have to do this sort of thing alone, though. They all expected it. "It's all right." Zoe tried to sound sure. This was probably like a job interview, or something. All she had to do was figure out what the woman—the *shaman*—wanted. "I'll be fine."

"You absolutely will. Jolie's downstairs as well." Allison's smile held no bright, false note; her every word had a soft soothing purr behind its syllables. "We thought you'd be more comfortable that way, and it's good for her own training."

"That means Mac'll be by this afternoon." Jack settled back in his chair, but he was still watching her. "Are you sure, Zo?"

Are you kidding? Not by a country mile. But she had to start doing what they expected, earning her place. "I am." At least she wasn't really underdressed for the occasion, since Allison was in jeans too.

It was nice to have decent clothes, but the stress of figuring out how to dress for each goddamn day was something else.

"I'll be right here. And there's the bond." Jack said it like there wasn't someone standing in the door, as if they were alone. "If you need me, all you have to do is think about it, all right?"

"That's absolutely right." Allison nodded, that slight, secret smile never altering. "He'll know if you're too anxious, Zoe. It's only natural."

I want to be that calm one day. It seemed magical—but of course, you could put up a good front and be boiling underneath.

Mama had done it all the time. So did Bea. Royal pretty much boiled openly, but that was different. The best policy was simply to never let anything show, and she had a great deal of practice. It was just...safer, but she was having increasing trouble keeping even the smallest shift in her mood from Jack.

He always knew, even if he didn't say anything.

"All right." She tried a smile, and Jack's in return was immediate. But he was tense.

Just like her.

"You don't have to be nervous." Allison didn't make her trot down the hall, though she probably knew the house as well as anyone living here. Instead, the shaman ambled, matching her boot-clad strides to Zoe's whispering along in black ballet flats. "I suppose Jack's told you about the Sorcerer's Gene?"

Wow, diving right in. Okay. "He says it's rare. That I can do things other...other Kith can't."

"That's all he said? Usually he's better at giving a *précis* than that."

Christ, now Zoe was giving a report without enough time to study. It figured. "He said it's instinctive. He needs data to work, but a shaman can do things just by feeling." *Intuition,* Jack called it. Of course she knew normal people couldn't follow their nose to a new job like she could, but her brother seemed to consider Zo's occasional witchery-tricks both completely natural and pretty special at the same time.

"Elegantly put." At least Allison sounded pleased now. She pushed her sweater-sleeves up, a silver bracelet glimmering on her left wrist. "I'm sure you have a thousand questions, though."

Not any I can ask. "It's confusing."

"Well, you were raised outside. I'll bet your mother used a great deal of religiosity, probably coupled with nearly random punishment and affection cycles." There was no judgment in the shaman's words, just quiet logic. "You're used to observing and anticipating to keep yourself as safe as possible, and not asking anything unless you're certain it's a safe subject."

"I guess." It was uncomfortably akin to being pinned under a microscope, like the harshly lit science slides in middle school. "Mama was Catholic until right before she met Pastor Bea." None of these people seemed to church, which was a relief even if it meant Zo had little idea where the closest charities, shelters, and soup kitchens were.

Even if you had to listen to a thundering sermon while you ate, free food had a powerful allure.

"Bea?" Allison's puzzlement was mild, and temporary. "Oh, McFisk. The misbegotten."

That's right. Jack had told her Bea's real name. *Beaton* was just another lie from the greasy jerk, but no wonder he'd changed it. She would have too if she'd been named *Leroy.* "Misbegotten?"

"Yes." Allison dropped back again, walking at Zoe's left shoulder as they descended. The staircase echoed their footsteps, its banister polished with beeswax just that morning and now softly fragrant. "That's the term for a Kith born...missing something. They're sort of caught halfway between us and the vast mass of *them*. Ordinaries."

"Skins." Shivers raced down Zoe's back, and she was cold. Was she a misbegotten? It would explain a lot. "Right?"

"Yes. You probably suspected McFisk wasn't quite normal." Allison sighed, trailing her fingertips along the banister. A stray draft played with the ends of her hair; it was like she carried her own personal breeze. "I can't imagine how baffled you must have been. And before you start worrying, no, *usanaugh* can't be misbegotten."

"That's good." Zoe tried not to hunch; *don't slouch*, Mama always said. A reddish glitter in her peripheral vision was the princess ring on her left hand, a comforting weight. The tennis bracelet was in a small, exquisitely carved cedar jewelry box on the white-painted vanity.

She was really thinking of the blue suite as 'hers' now. So far, she'd been able to stay here, so maybe midnight wishes on Christmas Eve did come true. Zoe turned to her right, the hall to the smaller study on the first floor now familiar instead of foreign territory.

If Bea was Kith too—misbegotten, halfway—what exactly did that *mean*? She had to ask Jack. He'd explain without making her feel stupid; he seemed to have a gift for it.

"It is." Allison's footsteps stopped because Zoe had halted at the dark-varnished door to the study. "And you knew exactly where we were headed, though I only said *downstairs*, nothing else."

It could be logic. Process of elimination. But there were plenty of other rooms, so maybe there was something to this shaman-stuff. Zoe folded her arms. "Mama called it witchery. Deviltry. Said it was Satanic."

"Sounds like she was very religious indeed." Allison's calm did not waver, but there was a tinge of sadness instead of amusement to it, the faintest breath of a different perfume. "She tried to make you fear what you are. It will take time to undo the damage."

"Do you..." Zoe glanced at the study door. It was closed, but if Jolie was in there she could probably hear everything anyway. "You really think something like that can be undone?"

"We're shamans; very little is impossible. And in any case, there's Jack. As long as you have your twin, you'll be all right." Now Allison smiled, fine lines radiating from the corners of her dark eyes. Even the grey-haired Kith looked impossibly vital, almost ageless at a certain point. "Shall we go in? Today you're going to help Jolie learn a few things."

She's going to learn? Not me? It was a relief, if Allison really meant it. The shaman was right about one thing, at least—Zo liked to keep her eyes open and figure things out without having to risk angering or bothering anyone. "Okay."

"You're my apprentice now too, you know." The older woman's voice was soft and pleasant, no hurtful edges. She acted like they had all the time in the world, but then again, everyone probably waited for *her* and not the other way 'round. "It's a high honor to train a *demie*. Training another shaman is also a very close bond. Almost parental."

Huh. "Does that mean you're going to marry Tr—ah, Dad?" Zoe hadn't missed her father's attentions in this direction—he was always getting Allison a drink, standing next to her, conferring with her. If Zo had to have a stepmother, she didn't think this woman would be an evil one.

"Marry him?" The shaman's laugh was like warm velvet. "He should be so lucky. Think of it this way instead: I'm teaching you to drive a car. If you run over someone because I haven't instructed you properly, it's at least partly my fault, and I will bear the responsibility along with you. Does that answer your question?"

I'm not sure. But she nodded, so Allison reached past, a breath of her cedar-edged perfume tickling Zoe's nose, and swept the study door open.

Jolie was by the fireplace, a heavy leatherbound book open in her hands. "*There* you are." She closed the volume with a snap, and she was in jeans as well, with a a red scoopneck blouse and dangling silverleaf earrings. The bright color suited her, from her velvety skin to huge dark eyes. "Welcome to the salt mines, Zo. This is gonna be fun."

Fun? Okay. Zoe pasted on a smile, glanced at the windows—it was a bright, sun-freezing day, the snow was blinding—and decided she'd learn everything they had to teach her, even if it was painful.

She'd learned a lot from Mama, and Bea, and even from Royal. If the Kith decided to throw her out, well...she'd survived once.

She could do it again. With or without this house, these clothes, or any of the luxuries the Kith took for granted.

And possibly, conceivably, maybe even without her brother.

46
FIRST LESSONS

N<small>ORMALLY SHAMANS NEVER LET ANYONE WITHOUT THE</small> G<small>ENE SEE THEIR</small> training; still, a *demi* couldn't be kept from his twin. Jack closed the study door softly, knowing Allison was well aware of his presence.

The three women were on a priceless, faded Persian rug before the gas insert—one of the newer remodels in the manor, Amelia was still considering changing over some of the other fireplaces. Sitting cross-legged, shining hair unbound and wearing almost identical expressions of concentration, the trio was a textbook illustration of the Kith's most sensitive and treasured talent.

A bar of golden winter sunlight, given strength and force by reflecting off snow, touched Zoe's denim-clad knee and brought out blue highlights in her curls. Her blue eyes burned softly, and she was utterly focused on Jolie. The pale streak at Allison's temple glowed too, and Jolie's earrings glittered fiercely.

"That's right." The elder shaman leaned forward, her manicured fingertips almost touching Jolie's, claws well retracted. Voice throbbed around the three of them in waves. "Perfect. Now, Zoe, I'd like you to disturb her again, just as we practiced."

Jolie had the deepest purr, and Allison's was freighted with uncanny power. But Zoe's lighter thrumming bathed Jack with skin-

tingling intensity as he folded his arms, leaning against the door to
watch his *demie* finish her first shaman lesson.

Zoe's gaze sharpened. Her pupils swelled, and a bright pinprick
of blue showed in each black well before she blinked, frowning a
little. "I don't want to hurt her." The words rang with Voice—but
lightly. She had a delicate touch, his twin.

Orbiting her at just the right distance was a pleasurable agony
he'd take, any day and anyplace, over the torment of her absence.
But, by Christ, he was beginning to think maybe he shouldn't be so
controlled.

"You won't," Jolie said softly, swaying a little. "It's just a little
shove."

Allison radiated deep, warm confidence, a shaman's characteristic peace. She said no more, merely waited.

Zoe bit her lower lip. She didn't look at him, but the twinbond
was suddenly alive, a stinging welter of confused impressions. She
looked calm, holding it together admirably, and even managed to
mute the connection most of the time—an entirely subconscious
effort, naturally. But the careful mask had slipped, and now he
received the full unfiltered jolt of his sweet *demie*'s feelings.

Bingo. His shoulders pressed into the door as his knees threatened to give. Heavy wood gave no betraying squeak; the fireplace
hissed softly. Elsewhere in the house was a formless mutter of voices
and footsteps, Dad's business running from the home office instead
of the Rouje building in Manhattan and Amelia putting the security
teams through their paces while the princess was distracted by Allison, but a heavy blanket of quiet enveloped this room.

Zoe tensed. He could almost, *almost* sense the unphysical shift of
her attention. Not even a patterner could predict a shaman, but he
had an edge with this particular one.

Or he would, eventually, when the bond settled.

Jolie's chin snapped aside. She inhaled sharply, swaying. The
contact between her and Allison broke with a soft unsound, the snap
of glass under several layers of cloth.

His *demie*'s hand flew to her mouth. She looked, of all things, horrified.

"Very good." Allison sounded pleased and thoughtful, nothing more. If the depth of Zoe's gift surprised her, it didn't show. "Jo?"

"A righteous hit." Jolie shook her head sharply. Her cheek flushed, a high angry beacon. "Damn, girl."

"I'm sorry," Zoe whispered into her palm. Her pupils shrank, losing the spark of shamanlight, and her baby blues were dark and wounded now. "Oh, God, I'm so sorry."

How had she survived out in the cold world, robbed of her own kind's comfort, surrounded by skins? Jack exhaled softly, willing her to stay calm, to look at him.

It worked. Her chin rose slowly, and so did her gaze, finding him like a magnetized needle pointed north.

It's all right, Jack whispered into the taut-humming twinbond. *I'm here.*

"Watch." Allison extended her hand again; Jolie presented her swelling cheek. Voice crested in a deep rumble, the elder shaman's fingers tensed...and the incipient bruise disappeared, retreating in fast-forward even more swiftly than a Kith's usual healing. "See? Not impossible, Zoe."

"Not even close," Jolie agreed. "Now, if you can just smack McKenna like that the next time he gets excited..."

"That's *your* job, and you need the practice." Laughter ran under Allison's words; she interlaced her fingers and stretched, catlike. "Besides, she's got enough to do keeping her *demi* on the straight and narrow. That's enough for today, ladies. Good work."

"Already?" Zoe pulled up her knees, hugging them, and though she did not look in his direction now, she was very aware of his presence.

Good. His beast shifted restlessly, sensing her distress and looking for its source.

"You've learned more than you thought." Jolie uncoiled, rising gracefully and offering her hand to the Pride's newest shaman.

"You'll crash early and sleep hard tonight. Hullo, Jack. How are you?"

"Tolerable well, Pindar." He watched Zoe accept the older girl's help, then it was Allison's turn to be lifted upright. "Just came to collect Zo for lunch with Dad."

"I'm really sorry." Zoe watched Jolie's expression closely, an anxious line between her eyebrows. Her sweater had slipped slightly, the V-neck showing delicate collarbones and a small slice of her shoulder. "I didn't mean to hurt you."

"Chill. You did exactly what you were supposed to." Pindar grinned and touched the *demie*'s arm, smoothing her sleeve. It was a rare, fleeting contact; shamans were mostly too sensitive to be handled. "And look, it's not hurting at all. Everything's copacetic."

Zoe didn't look like she believed it, but she accepted their good-byes with faultless politeness.

"See you tomorrow," Allison said on her way out the door, and that was that. She'd accepted Jack's *demie* as an apprentice instead of suggesting another shaman to train her, which wasn't unexpected but still a weight off Jack's mind.

It meant not only that his *demie* was powerful, but that Allison also agreed she was unbroken. Perhaps a little shy and strange after being raised by skins, but essentially whole.

A few moments later, farewells done, he was alone with his twin. She still stood by the fire, her hands hanging loose and empty, watching the doorway as if she suspected they were going to return.

"So." He longed to approach, to take her shoulders, press a kiss on her forehead. "How was your first shaman lesson? Looks like you did great."

"How can you tell?" Zoe now regarded him steadily, still wearing that worried line on her forehead. Every graceful line of her quivered with readiness.

Something like this might have made her retreat at high speed and possibly even bolt from the house in the first few weeks after her arrival. Now she was still uncertain, but far more willing.

"Allison only apprentices the best, and Dad wouldn't trust anyone else with your training. It's an honor, both for you and for her." Jack loosened his tie a fraction with a casual, hooked finger, glancing at the sideboard on the west wall. "You want a drink?"

Her eyes widened, sweetly shocked. "Before lunch?"

"Best time for it." *Nice and easy, Jack.* How far would her willingness extend? "I thought of going into town this afternoon, if you're not too tired."

His *demie* considered the prospect, still vibrating unsteadily. Her Voice had fled, but soon she'd start using it more. It was catching, when you hung around other Kith. "You can just go on your own, you know."

"Mh." He cocked his head, examining each fleeting expression crossing her pretty face. Underlaid by the twinbond, every emotion was written in neon, glowing softly. He was getting a lot better at reading that language. "Aren't you afraid I'll get into trouble?"

He was rewarded by her tension easing and a slight, secretive smile. Zoe brushed at her hair, pushing the silken mass back over her shoulder. "You did fine before I got here."

"No. I didn't." He ended up tucking his hands in his trouser pockets, since he couldn't seem to figure out what to do with them otherwise. "Want to tell me what's bothering you?"

"Allison said Pastor Beaton's misbegotten. That he's Kith." It spilled out in a breathless rush, and just after she finished Zoe looked very much like she wanted to cover her mouth again, jamming the words back in. Her chin lifted slightly, though, and her bright gaze was almost a challenge, dominance ready to rise if it met resistance.

An encouraging sign. "We didn't know until Sondra—Amerlane's oldest daughter, you met her at Christmas—went there to investigate. McFisk was related to Fantome; that's the Kith leader in that part of the country. A misbegotten shouldn't have access to a *demie*, much less a developing shaman." Jack paused. *Careful now.* "We'll probably take a good chunk of their holdings and require some kind of reparations as well. That's up to you."

Whatever she'd expected, it probably wasn't a calm, reasonable explanation. "To me?"

"Yeah. You get to decide, Zo. Always." *Then I'll make it happen.* "It's a pretty cut and dried case. McFisk should have alerted his pack-leader that there was a lone Kith on his territory, especially a young one. He didn't, or he did and Fantome didn't immediately notify Dad. There are consequences for that."

His twin stared at him for a long moment, and her undivided attention was one of the most pleasurable sensations in the world.

Then she turned her back on him, her hair moving in a heavy silken wave, and her shoulders came up. The sunlight had moved too and now caressed her hip, longingly attempted to touch her curls again.

Jack could relate. He paced silently across the room, avoiding the two leather couches and a comfortable, much-scarred ottoman. Her tension spiked, and the flood of emotion echoing down the link held a much darker undercurrent.

He didn't stop. She had to learn he wasn't going to disappear, and—useless to deny it—he wanted, *needed* to touch her. Once again she didn't withdraw, or make a polite excuse. She simply stood, trembling and staring at the fireplace, as his arms closed around her.

Better. "I'd've liked to kill both of them," he said softly, into her hair. So close to its other half, his beast retreated into quiescence. "Did you know that? To tear their guts out in front of you, *demie*, so you know nobody can ever hurt you again."

"I thought I had," she whispered. Tremors ran through her in waves; between shaman training and this, she was having a helluva day. On the other hand, she was clearly ready to hear his explanation, and—hallelujah—to offer one of her own. "Killed him, I mean. After Mama...after her funeral, he took me into the church cellar. He... well, after a while he went away, and I had to get out of the handcuffs. So I did, and...there was fire, I don't know if I did that. I knew he was coming back, though, and I had to escape. He opened the door and I..." Her right hand lifted, trembling like a leaf.

Be very careful, Jack. His own rage, sharply leashed, wouldn't help her now. "Brave girl." He mouthed the words, felt them hit home.

Her claws slid free with a slight crackling sound as bones shifted. Sharp and delicate, wickedly pointed, her fingers curled. The sunlight caressed her hand, glinted on razor edges. "It was the first time I hurt someone."

So there was more than once. "Sounds like self-defense to me." He couldn't help himself; Jack kissed her temple, his arms tightening. "I should have been there to keep you safe."

"I thought I'd killed him until you..."

Until I showed up, and told you he was still alive. Another piece fell into place. "You fired the church and clawed him, and you ran. Smart move."

She sagged against him then, so suddenly and completely he almost thought she'd passed out. But the relief singing through her was a tsunami, a dark reward for all his patience. Finally, *finally* she'd cracked, and he was right here to catch the pieces.

Perfect. "Very smart," he repeated. "You stayed under the radar, moving from place to place, and you survived. You're amazing, you know that?"

"That's not even the worst." The words were raw. "What if Bea— if McFisk tells them what I did?"

Is that what worries you? "He can't."

"How do you—"

"He's dead, Zo." There was no good time to tell her, but at least he could remove this worry. "That's why it's taking Sondra so long to negotiate. Fantome's cleaning up, because he can't admit he broke the codes by allowing a misbegotten to touch a *demie.*"

"Wait." She stiffened and might have pulled away, but Jack's arms turned to iron and she stopped, freezing like a rabbit. "Bea's *dead?*"

"Yep. Prison hit, probably." Was that too much detail? Jack

rubbed his chin against her hair, an absent-minded caress. If she was going to snap at least he had a good grip on her.

"When?" The twinbond was open and raw, and the sensations pouring through were both unsettling and comforting. Jack could bathe in what she was feeling, could bask in the closeness. Each wave of emotion locked them more closely together, and eventually she wouldn't be able to keep him out even if she tried.

"Just before Christmas." He wanted to nuzzle at her ear, tell her again in a whisper what he would do to anyone who had ever hurt her. "Dad and I both thought you didn't need the stress, so we didn't mention it."

"And is there anything else you *haven't mentioned?*" She surged against his grasp again, but Jack held her still. If she struggled much more his beast would answer hers in the only way it knew how.

And she wasn't ready for that. At all.

Steady, Jack. Be the good guy. "Maybe. But only to protect you, Zo-baby. Calm down."

She stopped trying to pull away, and Jack held her close. They fit together like puzzle pieces, edges aligned, a seamless whole. The fire hissed, the sideboard across the study rattled slightly, and a thin tracery of sweat dampened his lower back. His jaw ached, the change running inside his bones. His beast sensed her vulnerability, and wanted to savage whatever was unnerving his *demie* so badly.

"Good," he murmured. "Go ahead and be mad at me, I'll hold you until it's over." His control narrowed to a thread, but even that was strangely soothing. The worst that could happen was high emotion triggering the change, maybe her first one, and he could wrestle her until it receded.

The thought even held a certain charm, though it might break some furniture.

A thin cloud passed over the sun, robbing snowdrifts of their hurtful glare. His *demie* relaxed all at once, a sudden unloosing, and her ragged breathing rose and fell in tandem with his. "God," she said, softly. "*God.*"

Don't need him when I've got you, sweetheart. "The misbegotten was dead the moment he touched you, Zo. If it hadn't happened this way we would've taken care of it another. Do you think I'd let anyone who hurt you get away with it?"

"What if..." She shuddered, and he tensed, pressing her even harder into his safety. "What if I killed someone else? Or hurt them really badly?"

"I don't care if you left a trail of bodies from Hall City to Marquette. All I care about is that you're here now." How much simpler could it get? "And if anyone fucks with you, anyone *at all*, you won't have to lift a finger. I'll take them apart." *Hard.*

Zoe twitched, and he was so close to the edge he almost crushed her against him again. Control won out, just barely, and she softened.

"You can't..." Isolated from skins and their weird taboos, her reflexive disbelief would abate in time. But for right now, she still resisted.

It didn't matter.

"Of course I can." *Now do me a favor and relax, or Dad's going to be on his own for lunch.* "And I'll tell you as many times as it takes. Are you hungry?"

"I...let go, okay? I'm fine, I'm not going to claw you." Zoe wriggled again, and this time he had to reluctantly release her. She stepped away—but not far, and she turned on her heel, tugging at her sweater hem, smoothing her sleeves, and finally running her fingers through her hair, patting the curls down.

He wanted to help, but had to be content with watching. Still, that was a pleasure, too.

"Okay." Finally, her gaze rose to his again, shuttered and recalcitrant, all her walls back up. "That was...I'm sorry, it's just a shock. I didn't mean to—"

"You don't have to apologize." And certainly not over anything like this. "Not to me."

"I should." A faint note of belligerence, a kitten showing her teeth. She was testing his boundaries, both unnerved by the news and feeling the effects of Allison's lesson. "What if I want to?"

"That's different." He tried an imitation of Mac's easy grin, throttling the unsteady, explosive feeling triggered by her panicked withdrawal from the bond. "Now give your *demi* a break and let's go to lunch, hm? Dad'll want to hear about how your first shaman session went."

"Easier than I expected." Zoe crossed her arms, a defensive retreat he could allow, for now. "But...Jack, he's really dead?"

"As a doornail, Zo-baby." *Tell me who else hurt you, and they'll end up the same way.* "And for the record, we weren't hiding it, we were just waiting for you to ask. Figured you would in your own time."

"What a relief." Amazingly, she laughed—a short, bitter little burst of merriment, and her right hand moved as if she wanted to cover her mouth again to keep the sound from escaping. "God, that's a horrible thing to say. But it is. He's really gone."

"He is. And you're safe." Christ, he didn't know what to do—offer his arm, grab her again and trap her in a hug, attempt something, anything to ease that look from her face.

"Except for when guys in body armor invade at midnight." Another challenge as she eyed him; his *demie* was searching for a way to cover that gorgeous vulnerability. She'd learned to act careless and hard out among the skins, but it was just that—an act.

"They're only skins." He shrugged. "Don't worry, okay? I'm the analyst, worry's my job."

It must have been the right thing to say, because she relaxed again, another abrupt turn in her quicksilver moods. "What's a shaman's job?"

"Holding my leash and smoothing my hackles, naturally." He was rewarded by a tremulous smile, and the fact that his *demie* was right in front of him, a living, breathing mystery he could spend the rest of his life following the contours of, made up for every moment he'd spent without its comfort. "As well as taking Dad's mind off whatever disaster's currently occurring. Shall we?"

A somber nod, and she let him lead her across the study, opening the door as a gentleman always should for a lady. She even took his hand in the hallway, warm skin-contact tightening the link until his eyes prickled and he had to take a surreptitious deep breath.

She still had no idea what she meant to him, or to the Pride. But she was learning.

Better late than never.

47
FOREIGN OBJECT

HE'D MENTIONED GOING INTO TOWN, BUT THE WEATHER WAS TURNING, thick dark clouds streaming from the north. They ended up in the attic after lunch, Jack reclining on the unrolled futon while Zoe sat cross-legged, paging through old magazines and trying to absorb the news while his companionable quiet both soothed and daunted her.

By dinnertime it was snowing again. Trevor was still in his office so they ate at the breakfast bar, Amelia smiling at Jack's jokes and Lev cheerfully announcing that he'd been allowed to shape the pasta that very afternoon, cranking dough through a silver appliance that looked like an ancient torture device.

It would hit her at different times. Glancing at her father during lunch, turning a page, breathing in attic dust, listening to one of Jack's explanations, or swirling linguine onto her fork, the thought recurred. She would realize *Bea's dead, but I didn't do it*, and the relief would jolt all her innards, almost forcing a half-crazed giggle up her throat.

Nobody seemed to notice. Of course, Jack kept them busy, smoothly stepping into the conversation whenever she didn't want to talk. She'd become so used to him performing that little service; what would she do when he decided he didn't want to anymore?

Saying *goodnight* and closing the blue suite's door was even more difficult, because she didn't want him to leave. Her sigh of relief, while deep, was also packed with fresh anxiety.

Zoe Rouje wasn't a devil's whore, or a bad daughter. She was Kith, she was a *shaman*, and the weird things were perfectly natural among them. That was outlandish enough, but Jack also knew what Bea had done, and what she'd done to *him*.

The relief that she hadn't killed him or Royal had a sharper edge now. What if she told Jack about Roy? The prospect was alternately terrifying and deeply intriguing.

How would her brother—or Dad, for that matter—take the news about her working that way, though? First the dancing, then the dates, then...God.

The blue suite was a familiar friend now, though. She could turn off the lights and avoid the furniture from memory instead of with a Kith's night vision. Everything in the bathroom was right where she'd put it, and the faint scent of Amelia or Sarah only meant they'd dropped something off or cleaned.

Zoe scrubbed the toilet herself twice weekly though, and tried to keep things as neat as possible.

Her phone was on the nightstand—she was going to have to start carrying it around, since Bella and Jolie were both texting her and she'd been invited into a few group chats, all Kith. There was a text from Allison, too, inquiring how she felt after the day's lesson, and it was nice to go through the messages and answer them one by one. She'd agonized over whether or not to include emojis until she saw Dimitri's messages; he seemed to text little else.

Bell, of course, texted in full sentences and proper punctuation. Jolie rarely bothered with either, and Mac, in all the group chats, confined himself to short one-word answers whenever possible. Sort of like Jack, who sounded brusque and cold in chat the way he rarely did in person.

Even their father sent a text or two, mostly inconsequential pleasantries that probably meant *you kids and your newfangled toys.*

Kith using smartphones. It boggled the mind.

She brushed her teeth while she checked email—mostly empty, since nobody who knew her before probably ever thought about her now. It would be nice to find Jenny Scarsdale online, maybe, and tell her...what? *I found my real dad, and he's rich. Wanna come over for a slumber party?*

There was a fresh message on one of her very old accounts, one she barely remembered the password to. Probably spam, but she clicked to check anyway, and her hand went numb. The toothbrush fell into the sink, bouncing with a tiny distressed clatter.

AMBER ITS ROY
ANSER ME

Her heart leapt into her throat, pounding so hard she almost dropped the phone too. Flinging it across the room like a suddenly discovered venomous snake wasn't an option, but god*damn* she considered the notion.

There was a roaring in her ears. Her wrists hurt; her claws were poking free, fingernails lengthening to sharp amber points. Her jaw ached too, and a hard painful shiver went down her back, her skin prickling with tiny sharp ant-feet.

A sudden, weightless jolt, and Zoe was dimly aware Jack could feel her fear. His attention sharpened—he was only a short distance away, and she *felt* him striding out of his suite, heading for her door.

She somehow got there before he could, clutching her phone so hard aluminum and plastic squeaked, and she had to force her fingers to uncurl. The effort to retract her claws brought out a fine film of sweat on her forehead, dampness gathering in the hollows of her underarms and behind her knees. Her heart galloped, each beat a heavy hammerstroke felt in her wrists, her throat, her knees.

"Zoe?" Jack tapped at her suite's door, the worry in his tone clear through heavy wood. "You okay?"

No. I'm not. "Fine." The word quivered; she planted her hip against the door and took a deep breath. Allison talked about how important control was, how a shaman could affect the Kith around them. "It's just been a long day."

A ticking, pregnant pause. She felt him weighing whether or not he could push, the twinbond a blanket wrapping around her, heavy warmth that would have been comforting under other circumstances.

Any other circumstances.

Please don't, she pleaded silently. *Please just let me deal with this. Please.*

"You're upset." Very careful, very calm, his tone filtered through the door. "Can I come in?"

Oh, God. I can't take any more, not after today. "I'm just processing, okay? I need some rest. Please, Jack." She was going to break if this bullshit kept up; the strain of waiting for the axe to fall was terrible, and she had only herself to blame.

A slight creak from outside as he shifted his weight. "Okay," he said finally, and the edge of vibration to the word told her he wasn't happy about it. They could all produce that strange, sonorous purr; she didn't know how to turn hers on or off. "Just...it's all right, Zo. I promise."

It's not. She could hope and believe during daylight, but it was night now. The wind was rising, snow-laden eddies mouthing the edges of this beautiful house, and she was a foreign object in its magnificence even if she was a Kith shaman.

She would always be a stranger among their easy camaraderie. The difference was inside, where all their lessons and comfort couldn't reach.

Her twin finally went back to his own room, step by slow, unwilling step. Zoe scrubbed at her mouth with the back of her hand, mint toothpaste warring uneasily with bile.

It was just an email. She didn't have to respond. There was no good reason Royal Petterson would be trying to contact her now. And it was just like the asshole, too. He couldn't even spell.

Answer me, as if she was still one of his girls. One of his *bitches*.

How had he explained the deep slices down his face and chest, and all the blood? Her disappearance right afterward must've made some of the other girls think about things, and while he was in the hospital was a good time for them to hightail it too. Even those who only moved to another protector hopefully got a bit of breathing room before they had to start working again.

She hoped they'd stripped Roy's apartment clean before they left, and the club too. He'd had cash hidden everywhere in his rooms. Zoe had left every cent, solely concerned with escape, but now she hoped with a deep and abiding vengeance nobody else had been that restrained.

Zoe rescued her toothbrush and set about getting ready for bed. Then, her face tingling from a slap of cold water and hastily applied moisturizer, she settled in the window seat to think about things. The darkness outside could hide her, but where would she go? And she could feel Jack in his own rooms, pacing and worrying.

Her phone rested by her sock feet, its blank face giving no indication of what lurked inside. Why the fuck was Roy trying to contact her *now*?

Zoe's eyes half-lidded. *It's all right.* She could at least send a tentative tendril of soothing down the invisible twinbond.

Jack's response was instant, a flood of comfort. He didn't know why she was upset, probably thinking it was over Bea. Funny how no matter how bad her life got, a fresh problem could rear its ugly head and make everything else seem inconsequential.

Yeah, it's hilarious. A real riot. At least she could still think privately, though the twinbond kept growing. She could imagine it shifting inside her ribcage, invading her blood.

She had a good grip on herself now, though, as Mama would say. Zoe focused on her breathing, in and out, deep quiet swells—Allison had complimented her on that, Zoe accidentally stumbling on controlling her lungs as a coping method pretty early in life.

It's all right, she repeated, dropping the communication into the bond's deep, echoing well. D*on't worry so much. Just relax.*

He still wanted to be near her, but Zoe just kept breathing, sending whatever calm she could find into that peculiar inward space. Eventually the sense of motion faded—he was no longer pacing. Maybe he was settling for the night.

Now she could think.

She could just ignore Royal; God knew she'd tried her best to bury his memory ever since leaving Akron. He belonged in the past, along with every awful thing she'd had to do to survive.

In the beginning he hadn't forced her. She'd stupidly thought she was in love, though all she felt was cool revulsion at his actual touch. Still, he'd been nice enough at first, and she'd thought he actually, truly liked her, the way nobody ever had. She'd even agonized over lying to him about her name and where she came from.

Later, she was endlessly glad she had. At least she'd learned a few lessons from those shameful, degrading months. Valuable ones, and they'd stood her in good stead.

Zoe watched the blowing snow for a while, warm and safe. She was a shaman now, a *demie*, one of the Kith. But if Royal somehow found her, and told Jack and Dad what she'd done...

Maybe Jack would understand. But he'd also look at her the way men did when they found out what a girl had to do to get a meal sometimes. Could she risk that?

There was no answer to be found by sitting and brooding, for once, so she went to bed. She checked her phone again—Bella had sent a link to a pair of extremely expensive high-heeled boots she thought Zoe would like, and Jolie a cheery *See you tomorrow.*

The email from Roy still sat in that old, half-forgotten inbox. Maybe he hadn't found religion after all and was going back to his old game? There was no shortage of needy, desperate girls in the world to prey on, after all. Guys like him never wanted to let go, ever, and would fish through old victims to see if any could be roped back in again.

She thought about it, the covers pulled up over her head and the phone's ghostly glow illuminating her pillow, before deleting that account from her phone entirely. For good measure, she deleted a couple of the others, too.

They could sit in a digital graveyard and rot. She was a new person now, and besides, Roy only knew 'Amber', not Zoe Simmons *or* Rouje. She could stay off social media—most Kith did or only had locked accounts, Jolie said, because attention from ordinaries was dangerous—and money could definitely buy some kinds of anonymity.

Look at how little was on the internet about the Roujes, after all. And practically nothing about Mama, only that one old scanned-in article.

Her chances were good. All she had to do was be smart, play it safe, keep her mouth shut—and keep the twinbond from growing any more.

Easy.

Finally, she plugged her phone in, turned over, and closed her eyes, listening to the wind as it rasped at the house's corners.

It took a long time to fall asleep.

48

EASY MOOD

Jack had often prowled the house in a tank top and sweats at night, imagining his *demie* right behind him as he crept, Kith-quiet, through darkened halls and familiar rooms. It became easier as he got older, except for the aching absence of his twin. The sick crashing thump of disappointment when he turned, hoping against hope to find her in the shadows, grew progressively more intense until he'd stopped pretending during stealthy midnight rambles.

Now, of course, he didn't have to imagine. He could pad silently, slow-motion, across her sitting room, ease open her bedroom door inch by inch, and listen to her breathing. The place where the twin-bond nestled inside him was soft and hazy; she had finally dropped off.

At first he'd paced, driven almost to the change by her fear before the entire world shifted and she *reached* for him, flooding him with soothing. It was the first time she'd used the bond that way, and the relief was staggering. He had actually dropped to his knees on bare hardwood, head down, breathing deeply, all his attention focused inward.

Once he dragged himself to a chair with his eyes still closed, he'd simply waited for her to sleep. After that, it was only a matter of sensing her slumber was finally deep enough.

It was a tricky thing, sneaking up on a shaman. At least he had an edge.

He hopped lightly onto the padded top of the cedar chest at the foot of her bed. It was just the right height for a beautiful blue-eyed girl to perch upon while she slipped her heels off, her head tilted, wearing a soft abstract smile and listening to her *demi*'s banter.

Jack crouched easily. His *demie* slept on her side, her loosely braided hair a rivulet across the pillows and one hand outflung, slim pretty fingers loosely cupped. Her lashes were perfect charcoal arcs, her lips slightly parted in repose.

She was safe. Each time she inhaled, almost too softly for even Kith ears to hear, a fresh jolt of relief shot through him. He had to be careful, or it would break her rest—and she sorely needed it.

Shaman-work took a lot out of a Kith.

What had upset her so much? Was it just delayed reaction, or something else? It was hellish not to know, unable to offer a solution or even much comfort. A fitful rumble of Voice spread from him, steadying as he relaxed.

The purr pressed along every surface, stroking and teasing. It settled over his *demie*, a warm comforting blanket of sedation. The twinbond strengthened, humming with invisible force.

The years of isolation would take time to fully wash away, but he was no longer willing to let her face anything alone. The bond couldn't be *forced*, of course.

But it could be strengthened, bit by imperceptible bit. And an analyst's cold, one-pointed concentration was ideal for that task.

Dark eyes glinting like live coals in the darkness, his golden hair wildly rumpled, Jack stared at his sleeping *demie*, occasionally shifting slightly to keep his muscles fresh. It was akin to hunting a Broken, using a predator's stillness while waiting for prey to show, and his Voice took on a deeper throb.

Outside, the snow whirled endlessly. But his *demie* was warm and safe, and there were hours before dawn.

Plenty of time.

Any Kith, particularly an analyst, could function almost indefinitely on very little rest. Besides, watching his *demie* sleep without a care was as good as a solid twelve hours of unconsciousness. Consequently, Jack was in a reasonably easy mood by the time he finished his shower the next morning. The power had gone out in the wee hours, but was on again by six—someone out in the cold deserved a raise for that, indeed.

Zoe was still asleep, the bond a deep quiet softness settled comfortably in his bones. She was going to find it progressively more difficult to keep him at arm's length. Jack smiled at himself through the thin skin of condensation on the bathroom mirror, deciding he was presentable, and stalked into his bedroom to finish dressing.

He heard approaching footsteps while he shrugged into his suit jacket, and that managed to dent his happiness a fraction. By the time two sharp raps echoed at his door he was ready except for his tie, and when Mac swept into his sitting room—not waiting for a *come in* because he could hear damn well his quarry was up and moving around—Jack was at the bedroom door, eyebrows raised.

"Saddle up." McKenna had run his hands back through his dark hair more than once already by the look of it, and when added to his grim expression and the knifelike creases in his fresh suit, his presence added up to serious trouble on the brew. "And wake your sister up, too. Your old man's orders," he added hurriedly. "Not mine."

Shit. Did she sense something last night? It wasn't entirely out of the question; sometimes shamans could peer through time itself. "How bad is it?"

"Don't know yet." Mac didn't laugh. He simply fixed his best friend with a baleful glare. "They managed to kill the Golden's mate."

Jack froze, his thoughts racing furiously. "How the *fuck*?"

"Some kind of ambush, I don't have the details. Jolie rousted me out of bed two hours ago. Allison's on her way, Amerlane the elder and Traleski too. Weather's chancy, but they'll run if they can't drive. It'll take Bell and Dima some time to get here; I gather Bell's in a state."

"They visited the Golden on their last trip." And of course Bell, as an analyst, would be tormented at the thought of missing a small, crucial piece of data that could have saved one of their own. Jack's skin chilled as he settled his tie, knotting it swiftly. "How's Pindar?"

"Unhappy." Mac shrugged, but the fire in his dark gaze mounted another notch. Anything disturbing Jolie's peace would meet with swift reprisal if *he* had anything to say about it. "Your dad says we'll need all the shamans for this. Everyone's on edge."

"I'll get Zo up." He'd planned to let her rest, but... "Have Amelia send up some coffee, will you, and get the files arranged for me?"

"Of course." McKenna paused. "Are you...I have to ask, Jackson. Are you ready to work? We need you."

"My *demie*'s here and safe; I'm all four on the floor." Jack knew his smile was unsettling, but Mac's answered its feral glitter wholesale. "Don't worry about me, old man. Hey, where's Jasperson the younger?"

Mac tensed, a familiar move when potential prey was mentioned. "Still in detox, and it's not looking good." Which went without saying; skate addiction was pretty much fatal. "I'm not sure he's got anything more to give, but if you want him..."

There was probably no connection between the European skin hunters and whatever group Greg had been feeding intel to, but that was an assumption requiring rigorous testing before any weight could be placed on it. "I'll visit him myself when the roads are clear." And he'd have to take Zoe, too.

Jack felt her stir, rising from a deep well of unconsciousness.

If Greg had given up some tidbit that had crossed the Atlantic and made it easier to assassinate any Kith, much less a ruler's mate, skate wouldn't have to finish the traitor off. Either way, he was now a loose end, and those were best addressed sooner rather than later.

"I almost pity the little misbegotten." Mac's grin belied the words. "But not really. Anything else?"

"Not yet. We'll be along as soon as Zo's ready." Explaining this to his sweet *demie* was going to be a challenge. Wondering why the skins couldn't just leave Kith *alone* was a waste of time; the urge to pollute and kill was endemic to them. It didn't seem possible that they'd descended from common ancestors, even if Kith geneticists swore it was true. "Thanks, Mac."

"I live to serve," Mac said grimly, and left with a flippant salute. It was official, McKenna was downright furious.

He wouldn't be the only one this morning. Jack closed his eyes for a moment, taking solace in the soft blurring of the twinbond all through his nerves and veins. Zoe had just begun to glimpse the beauty of life with the Kith.

Now she'd see the danger, and he hated it. The skin hunters were about to disturb his *demie*'s peace along with everyone else's, and he found himself ready to level a few cities and salt the earth in response.

49

CALM, STORM

ONCE SHE DROPPED OFF ZOE SLEPT HARD, NOT EVEN WAKING FOR A DRINK OF water or trip to the bathroom. When she surfaced, she was genuinely unsure what day it was, or even *where* she was. It couldn't be the Marquette squat because there was no persistent scent of mildew, and besides, she was warm—in fact, downright cozy.

It took her a few seconds' worth of hazy blinking before she could place the pale wood and blue upholstery, the nightstand's stained-glass lamp, the bookshelves and the new, sleek black stereo, a Christmas gift.

The closet door was ajar. Grey light fell between the bay window's drapes, dust dancing in its slanted column. She had another day's performance to get through, but at the moment, the calm was welcome.

"Good morning," Jack said from the door to the sitting room, and Zoe almost screamed.

Cloth tore, her bare feet burned against hardwood, and she found herself by the bathroom door with no memory of crossing the intervening space, her shoulder clipping the jamb with a heavy, painful sound. It didn't hurt for a moment; she sucked in a gasp and felt utterly ridiculous.

"Easy, Zo." Jack held both hands up, silhouetted on her bedroom threshold with his dark eyes glinting. "It's just me; I didn't mean to scare you." His hair caught the dim light from the window, and he was already dressed. A dark suit, a subtly striped tie precisely knotted—he never laughed at her when she had trouble with a half-Windsor—and boots instead of wingtips, his trouser-hems breaking beautifully over well-buffed leather.

Great. He looked so *finished* and she was a barefoot mess, her blue flannel Christmas pajamas all awry, hair working out of its braid, and the weird dry taste of morning in her mouth.

Her heart pounded like it was going to bust out of her ribcage and go for a marathon over the snow-thick hills, and her wrists ached because her claws wanted to poke free. Her shoulder gave a flare of star-bright pain, finally catching up with the program. "Jesus," she managed around the dry rock in her throat. "Jesus *Christ*."

"It's all right." He kept his hands up, palms out, the classic *I'm harmless* stance. "Sorry, Zo-baby. Something's happened and Dad needs us, or I'd've waited. Be mellow, okay?"

Yeah. Sure. She'd torn the pretty blue sheets on her way out of the bed; a long fabric strip lay across varnished floor, silently accusing. And her shoulder hurt, the deep familiar pain that meant a bruise rising to the surface.

The space between a punch and the actual sensation of being hit arriving was hatefully familiar territory. Mama's pinches and shakes hurt in the moment, sure, but Bea's attentions—or Roy's, for that matter—were different.

"Oh. Okay." The words scraped Zoe's dry throat, her heart still buzzed like hummingbird wings, and her stomach flipped once, twice, before settling with a dark gurgle and a promise of trouble later. "Dad needs us?"

For a moment she was deeply, irrationally certain Royal had not only emailed her but also, somehow, her father and brother, telling them...what? It would be just like him, trying to ruin what he couldn't have, revenge for any insult imagined or real.

Not that he'd imagined her claws. Her wrists were braceleted with fiery pain, and her skin was suddenly two sizes too small. Rough prickles ran underneath, and she was suddenly, morbidly certain she was going to do something awful in the next few moments.

Probably to her brother, who just *stood* there, watching her.

"He does. There's bad news from Europe." Jack's gaze was level, and he looked relaxed. It was deceptive; she could *feel* his readiness. Which was powerfully, oddly comforting—he was fast, and strong, too. Maybe she wouldn't hurt him if she popped off.

But oh, God, she hated the thought of even trying to attack him. Anyone, really, but especially him.

"You're close to the change," he continued, quietly. "Probably feels really uncomfortable. Just focus on me, babygirl. Can you do that?"

The change? I'm too damn young for menopause. But he meant the other thing, the animal living inside all Kith. The terror she'd touched when she sprang at Bea, the fury that had raked its claws down Royal's face that horrible night, the struggling, wordless flood of rage that even now struggled for release.

A faint creaking sound ran under the bedroom's tense quiet. It came from Zoe's body, bones shifting, and the only thing scarier than the knowledge that her own flesh was changing at high speed was how much of a *relief* it was. She'd kept the animal leashed and muzzled for so long, but it knew where freedom lay.

And it wanted out.

"Zoe. Focus on me." Strangely, Jack didn't sound upset or frightened at all. He had to know she was trembling on the edge of doing something horrible. "I scared the hell out of you, didn't I? Sorry. Just be easy, Zo-baby. Focus."

I'm trying. The anger didn't want to go back into its cage, but as

Jack held her gaze it retreated. A soft sliding sensation went down her back like gentle fingers on a cat's fur, smoothing and soothing.

It came from the twinbond. *We used to think inside each other's heads*, he said, and it sounded alternately intriguing and frightening. Right now it was a lifeline, one she seized with desperate strength.

Her heart decided it wasn't going to hit warp speed and punch out through her ribs just yet. Ringing, panicked static in her ears retreated, and Jack took a step toward her, paused. Took another.

"Good. That's it." A slight, encouraging smile. "You're doing great, Zo. You're not in trouble, okay? Everything's fine."

Are you sure? Because I'm not. "What's happening?"

She wasn't quite sure if she was asking *what's happening to me* or *what's happening with Dad?* Either would do, as long as he kept talking, quiet and sure.

Jack cocked his head, giving the question due attention. He always did that, acted like anything she said was important. It was heady, comforting, and terrifying all at once. "You're startled, and you reacted just like any Kith struggling with the change would." Each word calm, evenly spaced. "Dad needs us because there's a problem overseas that might come here. Like those skins the other night."

The what now? Oh. "The people who want to hurt us. Because we're...different." So it wasn't about Royal—or Bea—at all. Jack knew what she'd done to Bea, sure.

But Pastor Beaton, the god of Righteous Savior, was dead in prison.

"Yeah." Jack approached, each footstep silent despite his shoes. Zoe let him draw nearer, though the uneasy itching under her skin struggled to return. It only retreated fully when his hand cupped her bruised shoulder, burning through flannel. "Ouch. That hurts, huh."

"You feel it." Zoe shivered, but not from cold or adrenaline. The movement came from something else, something she couldn't quite name. Conflicting emotions poured through her, a riptide of confusion.

"Yeah. Some Voice'll fix you right up, though. Allison will be here soon; Jolie's downstairs. We're going to have a full house again." He stroked her shoulder, a gentle polishing palm-touch. "Take a shower and get dressed, huh? Dad needs us both."

What the hell does he need me *for?* There was no point in asking, since her part of this bargain was showing up when summoned.

Or else. She wasn't quite sure what 'or else' entailed, but a lifetime's training in doing what she had to meant she knew when an offer couldn't be refused. "Okay."

"Amelia's sending up coffee. I'll come back in when it arrives, all right?" His body heat touched hers, and the closeness wasn't irritating at all. Under the edge of soap and shampoo—he must've just finished his own morning rituals—he smelled familiar, comforting. Like safety, and forgiveness. "Expect me, so I don't scare you again."

"Yeah." *Sure. That'll be easy.* How was she going to fix the sheet she'd ripped? Or anything else? "I'm sorry. I was sleeping pretty hard."

"That's a good thing. You needed rest." He smiled, then leaned even closer, and Zoe froze.

Jack kissed her forehead, a soft chaste press of lips like Trevor sometimes did to Amelia. The contact burned like Zoe's bruised arm, like a lit cigarette, like the change's fever in her bones.

"Get ready," he said, and let her go. Her bedroom door closed behind him. Zoe sagged, clutching her shoulder and wincing. Her heels were on cold bathroom tile, her toes on hardwood; she stayed right on the dividing line, tasting copper adrenaline and trapped by the trembling in her limbs, for a few long, endless moments.

Sure, she could be 'ready'. She spent her entire life bracing herself.

The question was, for *what*?

What on earth did you wear in situations like this? It was like dressing for dates; no matter *what* you chose it was going to be inadequate in some way, either for the weather, Royal's taste, or the clients' peccadilloes. Despite Janine's efforts the walk-in closet with its soft recessed lighting was still almost half empty, but what was there was enough to give Zoe a decision-making headache.

She decided anything Ms. Traleski had sent wouldn't be too bad, and since she was being summoned for something serious jeans wouldn't be appropriate. A skirt, then—and her gaze lit on a charcoal twinset with a silk shell-blouse.

Hallelujah, I'm saved.

A horrified giggle caught itself halfway in her throat, and she hurried to get dressed. There was no time to really dry her hair, but damp-dry was good enough and maybe she could excuse herself later and pull it back. A pair of suede kitten heels matching the twinset perched neatly in the shoe racks, so that was good. A slip but no hose, since she hated being wrapped up like a sausage. A pair of dangling silver earrings—a Christmas present from Amelia—and she was probably presentable.

Or so she hoped.

"Zo?" Two crisp taps on her bedroom door. "Coffee."

Maybe she was being too slow. Zoe hurried for the door and nearly tore it open, thankfully getting her second earring in just before arrival. Her shoulder ached, but the bruise wasn't nearly as bad as she'd feared. It would be gone soon anyway; she healed quickly.

She'd also tucked the torn sheet out of sight, making the bed as neatly as possible. "I'm sorry, I'm hurrying, I know it's—"

"Wow." Jack's hair was still damp, too, and he held two cups—a sleek tall black mug and a larger round red cappuccino number, familiar from other breakfasts. "You, uh. You look great."

Nice of you to say so. Zoe tried a smile, but it felt tight and unnatural. "Thank you. I'm ready; we can go."

"Slow down." He offered the red cup, and she wrapped her hands gratefully around its warmth. "I should tell you what's likely to happen, right? So you're prepared."

Oh, thank God. "That would be nice." Her heart wasn't settling itself quite properly in its cage; she probably didn't need the caffeine. "I don't want to embarrass you. Or Dad."

"You can't, okay? Come over here and sit down." He headed for the couch, and now she felt almost silly for zooming through the morning routine.

Almost, but not quite. Perched on blue cushions, she tried a sip of Amelia's newest concoction. To her relief, it was a plain, simple latte. Maybe the housekeeper was nervous about all this too, or she'd figured out not to waste fancy syrups on just-plain-Zo.

"Now." Jack settled easily, and inhaled the steam from his own mug. "Jeez, I have *got* to find out what she does to the coffee. Okay, listen."

Zoe crossed her ankles, made sure her skirt was properly smoothed down. *Don't slouch, hands in your lap, knees together, sip don't gulp, don't be tacky*—oh, Mama had taught her well, and now she was grateful for the endless reminders.

"We'll go downstairs, and everyone will be on edge because of the news." Today Jack's watch was the gold and black one with a leather strap; the morning had strengthened outside and the sitting room's window was full of snowlight vying with the electric glow of fixtures and LED bulbs. "Dad's going to need me for what I do best. He's also going to need to see you, see that you're here and safe, because one of the things we always worried about was something bad happening while Angelina had you. All right? Just seeing you will calm him down, and you're a shaman, too. You'll make everyone better just by being in the room."

I doubt that. But this was important, so Zoe simply shifted uneasily, listening hard. The red mug's warmth sank into her hands, eased the tension in her wrists.

"You've got one job," Jack continued. "Stay with me, and stay as calm as possible. Can you do that?"

That can't be all. "I can. But..." Her hand shook slightly, and the coffee's surface trembled.

"But what?" Jack didn't sound angry, just thoughtful. He regarded her intently, his golden head slightly cocked. "Tell me."

His calm was infectious. Zoe took a deep breath, the twinbond twitched inside her chest, and questions spilled free. "What's going on? What are you going to be doing? What happens if I mess up?"

"I hate having to tell you this." Her twin shifted, glancing at the window. "There's been an assassination. One of ours, in France. It's probably not connected to the skins who attacked us before Christmas, but either way I'm going to be looking at the data to find out what I can in order to coordinate our response. Kith from different countries work together as a matter of course—we *have* to, especially with skins the way they are. Do you understand?"

Oh, God. She nodded, wishing she didn't have a mug of hot liquid to keep steady. This sounded worse than any of Mama's ramblings about monsters and deviltry. Had she thought she was protecting Zoe from *this*? Maybe it had been a big swirling ball of interlocking things forcing her mother to take Zoe and run.

But if Angelina honestly thought there was danger, why would she leave her other child behind? Jack probably had some trauma from being the one she didn't take, and the realization hurt Zoe's heart just like Mama's constant sawblade fear had.

So much pain, and it all collected in her own chest. She had no earthly idea what she'd do when the cup overflowed.

"Good." Jack took a small sip of his coffee, testing its temperature, and looked relieved. "As for messing up, you can't. It's literally impossible. All right?"

She didn't believe that, but Dad was expecting them and by now Zoe knew nobody but *nobody* made Trevor Rouje wait. He was always kind, of course, and sometimes even laughed with his children. But mostly he was stern, and she'd glimpsed the thunderclouds on him once or twice. She devoutly hoped she'd never be the focus of his disapproval.

If Royal sent him pictures of 'Amber', what would he do? Would Jolie and Bella smirk behind her back, would the guys look at her with that faint nasty smile she'd seen on too many male faces to count? Would Amelia sniff the way she did at a substandard dish?

"All right." Zoe tried her own coffee, finding out it was still too hot for drinking. *Might as well get this over with.* "We should go."

Jack shook his head, immobile. "Hang on."

Of course. There's always more bad news. "For what?"

"I want a few nice moments before I have to do this. Just you and me. Please."

Her heart expanded, and the pain vanished. Zoe nodded.

A fire was laid in the sitting room, but it hadn't been lit. There was a faint sound—the wind across the chimney, a faraway breath. Zoe waited, watching Jack's face. He studied her in return, finally sampling more of his coffee. That meant she could try her own, and found her stomach had settled.

If she had to leave, she could at least remember this.

The tension felt like a tornado approaching, the moment just before the sirens started wailing *get to shelter.* Twisters whirled around a pinprick center, and hurricanes had a much larger eye. Drinking coffee on the couch with her twin felt very much like the calm in the exact middle of a vast spinning storm.

Stay with me, he said. And God but Zoe wanted to, because that stillness was the only real safety she'd ever found.

It was also over too soon. Jack exhaled sharply and rose, offering his free hand. "Ready?"

No. "Sure." She let him draw her upright—all that leashed strength was scary, too. But exhilarating as well, like a carnival ride. She'd only been on one rollercoaster, back before Mama was hooked too badly on her medicine; still, the memory was a bright spot. That entire day had been nice, Angelina's then-boyfriend expansive and relaxed, paying for tickets and letting child-Zoe ride on his shoulders. "Jack?"

She never found out what happened to that guy. He was just

gone one day, coming to nothing like all Mama's other attempts to find a man to take care of the bills.

Until Bea.

"Hm?" Jack didn't let go of her fingers, gazing down at her, and the edge of his body heat brushed her lightly, like a stray cat who knew you could be counted on for gentle pats.

"Will you stay with me too?" Her lungs weren't working quite right, so the question came out soft and breathy. She sounded about five years old, and frightened.

"Always." Instant, and utterly certain. It was unnerving, because the twinbond flowered between them and she *felt* that certainty. He didn't second-guess or dither, like she did.

No, Jack was *sure*. Even if the certainty was temporary, it was deeply welcome.

"Okay." Zoe tried to sound equally confident, and probably failed miserably. "Let's go."

50
NEW FORMULAS

His *demie* had lovely long legs, but her strides were shorter than his and she was in heels as well. Jack had to force himself to move at her pace, which did him nothing but good. The coffee helped too, but most importantly, Zoe had calmed down.

Blue eyes wide, her hair a glorious mass of inky curls, demure in charcoal cashmere and silk, his twin was the very picture of a Kith *demie*. Of course, wildly mussed and panicked earlier she'd looked the same, an almost feral beauty, bright as a star.

His shoulder ached, a ghost of her pain. He longed to use a little Voice and help her with the healing, but if he started that now he might halt midstride, pull her into a side room, and prove beyond a shadow of a doubt that he was never going to let her go.

Ever.

The house rang with activity—footsteps, voices, all Kith. The front door opened and there was a burst of half-heard conversation —he could hear Janine's alto purr, crackling with authority. She must have run to arrive so quickly, the roads were a mess.

He turned them down the hall for Dad's office, and braced himself. This was going to be unpleasant—but at least she was right next to him. "As calm as possible," he murmured, and she nodded as he swept the door open.

"—so we may have to firewall that," Dad said. Every crease in his suit was sharp enough to cut paper with, his mane was immaculate, and the catseye signet on his left hand gave a single bloody glitter. A heat-haze hung on him, and even Jolie's calm—Pindar was next to the fireplace, listening as Mac leaned close, tapping an index finger into his palm for emphasis—couldn't cover the unphysical scent of smoky rage pouring from the Pride's leader.

Big blond Gessel hovered near the door, looking somewhat green. Hermann was busy attending to the laser printer, which was spitting out paper at a rapid rate. Janine Traleski glanced at Jack, taking in Zoe too before returning her attention to Trevor.

"I can be there in a few hours," she said, softly. "And I can hunt down these bastards."

Uh-oh. Jack finished his coffee in two long swallows; Gessel hurried to take the cup and dart out the door kitchenward, relieved to have an errand. "Zo?" He offered his arm, and his *demie* took it, hesitantly, still balancing her own mug in her other hand.

Good. He wanted her concentrating on that instead of on her own anxiety; he shepherded her across the room. Dad's desk was littered with paper already, and Shanice, gems of melted snow jeweling her mass of amber-beaded braids, frowned at Dad's primary computer as she tapped at a keyboard. Her attaché case sat next to her chair, a faithful pet.

The office's secondary desktop was alive too, its screen flickering between two different video meetings—probably Michel the Golden's second-in-command Idris on one, war-rooming with the other European packs, prides, and sleuths, and Simon Elmalik on the other since he held a good chunk of North Africa. Klara Livesett, tall, blonde, and impeccable in a grey silk sheath, sat next to Shanice. Klara rolled her head from side to side to loosen stiff neck muscles, and spoke in a low clear tone, translating something. She was a patterner, a linguist—and Traleski's mate.

Klara's right hand reached out, questing; Shanice slid a pad of lined paper and a pen over with her left, still focusing intently on her own work. One of the phones rang and Hermann whirled, scooping the handset up; it was the dedicated line from the Rouje building downtown.

The Kith had swung into action. It was heartening.

"There you are." Dad's gaze fell on them both, blue eyes softening as he took in Zoe. "My apologies, little dancer. A terrible thing to wake up to."

Zoe slid free of Jack and set her red mug down on the desk. She wore a shaman's thoughtful, listening expression; Jolie glanced across the room and probably heaved a sigh of relief at the presence of another of her kind. The calming effect would be exponential.

"Good morning." His *demie*'s voice held all the restful soothing in the world. "It seems really bad. Are you all right?"

Trevor's shoulders relaxed a fraction, and the line between his dak-golden eyebrows eased somewhat. "Am I...you know, I think you're the first person to ask in years."

A tinge of nervousness still clung to Zoe's scent. Yet she approached Trevor with inquisitive grace, almost fearlessly, as if impelled. After a short, breathless pause, she gingerly slid her arms around her father, a shy hug.

Watching the ruler of the Pride all but melt was an amazing experience. Jack's jaw was suspiciously loose.

"I suppose that's one of my jobs, right?" She stepped away, and her nervousness had almost vanished. So had the sharp gunpowder edge of their father's anger.

It was still there, merely submerged.

"Only if you like the work." Trevor patted her shoulder, carefully reined strength evident even in that small motion. "Don't worry, we've weathered these storms before. And you're here and safe now; we're fortunate in that."

"I told her the same thing." Jack scooped up Zoe's coffee; she'd want the rest of it soon. "How's Michel?"

"Inconsolable, of course. And enraged." Dad's expression turned remote. "It's taking four shamans and his daughter to hold him back. Keisha Stanwyck in Dijon just sent over another tranche of documents, everything they've acquired so far. Elmalik's family home was attacked as well, and the Howler called not ten minutes ago."

"Huh." Jack absorbed this; for the Howler to reach out like this was extraordinary, even after the diplomatic success of returning a lost *demie* to her family. "A concerted, intercontinental effort?" Everyone had been certain the skin hunters were too busy jostling each other for position to work effectively together; perhaps that centuries-long certainty had reached its end.

"Don't know yet. Skins tried to kidnap a pair of kids on their way to school, right in Houston." Trevor's gaze rested on Zoe, who regarded them both solemnly. "Fortunately the security measures held, but two jägers were badly wounded and they're not healing as they should. Belmario and her crew say it's the new tranquilizers; as far as they can discern the formulas are loosely based on skate. Which makes sense."

"We'll figure out a counter, given enough time." Jack hated that his *demie* had to listen to this. An icicle had settled in his guts. "But... they wanted to kidnap cubs?"

"A liquidation team wouldn't carry restraints." Dad's tone was even and calm, but his blue eyes flamed.

"Which kids?" The icicle was turning into a sword. This pattern was clear, and he didn't like it at *all*.

"Mirabel's cubs." Dad patted Zoe's shoulder again, possibly more to soothe himself than his daughter. "Boy and girl."

The Howler's heir didn't have a defined talent, but made up for it in general dominance. It never paid to underestimate Mirabel de la Casa, and her mate Roger just missed being a shaman by a hair or two. "*Usanaugh?*" He didn't think so, but it was best to be sure.

"No, singles. Elder girl, younger brother." Trevor's hands tensed briefly as they dropped. He glanced at Zoe, and the strain eased. "What are you thinking, Jack?"

"Nothing yet." Jack indicated one of the couches, a polished wooden table sitting ready before it. "Sit down, Zo—right over there, please. Mac?"

McKenna was already on his way toward Jack, bearing an armful of manila file folders. "Thank God you're back. There's a lot of paper."

Jolie trailed him. "Hey, Zo. You hungry?"

His *demie* shook her head, but she looked grateful. "I don't think I can eat. This all seems...terrible."

Well, that's one way to put it. "Did they manage to question any of them? In France or down the Howler's way?" Jack hoped they had, but it wasn't really necessary. Each detail was worse than the last, and the picture becoming clearer was nightmarish.

"Unfortunately not." Dad's sigh was only partly weariness. His anger was banked now, but it would burst into fresh flame as soon as Jack's talent—or Bella's, or a shaman's leap of insight, or any other break—gave them a direction. "The ones we had before Christmas didn't know much, they were only mercenaries. Their money was washed so many times it's impossible to track, though Gibson's got a couple of his hackers on it now."

"That's good, though I'd wager the group before Christmas and the Houston mess are probably unrelated to overseas." The risk of said hackers alerting their enemies to security holes and Kith attention was negligible when compared to the utility of gathering intel and causing damage to the hunters' digital infrastructure.

"Really?" Dad frowned, but he knew better than to mistrust his heir's assertions at this point.

"If other data comes in, I'll scrap that assumption." Jack waited until Zoe had perched on the couch; Jolie hovered near her, their dual auras of calm washing out in concentric rings. It was almost as pleasant as Voice, but starting to rumble now might have a less-than-sedative effect on already angered Kith. "What's on top, Mac?"

"Site photos from Louveciennes." McKenna handed them over. "Be prepared."

"Always," Jack murmured, and flipped the first file open. Glossy color photos paper-clipped to reports—his gorge rose briefly before an analyst's chill reasserted itself, clamping down with a vengeance. It looked like the bodies of Lucile Davencourt and the jägers protecting her had been desecrated after death, and given how quickly Kith tissues broke down there was no way of telling if the skate tranqs had been used. "They had time to do this? Interesting."

"Yeah, well." Mac looked a little green. "Michel won't ever recover. But Orodilla from Madrid said something interesting, she thinks—"

Zoe leaned close, peering at the photos.

Don't. Jack snapped the file closed. "No. I don't want you to see this."

"Shouldn't I, though?" Those wide blue eyes, innocent and clear, fastened on him. It was unfair—his *demie* could get anything her heart desired out of him with that look, but this would hurt her. "If this happens a lot, sooner or later I'll have to. Right?"

"It doesn't happen *often,*" Jolie said softly. "But..."

Jack's *demie* simply regarded him, steadily. He hated the thought of those quiet baby blues taking in anything so awful as the sight of ravaged Kith bodies. "It's bad." *Don't do this, Zo.*

His beautiful, uncertain twin held out one slim hand. "I have to see."

Jack should have snatched the file away. But he—the stubborn analyst, the contrary heir—was helpless. All she ever had to do was ask, and his resistance melted.

Zoe flipped the file open. All color drained from her face. The spreading shaman-calm from Jolie echoed in her, but a tide of devouring sadness washed through the room. Janine was at the desk now, her hand on Klara's shoulder; Dad glanced at his children, and it was clear now that his daughter had inherited the worry-line between his eyebrows.

"Jesus," Zoe whispered. Even her lips had turned bloodless-pale. "Why...why would anyone..."

"Because they're skins." Jack subtracted the file, whisking it away before she could take it into her head to do more damage to herself. "And they hate what they can't control. We're going to make sure they can't do it again."

Thankfully, she didn't protest, and she didn't reach for any more papers. She just sat, her hands so tightly clasped her knuckles turned white and her eyes brimming.

Most of the time, his feelings on skins were neutral verging on amusement. Now he was perilously close to hating them, but not nearly as much as he hated himself for showing her any of this.

51
HAT TRICK

IT SHOULDN'T HAVE SURPRISED HER. THE WORLD WAS CRUEL, AND GROWING up was all about learning that fact over and over again.

The first photo in the folder had refused to make sense at first, shapes blurring and mutating until Zoe realized what she was seeing was a dead body. No—more than one corpse, all tangled together amid the shattered smoking remains of a car, limbs splayed indecently and someone had cut...had *torn*...

The vision wouldn't go away, burned into her retinas *and* her mind. She was glad the only thing in her stomach was coffee, and the rushing in her ears rose in waves. She had to breathe deeply, pushing the sound away.

Nobody else in the office looked like they were going to vomit, though Jolie was pale and a muscle in McKenna's cheek flickered. Dad seemed calm enough, but an invisible shimmerhaze of fury hung on his broad shoulders, far worse than Pastor Bea's deceptively quiet, brass-scented rage.

Even Janine cast a few measuring, almost-apprehensive glances in Trevor's direction. Only Hermann and Gessel seemed immune to trepidation, hurrying to and fro with such alacrity they probably didn't have time to be scared.

Jack sat very still, only stirring to turn a page as he went through the file front to back, his disgust invisible from outside. It echoed in the twinbond, though, and every once in a while he would exhale softly and look at her.

Zoe found out she was indeed a coward, because she had zero desire to see any other pictures even after making a big production out of how she should.

Well, she'd always suspected she wasn't very brave. But she just couldn't make herself look again.

Once was enough. It was the worst thing she'd ever seen, and that included the body in the squat in Illinois after she'd left Royal—the heat had killed a lot of homeless people that summer, while she worked at the landscaping company. The ramshackle abandoned house serving as her temporary refuge had held a half-dozen people of varying age, sobriety, and desperation; one morning, they woke up to find only five still breathing.

The old man who'd laid claim to a corner of the living room downstairs had begun to stink and swell, his face blackening; *when* he'd actually died was an open question. Things—especially roadkill —spoiled fast that time of year, but he hadn't moved for at least forty-eight hours before that, only rousing enough to shout filthy words at anyone who asked if he was okay.

Death did indeed have a particular smell, and it lingered in memory once you'd been exposed to it. The day they'd found out he was definitely deceased Zoe had packed up, left half a week's pay behind, called 911 from a payphone at the bus station—someone had to at least bury him decently—and kept moving south despite the heat. The weather had broken when she reached Marquette, and that had seemed a good enough reason to halt. Maybe she should've gone north instead, but that would've taken her too near Ohio—and Royal, who at that point she was almost certain she'd killed.

Would the Kith have found her sooner if she'd ever traveled closer to New York? She couldn't even guess.

McKenna kept bringing Jack other files and random papers, as well as murmured pieces of information from the phone or the two Kith at the desk. Dad and Janine conferred quietly near the desk, peppered with questions from the women at the pair of computers. Jolie rose and wandered the room, her shaman's calm spreading in rippling waves Zo could almost see.

It helped, a little. And when Jack turned to her or reached through the bond, that helped too. He seemed to take just as much comfort from the contact as she did. Trevor glanced often in her direction too, and each time he did, his expression eased for a short while.

But the rage remained, hazy like heat-ripples over pavement. And though she absolutely, positively did *not* want to know any more, she couldn't very well turn off her ears.

"Different chemicals?" Jack leaned forward, his dark gaze sharpening. "In each batch?"

"Yeah. Elmalik's science division agrees that they're testing skate-based sedatives, trying to get full paralysis and stop it burning off so quickly. All the labs have moved this to the top of the list. Buenos Aires and Shanghai are looking into where some of the more exotic fixatives and compounds were sourced." McKenna gathered some of the scattered papers and color-coded folders on the table. "Those two crazy cats in the Philippines are going through their pharmaceutical holdings too, and the Jakarta contingent is offering specialist hunting teams. So are the Russian sleuths."

Jesus. How many Kith are there? Each time Zoe thought she had a handle on what was happening, another casual mention of something-or-another walloped her.

"Michel won't say no to that, and I wouldn't either." Jack thought for a moment, then nodded briskly. "Let's let it be known we agree, unless Dad vetoes. It's a good sign that there aren't tranqs left at the Louveciennes site."

McKenna's dark hair was almost bristling with anger; it was a good thing he wasn't paying any attention to her. "They could have cleaned up after themselves, they had time."

Jack nodded, exhaling sharply. "Can we get all Gibson's hackers on the money trails?"

"I'd be surprised if they aren't following it already just to *do* something. Including Fyodor's bunch." Mac set off for the desk; the two women—one was from Janine's shop, Zoe remembered her—were both speaking softly into headsets, occasionally muting their mics to say something to Trevor.

She felt Allison before the shaman arrived, a sense of pressure like a storm front moving over the prairie. The doors opened, there was a flash of silver from the stripe in her dark hair, and Zoe dragged in a deep breath. A high pretty flush made the shaman glow, and tiny stars of snowmelt dewed her clothes. She made a beeline straight for the desk; everyone in the room stopped, staring at her.

Except Jack. He merely gave a brief glance, looked at Zoe again, and returned his attention to yet another file in his lap. "Zo? Take a look at this."

Oh, God. Maybe he was mad at her for insisting. She took the thick pile of paper with trembling hands, and flipped the blue cardboard cover aside.

"Not Lucile," Allison said softly, but since the silence was almost pin-drop absolute the words were clear and distinct. Her characteristic aura of peace had turned into a thick cloak of sorrow. "Please, tell me she's all right. Tell me *everyone* is all right."

Trevor's eyes had darkened too, and his shoulders tensed, the burden dropping a little more heavily on their broad expanse. "I'm sorry, Allison."

"Son of a..." The shaman turned away, her hair swinging, and dropped her chin. Her shoulders curved inward, and she flinched like an uneasy teenager listening to Bea thunder about hellfire from Righteous Savior's spotlit pulpit.

Jolie crossed the office, slid her arms around the older woman. "Alain and Marie-Claire are with Michel," she said softly. "They'll keep him from doing anything...rash. And from falling, too."

"At least that." Allison's sigh caused a soft warm breeze through the room, rippling paper and folders, brushing at polished wood, lifting stray hairs. She leaned into Jolie's comforting, an easy, natural movement. "I'm all right, I swear. What needs doing?"

"Jack?" Trevor looked past the shamans.

Zoe's brother nodded, though his hot dark gaze was still on Zoe. "Just look through those," he said, and she knew an order when she heard one. "Tell me if anything sticks out, even slightly." His tone turned sharper, far more businesslike. "Jolie, I want you and Mac to go downtown and triage what the scientists are sending, we don't have the resources to process it here. Allison, we're already at code red, but we need everyone checked—every house needs to be on wartime footing, and watch the cubs. I don't know about overseas yet, but here they're after small targets, ones they consider weaker."

Zoe braced herself, looking at the papers. A hot, squirming sense of relief slid through her stomach when she found there were no pictures, just columns of names and numbers. Looked like businesses, with addresses and short descriptions, and the numbers were likewise prosaic—phone, percentages, estimated yearly profit or loss.

Maybe it was make-work presented as a treat, like coloring a single Xeroxed page with anemic, chewed-down crayons when an elementary school teacher needed a few minutes to think.

Fine. She'd take it, especially if it meant she could pretend not to hear more terrible things and think about their horrifying implications.

Allison conferred with Dad and Janine, then turned away and took out her cell phone. She began dialing, and the video meetings at the desk changed tone—less shocked and grieving, more determined. Hermann murmured into the sleek black cordless landline, switching between English and a different language, sounding like German but with harsher consonants. McKenna and Jolie said hurried farewells and left, Jolie touching Zoe's shoulder as she passed.

Zo barely felt it. The papers riffled in her hands like tiny living creatures, and her immediate reflex was to freeze. *Don't you do that deviltry. Don't you dare.*

But she was well and truly caught. The feeling had never been so strong before, and she could no more stop than she could halt an entire mountainside's avalanche.

"Good," her brother said softly. "What've you got, *demie?*"

Her finger had glued itself to a specific point. Zoe's entire body tensed. "It won't move," she whispered.

"That's the Gene waking up." He leaned over, peering at her lap. "Sundown Limited. Good." He made a notation on a legal pad that had appeared out of nowhere, a heavy silver pen from Dad's desk glinting as he wrote. "Give me another one."

Oh, God. "I don't..." But her hands were moving, as if they'd just waited for him to ask. "Krogfeld-Annam. It says it's a holding company."

"Great." Her brother made another note. Gessel approached with a sleek silver laptop, he set it on the table and Jack nodded thanks. "Now for the hat trick, babygirl. Anything else in that file?"

Zoe watched her hands shuffle more pages, the ink-marks turned into swarming ants. *I don't know what I'm doing.* But she did, in some way—it was almost the same as scrolling through job postings, letting her eyes unfocus until something jumped out at her. Or following her nose in a new town, looking for a cheap room or a likely squat. "Two. Higgins International and Liftvalla."

"Sheer magic," he muttered. "Good. Put it down and take a rest."

I didn't do anything. Zoe blinked, the world returning to its usual color and sharpness again. A cool, strange breeze freighted with a silver tinge-scent of moonlight caressed her cheeks, and her stomach flipped. "Ugh."

"Well done, kitten." Allison was suddenly standing at the couch's armrest, leaning over to lay a cool, gentle fingertip on Zoe's forehead.

It was hard not to flinch; the shaman just appeared out of nowhere. "Have you had breakfast?" A strange, undeniable flood of peace flowed from the touch, unfamiliar relaxation spilling down Zoe's back.

"Not yet?" For a moment, she couldn't remember what time it was, or even what day.

"No more until you eat something, then." Allison's smile was weary but genuine.

"I, uh..." *Oh, God.* Sudden panic rasped behind Zoe's breastbone. "I think I should...excuse me."

She would have lunged upright, probably running into the older woman, but Jack's hand shot out and closed around Zoe's wrist. It stopped her dead; the twinbond was a painful stinging between them for a moment, her own fear and his sudden...whatever he was feeling, it was hot and uncomfortable.

"Jackson," the shaman said, softly, "she's not in any danger."

"I want to go to the restroom, please." It was the only thing Zo could think of. She sounded like a six-year-old embarrassed at a birthday party—Mama had never let her attend any even in elementary school, because most of the other kids weren't 'good family' and it wasn't like it mattered anyway, they wouldn't be there long.

But Zoe could *imagine* the blush and the hot bite of shame very well, especially since she'd attended uncomfortable work-related shindigs. No retail job was so terrible the higher-ups didn't actively try to make it worse with mandatory 'celebrations'.

"Zo..." The heat faded from the link, and Jack was his usual self again. "Sorry. This stuff's upsetting."

That was certainly one way of putting it. "Excuse me," Zoe repeated in a strangled whisper, tugged free of his grasp, and when she rose Allison stepped back in one coordinated, graceful motion, like dancing.

Zoe's heels made small unhappy sounds as she hurried into the hall. The lump in her throat swelled, her eyes smarted, and she had the unsettling idea that while she might not spew outright, she was probably going to retch helplessly once she found a sink, the way she had after her first date with one of Royal's 'friends' from the club.

The closest bathroom was on the other side of the downstairs library, and as she passed the half-open door a flicker of motion caught her peripheral vision. She froze, swallowing hard against her stomach's rebellion, and turned her head slightly.

Bright light from two chandelier fixtures and grey snowshine spilling through the tall windows filled the library, gilding the shelves, the small mahogany letter-writing desk, and dark heavy furniture. A fire snapped and chortled to itself under a heavy oaken mantel, and the books all stood primly, brought to the very edge of each shelf.

Someone was on one of the leather couches—no, two someones. It was Dimitri and Bella; the boy twin's arm was over his *demie's* shoulders and he hugged her, his curly head bent.

Bella's face was buried in her hands, and her slim shoulders shook. A powerful mixture of shame, fear, and grief spread from her in near-visible waves, and when she surfaced to blow her nose into a snowy handkerchief Dimitri produced, the soft mutter of her words turned distinct.

"—should have seen it," Bell said, raggedly. It was the first time she'd appeared anything less than perfectly poised and polished, her auburn bob ruffled and her green blouse a fraction askew. "I should have seen *something*. What did I miss?"

Dimitri's response was a mere whisper, only the tone—comforting, consoling—discernible. He kissed her hair, and squeezed her shoulders more tightly.

"It's not enough." Bell mashed the handkerchief into a ball, rolling it in her palm and squeezing hard. "I missed something, Dima. It's my fault."

"No." *That* earned a sharp, audible reply, but Dimitri's tone dropped again. Soft and urgent, it sounded like he was explaining something.

Finally, Bell's shoulders sagged, and she sucked in a sobbing breath. Dimitri hugged her even more tightly with one arm, and raised his free hand to trail his fingertips along her cheek, catching her chin, tipping her face up.

Zoe's lungs burned; her breath was stoppered. She knew she shouldn't be watching this, it was *private*, but she couldn't look away.

It was no chaste peck, or awkward forehead-kiss. Bella freed a hand from her lap, her slim fingers tangling in Dima's dark hair as he leaned into her, their bodies melting together for a short, endless eternity.

Zoe's cheeks were afire too. Her heart beat thinly; she had to slink away, hoping she was quiet—her heels were now muffled by the carpet runner, a faded red-and-yellow antique—and quick enough at the same time.

She reached the bathroom, eased the door shut, and locked it by touch before flicking the light on. Then she slumped against heavy wood, looking at the bright, clean tiled room with brass fixtures and pretty wine-red towels. A black-haired girl watched her from the spotless mirror over the sink, blue eyes wide, cheeks scarlet, her ribs heaving.

Strangely, her reflected self looked indisputably Kith. Spending so much time around them meant Zoe could pick out the similarity in cheekbones, in the way she held her head, in the shape of her arms. Her heart gave another violent, shattering leap though her stomach was now behaving itself, and if she didn't calm down Jack might feel this through the twinbond.

If he did, he would probably come looking for her. She couldn't tell if that was a good thing, or a very, very bad one.

Mama would just die. She was going to hell because the thought was funny, in a bleak, ironic way.

Was this, along with the danger and the luxury, what it meant to be one of them?

And if it was, what, in God's name, was she going to do?

52
CONTEXT

A PROBLEM FOR ONE KITH WAS A PROBLEM FOR ALL, AND ONE OF THEIR advantages over skins was the nature of their cooperation. Resources were pooled, ego and primacy set aside, and every pride, pack, or sleuth in the world was now alerted to the threat and sending help.

Not only that, but his *demie* had the Gene, and with her safely at his side Jack could do anything. Or at least, he felt like he could.

By noon, there were more-than-promising signs. The components and fixatives—including the exact strain of skate the stateside hunters were using—in the tranqs had mostly been sourced and the actual customers were being run down, every major clan had gone into lockdown and onto wartime footing, and the Kith's overarching strategy and stage-by-stage response to the skin hunters—both local and overseas—upping the ante was measured, resolved on, decided, and put into play.

Dima and Bell appeared; the *demie* analyst's lashes were matted and her nose faintly pink. Her *demi* glowered, all his easy temper submerged in cold watchfulness.

Jack could relate. And with another analyst in the room, the workload was halved.

"They can't be cooperating," Bell confirmed, tucking a pencil behind one shapely ear as she frowned at her laptop. "Overseas they're looking to kill, and don't have the tranquilizers. Here, they're looking to drug and capture. We have two different problems here."

"*Thank* you." It was good to have his work checked and found up to par; Jack could heave a sigh of relief. "Which half do you want, foreign or domestic?"

"Oh, I'll take the European bastards." The gleam in Bell's hazel eyes could only be described as *predatory*. "Unless you've got an objection."

From there it was relatively straightforward work, but Zoe was pale and quiet. She huddled next to him on the couch, not even glancing at his impromptu workstation, and barely ate even under Allison's gentle urging. Still, every time Dad looked in her direction his expression eased, and Jack found he liked working without the distraction of a missing half, the wound bleeding away critically required energy.

A bird kept caged and flightless all its life suddenly bolting into the blue could not have felt more exhilarated. The only cloud was the nature of the emergency making flight necessary.

"I can handle everything else," Bella finally said, settled in one of the wingback chairs, with a small table dragged over to serve as footrest and file holder at the same time. Dimitri hovered at her right hand, ready to track down and bring anything she would need, no matter how small.

Jägers thought better on their feet, and best of all while in pursuit. Sometimes, when younger, Jack had wondered if it was better to be a runner than suffering an analyst's constant, cold weighing of every potential avenue. Of course any talent or dominance was pressed into service by the Kith, with rights accompanying the heavy responsibilities, but...an analyst's chill weighing of every possible contingency, not to mention the inability to let certain conundrums rest until solved, was uncomfortable even at the best of times.

"You two should get some rest," Allison said from Zoe's other side, stretching lithely upward from sitting. "And a snack."

"I'm fine," his *demie* murmured, but the bond was reverberating with her unease.

He didn't blame her. This was terrible, and she was hearing far more than he liked about violence, not to mention casualties. At least three clans in western Europe had been attacked; Lucile and her guard were the only deaths, but even one injury was far too many.

"Jackson?" Dad turned from the desk, tucking his sleek silver cellphone back into his pocket. "A moment, before you go?"

What Jack really wanted was to spirit his *demie* out of this room and somewhere quiet; he didn't like the way she shrank further into herself each time Allison pressed her to take a morsel. Amelia was showing her concern in her usual way, cooking up a storm and probably worrying over every scrap sent back untouched or barely nibbled.

Shamans needed the solidity of food and companionship after using their gifts. The stateside hunters were a wholly separate problem, even Bell agreed, but in the process of confirming as much Zoe's talent had given him the missing piece to a particularly complex puzzle, research into the business she pinpointed triggering a cascade of intel that would eventually bring them to the authors of several kidnap attempts.

And she'd done it so simply, too. Just paging through the papers, frowning a little, before her blue gaze sharpened and she tapped with an elegant fingertip, her wrist held beautifully. Whether it was childhood ballet or natural Kith grace was an open question.

Jack rose, and she made no move to follow. Instead, Zoe sat, shoulders rounded and gaze downcast, her hair curtaining her expression.

Well, no wonder. This was a horrible thing to wake up to, and with Angelina's training, she was probably on tenterhooks waiting to see if someone would take exception to her perfectly natural performance of deep intuition. Jackson ambled across the office, his hands stuffed in his pockets as if he was Mac.

"Can it be quick?" he asked, *sotto voce*, as he halted at his father's side. "She's upset."

"I can tell." Trevor's expression was the mask of grave thoughtfulness reserved for major emergencies and disasters. "That was Amerlane the younger. Fantome's sister is making a bid for the Plainswalkers."

What? "Now?" Battles for primacy happened, of course—but during something like this, when everyone needed to be fully focused on responding to skin hunters both at home and otherwise upping the ante?

He'd suspected a challenge to Fantome's power, but this was...huh.

"Apparently it was made official this morning. Sondra seems to think Louisa has a shot, too. She's got the pack elders behind her." A faint edge of amusement touched Dad's tone; he welcomed any good-faith challenge to his own rulership with something approaching relish, but many other Kith leaders felt differently. "George is still in control, but nobody knows how much longer. Our team is uneasy; they want to peel off financials and territory before there's a new leader to start renegotiating with."

"Do it." Jack didn't hesitate. A new Plainswalker leader would be too busy to challenge the Rouje Pride for any right-of-return, and by the time Fantome's sister had power securely in her grasp it would be too late. "Why now, though? Hasn't she been held in seclusion for years? There was some old scandal, right?"

"Nothing more than rumors." But there was a deep line between Trevor's golden eyebrows. "I wondered if the misbegotten was her get. Seems likely, what with Fantome's reaction."

"I never heard she had a mate. But that's no indication." A Kith female bred as she pleased, and nobody with any sense argued the point. Had Fantome's sister tried this before? Putting her in seclusion might have been the Kith leader's solution to a sibling with enough brains and dominance to be a serious threat.

Jack shelved the mystery for later thought; McFisk was already dead and Zoe was safely home, protected and secure. The finer points of the Plainswalkers' leadership struggles would keep him occupied if he suffered a bout of insomnia from his *demie*'s aching nearness and constant reticence, though.

That prospect, while unpleasant, was far better than being sleepless from the agony of her absence. He'd take it. Gratefully, even.

"Indeed." A flash of worry married to distaste crossed Trevor's face, which was interesting in and of itself. "Off you go, then. If we need you—"

"—Zo will know, or Allison will come get us. Understood." Jack nodded, restrained himself from tipping the old man a salute, and turned to find Zoe had risen and was halfway across the office. The twin-bond was full of a hot, scratching impatience mixed with wine-red fear; Gessel stepped aside smartly, opening the door for the Pride's princess.

Usually so polite, Zoe didn't pause or thank the myrmidon. Her stride lengthened as she hit the hall, and Jack doubted she knew where she was going. His *demie* simply wanted...away.

So he hurried to follow, using his greater stride length to advantage. It was where he belonged, and even though the Kith waters were roiling, he was an island of absolute calm.

Zoe took the stairs almost two at a time, her heels clicking and her calves working just like a dancer's, but stopped on a dime once she reached the third floor, whirling to regard him narrowly. "I'm *fine*," his *demie* repeated, no doubt her deepest prayer in times of stress. "You can go back. They probably need you."

Not as much as you do. She didn't quite understand the nature of the *usanaugh* bond yet, and they had time for her to learn just how impossible any separation was. Jack halted two steps below her. "If they do, you'll know."

"I don't know anything." Zoe folded her arms, her chin lifting, and from her suede-clad toes to the top of her pretty head she was the very definition of *beautiful* and *unnerved* at once. "One minute I'm stocking shelves in Marquette, the next I'm here in all this and those...those *pictures*..."

I told you not to look. But every kid had to touch a hot stove at least once. "There are dangers to being what we are. I didn't want you to know that." Jack let her keep the high ground, which meant she could eye him directly instead of having to look up. "Not yet. I guess not ever, if I could help it."

After being on her own for so long, no wonder she had difficulty with the idea of being protected, let alone cherished. There was time to handle that too, and this was a good first step no matter how much he wished the lesson could be otherwise applied.

"I just..." Tense, vibrating like a violin string under a sustained bowstroke, Zoe took a deep breath. "Those men, the other night. They were looking for me, and I heard all of you talking about tranquilizers."

"Yeah. Over here they're going after smaller targets—Kith children, females." Jack shrugged, a carefully considered display of calm unconcern. He didn't want to inform his *demie* that her father and brother—the ones who should be protecting her, anticipating every danger—had only barely won the race to find her, either. "Though they'll get a lot more than they bargained for if they ever try that shit on a jäger like Amelia."

"Yagger?" She said it like a challenge, her chin lifting and those baby blues flashing; Jack had to banish a smile. "What is that, really?"

"Jäger," he repeated, patiently. Waiting for her to ask questions was maddening but indubitably the best policy. His *demie* needed time to absorb the smallest, most basic things about the Kith, and hurrying would get them nowhere. "She tracks things, hunts. Like

Janine. There's patterners too, and myrmidons like Gessel. Plus analysts like me, and shamans like you. Specialized talents, and they all serve the Pride."

A single angry headshake, like a cat annoyed with drops of cold water. Zoe's silky hair swayed with the movement. "The woman in the picture, Jack."

"Lucile Duhalde, Michel d'Aventine's mate. She was a patterner." *May the Moon hold her.* Jack took care to space the words evenly, keep his tone low and matter-of-fact. His own loathing and worry had to take a backseat. "And the other bodies were the two jägers guarding her. Skins killed them."

"But *why?*" Her pretty hands curled into fists.

There was an edge Jack couldn't quite place to the emotions pouring through the twinbond. "The shamans say we once lived in harmony and all that, but I don't believe it. They've always hated us, and we've always let them."

A shudder rippled through her, and her skirt moved slightly. So did her earrings, swaying like wind-brushed branches. "Is this why Mama left?"

"I don't know." *I doubt it.* "You're angry at me."

"I'm not." A sudden flood of panicked denial through the link matched her instant retreat, two quick skipping steps, each with a crisp heel-tap. "I'm sorry." The hall behind her watched them both, shafts of snowy light falling through the windows in regulated bars, framing her beautifully.

"It's all right." Jack climbed the last two steps, drawn just as surely as iron filings after a magnet. "You know I'm safe, that's why you can—"

"*None* of this is safe!" Two spots of color bloomed high on her cheeks, and she retreated still further, each step unerringly graceful. "I was safer back in Marquette!"

"Were you?" He still followed, aware of the change burning in them both. "Because you were being tracked from Ohio, you know. We were ahead of someone else finding you, but we don't know how

far." *Crap. Didn't mean to say that.* His childhood temper, the unreliable, explosive unsteadiness suffered without his twin, had packed
up and left with her arrival. Other Kith didn't have to fear his rage
now, just his calm clinical response when they stepped out of line.

Only his *demie* could provoke him. And she was doing an absolutely fantastic job at the moment.

Zoe regarded him, shocked, her mouth open slightly and her blue
eyes burning almost like Dad's. She looked adorable when she was
surprised, and he wished they were having any other conversation
but this.

"Skins hunt us," he continued. *Get back on track, for God's sake.
Explain something, anything, so she doesn't feel like this. Help her.* "Some
of them are fanatics, some are bigots. Some think they can strip out
what makes us Kith and use it for themselves." A shiver of loathing
ran down his back—whatever skins didn't have, they both feared
and wanted to steal. It was a law of the universe, like gravity or
entropy, or the bond between *usanaugh*. "Dad was always afraid you
and Angelina would run across them."

And so was I. Had nightmares about it, in fact. Should he tell her as
much?

Her shoulders touched the wall. He'd backed her into a space
between one of Jolie's big white avant-garde sculptures and the door
to the lounge, a small rectangular room with a bar and two couches,
not to mention a liquor cabinet he and McKenna had plundered
more than once growing up.

Jack used his height ruthlessly, boxing her in, his hands flattening on either side of her shoulders. If the change took hold, he
had her nicely corralled. And if she was trapped between him and
the heavy wood paneling, he could be sure she was safe, and that
soothed him as nothing else could.

"Jack..." The word died on her lips. That strange feeling pouring
through the twinbond was a torment, he couldn't quite name it.
"Stop."

Oh, sure. Anytime, my sweet demie. *Certainly.* Except he didn't want to. "I'm not going to hurt you." *That's the very last thing on my mind.* Hopefully she could tell, but all the confusion roaring through her might drown him out.

Her nose was a bare inch from his. The entire world revolved inside those big, blue, thickly lashed eyes. "What else aren't you telling me?"

The faint touch of her breath against his almost undid him, and Jack had to make a serious internal effort to speak quietly, calmly. "I tell you too little, it scares you. I tell you too much, it'll scare you. Can't win." Not that he minded—even a losing battle was a pleasure, if you had the right partner.

It might even have been the best thing to say, because the tension in his twin drained, bit by bit. Zoe exhaled shakily and her scent changed a fraction, the stinging yellow of fresh fear fading as a thread of warm comfort worked against its grain. The arch of her collarbones, the shape of her top lip were both works of art; he liked contemplating them, not to mention a thousand other little things.

"Just trust me." He made it as soft, as persuasive as he could. "Ask me anything you want. You know I'll answer."

"But will you tell the truth?" Zoe stiffened, as if expecting violence—a slap, a sudden eruption of anger.

"Why wouldn't I?" It baffled him for a moment, and his heart ached. Growing up among skins must have been pure unadulterated hell for her, twice as bad as his own suffering. "I'm not one of *them*, Zo."

"What if I am?" A quick flicker of her tongue, wetting dry lips— oh, it wasn't fair at all, she had him right on the ropes. "What if being raised by...by Angelina means I'm one?"

Is that what you're afraid of? "You're Kith all the way through, babygirl. It's instinct, you can't help it. All you need is context, and I've got a lifetime of it, okay? I'm *here*. We won't ever be apart again."

"Promise?" And, God help him, she bit her lower lip like she always did when she was uncertain. At least he'd figured out that much about her, and he didn't mind her scrutiny.

Being under her gaze was a torment, but a delightful one. "Scout's honor." He had to back off a bit, straighten, and engage in a completely unnecessary settling of his suit jacket's sleeves. *Don't give her any more time to get nervous.* "You need lunch; Amelia'll send something up. Want to watch TV in my room?"

"I saw pictures of a corpse this morning—more than one, actually. I don't feel like eating. Or television." Now Zoe watched him very carefully, her pulse visible in her slim throat, tense and alert to any sign of displeasure.

Oh, she was still a riddle, but he knew its dimensions now. Even if he never solved even a fraction of the enigma, he didn't mind bumbling along in the dark.

As long as she was here. As long as she *stayed.*

"Fine. But I'm hungry. Come on." He offered his hand, hoping businesslike composure would soothe her. "You've never dealt with something like this before, and you were great. You gave me everything I needed to do my own work, you know."

"I didn't..." But her fingers threaded through his, cool and trembling. He tugged, gently, and they set off down the hall. "Did I?"

"Did you ever." He could make a game of it, walking in unison so the sound of his footsteps melded completely with hers. "Cut at least a month's work down to thirty seconds. Which will save lives."

"Save lives." Now distrustful, but fascinated with the idea. "Really?"

"Yes." He hustled her past the doors to the blue suite; if she retreated now he might not see her for hours. She was nerve-abraded enough to try for panicked retreat when what she needed instead was her *demi.* "Now you're going to sit down, put your feet up, and hang out for a while so I can relax. I'd prefer not to think about what I had to read, okay? I need coping mechanisms too."

"Oh." She would have halted, but was pulled along by his steady pressure. "You're just as upset as I am." As if she'd just realized it.

"We keep tabs on skin hunters as a matter of course; maybe I overlooked something. I'm an analyst, I'm supposed to see everything. It's..." Now he had to search for the precise word. "It's painful, to wonder if I could have averted...this. Anything. All of it."

Zoe squeezed his hand with surprising strength; she was forgetting to impersonate a skin. "Nobody can see everything."

I'm Kith. I'm an analyst, too. I should see everything. It bothered him more than he'd ever admitted to anyone, even Mac.

Even Dad.

And yet she drew it out of him just by being nearby; he also didn't miss how she was more worried about his suffering than her own, her instant, instinctive response to comfort him. A *demie* was a wonder; all the missing pieces right where they belonged. Jack's eyes prickled slightly as he swept open his door, motioning her in. "Keep telling me that, and I'll try to believe."

53
STRANGE SECRETS

THE HOUSE BRIMMED WITH FRANTIC, HUSHED ACTIVITY UNDER AN IRON-colored sky, but nobody came upstairs to collect them and Jack apparently felt no need to go check on events. He did glance at his phone occasionally, and Zoe was kind of glad hers was back in the blue bedroom because the urge to re-add that old email account and see if Roy had tried contacting her again poked at her brain, a steady torment.

Amelia sent up a covered tray with a variety of sandwiches and crudités, carried by a grave, quiet Lev; the flatscreen on the wall in Jack's sitting room held a truly staggering number of channels and streaming services. Flicking through them induced a strange meditative state, helped by the weird stormy light through the windows— he didn't have a French door or a balcony.

That was hers alone.

Zoe found herself eating, almost guiltily; she was outright famished. The sandwiches could have been cardboard and she still would have scarfed them. She hadn't been this hungry since the terrible first few days after leaving Hall City and the burning Righteous Savior.

Jack helped himself in far more leisurely fashion since he hadn't refused breakfast, watching the television without any change of expression or murmur of protest no matter how often she flipped the station. He didn't seem to mind her playing with the remote, either. As soon as she finished her third sandwich, Zoe's eyelids turned leaden and her entire body followed suit. A series of deep yawns shook her; she caught Jack's sideways look and almost flinched, dabbing at the corner of her mouth with a striped, cheerful yellow linen napkin. "Sorry."

Quit stuffing your face and don't yawn at the table, Mama would have hissed. It was probably time to admit she was glad her mother was gone, and maybe she could start working on figuring out if Angelina should have stayed here instead of dragging Zo off across the continent, living miserable and hand-to-mouth.

Then again, what normal person was equipped to handle all this?

"Why be sorry? You did shaman-stuff." Jack settled his sock feet on the table. With his tie loosened and his hair disarranged, he was the picture of relaxation. "It wears out the body. You need fuel, and a nap."

A nap sounded fantastic, but trudging back to the blue suite also felt impossible at the moment. Zoe stared at the muted game show on the huge screen, closed captioning scrolling across the bottom. She hadn't watched television in *ages*. Not since Nebraska, really, unless there was an old sclerotic set in an employee breakroom. The scramble to survive took up all her time and energy.

And the vision of Dimitri and Bella on the library couch just wouldn't go away. Had she misinterpreted it? Or maybe it was a hallucination, like Mama had on her medicine?

Mama was a junkie, Zo. Call it what it is. Her feet tingled as she worked them out of the heels, an involuntary sigh of relief escaping her lips. She was trapped in a funhouse, every mirror warped and every corner holding some strange, dangerous secret.

Kith. Skin hunters. Jägers. Shamans. *Usanaugh.*

A hot flush went through her once more, her internal thermostat malfunctioning. Did everyone know about Dima and Bella? Did they just pretend *not* to know, like an entire church congregation could ignore a pastor carrying on with at least three of the wives in his congregation and doing horrible things to at least one of the youth group girls for good measure? Not to mention what he'd done to his almost-stepdaughter, but at least Mama had never outright married Bea.

Jack kept telling her he'd answer questions, but how on earth could she ask him about what she'd witnessed? It was just the same as anywhere else—you learned by keeping your eyes open and listening around the edges and corners, because even if someone would tell you the truth, there were always limits to their willingness.

Or their honesty.

Zoe straightened, self-consciously. I think I'll go lie down," she said, and handed Jack the remote. Her legs felt like noodles, and her eyes were grainy-hot.

"Just stretch out here." He indicated her half of the black couch with a single, languid wave. "I can get you a pillow."

"No, I'm okay." If she could retreat to the blue bedroom and sit in the window, maybe she could think about things without scaring herself. Or she could slither under the bed. It was sounding more and more attractive all the time. "I'll just go back to my—"

"Please." Her twin turned slightly, and his dark eyes all but glowed with intensity. His lips twitched, as if he wanted to grimace —or snarl. "I need you close, all right? It's a *usanaugh* thing. After something disturbing, you need your twin to sort of...calm you down."

It made sense, but now her cheeks were on fire again. He could probably feel it through the link, and the embarrassment sent another scorch through her entire body. How could you be ashamed and half-asleep at the same time? "Wouldn't you rather be alone?" None of her conversational tricks for keeping a stranger at bay were going to work, she could just tell.

Because he wasn't a stranger. Not by a long shot.

Not now.

"I had seventeen years of *alone*, thanks, and I'm not after more." At least he didn't sound angry, just very...definite. "But if you need to go back to your room, go ahead."

It was something Royal might have said, but Jack didn't need Roy's passive-aggressiveness. Of course, when you were stronger, faster, and had razor-sharp claws, maybe all that bullshit was discarded in favor of outright, open aggression.

The realization sent a strange shiver down her back. Still, with a lump of food safely in her stomach and the quiet of the room, a nap sounded downright glorious.

Slowly, carefully, she arranged herself on less than half the couch, trying not to take up too much room. Tucking an arm instead of a pillow under her head brought back memories—still, it was much nicer than a bus station bench or fitful dozing in a squat. For one thing, it was quiet except for the slight hum of others in the house's depths and the faint electronic buzz of the muted television. Zoe tugged at her skirt; Jack wasn't looking. He'd turned his attention to the flatscreen, taking another bite of a prosciutto-and-Swiss sandwich, cut neatly on the diagonal like Amelia always did.

She meant to just lie quietly with her eyes closed and think about things, but as soon as Zoe truly settled a heavy black curtain dropped, and she was lost.

The window opened easily enough, though it took some tugging and flakes of paint peeled free of the sash. Zoe settled a hip on the sill and stared down at the roof of the building next door; you could also see a piece of Akron's skyline, which accounted for the price of this apartment, but it wasn't the best slice.

Roy was moving up, though. That was the important thing, at least as far as he was concerned.

"What the fuck are you doing?" Shirtless, his sparsely furred chest *gleaming with water droplets, the lean dark-eyed man she'd thought she loved—even as recently as a month ago—scrubbed at his wet hair with a threadbare towel. "Close that, it's cold."*

It was a beautiful early-spring night, a hard sharp breeze bringing freshness laden with rain instead of ice from the Little Cuyahoga. Clouds like sop-wet rags raced across the sky, and the skyscraper lights were beginning to come up as dusk finished falling earthward. Zoe filled her lungs with the night, a galvanic thrill running under her skin, and moved to obey.

Apparently she didn't move fast enough, though, because Roy dropped the towel and stalked across the living room. "God damn it, Amber," he said, softly, and it was the very worst of all his voices, a rasp of irritation cutting every syllable short. "What I gotta do, huh? What do I gotta do to get it through your head?"

The sudden rasp of violence in his scent was familiar too, for all it was watered down. The only time he smelled nearly as vivid as Bea was when he was furious, and Zoe had taken to wondering lately if that was why she stayed.

Roy grabbed her shoulders, his fingers sinking in. He didn't squeeze as hard as Bea, and sometimes she dared to dancingly avoid him while he was trying to whale on her. Not too often—it usually enraged him even more —but sometimes you could dodge even the worst petty tyrant.

You just had to figure out if it was worth the cost.

A sticky, suffocating blanket of fear, tight as a python in an old National Geographic she'd leafed through once, the snake coiled around some small, dying jungle creature. Royal shook her until her head bobbled, but Zoe was looking inward, *because sometimes when she disconnected from her body during a man's rages there was a glimpse of something else, something better, lingering just out of her mental reach.*

And sometimes that glimpse spoke, a soft despairing cry she longed to answer.

Where are you? Just show me a sign.

When she'd met Royal she thought maybe it was his *voice, but now she knew better. Things were getting bad here. Just last night he'd punched*

Gilly in the face, which meant she couldn't really work until the bruising went down.

And that just made Roy even madder.

None of the other girls envied 'Amber' being up here tonight except maybe Cassie, who was number one now. Roy liked using her to corral the others; since she was older, she was kind of desperate to keep the position. She thought 'Amber' was looking to take it, and Zoe couldn't convince her otherwise.

Look, it's not even my real name. I can leave, I'm just...

She heard the snick *of the switchblade, and realized Roy hadn't just gotten mad, he was well and truly worked up. Something must have happened earlier that afternoon—just what didn't matter, because she had failed to notice the signs and he was too close, yelling that he had to get it through her fucking head one way or another and shaking her with one hand locked around her left arm while his other fist, full of a hilt and sharp metal, approached her face.*

He probably just meant to scare her; 'Amber' was a top-tier girl and brought in a lot even on slow nights. But something inside Zoe snapped, a hard clear sound she was surprised didn't echo through the entire building and register on the Richter scale as well. Her wrists ached, her hands tingled with sweet pain, and for one glorious moment she was completely unafraid.

The animal living inside her skin—a ball of appetite, nerves, and reflex—was fully awake.

And it wanted out.

Her knee jerked sharply up, nailing him right in the groin with considerable, nearly inhuman strength. Roy folded mid-syllable, making a woof *sound that would have been funny if the knife hadn't grazed her collarbone on the way down. The shallow slice was barely a papercut, but Zoe's hands flickered like hummingbird wings. The switchblade went flying, hit the glass coffee table with a clatter; a splatter of blood hung in the air, a strangely beautiful suspended arc, before her hands moved again, hey presto, just like a magic trick.*

It was so easy, after all. Four deep parallel slices opened on Roy's naked chest to match the ones swiped down his face, muscle showing raw and red before the blood began, and that was when he started to scream.

Unfortunately, Zoe—the girl he called Amber, the patient one, the top-tier who didn't need more than a token slap or shake to stay in line— was making a sound too. A glassy high-pitched cry laden with icy moon- light, swallowing the sound of Roy's howl.

Which was probably a good thing, because if the animal had heard him, she might have clawed him again just to get him to shut up. As it was, Zoe bolted, the apartment's front door shattering off its hinges and the tiny sequined working bag at her hip bouncing. No cash, no ID because Roy kept her fake one from the town before Akron, no clothes but the miniskirt and tank top she was wearing. She took only her bare hands and the purse carrying a broken plastic comb, some lip gloss, and a small stack of prophylactics.

'Amber' disappeared that cold, wet almost-spring night. Zoe fled south; she might not have stopped in Marquette if she'd had any real choice, because she had been certain she'd killed him.

Or maybe she was afraid that if she hadn't, the chained, tightly controlled animal in her would want to turn around, return to Akron, and hunt him down...

54
DOING BRILLIANTLY

THE FIRST TIME USING THE GENE IN CONTROLLED FASHION WAS ALWAYS A doozy, the shamans said. Unbidden flashes of intuition were common and only slightly wearying, training was a real workout, but deliberate invocation was something else. Which was why his *demie* was out like a light when Jack tucked her into her own soft blue bed, and perhaps why she mumbled restlessly, tossing while she dreamed.

He didn't mind. His usual insomnia after a disaster—his talent restlessly chewing over each scenario, attempting to dig deeper, to find more—vanished, and when he stretched out next to her, carefully atop the covers, the consciousness of his softly breathing *demie* wrapped around him in a warm cloud.

Every time she elbowed him, he half-woke and smiled. It was better than mere sleep or even unconsciousness.

Well before dawn, footsteps in the dark hall roused him, and Jack was up in half a heartbeat. He stepped out of Zoe's suite, shrugging back into his suit jacket, just as Dad halted a few paces away. The old man's eyes glowed soft blue, and his teeth flashed briefly in a hard, predatory grin.

"More bad news?" Jack swept the door closed, and pitched the words very low indeed to avoid waking his *demie*.

"Two more attempted kidnappings and a sniper attempt on Jorge Luzon down in Baja. He's furious at the insult—a skin with a gun? What next, you know?" Dad shrugged, the motion invisible to skin eyes but plainly evident to a Kith, even in the gloom. "How is she?"

"Tired." *And dreaming.* His twin's thoughts moved in dark shoals, only a few flickering fins visible. Still, Jack could tell the emotional direction they were swimming. Her nighttime landscape was dangerous, even if she was was comforted by her *demi*'s presence. "What do you need?"

"Just came to tell you we're moving the hunt downtown. The hackers cracked a single stream on the financials, Bella put it together with your work—and Zoe's." Dad's teeth glittered; his snarl was mirrored by Jack's own beast. "We've got a direction for our stateside hunters, and we'll take their money first."

"Good. What about the Plainswalkers?"

"Amerlane and the rest will land at Albany in about an hour. We've taken a great deal, territory as well as cash. Fantome's shoring up his remaining position, but who knows?" Clearly, Dad's tone said, he didn't care whether or not the Plainswalker stayed in power. "We've made our point, McFisk is already dead, and if Louisa takes over she's still bloodkin to McFisk, so we can require atonement if necessary. If our little dancer decides she wants it."

"Unlikely." Jack wouldn't mind tearing the life from any of McFisk's kin, blood or otherwise, but his sweet *demie* had suffered enough, and he wasn't going to disturb her peace any more than absolutely necessary. "She's...kind."

Nothing stirred in the house, a profound hush filling every corner. The peculiar quiet meant it was snowing again, and was tinged with the exhaustion of a day spent dealing with what turned out to be two separate but equally ugly disasters. Still, there would be Kith running the perimeter even in this weather, shaking off the cold, standing guard. Amelia would keep the kitchen warm all night, ready to ply them with calories and her approval.

"Well, she can afford to be." Dad sounded relieved; a Pride daughter was to be shielded and cosseted to the best of her parents' abilities, and he had a lot of catching up to do. "Moonfall's next week. Can she be ready? I know we wanted to give her time, but..."

Jack stilled. There was only one reason why Trevor would contemplate pushing Zo out of her comfort zone, especially since she still hadn't taken the change fully. "They found something else."

"The hackers have been busy; these stateside hunters had a whole dossier on my daughter. It fills in some gaps." The faintest whisper of Voice edged Dad's tone, and a dark edge invaded his familiar scent. "Bella's confirmed they were the other players after her. Zoe came to their attention in Ohio and they were tracing her south. We were about a month ahead of them, but still."

A month was far too close for Jack's liking. "And we have the whole thing?" Chill sharp prickles traced down his back at the thought of an oblivious, nervous Zoe wandering near skin hunters, especially this group with its restraints and tranquilizers instead of the usual assassination gear. "The whole thing?"

"Yes." Trevor paused, and his quiet strength was comforting. The damage, while severe, was well on its way to being contained. "It's... difficult reading; you won't like some parts. But now we know."

"And you want her at Moonfall. We did promise she didn't have to." It would make her safer, Jack supposed...but he wouldn't break a promise given to his *demie*. She was holding up like a champ despite seeing ugly, murderous skin jealousy; she was learning about the Kith, forgetting to be quite so afraid, and learning to accept his presence.

He wanted that trend to continue.

"Maybe you can make it sound intriguing?" Dad settled his jacket sleeves, quick habitual tugs. A slight untidiness to his golden mane and certain looseness to his tie were the only signs of stress allowed. Eventually Zoe might get him to unbend a bit, and Jack was looking forward to the event. "Allison thinks it's a good idea. Just...have her consider it?"

"I'll do my best." He eyed his father. "I see you didn't bring the file with you."

"It's in my office safe for whenever you're ready; cracking the combination again will do you good. I wanted you to hear this from me, though."

Ah. "That bad?"

"We should have found her years earlier," Dad said, and only his heir would ever hear such open pain in his voice. Any other Kith would receive the imperturbability of a leader—the rock to lean on, no whisper of uncertainty or agony escaping. Such was the price of dominance, and rule. "It never occurred to anyone she could have the Gene, even Allison—which shows just how powerful she is. And being raised as a skin? It's terrifying. What if I—what if we fail her?"

"I'll be right next to her," Jack promised softly. "Twenty-four-seven. Any problems won't have a chance to develop."

"I'm more worried she'll withdraw, or need seclusion. We've spent long enough without her already." Dad pushed stiff fingers through his hair, raking the mane, but the glow of anger in his eyes had abated somewhat. "Do what you can. If she can't attend I'll have a double security complement here."

Put like that, the suggestion took on a far more ominous cast. "You and Allison think they're after her specifically." *No wonder you had to be the one giving me the news.* Any other Kith, even a shaman, might have a little difficulty dealing with a *demi* who had not only suffered years of estrangement from his twin but also received confirmation she was targeted by filthy skin hunters.

"The overseas ones seem merely intent on murder. We think it's that Swiss group, and Michel's sworn vengeance." It was the mark of a Kith ruler that Trevor could say it so calmly, with only a faint tinge of distaste accompanied by a brief shrug. "Our local set obviously wants to carve us up for research, or just for torture's sake. And I can think of even worse scenarios."

"So can I." At least Jack could return to his twin's sleeping warmth in the next few minutes. "Try not to worry, Dad. She'll be fine."

"I hope so." Dad clasped Jack's shoulder, fingers digging in briefly. "I have to say, you're doing brilliantly. Good work."

The lump in his throat was small—but it was definite. "Happy to hear it, sir. I'm going back to bed." At least he had never doubted his father's affection, though it was sometimes harshly applied.

Trevor padded away, just loudly enough to warn another Kith of his approach. His shoulders were ruler-straight, but a little of the weight on them had eased.

Which was good to see. Jack slipped back through the door into the blue suite. As nice as it was to help Dad, returning to his *demie* was better.

And listening to her quiet breathing in the darkness was best of all.

55
WE'LL OBLIGE

THE SOLARIUM WAS BRIGHT AND RUSTLING, FULL OF DIRECTIONLESS snowglare and the smell of damp green since someone had watered the plants that morning. Probably Hermann—the retainer liked gardening, and said he thought better with his claws buried in earth.

"But...we should help." Zoe's eyebrows drew together and her mouth turned slightly down; even her frown was adorable. She'd chosen a bulky hunter-green cardigan today, wrapping herself in thick wool as if she needed armor. The sleeves were long enough to swallow her hands to the knuckles; when she played with the tortoiseshell buttons she looked like a little girl playing dress-up. Her hair was pulled severely back, braided with a vengeance, and the trace of damp at her nape was leftover from her morning bath.

"It's all moved to the building downtown," Jack repeated. It was strange to not be working himself round the clock after an attack, and perhaps she sensed his faint guilty unease at the change in responsibilities. Regardless, his *demie* needed him, and all business took a backseat to that imperative. "More resources there, and Dad said you need peace and quiet anyway. Allison won't be by for shaman lessons today either. We're gonna have some fun instead."

"Fun?" His *demie* set her tiny espresso cup down; clearly Amelia suspected the princess preferred rocket fuel this morning. "Is that even...I mean, someone's gone to heaven, Jack. More than one person."

Gone to heaven was a particularly Midwest euphemism. Maybe she'd heard it from McFisk. "The entire Kith mourns," Jack said, with traditional, reflexive politeness. His own coffee was straight black and thick as sin, just what he needed. The ten seconds of caffeine buzz would clear his head before vanishing, but even that was welcome. "We're hunting down those responsible. They'll face the wrath soon enough." No suit for him today, just jeans and a heavy black sweater; his *demie* had chosen a likewise outfit.

When her left hand moved the cardigan's cuff did too, and the princess signet's ruddy gleam was revealed. Seeing it was enough to make even an analyst believe in miracles. She also wore the first pair of boots he'd ordered for her, probably seeking some comfort in any familiarity.

His *demie* had arrived with nothing; hopefully some items since had begun to look like friends. The years without her receded into the blur-haze of a bad dream, and he liked it that way.

"Wrath, huh?" She hadn't seemed surprised at his presence in her bedroom that morning, but her baby blues were shadowed as if she hadn't had enough rest. A faint breeze touched green fronds and leaves, a shaman's restlessness echoing through warm air. "And hell-fire? I know a little bit about that."

"Skin theology." He wondered if she wanted to know about Kith funerals, about singing the dead to the ancestors, about resting in the Sun's heart or on the dark side of the Moon. "If they want hell so badly, we'll oblige. But *you* need to quit worrying. Dad'll be home for dinner and wanting to see you're all right."

"Breakfast!" Amelia chirped, appearing in the solarium door followed by a solemn-faced Lev, who carried a bulky tray. "Omelets for good children, you will need the strength today."

"Good morning." At least Zoe looked pleased to see the house-keeper. "I thought you'd be with Dad."

"Why? I stay to watch the hearth, and the little girl." Amelia began unloading the tray at high speed. Lev glanced uneasily at Jack —old habits died hard, but the kid brightened when Zoe spared him a good-morning smile. "My mate is with Mr. Trevor, and Allison too. Don't worry, he is very safe."

It was laughable to think of Dad needing protection, but Zoe's expression eased as the jäger and Lev left. The young Kith's boots and curls both bore traces of snow, since he'd been running the perimeter that morning. He was probably near to bursting with pride that Meel let him take that duty, too.

Thankfully, Zoe set about consuming her spinach and feta omelet with something approaching real appetite instead of her usual mannerly, painful reticence. "So you don't think Dad needs us?" Her eyebrows rose, and Jack was a fool, because he was ready to agree to just about anything she wanted, despite every consideration of safety and good sense.

"You already helped immensely, and he was very emphatic that you stay here and rest." *I happen to agree with him.* But he'd prepared a counter to her possible objections, and it was ready for deployment. "I thought we'd get out of the house a little, though, if you were up for it. We can go for a run."

"In eight feet of snow?" Now she smiled, reaching for the wooden salt shaker. There was also a small mountain of sourdough toast, whipped butter, three different pots of jam, and a fat-bellied glass jar of honey.

Amelia was leaving nothing to chance.

"Less than a meter of snow, Zo-baby." Jack watched her smile at his pedantic tone; to be understood was a gift, rain after years of drought. "That doesn't trouble us."

"Running." Testing the word, and her swift glance at his expression lingered. "I hated gym class."

"It's not like that." He applied himself to his own omelet and wheat toast; Meel had even cut the crusts off, as if he was six years old again. "Trust me."

"Can I?" All seriousness now, gravely pretty in the solarium's brightness, her raven braid gleaming as she regarded him. It was increasingly easier to pretend she'd been here all along; he hoped she found it as soothing as he did.

"I won't leave you in a snowdrift, if that's what you're asking." What else could he say? For all the pretense she gracefully acceded to, a *demie*'s easy reliance on her twin might take years to develop. Hopefully, seeing Dima and Bell model healthy *usanaugh* interactions would rub off on her. "I promise you'll enjoy it."

"We'll see." But a shy smile returned, lurking at the corners of her mouth, and she pushed her cardigan sleeves up, showing delicate wrists. The tennis bracelet glittered sharply, and seeing her wearing traditional Pride gifts was a blessing in and of itself. "Do I have to wear exercise clothes? I think Janine sent some."

"If you want." The thought had definite possibilities. Jack didn't have to guard against the constant devouring worry of her absence; the relief was daily, intense, and showed no sign of abating. "But what you have on now is fine."

"Maybe different shoes?" She had practically consented, and now she was working on logistics. No doubt she'd attempted to mother Angelina; Jack would bet his favorite watch and all his cufflinks that all her skin coworkers had felt the benefit of that anxious caretaking reflex.

Some of them might even have mistaken it for weakness.

"We could run barefoot if we wanted to, even in this weather." Today's lesson would start the process of training her for Moonfall, assuming she agreed to attend the celebration. The dossier in Dad's office safe could wait until Jack had a few quiet moments to crack the combination—Dad was probably using a randomizer now—and swallow the file whole, tucking its contents in mental drawers for later absorption. "We're Kith, *demie*. Eat up."

56
SNOWRUNNING

Lev or Gessel had been out shoveling, so there was a relatively clear path through what Jack said was a rose garden in summer— though it seemed impossible that any season other than white winter could exist. Tiny ice-pellets spattered down at random intervals, and the wind was a knife.

Still, even the dreary grey sky was somehow alive today, and the cold pressed against Zoe without reaching a warm inner core now that she had...enough.

It was a luxurious feeling. She could stay like this forever, in a comfortable, cushioned snowglobe. But the image from yesterday— the bodies, the blood, the shredded car surrounded by diamond glitters of broken safety glass—wouldn't go away.

Outside this thin glass sphere of calm, terrible things lurked.

"You probably already know about this." Jack bounced slightly on his booted toes before settling. He would have left the house in just sweater-and-jeans, but Zoe insisted he wear a coat—and he gave in, grinning sheepishly.

It was nice to feel like she had some control, even if it was simply nagging someone to wear a jacket like sitcom parents always did. "I know how to run." After all, she'd been doing it almost all her life.

"Yeah, you were pretty fast when I found you, but I'm familiar with the ground here." Jack set off down the shovel-scraped walk. "And I'm gonna teach you something cool. This way."

Their footsteps crunched companionably on frozen pavement, the house a warm solid bulk watching them with golden windows, its solid roof heavily frosted. All the Christmas lights were packed away, and a few chimneys sent up thin curls of woodsmoke.

The pool—drained and covered for the winter—was behind a wrought-iron fence, and the gate was frozen solid. The poolhouse was larger than many an apartment she'd seen, let alone lived in, and the mounded shapes of bushes under heavy snow sat stolid, patient, waiting for any thaw. The back of Jack's black wool coat was starred with tiny clear droplets, melted ice beginning a slow buildup.

"This'll work." He stopped, golden head slightly tilted as he inspected the snow, and indicated an unbroken sweep of drifts going down a slight incline. It would be a field in summer, she thought, and there was a crooked wooden fence in the distance. Dark smudges—copse and grove—dotted the paper-white hillocks and hollows. "We won't go too far. Give me your hand."

It was scary, how her arm extended without any real effort on her part. Her ungloved fingers laced with his, again without conscious effort. It felt...

...well, it felt *right*. Warm, and safe. Natural.

"Okay, now step up. Like this." Jack took a single step off the cleared walk, lifting his foot absurdly high.

Amazingly, the snow didn't give under his boot. It stayed pristine, unbroken, and he tugged at her hand.

She expected to plunge right through and flounder while he laughed. But a strange vibration poured over her bones, a hummingbird flutter, and it came from the feel of his skin against hers.

"Oh." So that was how he did it. Simple, it was even *easy*, and she wondered why she hadn't figured this out before.

"Fun, huh?" He grinned down at her, balancing on the thin top-crust of a snowdrift. "Take a step. Real light, just roll through. See, you're a natural."

"You're doing it." Zoe could feel him reaching through the twin-bond somehow, quiet glowing strength bridging gaps, filling in broken places. Instinct leapt between them, the wordless understanding of muscle and bone.

"Same way I'll teach you about the change if you have trouble." He tugged at her again, their soles only making the lightest feathery impression on drift-tops. The wind combed his hair, pressed damp cold fingers against Zoe's cheek. "Try it again, roll through. Perfect. There's a party soon, the whole Pride. You want to go?"

Oh, God, I barely got through the last one. How many parties do you guys need? Still, she'd endured Christmas and New Year's without any huge problems. "Do I have to?" She let him help her to the top of a snow-covered boulder, its sides striped with darker bands of ice and melt.

"Of course not." He hopped, landing feline-soft. "But Dad thinks it's a good idea."

She followed suit without thinking and landed beside the rock, just as lightly. A hot, happy flower bloomed inside her ribs, and Zoe found she was wearing a dopey, disbelieving grin. "Wow. I never..." Why hadn't she figured this out before?

"That's not even the best part." Jack pulled on her hand again—gentle, irresistible pressure. "Come on, *demie*. Let's run."

Her boots were butterflies, wings drumming sensitive air. Jack's hand fell away from hers, but the twinbond still blazed between them, a bright star dilating until it was a tunnel pouring strength into her bones.

Zoe unfolded into an effortless leap, hanging over a small steep-sided gully with a trickle of ice at its bottom before touching down on the other side, dodging trees like rollerskating while carrying a full drinks tray and not spilling a drop, curving away from Jack and finding herself almost alone under a flat hard iron-pan sky, ice crystals stinging her cheeks and her heart flutter-pumping.

But he caught up a half-breath later, matching her stride for stride. A high soprano cry burst from Zoe's throat, surprising her. Jack's howl was different, a basso grumble shaking spatters of snow from ice-freighted branches as they plunged into a frozen grove and out the other side. He veered and she followed, sensing his caution— there was a ribbon of asphalt nearby, a nose-stinging tang of exhaust, and that meant unfriendly eyes.

Skins.

Now, after plenty of good meals and a few shaman lessons—not to mention sleep—power sang in her veins and she was faster than her brother. Just a fraction, just a hair.

But that was enough, and she knew she could have eluded him in Marquette if she hadn't hesitated. If she hadn't been so exhausted, on the verge of giving up.

There were very few marks to show their passage—they simply skimmed above the snowcrust, hanging in place while the world turned underneath. All she had to do was touch her toes lightly every now and again. Zoe skidded to a stop in a clearing, head upflung, every muscle alive and aware, a statue of listening. Her ribs heaved, puffs of warm breath flashing into silvery cloud.

Was this what happiness felt like? Her heart was going to explode.

"See?" Jack's heat touched her shoulder, her entire right side. He wasn't gasping, but his hair was mussed, freighted with shimmering icy drops, and a flush painted his cheeks. "Told you. Instinct."

The air was bright champagne, bubbling and sparkling all the way down. She tasted a thaw coming, the weather shifting in a few days. Eventually this would all melt and a muddy green spring would emerge.

For the first time, she thought maybe she'd be here to see it.

Zoe bolted, slipping between trees—the deciduous ones raising naked arms, sugar-frosted evergreens hushed and secretive—and cutting across a gently rolling field of white. No footprint, almost no sound, icy pellets kissing her cheeks and peppering her coat, catching in the curls springing free of her braid. It was like running on the prairie during a thunderstorm, daring or begging Mama's terrifying, never-satisfied God to strike her down.

Leaping, dodging, cold air pouring down her throat and her eyes stinging, she ran. A stone wall curved before her and Jack was suddenly to her left, darting in to herd her away—that was probably the property line, and now she knew just how far he was willing to let her go. She reversed, streaking away over drifts and deadfalls, sure deep inner knowledge keeping her from tripping or falling. The house flashed by, an icy confection starred with golden lights, and she ran until another stone wall reared before her.

This time Jack appeared from her right. Zoe halted, her braid a heavy damp whip. This was amazing, it was uncanny, and worst of all, it was *fun*. Mama would have a fit.

No, she won't. Not ever again. You're free.

Well, if not free, at least in an endurable situation. But there were people with guns and tranquilizers hunting this side of her family. And now she knew Bea hadn't been entirely human after all.

Apparently Zoe wasn't either, but as she reached blindly for the stone wall to steady herself, hoping her side wouldn't cramp up—it felt just on the verge, muscles protesting unfamiliar use—it also occurred to her that being human was no great shakes, after all. Wars and murders and other terrible things were everywhere; in contrast, the Kith just seemed to...get along.

At least, she hadn't seen any disagreements or violence yet. How long would it take?

"Deep breaths," Jack said. He hovered at her shoulder; she hadn't managed to outrun him after all. Nobody would find their tracks; the snow was practically unbroken in every direction. "You feeling dizzy at all? Hungry?"

Her stomach was an empty aching. It was the same feeling she'd get as a kid after recess; she realized the daylight had changed. The sun had reached apogee and begun its daily descent, a barely brighter smear cloaked in heavy grey cloud. They'd been running longer than she thought.

"A little," she said, cautiously, and studied him, her fingers hovering a fraction from rough stone, blocks piled up and held together by heavy frost.

"First few times you can get dizzy, until you learn to pace yourself." Jack's dark eyes glowed, his hair stood up in all directions, and his coat was unbuttoned. "Amelia'll have a snack for us. When you're ready."

That's the question. What, exactly, am I ready for?

The terrible itching of uncertainty under her skin had receded. Zoe felt clear-headed again, and that was a welcome change. A shadow of an idea lingering at the back of her head glowed reassuringly, and it was another good feeling to have a definable goal.

She could start testing limits now. How far would they really let her go?

Did she really want to find out?

"Race you back," Zoe said, whirled once more, and took off for the house.

57
UNPLEASANT READING

IT WAS ENJOYABLE TO HAVE A DRINK BEFORE DINNER WHILE WAITING FOR HIS *demie* to change out of damp clothes and reappear. Trevor's study was an island of calm, his desk had been cleared, and the fire snap-popped companionably.

"Tested it on herself, of course." Dad's golden head gleamed; he gave an uncharacteristic deep sigh. Belmario was making good progress with the tranquilizer, but her methods were a little...enthusiastic. "Calls it *commitment to the process*."

"Well, she's a chemist." Pleasant tingles raced along Jack's limbs as he poured brandy. Running with his *demie* was welcome exercise, and after lunch they'd played tag almost all afternoon as the sky cleared and the temperature dropped. A hard freeze was on its way, but the dirty grey scent of a thaw in the not too distant future rode the back of the wind. "They're all crazy."

The good news was that the European skin hunters had been identified—it was indeed the Swiss bastards—and their tenuous alliance with the Vatican's costumed bigots, not to mention a certain Chechen group, had already begun to fray under the pressure of Kith response. Skins were laughably easy to divide-and-conquer; they did it so often to themselves any outside force was naturally assisted by the habit.

It was also clear the stateside and foreign hunters weren't cooperating. The ravaging of Lucile Duhalde's corpse—and the bodies of her guards—had merely been fanatical, not the taking of tissue samples as Jack had initially feared.

If this new tranquilizer became a global thing, though, they'd have problems.

"I seem to remember you receiving high marks in your own chemistry studies, son. Anyway, she'll have full countermeasures ready soon." Trevor accepted a tumbler of spiced rum, his ring glittering venomously, and his gaze roved beyond the window, searching and restless. "We have a few teams are going after high-value staff at the pharma companies—we can either turn them or rob the skins of their expertise. The hackers had a breakthrough just before the markets closed, and they'll spend all night siphoning and tracking. Our particular problem is well-funded. Guess."

"Not religious, though I'm sure the overseas hunters probably got at least thirty percent of their operating funds from the Vatican." It was a good thing the Church Militant wasn't in full control of more than a few square miles of rotting Tiber-adjacent real estate anymore. Jack held the brandy snifter under his nose, enjoying the sharp, balanced aroma. "That's the most likely carrot getting all the mules to pull together. But I'd wager our homegrown bastards are more scientific. Some oligarchs looking for a fountain of youth."

"That's what Bella said. The shell companies are clustered, which was sloppy of them. Your sister seems to have found all the major funding streams, and following the threads will give us the whole spiderweb." Dad's grin held a shadow of fatigue; a leader, whether of pride, pack, or sleuth, did not rest until a threat had been neutralized. "Mac wants to interview Jasperson again. I told him he'd have to wait for you."

"I appreciate that. I've got an uneasy feeling, even if I trust Mac's ability to squeeze a little shit like Greg." The last thing they needed was McKenna tearing the traitor to pieces before all his secrets— including the ones Jasperson the younger didn't know he was holding —were plumbed. "I don't know what that waste is likely to have that skate won't have burned out of his brain, but we need be sure."

It was an unpleasant prospect. He didn't want Zoe to see what he might have to do in order to induce a treasonous Kith to be even more forthcoming...but there was no help for it. The sense of a missing piece, an instrument just slightly out of tune, returned each time Jack thought about the attempts to kidnap Kith women and cubs.

"Pays to be thorough." Dad stared out the window, probably not even seeing the clear, subzero night full of glimmering stars and waxing moon. "Gibs and his crew will be unraveling shell companies all night, tracking the real players. Michel wants to eviscerate them all, near and far, and sow salt over the remains. Nobody really disagrees, but the shamans are adamant the innocent can't be touched. Since we're better than that." A faint shade of anger perilously close to disbelief tinted Trevor's tone.

"They're right." Jack's own tightly reined bloodlust would be audible, too. "At least we have her home."

Trevor's stony mask broke, and a smile teased at his lips. "Played in the snow today, did you?"

"She's fast. Pasted me with a snowball, even." And his *demie*'s laughter at his surprise was like silver bells; Jack hadn't wanted even mock-vengeance. "She seems to be—"

"She seems to be what?" The door ghosted open, and Zoe appeared. A pale peach twinset, the princess signet a bloody glitter on her left hand and the tennis bracelet on her right wrist, she tilted her head and a raven curl fell into her face. She blew it away with a mischievous smile, her lips pursing briefly, and Jack's heart stopped. "Hi, Dad." No hint of shyness in the greeting, either.

Dressing for dinner was a damn civilized custom, and now Jack wished he'd changed into a suit. Had she been listening?

"Little dancer." Trevor skirted the desk, set his drink down, and offered himself for a brief hug—which Zoe gave with every evidence of calm enjoyment. The wound in the Pride was healing. "You look lovely. Did you have a good day?"

"We went running." A quick glance at Jack, those baby blues darkening, made the link ignite in his chest. "Is everyone all right?"

Of course she'd worry, but at least she'd had an entire day of moving too fast to brood. It was a gift Jack longed to repeat.

"Everyone's fine." Trevor patted her shoulder, carefully, all claws velveted. "The unpleasantness will be over soon; you shouldn't worry."

A shadow crossed her face—did she think Dad was being dismissive? Being protected was probably a new sensation for a girl raised as a skin.

The fire gave a subdued pop, and if the thread of mouthwatering scent tiptoeing through the house from the kitchens wasn't Amelia's famous herb bread, he'd eat his hat.

"I was thinking." Tension invaded Zoe's slim shoulders, and she watched their father very carefully indeed. "Can I go into the city tomorrow?"

Hallelujah. "Sure thing," Jack said, immediately. He'd been hoping for a field trip, if only to make her more accustomed to little courtesies—her door opened, her coat held, an arm to lean on. "I've got some errands too, so—"

But his *demie* had other ideas. "By myself." Zoe took a step back, still watching Dad as if Jack hadn't spoken.

So, the princess was testing the kingdom's borders. It had to happen sooner or later, and *that* was why she was wearing the jewelry.

It was armor. So was her carefully applied lip gloss, and the peach cashmere.

"Well..." Trevor scooped his drink back up, but he moved a fraction more slowly than usual, careful not to startle or unnerve. "It's best not to go alone. Will you consider taking your brother with you? Get him out of the house, give him something to do."

"He has work." Zoe gave Jack a quick, breathlessly blue glance. Cold fresh air clung to her despite the change in outfit; the dirty yellow scrape of fear hadn't quite invaded her scent yet, but it was close. "Right?"

Be careful. "Nothing that can't be put off. You know how lazy I am." Jack shrugged; if she wanted the illusion of solitude, he could give it. Trailing his *demie* without being noticed would be an enjoyable game. "Sarah or Jolie might want to go into town too, though. Girls' day out."

"Never mind, it was just an idea." His *demie* swung away, nervous and delicate as a doe returning to cover. "The weather's bad anyway, right? I'm going to see if Amelia needs help."

Dad might have said something else, but she was already on her way to the door, her heels making soft, authoritative little noises. The sway of her hips was pleasantly distracting; still, the tension vibrating in the twinbond gave Jack pause. "Zo?"

"Hm?" She froze, her shoulders coming up—a slight twitch, ready and braced. It hurt to see; he'd been so careful, so endlessly patient.

Still, when nothing bad happened, she'd relax eventually. It might take years, but they had plenty of those to spend now.

"We can go wherever you want," Jack pointed out. "Dad just worries about security. Especially with all this going on."

"I get it." Bright, brittle cheerfulness filled the words, a distinct change from a carefree afternoon playing in the snow. She vanished again, retreating down the hall and obviously making no effort to be silent now.

"Is she..." Dad looked baffled, for once, and it was the first time Jack could remember the old man looking to his heir for direction instead of the other way 'round.

"She's testing limits." Conflicting emotions poured through the twinbond, rasping along Jack's nerves—but at least she wasn't attempting to shut him out, nor was she contemplating escape of a different sort. Which was a distinct relief. "It's a lot to take in."

"I didn't hear her approach." Trevor took a hit off his rum, blue eyes narrowed and the cufflinks she'd given him for Christmas glinting. "A quick study, just like her brother."

Jack made a soft noise of assent, most of his attention on the steady waves of feeling echoing through the link. Maybe it was a psychological reaction to the closeness of the bond, or perhaps she felt safe enough to truly express her preferences now. "I'll take her into the city after Moonfall, I think. We can wait that long."

"Ah." Their father nodded, and his relief was almost transparent. "So she'll join us?"

"I think I've got her talked into it." And today had proved beyond a doubt that she could run, the change spilling through her in fierce waves but not quite breaking free. All she needed was the last little piece, and the collective pressure of other Kith all around her would provide it.

"*That* is good news." Trevor tossed the rest of his rum down, baring his teeth afterward. His reflection in the window copied the motion, almost snarling with relief. "Well, when you *do* take her into town, will you want security?"

Which meant Dad was counting on Jack to know what was best for his *demie*, and he appreciated the vote of confidence. "I don't, and she'll sense it. But if it makes you feel better, by all means." Jack finished his brandy too, grimacing slightly at the brief flare of sharp alcoholic heat. Maybe he even looked like Trevor when he did so; he wouldn't mind that at all. "We'll have to visit Jasperson together, after all."

Dad didn't ask if she was ready for *that*. He simply nodded, consigning the prospect to its proper place in a never-ending cavalcade of a Kith ruler's worries, and pointed out it was nearly time for dinner.

He wanted to be in the blue suite, listening to his *demie* breathe as she slept. Instead, he was in his own rooms, lounging in a sleek black leather chair with his sock feet propped on the glass coffee table, sipping a brandy and paging through a dossier skin hunters had compiled on his twin.

It was highly unpleasant reading. A young, vulnerable girl alone in the world, running on an explosive cocktail of shaman's sensitivity and Kith-sharp reflexes—it was a good thing *demie* couldn't become Broken, because another of their kind might well have needed hunting down and dispatching after that.

And while girl *usanaugh* were completely immune from falling, they could very well decide existence was unendurable and withdraw into suicidal apathy. Even an analyst had trouble contemplating such a prospect calmly; Jack had to look across the room and exhale sharply after reading about a few...incidents, in his twin's prior life.

She'd vanished from Hall City after a fire at McFisk's Righteous Savior Church, the blaze probably shaman-fueled because it stubbornly resisted any control until it had consumed the entire building. A series of small-time jobs on either side of the law followed, as she drifted eastward—she'd moved pretty steadily, as if unconsciously drawn in her *demi*'s direction, changing names and Social Security numbers almost constantly. This collection of sightings and filings filled great gaps in the Pride's research of her movements after Angelina's death—which had been more blank spots than anything else until she arrived on the Howler's turf—and as Jack read he turned alternately cold and feverish, because the skin hunters had been practically breathing down her neck.

She'd tangled Kith *and* skin pursuit. Both were startling achievements for an untrained girl who thought she was a skin herself. She wasn't even twenty-one yet—their birthday was in May, he had to think of presents—and had managed all this.

Zoe never spoke of the time between Hall City and Marquette.

Now he could see why. Her restless motion took a brief break in Akron, Ohio, where she did a six-month stint in a 'gentleman's club'.

Which was interesting, and ended with the owner of the club in the hospital.

Said owner was a reasonably young skin male, and the collection of emergency-room photos were pitilessly lit by flash and fluorescents. Looked like he'd mouthed off to a Kith and would wear the proof for the rest of his wasted life.

Jack hated the bastard on sight, and there was a definite similarity—strong jaw, dark hair cut douchebag-style, a certain crafty glitter in the eyes—to the skin on the train New Year's Day. Zoe had clearly seen the resemblance; they were probably lucky she hadn't run screaming from the subway.

No arrests from that Akron incident, naturally. The police report was interesting reading and the officer producing it was most probably a low-level contact for the stateside skin hunters, but that wasn't unusual. Everyone with any real pull knew it was good business practice to keep a cop or two in the pocket.

Possible animal attack was written carefully on the report, and Jack's smile was a cold, thin curve.

Zoe wasn't overtly mentioned, so at least the skin—Royal Petterson, he even *sounded* like a dickwad—had enough sense to keep his mouth off a *demie*'s name. On the other hand, she'd no doubt been using one of many fake monikers, chosen at what she probably thought was random but was no doubt the subtle inner prompting of the Gene.

After marking Petterson she'd run southwest, and the trail was not just cold but frigid until she showed up in Marquette, deep within the Howler's territory.

The skin hunters had been hampered once she crossed the Howler's borders because he ran a tight security ship, comparable to Dad's own, and they couldn't find much purchase inside his borders. Ironically, that very apparatus had finally caught on to the presence of a stray Kith girl on the packleader's turf, which had set off all sorts of alarm bells.

Maybe by that point she'd wanted to be found, or some part of her had? It looked like marking the skin in Akron had frightened her so badly she'd fled even the subtle pull toward her *demi*, if indeed that had been drawing her eastward from Nebraska.

Jack closed the dossier and took another hit of brandy to wash the taste out of his mouth. A clear hard freeze had descended with full dark, and the house was silent except for stealthy creaks as it dozed, its hide protecting inhabitants from the weather's fury. He could sense his *demie* settled for the night next door, either asleep or getting there.

Warm and safe, where she belonged. Now she wanted to go into the city by herself; what on earth was she thinking? Was she simply testing boundaries, or was there a darker reason? Some battered creatures fought any attempt to provide aid, driven so far past trust any refuge was treated as a life-threatening trap.

At least the twinbond, strengthening daily, could communicate her emotional weather and strong, specific thoughts intended for her *demi*. It would only intensify. Soon they would have very few secrets, if any.

All he had to do was wait.

58
EYE AND CLAW

THE ANTICIPATED THAW TUNNELED THROUGH PILED DRIFTS, TURNING THEM sloppy grey during daylight before freezing sugarcrust-hard once dark fell. Dusk probably wasn't a great time to be driving, even with a bright full silver moon a little above the horizon, but the cloud-grey SUV slipped smoothy over well-plowed roads, snow tires faithfully performing their duty.

Zoe's fingers twisted together so hard they hurt. It was a nice car, with privacy tinting plus all the bells and whistles. The leather seats even had heaters, in case a tender rich tush caught the shivers.

The windshield filled briefly with oncoming headlights, a bright glare draining quickly. It would have been a sedate, pleasant snowy drive, if not for the destination. Sure, they were studiously casual about this particular gathering, especially Jack, but they had to suspect Zoe's hearing was sharp as theirs. *Moonfall*, they called it.

A Kith thing, and she had to measure up. She just *had* to.

"I'd tell you to relax." Jack kept glancing at her sidelong, though his hands were steady on the wheel. "But I don't think you're going to." Ahead of them, another SUV, matching grey, held Amelia, Hermann, and Trevor. The big house stood empty except for the electronic security system, because the staff, including Lev and Sarah, had left earlier that afternoon.

Zoe would have preferred to stay there, wandering the halls and listening to the silence. There was nothing better than the absolute freedom of being left home alone, though young Zoe had sometimes been paralyzed with the fear of Mama simply leaving her behind like a broken suitcase.

And besides, she'd miss Jack. It was deeply unsettling to admit as much, even if only to herself. Closing herself up alone in the suite every evening meant she had time to think, true—but she ended up pacing or brooding instead of enjoying the space and quiet, and the discomfort would mount until she went to bed or was driven out into the hall in the middle of the night.

Each time she stepped out of the blue suite, he was waiting. Which should have been creepy as fuck but instead was a relief, like finally reaching a persistent itch right between the shoulderblades.

And in the absence of shaman lessons, since Allison was busy with the current crisis, Jack was teaching her to run the way Kith did, though 'teaching' was kind of a strong term for showing her the way and letting instinct take over. All these years she hadn't really had a clue how strong or fast she really was.

Could've used that in Akron. Or hell, anywhere else. "I could run back." She stared at the taillights ahead, two glowing-bloody blots. Dad would be disappointed if she didn't do attend this thing, and so would her brother. "Just watch a movie and wait for everyone to get home."

"I'm glad you're finally calling it home. And this is gonna be fun. I promise." More headlights cast sharp shadows across Jack's face. *Dress comfortably*, he'd said, but she knew 'party' didn't mean 'comfort'.

"Allison thinks I can do it." She hated the nervous-talking thing, and had thought she'd successfully trained herself out of it. "Dad thinks I can. You think I can too."

"I *know* you can." God bless him, he sounded certain. But when didn't he?

Jack was always so sure, and she was a ball of bare, sparking nerves.

What if I hurt someone? What if I somehow turn into a misbegotten because of Mama? What if... Every prospect was worse than the one before, and all the encouragement from everyone was a torment because it just made her inevitable failure worse.

She couldn't figure out if she was truly trapped, either. On the one hand, everyone seemed to assume she and Jack were joined at the hip, and if there were people hunting Kith with tranquilizers and real bullets it made sense not to go wandering around alone. On the other, she'd survived since Hall City by sensing pursuit and knowing when to jump, and her instincts were screaming in weird, uncoordinated bursts like they couldn't figure out which direction the threat was coming from.

But was it just good old-fashioned paranoia? If she had some alone time Zoe could probably figure it out, but there wasn't any solitude unless it was in the blue suite, and not even then because of the twinbond—which seemed to be getting stronger, if that were possible.

The image of Dimitri and Bella on the library couch returned at odd intervals, and she wished she didn't blush like an idiot each time. It wasn't like seeing Mama with her boyfriends, either. The complex tangle of feelings was all but inarticulate, which made it doubly frightening.

Everything was worse when you couldn't find a name for it. Even running on the property with Jack didn't halt the restlessness, her brain jumping from one worry to the next like a flea on a hot tin cat, her nerves rubbed crossways with the constant sense of unfriendly attention creeping closer.

The two SUVs banked carefully into a right-hand turn, slipping through an open wrought-iron gate with wicked frost-starred spikes.

The driveway was just as sealed and ice-free as the one at Trevor's house.

"It's a nice estate," Jack continued. "Quiet for the shamans and plenty of room, but I like home better. Frankly I like the carriage house most. Lived there for a couple years before we found you."

Before we found you. Four little words. She was well and truly in the fairytale now, and waiting for the dark, terrible punishment part to begin was driving her batshit.

She knew where the carriage house was, and had run past it several times with him. Imagine, having whole *houses* to leave empty —and then there was this, the shamans' estate, which was either Allisons's home or just a gathering place.

'Plenty of room' was the understatement of the year. The shamans' estate looked like a honest-to-God chateau that should have been surrounded by vineyards, and every window was lit though no Christmas lights were in evidence here either. Some places left decorations up until spring, but not these people.

Of course with the number of parties these people seemed to throw, no wonder they had so many color-coded tubs of ornaments, hangings, and the like. It was exhausting; how did they *do* it?

A knot of Kith stood on wide, shallow stone steps before a massive bronze-colored door, but there were surprisingly few cars in the barnlike garage that looked like it had once been a stable, its wooden doors pushed wide. She had to wait for Jack to open her door, again.

It was expected, so she stayed in the passenger seat, smoothing her skirt nervously and taking deep breaths of leather-scented still-ness. This wine-red woolen dress was really more autumn than winter, but the skirt fell to mid-shin as well as having plenty of swing, and she could wear it with the long black coat and a pair of heavy silver-buckled boots. The outfit had seemed daring and artistic in the full-length closet mirror, especially with earrings, her signet, and a few of the glittering hair clips Janine had sent for the

Christmas party providing a bit of sparkle, but now she was deadly certain she was ridiculously underdressed.

Either that or she'd missed some sort of invisible rich-person memo and would be laughed out the party.

"You look great, by the way." Jack swung the passenger door closed, gauging the force perfectly. The alarm turned on with a chirp, and he offered his arm. In charcoal trousers and V-neck sweater over a crisp white button-down, he looked like what Royal's girls would have called an easy date, meaning good payment, nothing too strenuous, and perhaps even a modicum of politeness. "Just like a shaman."

Oh, God. But she had to smile like she agreed, so she did. Her heart kept trying to hop into her throat, even the moon-tinged night outside the house was too uncomfortably bright, and if not for Jack's free hand locked over hers in the crook of his elbow she might decide to put all the running lessons to good use. His ring gave a blood-tinged glitter—at least they matched that way, though his was gold and hers silver.

Dad was already at the door, listening to an older Kith man with a greying mane and a bloodless mouth moving swiftly as he muttered what had to be news. Probably about the hunters.

Skin hunters.

"Happy Moonfall!" The streak in Allison's hair glowed. The head shaman wore a broomstick skirt and a silky black peasant blouse; a loose belt with silver conchas rested easily on her hips. A great wave of relief poured from Zoe's scalp all the way down to her toes; she wasn't over- or underdressed. For once, she'd guessed correctly.

"We're finally complete again, it's great," Allison continued, and actually bounced a little, like an excited child. "Come in, come in, let's get started."

The floor-to-ceiling windows on either side of a vast vaulted ballroom were wide open, cold air pouring through. Zoe hoped the heat was turned off; then again, they probably had enough to pay whatever bill presented itself, which just made her wonder—once again—just how in the hell she'd managed to get swept up by these people.

Maybe their eyes hurt too, because the lights were low, the two massive, tinkling crystal chandeliers dimmed. The assembled Kith were restless, electric mutters racing through small groups as they formed and broke apart amid mutters of conversation and bright spangles of laughter.

McKenna sidled up, punched Jack lightly on the shoulder. "There he is." His khakis were neatly pressed, and like Jack, he wore no watch tonight. "Gonna run you ragged this fine evening, old man."

"So what else is new?" Jack tipped his chin, still holding onto her almost for dear life. "Hey, Pindar."

"Thank goodness you're here." Jolie's smile was as serene as ever, and she gave Zoe its full benefit, her long black skirt—very much like Allison's—swaying as she halted at McKenna's side. Her sandalwood hair was loose except for a clip holding her bangs aside, and she wore a heart-shaped silver locket with a small but undoubtedly real emerald glinting on its curved face. "Another shaman is always welcome with this crowd."

"We're strong-willed." Janine Traleski appeared, all but rubbing her elegant hands together with glee. She was in butter-soft designer jeans and a black velvet blazer over a silk shell, so maybe that was what they meant when they said 'comfortable'. Her ruddy hair was down, for once, and the soft mass suited her. "Oh, my dear, you look *lovely*. Happy Moonfall."

"Thank you," Zoe managed faintly. "Happy Moonfall."

It took her a few moments to realize what unnerved her so much. Not a single one of them held anything resembling a glass of alcohol or anything else. And the youngest Kith here were in late adolescence, none of the children or preteens.

This was a grown-up family party. She wondered where the parents of the truly young kids were, and if they resented being home while everyone else did...whatever this was. God knew Mama would have.

Don't think about that. Zoe kept her smile plastered firmly on, and for once she wished there was booze available. Taking a belt or two of bourbon sounded heavenly, though it wouldn't get her even mildly tipsy.

"You're doing great." Jack drew her away from Mac and Jolie; Janine gave a cheeky farewell wink before gliding away with a statuesque blonde woman in a lace-edged pink dress, a silk hibiscus over her left ear. "Pretty soon Dad'll give the signal, and we'll sing. Then..."

"Have you done this a lot?" Zoe caught sight of Dimitri and Bella through a gap in the crowd; Dima's arm was over Bell's shoulders, and he nuzzled her hair while the *demie* chatted animatedly with Lev.

Zo looked away, hurriedly, her cheeks suddenly furnace-hot.

"Once, to prove the change." Jack shrugged, steering them through the crowd, and didn't let her pull away. His hand clamped over hers as if he suspected just how longingly she was thinking about escape. "Couldn't after that, because my *demie* was gone. I think I'm as nervous as you are."

It didn't seem possible. "I don't believe you." Yet despite the knot in her stomach, she found herself smiling.

How did he *do* that?

"Check and see." Jack glanced down at her, wearing the most lopsided and charming of his many grins. "Half of what you're marinating in right now is my stress. I could use a drink."

"Well, you've got the car keys right in your pocket." Oddly, she felt better now. The other Kith seemed to sense her anxiety, or it was tradition to leave someone alone their first time doing...whatever this was. Or maybe Jack warned them to stay away, in that mannerly but no-nonsense way of his. "We could just drive back to—"

"Ladies and gentlemen." Trevor's tone pierced the crowd's murmur effortlessly. Dad strode into the ballroom, for once in trousers and a sweater like Jack's instead of a crisply pressed dark suit, and Kith parted like he was Moses taking a seashore stroll. "Tonight is a blessed night."

"So let's get on with it," someone said, in a clearly audible undertone. It sounded an awful lot like McKenna, and Trevor's smile, while truly amused, was also somehow forbidding as a glacier. A rustle of amusement slid through the crowd.

"It's the first Moonfall of the year, and the Pride is whole again." Dad's gaze settled on Zoe, and she was glad Jack was protectively close. Waiting for her father or brother to finally snap was nerve-shredding, but at least she'd have some warning if her twin was angry at her.

She'd *feel* it.

"The lady of the night rises." Allison's voice was soft but clear at the opposite end of the ballroom, and a profound hush fell over the crowd. The crowd moved away from her, too, and the shaman stood with her head tipped back, her gaze on the ceiling as if she saw the sky instead. "We are Her children."

"*We are Her children,*" the Kith answered, except Jack and Zoe. Her twin didn't look at Allison, either—instead, he turned his head and gazed down at Zoe, who shivered. The ballroom was vast; the night full of freezing slush and the iron smell of more snow breathed softly through its throat. There were more Kith just outside on a broad icy patio, and they were lit not only by the house's soft glow but also a faint silver.

Moonlight.

"We are strong, we are quick, we are bright." This came from Jolie, her dark eyes lambent and her hair stirring on the chill breeze.

Again, the Kith answered. "*We are strong, we are quick, we are bright.*"

"Eye and claw." Trevor's baritone, underlaid by an eerily modulated humming. "Fang and hide."

"*Eye and claw.*" The hum mounted. "*Fang and hide.*"

Jack's lips twitched. He clearly knew the ritual responses, but wasn't saying them because she didn't. A great burst of red-tinged relief and another, more scalding emotion passed through her; Zoe's skin felt shrinking-tight, as if she'd just opened a hot oven.

The hum mounted. It was like the end of the Christmas party, but this time the sound went on and on, the shamans producing a glassy soprano note like foam atop a dark wave. Zoe shifted uneasily, her throat aching, and finally couldn't stop her own piercing addition to the noise.

Anticipation crested. Her skin rippled, each hair awake, alive, and stretching. She shifted again, desperately trying to contain the animal locked in her bones. It wanted out, like in Hall City or Akron; it wanted freedom.

It wanted to *run*.

The link vibrated through her entire body, and suddenly her twin was in her head, a hot welcoming flood of sunshine. The animal recognized him, stretching with relief, and her surroundings—singing Kith, open ballroom, the chill of winter night, snow and slush and the rising dish of the moon thrumming its own massive chord to add to the chorus—fell away.

There was only Jack, and the need to *move*.

A single coughing roar lifted from the mass of Kith, glass shattered, and a cold draught poured down Zoe's throat because her lips were slightly parted. The chill tasted of silver, of darkness, of fur and wild white wine.

And the animal in her bones, her oldest, most faithful companion, swallowed her whole.

59
MOONFALL

A Kith's first Moonfall was disorienting, and normally the entire Pride closed around the young ones, guiding and protecting as they learned the change. They had to try to keep her on the estate, but Zoe was *demie*, not to mention bearing the Gene. Her beast was strong, and for once she wasn't fighting it.

At least a few days' worth of running practice meant Jack knew how she liked to move, and he was right—it couldn't be her first time using the change. She'd shifted enough to claw the shit out of a skin in Ohio, and he might have cheered if the Kith's inheritance wasn't burning in him as well, his beast focused unblinkingly on its counterpart inside her skin.

The shamans' estate was relatively large, and normally the Pride ran clockwise in its confines, a tide of half-seen forms with bright eyes, glossy hair, glittering teeth. They flowed from skinform to beast and back again, dancing on the edge between perfect control and complete abandon.

In the center of the wild mass his twin ran, and he was a half-step behind her. Leaping deadfall, sliding over frozen drifts, cresting hills and plunging into ink-black valleys, her beast lunged and twisted, attempting to break the wall of bodies. The other shamans were endless wells of stillness even as they moved, their calm swallowing any stray aggression or ill temper, and the deep satisfaction of collective consensus flooded every Kith.

Except one. His *demie* was used to being alone, apart; she feared union.

Still, he was inside her skin and she stretched into his, a splitskin ecstasy ringing in every footstep like ripe fruit just before bursting, filling lungs and heart and bones with hot satisfaction.

Was this what skins felt when drunk or drugged? Other Kith sometimes talked about the Moon suffusing them during these celebrations, but his twin was all he needed, and when she broke for the edge of the group again he was with her, feeling her irritation when a solid wall of others blocked her way.

Let me out, her keening silvery cry pleaded, and he longed to do whatever pleased her, give her whatever she wanted—no matter how deadly, no matter how dangerous.

The Kith survived by keeping this private; skins were weak and divided but had the weight of numbers on their side. Besides, every good predator knew to respect prey to some degree.

Even a rabbit could turn on its tormentors, and draw blood.

The Pride ran with its returned daughter, the wheel now whole, not missing a single spoke. Dad was in the vanguard, Allison at his side. Between the two poles, ruler and shaman, the track was laid and the Pride followed like a needle in a vinyl groove.

McKenna and Jolie pressed close; so did Dima and Bell, a hedge of protection around a newly returned *demie*. Zoe slipped from side to side, feinting and reversing with natural grace; her beast was dark and lithe, blue eyes burning like Dad's.

Jack was simply lost in the glory of her presence. The change was clearly no problem for his beautiful, uncertain twin. *See*, he wanted to howl, *you worried for nothing, it's fine, you're all right.*

She darted behind Jolie but McKenna moved, cutting her off; Jack's snarl was answered wholeheartedly. Mac's beast understood his, but *back down* wasn't in either animal's vocabulary. Jolie paused,

her deep calm swallowing them both—but apparently Zoe's
instincts had anticipated that, because she bolted through the fractional gap.

Dodging, ducking, leaping, catching an overhead branch and
ignoring the load of sopping-cold snow shaken from the rest of an
evergreen, his twin launched herself past the stream of running Kith
and into the night.

Now Jack had to use all his speed simply to keep up. Cold air
poured through him, his lungs heaving, and his feet drummed the
earth, each step landing as his *demie's* did.

They ran as one, breathed as one, and his heart sang inside his
ribs as it matched hers beat for beat. *Don't*, his beast said, understanding the danger better than hers.

Her only reply was a wash of deep red fear, a beaten creature
lunging for freedom, pushed past endurance.

All right, demie. *If that's what you want, do it this way.* A
sudden breathtaking expansion, one self in two bodies as if they
were infants again, nose-to-nose in the cradle and blinking at
each other with astonishment. He edged past her, and his twin
let him. A ravine loomed before them, a fissure in the earth's
wrinkled face; he leapt and she did a moment later, hanging
seraph-like with her hair a wild curling mass combed by night
wind, the shimmer of her blue, blue eyes leaving a streak on the
face of an icy night. Landing with a jolt, snapping forward again,
and he didn't care what happened next as long as the connection
stayed.

The Pride howled behind them, a chorus of caution, but the roar
of cloven air swallowed the sound. The tumbledown stone wall
marking the edge of the estate was fast approaching, and a flickering
from the right was a trio of myrmidons running the boundary,
pursuit predators a trifle slower than other Kith but thickly armored
to make up for it.

Jack veered, and Zoe moved with him. She was *trusting* her twin,
the bond wide open and flooding them both with sensation. All the

patience, waiting, and caution exploded; the running Kith accepted them again like a puddle closing over a raindrop.

Night's great silver lamp mounted higher in the sky, beaming at her most favored children. Lost in the dream of Moonfall, the *usanaugh* ran, a tiny Pride within the larger community.

Jack's only regret was that it could not last forever.

There was a lot of uncertainty and aggression to purge, between the news of skin hunters and the frustrations of daily life. Relief and joy at a missing Kith's return was potent fuel as well, along with the sheer natural exhilaration of moving with others of their own kind upon a moonlit night.

One by one, though, the Pride members began to slow. The more experienced among them guided the faltering back to the estate house, and the shamans' calm spread in overlapping rings, a soothing galaxy-whirl.

He knew the precise moment his *demie* flagged. Eventually she'd learn to pace herself, conserve enough energy to reach home again. Or perhaps she never would, because when she fell her *demi* would always be ready to catch her. He barely broke stride, the Moon's strength humming in his veins as he scooped her up and turned sharply, the thinning crowd separating to let him pass. McKenna and Jolie swept away with the rest, Allison's high trilling cry fading into the distance. Jack slowed to half-speed, his twin caught in his arms, her sooty eyelashes fluttering and slim beautiful limbs twitching.

Even after being run to exhaustion, she still refused to give up.

Most would stay overnight at the estate, snacking and napping or having quiet conversations, and run home in family groups just before dawn, avoiding skin notice just as other animals learned to. Jack stepped through a wide-open window into the ballroom, nodding at Amerlane the elder—the old myrmidon was watching the night, waiting for his mate to return.

Maria always ran until the shamans stopped. Sondra took after her, and probably had a good few hours' worth of motion in her yet.

Zoe made a soft protesting noise. Her hair was a wild silken cloud, tiny glittering clips knocked askew; her boots were damp and her skirt swung as he carried her, fresh air mixing with the intoxicating healthy musk that was his *demie*, fully integrated into the Pride and nearly unconscious.

She was trusting him to deal with everything else, and he was more than happy to do so.

It was about goddamn time.

60

ANSER ME

For a long time she floated in deep darkness, broken not by dreams but faint, starry flashes of movement. When she rolled over, throwing an arm across her eyes, she realized she wasn't in the blue suite.

Jack's mattress was a lot firmer than hers. He didn't like softness, rounded corners, padded edges. Straight, direct, largely uncomplicated—God, she wished she was more like that.

Her entire body ached, each muscle protesting as if sprained. Even her ribs hurt. It felt like dull spikes had been driven through her temples, and her stomach was sour.

"Easy," her twin said, softly. "You might feel a little hungover. It'll pass in a few minutes, just lie still."

What the hell happened? She remembered the humming, the ballroom, and a few disconnected patches of running under a huge, ice-pale moon. Bits and pieces swirled inside her head, refusing to make a coherent whole.

Her throat was dry as the Sahara. "Did I..." *Did I do something wrong? How did we get home?* Then she realized she was in his bed, and all other considerations became secondary because she further realized she wasn't wearing a single stitch except the princess ring on her left hand. She hurriedly peeled her arm away from her eyes, wincing—even with the curtains drawn it was too bright, her eyes watered—and making sure the covers were appropriately tucked.

Good God, what am I doing here?

"You did great." Jack had dragged a straight-backed black-and-chrome chair from his sitting room to the bedside, and perched easily, leaning forward, his elbows propped on his knees. Watching her intently, as if he thought she was sick.

Had she thrown up on her dress? Jesus *Christ*. "I, uh…"

"It'll go away in about ten minutes. It only happens the first time, something about adapting to Moonfall." Did he sound anxious? He certainly didn't look it—black sweater, jeans, no watch but his signet gleaming, and his hair was immaculate. Looked like he wasn't suffering a hangover, but then again, he'd done this before. "I know you were worried."

"My dress?" Maybe she'd ruined her clothes. They'd all been running around in the dark; it was amazing nobody got hurt.

They could see a lot better than skins, but if Zoe had been the only one to stumble it would be par for the fucking course.

"I thought you'd be more comfortable without it." Jack didn't move, studying her face. A thin line of morning light showed around the drawn curtains, poking at her tender eyes. His room was almost as familiar as the blue suite by now. "You were out pretty hard and I was too tired to get you into pajamas. Sorry."

"Oh." That was kind of reasonable. But still, another of those embarrassing flushes suffused her cheeks and she had to look away, gauging her chances of looking utterly ridiculous if she bolted for the door and took the sheet with her.

Still, it wasn't like…she couldn't finish the thought. He was her twin, right? This was evidently normal.

What about Dima and Bella? Is that 'normal' too? He kept telling her to ask questions, but that one couldn't be given any air.

"I'll get you a sweatshirt if you want. Amelia will send up breakfast, she always does something nice after Moonfall." There it was again, that faintly nervous note. He didn't shift, watching her intently. "Now you're a full member of the Pride. Well, we both are. Congratulations."

That's nice, I guess. Royal's other girls had talked about hangovers; was this what they felt like to skins? "I...uh, thank you." Zoe's entire body ached, as if she was growing again. It would be nice to be a little taller, but she hated the pain and Mama's deep sighs when clothes no longer fit. Her shoulders were cold and the comforter was rumpled, but she had the sheet and blankets securely tucked. "It feels weird."

"It'll pass, I promise." Jack paused, his gaze fastened on her face. At least he wasn't looking anywhere else. "I know you wanted a trip into the city, and I have something to do there. Wanna go?"

God, not right now. "When?" She could drag herself up, she supposed; it was no different than the exhaustion in the middle of a double shift, when you had just enough energy to realize how tired you were and how little it mattered because there were hours yet to go.

She'd endured worse. Maybe with a shower and a gallon of Amelia's coffee she could even be cheerful about it, but she wouldn't wash her hair. The very thought filled her with weariness.

"After breakfast? Or we should probably call it brunch, since we slept in. The roads are clear, and..." Her brother paused again, still examining her. She probably looked like hell; God knew she felt it. "Don't try to move just yet, okay? Just wait for it to get better. It'll happen soon."

Sure. If he was going into the city, she could see how far they'd let her go in that direction, not to mention start learning her way around outside the house's warm safety.

When the inevitable happened, she'd be glad she spent the effort. Getting lost in New York was no doubt easy, hiding there after the inevitable and until she figured out where to go next couldn't be much harder. "I should get ready."

"There's really no rush." Jack straightened, pushing his sweater-sleeves up tanned forearms. "First Moonfall's a big deal. Dad'll have a present for you."

"Another one?" *Good Lord.* Zoe sagged against the pillows; at least Jack had no shortage of those. "He shouldn't waste them on me." Then she sucked in a sharp breath, because it wasn't the sort of thing the girl they wanted her to be could—or would—say.

Flat on her back and cocooned in blankets, she wasn't equipped to handle any of this bullshit at the moment.

"He wants to make up for lost time." Jack's tone said it was perfectly logical, as if everything about this was even *close* to normal. "Besides, it's traditional for First Moonfall. He gave me my first real watch on mine. You'll get something better, I'm sure."

Oh, God, now she had another potentially valuable thing to worry about losing. "I'm sorry." She was so, so tired of waiting for the other shoe to drop. Or more precisely, for the first shoe, because so far they'd been insanely nice.

"What? Why?" Jack smiled, but his forehead wrinkled with slight puzzlement as if he suspected she might be joking. "You did *amazing*. Next time you'll probably keep the entire Pride on track. Won't even need the other shamans."

Wait, did she have to do last night again? Right now it sounded like the worst punishment in the world. "I don't even remember what I did."

"That's usual too. Couple of times you wanted to leave the estate, but we kept you safe. That's why we all run together." He rose slowly, unfolding from the chair like a cat stretching after a nap. There were footsteps in the hall, making zero effort to be silent, and a cheerful whistle accompanied them. "That'll be Lev. I'll knock before I come back in."

"Where's my dress?" Honestly, Zoe didn't even want to sit up, but the world didn't wait around for anyone to feel better. It kept going, whether you felt like hammered shit or not.

"In the laundry. If it bugs you, grab something from my closet, but wait until you feel better, okay?" Then Jack was gone, swinging the door mostly shut, and Zoe had to suppress a groan.

He was right, though. The aching and nausea receded rapidly, especially if she kept still and breathed deeply. In its place, a steadily rising wave of almost ridiculous well-being began at her fingers and toes, working inward.

A few more minutes later, as Jack and Lev exchanged murmurs in the sitting room, Zoe tentatively pushed herself up on her elbows. The hangover gave one last throb and vanished, swirling away like rinsed dirt down a drain.

She hadn't felt this good in ages—or, indeed, ever, that she could remember. If she hadn't been naked as a jaybird, she might even have enjoyed it.

Tearing the sheet off the bed and walking around toga-style wasn't an option, no matter how tempting it seemed. At least Jack had sweats, even if they were comically large. As soon as she was halfway dressed, a fresh flash-flood of relief almost knocked her off her feet. She couldn't tell if it was hers or Jack's, but what did he have to be relieved about? Maybe he'd been counting on her not to mess up last night.

But then it hit her—she'd been too physically miserable to really hear Jack's casual, life-changing assertion.

A full member of the Pride. Did it mean she finally, at long last, actually belonged somewhere? If so, all she had to do was keep up. Maybe practice would make it easier.

"Zo?" A tap at the door. "You feeling better? There's coffee."

Rolling up the sweatshirt's sleeves, she hurried for the door, for once not even pausing to make the bed.

A Kith metabolism ran hot to fuel the change, Jack said, and Zoe figured maybe they drank all the time to provide a few more calories. It also explained why the breakfast was massive; it was a good thing

Lev was strong, or he couldn't have handled the vast wooden tray. Jack carried it into her suite, and that's where they ate.

Dad's present—wrapped in shiny silver paper, set carefully on the coffee table in her sitting room—turned out to be a string of pinkish pearls hand-knotted on silk, and a pair of tickets to *Swan Lake*. Box seats, and the date was in two weeks. The card said, *Happy First Moonfall, little dancer*, and Dad's signature was a newly familiar scrawl.

"My God." The words were hushed and awestruck, as if High Mass was about to start. Zoe stared at the tickets, each held in a glossy brochure swarming with publicity photos. "This can't be real."

Jack grinned, peering over her shoulder. "Looks like we're going to the ballet. The other one's from me."

The other present was wrapped in bright red, a tiny box with a pair of diamond solitaire earrings, a larger rectangle proving to be a book. Not just any book, but a first edition of Murakami's *Hard-Boiled Wonderland and the End of the World*.

Zoe's heart was having a hard time keeping its walls up, with all this dangerous happiness pouring in. "Jack..."

"You already have a copy, I know, but it's not a first." He poured another cup of coffee from the thermal carafe and sighed contentedly, leaning back into the blue velvet couch. "Thank you, by the way."

"I didn't do anything." She ran her fingertips lightly, reverently over the cover. Jewelry was great, and it could be sold if you were in a pinch. She might not get to see the performance, if she messed up badly enough before the date.

But a book...that was special. If she had to leave, she would take this one small thing with her.

"You came back from Texas with me, and you've stayed." Jack's dark eyes half-lidded. He inhaled the coffee's aroma and smiled, a sweet, almost misty expression. "Don't think I don't know you've got one foot out the door, *demie*. I keep wondering if you'll be here in the morning."

Her silly, stupid heart gave a strange, half-hopeful leap. "I want to be." The weird flood of well-being, after washing the hangover away, hadn't abated yet. And though she felt a little ridiculous in Jack's comically large black sweatshirt and a pair of boxers also plundered from his closet, maybe it wasn't so bad. "So I guess...I'm really part of the Pride now?"

"We both are." Jack considered the remains of the breakfast tray with bright interest. "I feel like I could handle some pancakes, too."

Zoe might've teased him, but her own appetite was just as keen. "All that running. Maybe you should go down to the kitchen and..."

The phone on her nightstand chimed, a soft sweet message-sound barely tiptoeing into the sitting room. She almost flinched, bouncing upright and hurrying into the bedroom.

"...ask Amelia nicely? Probably will, once I finish this." Jack's voice rose slightly, pitched to carry through the bedroom door. "I wonder if she'll send up more eggs?" He said something else, too, but Zoe couldn't hear it over the sudden rushing in her ears as she scooped up her phone and stared disbelievingly.

It was a text, but not from Dad. An unknown number, and a single line of angry letters.

Amber its Roy ANSER ME

Christ, Royal couldn't even spell, and he was harassing her. Then the implications hit, thunder trundling along after a lightning flash.

How the *hell* did he get her number? Did he have Dad's too? Or Jack's? What was he telling them? He certainly had pictures of Zoe working at the club, or worse.

Was he going to use them?

"Hey." Jack's voice, accompanied by hurried footsteps far too quiet for his size. "Zo? Zoe, what's wrong?"

"Nothing," she managed. Her tongue felt too thick for her mouth, and a cold trickle that wasn't sweat slid down her back. It was pure, unadulterated fear, and she'd thought she was over that particular feeling. Was she sweating? She hit the phone's side button and the rectangular screen went blank, a baleful glassy eye, just in time. "I'm fine, just...just a little..."

"Sit down." Her twin had her shoulders, a warm solid comforting grasp, and he guided her to sit on the neatly made blue bed. The twinbond throbbed between them, an incoherent swirl. "Here. Breathe, that's it. Look at me. *Look* at me, Zo."

The snap of command in his tone was like a pinch on an already-sore bruise. Zoe flinched but obeyed, reflexively letting her gaze unfocus.

It didn't make whatever a man would do hurt less, but it gave a little distance from the event. Jack turned into a golden-topped smear, his eyes burning despite their darkness. "You're all right," he continued. "You're safe, I'm here. Just breathe."

His palms cupped her face, his skin fever-hot. Or maybe she was just frozen, a block of icy terror.

I can't do this. I just can't. "I'm sorry," she whispered.

This wasn't a fairytale. It was a nightmare, or it was hell.

And she deserved every bit of it for what she'd done, even if she was just attempting to survive. God, like Mama and Bea, didn't give a damn how hard you tried. He set up the game, let you fail, then took vengeance while loudly declaring it was all your own fault anyway. That was what power really consisted of—and she had none except for when she turned on her tormentors, claws out and rage filling her entire body.

But a Kith had to control their temper. It was their biggest rule.

"We'll stay home today." Jack's thumb caressed her cheek, a soft absentminded stroke. "You can go back to bed, or we'll watch movies while Meel sends up snacks. Okay?"

"No." She hunched, shoulders rising protectively, the sweatshirt slipping and her bare legs under the boxers prickling with gooseflesh as if last night's cold was working its way into this pretty warm room she had just begun—deep in the secret recesses of her heart—to think of as her own. "I'm fine."

"You're not, I can feel it. Come on, into bed."

"*No.*" If she was already damned, she might as well refuse. "I was just dizzy for a moment, that's all." What would Mama do?

Well, Angelina had waited, laid her plans, and escaped. Maybe the Kith had scared her so much it seemed like a good idea.

Zoe summoned a paper-thin grimace, attempting to impersonate a smile. Pretty soon Jack would look at his own phone and probably see messages from an unknown number—or was Royal keeping that in reserve?

What the fuck did Roy *want?* As soon as the question rose, she had her answer.

Money, probably. Zoe could get her hands on some, and pay him off—the only hard part would be her own anxiety over visiting a bank with the brand-new cards and ID—but she knew blackmailers never stopped at one helping.

A worse prospect was facing Trevor's disappointment, or Jack's. Sure, they *said* nothing she'd been forced to do would make them feel differently about her, but she knew better. Not only had she lost her temper and clawed both Royal and Bea, but she'd also done...other things, bringing in money for Royal.

One of his girls. One of his *bitches.*

Her twin would turn away in disgust, and she'd lose everything. The house, the shaman lessons, the presents, the clothes...

She'd be right back where she started. Some part of her had always known all this was temporary, so it wasn't really any surprise.

But oh, her heart hurt. Despite holding herself in readiness, the suddenness of the dream's shattering still shocked the breath right out of her.

"Hey." Jack's nose hovered an inch from hers. He peered into her eyes like he could see the wheels turning in her brain; they were revolving faster and faster now, just like they always did when it was time to jump out of a bad squat or a worse job. "What is it? Don't shut me out, Zo."

I didn't think I could. Maybe she just had to be miserable to do so. The twinbond resonated unhappily between them; she could almost *see* how she was partially damming its invisible flow.

Allison said they hadn't found Mama and Zoe because of the shaman-stuff. *You helped your mother, didn't you.* Oh, now Zoe could remember her first meeting with the older shaman, clear as a bell.

All those years, she'd been somehow keeping the Kith at bay, hiding both herself and Angelina because that was how her mother wanted it. She could do it again, couldn't she? And Zoe Simmons— no, Zoe Rouje, even if they threw her out—wasn't helpless anymore. She had claws, and the Sorcerer's Gene; she knew how to run like a Kith now.

That had to be worth something. At the very least, it would make survival out in the real world a little more possible.

Zoe took a deep breath, leaning away from her twin. He let go, reluctantly, and thank God he wasn't looking at her phone. Instead, Jack studied her as if she was a new creature, one he wasn't entirely sure he liked.

Her heart hurt even worse. "I'm probably just adjusting." A lame excuse, but a better one would have to wait. She needed a plan, unless she saw a good chance and could use it. Either way, it was time to get serious. "I should get dressed if we're going to the city today."

"It can wait." Jack didn't step back, still regarding her with that strange expression. The edge of his warmth touched her, a refuge she didn't deserve and couldn't afford. "I'll call Allison, since you're not feeling well—"

"No. Please." God, if he just left her alone for a minute she'd be able to *think.* "Just a hot shower and some more coffee, and I'll be fine. And we can go into the city, right? I have things I want to do too."

"Like what?" His hands hung, loose and relaxed, and he didn't quite loom over her. But it was close. "I'm serious, Zo. You should stay in bed and I should call Allison. If you're still woozy this long after waking up, it could be serious."

It is. But he wouldn't know it. Maybe he'd never find out, but she couldn't count on that. "It's already over." To prove it, she rose, and her legs weren't unsteady at all. She even tried another, more natural smile. "See?"

"Yeah." Jack's expression changed, but with all the ringing, staticky interference in the bond she couldn't sense his true feelings. "I see."

Zoe was suddenly very aware she was in a too-big sweatshirt and boxers, the ring on her left hand a heavy weight reminding her of everything she would be giving up soon. "I'll put these in the wash." Her phone buzzed again in her hand, and his eyes narrowed slightly. "Thank you."

"Okay. I'll get you more coffee." But Jack still didn't move. Instead, he leaned forward, and she tensed. Just a fraction, just in case.

He pressed his lips to her forehead, and the flood of scalding down her entire body temporarily chased away the cold.

"There," he said, quietly. "If you get dizzy again, just sit down and wait for me."

"All right." She watched him retreat, each step graceful and silent, and wished she could.

PART FOUR
THE TRAP

61

BETTER MYSTERY

THE SLIGHT DAYTIME MELT WAS ARRESTED HALFWAY BY ANOTHER FRIGID blast from the northeast, delighting and exciting local meteorologists, but the roads were clear and Gessel drove carefully. If the myrmidon was uneasy at chauffeuring the Pride's treasure, no whisper of the feeling leaked free.

Which was good, because Jack's *demie*, rather than being soothed and energized by her first Moonfall, was pale and distracted.

Still, it stole Jack's breath to see her in an oxblood V-neck sweater and black slacks, shiny brogans on her delicate feet, a heavy knitted scarf wrapped solicitously around her slim throat, and the protection of the long black woolen coat. She held the small leather purse—Hermann's hobby was making bags for everyone—in her lovely lap, staring out the window as the freeway unreeled and small spatters of slush dewed the windshield.

The twinbond ached in his chest. She needed privacy, they were both accustomed to being alone—but still, he hated it. Had he put a foot wrong somewhere? Was the Gene warning her of trouble? Or did it have something to do with her phone? She'd checked the thing twice already and they hadn't been in the car for long at all.

None of the Kith would insult her, at the estate or anywhere else.

So perhaps she was sensing some fresh disaster, or something about her first Moonfall had gone wrong? She'd slept deeply enough for full recovery; he should know, since he'd been right next to her.

Where he belonged.

The quiet should have been restful. Gessel hummed along with a concerto on the radio, a soft counterpoint to the windshield wipers and the almost subliminal hum of the engine. Jack wouldn't have minded taking a commuter train in, especially business class, but he wanted both security and privacy for his *demie*.

How could he explain what was about to happen? He had to find at least some way, and once they arrived it would be too late. "Zo?"

"Hm?" A startled, very blue glance. She didn't quite huddle against the door like she had in Texas, but he suspected it was close.

"I'm afraid you might not be very proud of me this afternoon." If he could get her focused on aiding her twin, he might be able to pry up a corner of the twinbond and peek at what was bothering her so much.

One way, or another.

"Why?" Her eyes all but glowed; now that she had attended her first Moonfall she burned even brighter with Kith vitality. Nothing seemed wrong with her physically, except the way she held herself, achingly tense.

"Because we're going to visit a traitor." He had to choose each word carefully, and his tone as well—calm, matter-of-fact. "A Kith who betrayed the Pride."

"How?" Her nervousness mounted another notch. "I mean...is that even possible?"

"Not often." Jack suspected his fragile, sensitive *demie* was a hairsbreadth from attempting to throw herself from a moving vehicle. The cold, one-pointed concentration of an analyst settled over him, ready for any snippet of data, no matter how small, to illuminate her unease. "This guy—Greg—has been feeding information to a collection of skin hunters in return for drugs." *And a few other things, I'm sure.*

Not to mention the brat had topped it off with claiming to believe he could mate with a skin and possibly throw a pair of *usanaugh*. If young Jasperson had been truly set on marrying the honeypot skin he would've brought her to his parents, and Dad—as the Pride's ruler—would have been told, both so the prospective mate could be vetted and security set in place to shield her from various dangers.

Including the hunters who had been running her to entrap a dumbass, skate-addicted waste of fur.

"Drugs?" Zoe's complete attention settled on him, finally, and it was a welcome warmth. "But when I...huh."

So his *demie* had experimented, and found most if not all recreational drugs only provided a few seconds' worth of effects. It made complete sense, anyone living on the edge of survival wanted any relief they could find. "Most street trash doesn't affect us, our metabolisms just shake it off. But there's one that does—it's designer, expensive, and nasty. That's not the point, though."

"Okay." A powerful burst of relief resonated along the link; something about that particular piece of information comforted her. Zoe regarded him somberly. "What's the point?"

"Greg might be holding out under questioning, or there might be things he doesn't know he knows." Jack's stomach settled, and he wondered if he could take her hand. He decided not to—for the moment. "I may have to play a little rough in order to drag something useful out of him."

She tilted her head; her hair glowed even though tightly braided, its curl ruthlessly contained. "I've seen rough before."

His beast, easy and satisfied inside its cage of bone after last night's luxurious freedom, raised one sleepy eyelid at the thought of anyone interrogating his *demie*. "I don't want to scare you."

"Because all the rest of this is so normal and un-scary?" Zoe's wry, fleeting smile was a gift. At least he was easing her mind, to some degree.

"Well, maybe not normal for you *yet*." He could allow as much. "I still think we should call Allison about your dizziness. It could be a shaman thing."

"I'm fine," Zoe repeated. She said that a lot, along with the apologies skin females learned to use, propitiating their way through society. "So I can go do what I need to while you're asking this guy questions, right?"

Nice try. "You'll be right next to me when I ask him, my sweet *demie.*" On the one hand, he wished she didn't have to see anything like this; on the other, sooner or later she would have to. And McKenna would be irritated that his own no doubt strenuous efforts hadn't dug everything out of a bit of prey. Jack's attention sharpened. "Where do you need to go? We can do that first."

She weighed the offer, a bright blue glance at the back of Gessel's head, then a quick look at Jack. Uncertain, watchful, wary—the day she didn't feel the need to be so cautious would be a happy one. "I just wanted to go to a library, that's all."

The twinbond vibrated between them, saturated with her unwillingness. Pushing would get him nowhere. "There's a good one close to home—well, near Janine's office, but you get the idea. We can hit it on the way back unless you're too tired or you want a card from the New York Public."

"We might not have time; Amelia said she was expecting us for dinner." She shifted nervously, and he felt the movement in his own limbs. "This Greg guy. What kind of information was he giving?"

"We already know most of what he's done, I think. But I'd like to know more." The nagging sense of something slightly out of tune, a mere breath out of place, would not leave him alone. Jack also wanted to know why she needed a library.

It could be simple comfort—where else did a bright, terrified child find some kind of security? Yet he could not for the life of him find the missing piece, either to her reticence or to the situation with the stateside hunters.

The whole situation irked him, and he suspected it would only get worse.

"And I should see it," Zoe said softly. Pointed chin, high cheek-bones, the arch of her eyebrows—she resembled Angelina in some of the photo albums, except for her eyes. Those were all Trevor, and what was handsome in Dad was outright stunning on her. "So I know what happens to traitors."

"What? No." *Why would you think that?* Jack simply wanted her to know what would happen to any threat, direct or otherwise. "I just have to do some unpleasant things to keep you and the Pride safe. Besides, I need you there. You'll sense things I don't."

"Maybe." She returned to staring out the window, watching shiny beetle-like cars trundling through the cold.

It was agonizing to hear the distrust of her own talents, and further agonizing to feel her frantic, determined blocking of the link. The only cure was time and support; sooner or later, she'd run out of ways to keep him at bay. "Don't worry. It's instinctive."

His *demie* nodded. That was all.

And Jack was even more uneasy, if that were possible.

The building could be mistaken for an abandoned warehouse; it slumped under spatters of sleet and the only movement was a *No Trespassing* sign on a rusting chain-link fence, flapping under a stiff cold breeze.

At least, that was the only movement a skin would spot.

Despite its air of disrepair, the warehouse grudgingly opened one of its side-doors; Gessel nosed the SUV into a dark hole. The myrmidon had taken a few extra turnings along the route as a precaution, and he didn't cut the engine until a flicker of movement deeper in the shadows resolved into a pair of bright-eyed jäger hurrying to greet visitors.

Jack didn't wait for Gessel to perform a chauffeur's door-opening duty. Zoe's pulse was humming in his throat and wrists, and her anxiety had a diesel kick to it, echoing down the twinbond. However, she *did* wait, like the good little *demie* she was.

"Sir." The more dominant of the two jägers was Alice Creste in jeans and a sleek hip-length leather jacket, her brunette ponytail swinging as she halted. "Surprised to see you here."

"Oh, wow." Her teammate Billy Shourif—blond, curly-headed, and dimpled—blinked as Gessel shepherded Zoe around the back of the SUV. "That's...oh, *wow*."

Alice elbowed him, but Jack was feeling magnanimous. Of course the kid would be stunned at Zoe's appearance; she was a Rouje down to her toenails and the soft shaman breeze accompanying her was a few fractions warmer than the chill outside. Bars of weak sunlight filtered through windows deliberately left dirty and in some cases even boarded up, but further in it would be well-lit and warm.

This structure was meant to hold living secrets while their depths were fully explored, but that didn't have to mean uncomfortable.

Not for the questioners, at least.

"Zo, this is Creste and Shourif, on duty today." He didn't miss how his *demie* hurried to stand near him, watching the other Kith with large, lambent baby blues. "You're feeling more Kith in here too, but don't worry. They're just on watch."

As if summoned by the words, a scraping, lonely sound rose from the warehouse's depths. Too soft for skin senses, it carried a weight of desperation that raised Jack's hackles.

The only good thing about the cry was that it pushed his twin closer, and she grabbed for his hand. Her gloved fingers slipped between his, and the lump of her signet under custom-cut leather was a reminder that she was safe, she was within arm's reach, and he was whole again.

Contact soothed them both, and the twinbond cleared like a cold mountain stream after the silt of a disturbance settled.

"That's Jasperson." Alice shrugged, and did *not* eye Zoe with bright interest. Instead, she stood at quasi-attention, and after a moment Billy did too. "He's detoxing hard today, and all the shamans are taking care of other business. Or..." Belatedly and visibly, the jäger realized a shaman was standing right before her. "Are you here for treatment? He could use it."

"Just going to ask a few questions." Jack squeezed Zoe's hand, gently. Now that he was concentrating on something else, her attempt to keep him out of the bond eased—perhaps she was simply uncomfortable with the intensity of an analyst's attention. "Who's watching him?"

"Syl and Marcus. They don't have any kin-link." Alice's elbow jutted out again, just brushing Billy's lean-muscled upper arm. "Billy's a Jasperson cousin on his father's side, so he's hanging out with me." The explanation had to be for Zoe's benefit. "Skate, you know. It's...hard to see."

Skate addiction ate a Kith from the inside out unless a shaman could work some kind of deep, draining, dangerous miracle to free the sufferer. Most Kith leaders banned the attempt, since it often ended with the death of the addict and severe damage to the shaman; the bearers of the Gene were simply too precious to waste.

"No doubt." Jack moved, and found Zoe moving with him, natural as breathing. The cry came again, and she shivered.

"Sir?" Gessel, his baritone rumbling. "Do you need me?"

"Grab a drink, Ges. We won't be long." Jack didn't miss Alice's brightening, and of course the myrmidon would be blushing, as much as one of his kind ever did.

Creste and Gessel would probably end up mated before long, and Jack wished the myrmidon luck. Alice's mother would put any prospective mate through their paces in exemplary fashion.

Plunging through a pair of swinging doors into the warehouse's labyrinthine innards, he took care to keep his strides short so Zo didn't have to hurry. Her grip on his hand tightened, as if afraid he'd leave her behind.

"It sounds bad," Jack said softly. "But believe me, he deserves every bit."

"People get addicted for a lot of reasons." Her quiet thoughtfulness matched his, but a faint tremor hid under the words. "You can't judge."

I can. In fact, it's my job to do so. "There are Kith who get addicted and don't betray their own, Zo-baby." Two right turns, a left, concrete floor and many-painted walls—it was depressingly easy to navigate this space. "Stay behind me when we get there, all right?"

"Is he..." She shivered again as yet another muffled cry filtered through the quiet.

"He won't hurt you." *Nothing will.* "But if he tries, I'll have to tear his guts out through his nose."

"Ugh." The sound held a trace of pained amusement, as if she thought he was joking.

He wasn't. Jack held her hand, leading her through the passages, and wished this were already over so he could solve a better mystery.

62

PRISONER, PATTERNS

A DOOR OPENED, JACK USHERED HER THROUGH, AND ZOE FOUND HERSELF IN a small space looking very much like a supermarket's break room. Except the couch and television weren't cheap leftovers, the mini fridge was a whisper-quiet stainless-steel number, there was a high-end espresso maker instead of an ancient arthritic boil-your-grounds antique, and the two Kith in their impeccable suits and well-buffed wingtips with thicker industrial soles weren't the usual dispirited retail employees.

"Holy hell," the tall brunet one said. "And hello, Jackson. Good to see you."

"Hi, Syl. How are your parents?" Jack let go of her hand, but only to slip his arm over her shoulder. And maybe she was a coward, because Zoe was glad for that. None of this seemed as scary with his solidity next to her—even if she suspected this was going to be what Mama would call an Object Lesson, like the time she'd threatened to leave Zoe at the fire station in Cedar Falls.

They put bad little girls in jail, and beat the devil out of them.

She hadn't thought of that in years, and suddenly Zoe was six years old and panicked again. The feeling passed in an eyeblink—for God's sake, she was almost twenty-one now, an adult by any measure—but her heart still hurt and there was a distinct taste of copper at the back of her palate.

The door on the other side of the room was a big heavy metal rectangle very much like an industrial freezer's, not only latched but sporting a padlock on a hasp. The walls on either side looked heavy-duty, too. Another weird, muffled scream burrowed through the door, lingering just on the edge of sharp Kith hearing.

The idea that Jack and Trevor believed in object lessons too wouldn't go away. And neither would her imagination, lightly playing with the idea of being trapped in a place like this, howling with despair.

Royal was no doubt making plans to tell her father and brother everything. When he did, would they stick her here and drive away without a glance in the rearview, like Mama had threatened to?

"Fine and healthy, thanks for asking." Dark-haired Syl, broad-shouldered and grey-eyed, regarded Zoe with some curiosity. "Uh..."

"Zo, this is Syl Drake and Marcus Harriman." Jack squeezed her shoulders slightly, probably to make sure she was listening. "They're myrmidons, like Gessel."

"How do you do," she managed. Would they be her jailers? Zoe had claws, but these people did too—and they were much stronger than Bea.

He was—or had been—merely misbegotten, and they were full Kith.

"Pleasedtameetcha." The other man, silent until now, had a beaky nose and an engaging smile, his honey-colored hair falling in a soft wave over his forehead. "Always good to have a shaman around."

"Let's get this over with." Her brother forestalled any further pleasantries, stepping forward so she had to as well. "My *demie* wants to go to the library today, too."

Oh, God. Zoe watched as the two other Kith moved, lithe and graceful, to either side of the door.

"I don't think he'll try again," the honey-haired one said.

His companion grinned, and produced a key from his suit jacket's breast pocket. "Bet ten?"

"Five." They did this a lot, to judge by the banter.

The padlock clicked open. "Coward."

"I'm just not a sucker, Syl." The almost-blond stretched his neck, a quick supple movement of his head first to one side, then the other.

She was ready for just about anything when the door freed itself with a click, popping slightly out and sliding to the left instead of opening into either room. The motion was quiet, well-oiled, and the resultant deep hush held a crackling edge.

The room beyond was softly lit, and every corner and edge was padded. Even the walls and floor were covered with vinyl mats. A bed, a chair, both bolted to the floor. A washbasin and a commode, both made of stainless steel, also had vinyl wrapping anywhere someone was likely to attempt hurting themselves—or others.

At least it smelled clean, like bleach and lemon polish. Sheets and blankets were tangled on the bed, thin pillows without cases twisted into weird shapes, and crouched with his back against the wall across from the door was a skinny Kith, his shoulders so sharp they threatened to wear through his black T-shirt. His jeans were torn but freshly laundered, and the rips in tough denim looked fresh. He stared, dark eyes protruding and almost-vacant; his lips parted slightly.

His skin, instead of a glow of health, held a terrible yellowish tinge. The prisoner's gaze drifted a bit before focusing, intent and bright like he wanted to drill a hole in her. He went still, and made a soft noise in the back of his throat—not quite a growl, not quite a whine.

She shivered again, but her brother didn't seem fazed in the least.

"Hello, Greg." Jack halted just inside the door, his arm tense against her shoulders; the other two Kith crowded into the opening, cutting off any possible escape.

Greg didn't respond. He just stared at Zoe, and when he

blinked his eyelids didn't quite sync. A shudder worked through him, each limb moving just a shade out of time, and because Kith were usually so coordinated and graceful the difference was startling.

Jack waited. The quiet was like snow falling, except for a sharp, static-laden undercurrent scraping Zoe's skin. It was irritation—but it wasn't hers.

No, it was Jack's. And it wasn't quite anger, either.

The emotion was pure, hot, tightly leashed rage.

Greg began to rock, slowly. His back brushed the wall each time, and even though the light from a recessed, well-padded fixture over-head was soft and forgiving he looked sallow. His thin cheeks flushed, and sweat gleamed at his temples.

"Rouje," he finally husked, a hoarse, broken word. "You found her after all."

"Can't keep *usanaugh* apart." Jack's arm loosened, but he didn't quite let go of her. Humming readiness filled him; finally, his atten-tion was off her and the twinbond stopped trying to expand inside her chest.

Which was a relief, but her lungs refused to work quite right. She stared at the thin, shuddering Kith, and wondered if she was looking at her own future. She didn't know what drug would do this, but ignorance was no insurance.

The world didn't care about your innocence. It would sucker-punch you just the same.

"Knew you'd to come see me eventually." Greg laughed, a ruined croak. "Finally part of the Pride now, huh? You bastard."

"Mind your language." Jack's expression was set and calm, his tone mild. If not for the bond, she wouldn't guess how furious he was. "My *demie* has tender ears."

"Fuck her ears." Greg's lips skinned back, and his teeth gleamed white. They looked wrong—entirely too large, and too sharp as well. "And fuck you, too."

Jack sighed. "Stay here," he murmured, and stepped away from her. Now she was free, but she couldn't move. Her body simply refused.

Her twin bore down on Greg, slow graceful slinking steps. The crouching prisoner didn't seem to notice, still staring at Zoe. She watched him in return, and realized why all this seemed so familiar.

It was just like being trapped in a squat with a batshit crazy guy who could snap into violence at any moment, or one of Royal's clients who liked fear and pain instead of just the usual. Or a club 'guest' showing his true colors, all inhibitions drowned in a pool of alcohol.

"Yeah," he said, suddenly. "You're the one they want. Bet you don't know why, though."

Zoe realized she was swaying slightly, matching his steady rocking motion. Now she could smell him—Kith, male, and a terrible fatty, rancid edge to the scent, like a short-order grill left uncleaned for weeks in hot humid weather. How many small-time diners or chain restaurants had she waited tables in, smiling for tips, complimenting, avoiding the pinches of dirty old men and the notice of petty middle managers?

"So you gave them access to the search programs for my *demie*." Jack folded down in front of the prisoner, crouching easily. Zoe's shoulders hunched, a reflexive movement, as her view of the skinny Kith was blocked. "Anything else was gravy, or cover."

Greg craned his neck, trying to see around Jack. Zoe stopped swaying, rooted to the spot.

"Think about it." If the screaming hadn't damaged something in his throat, Greg might've had a nice voice. "A *demie* raised to be one of them? They think she's the missing link or some shit. A cooperative subject for study, and when that's done they can just put her on a fuckin' autopsy table and—"

Jack moved, a snakelike, blurring slap. The sound hit padded walls, was swallowed, and Zoe flinched. Her left hand stung briefly, but again the sensation wasn't hers.

It was her twin's.

"I said *watch your language*." The scary thing wasn't Jack's speed, or the way the blow knocked Greg onto his side.

No, the truly terrifying thing was how nonchalant he sounded. Just a mild reminder, a bored crossing guard reciting *move along, nothing to see here folks, get going.*

Greg curled up like a pillbug, his knees almost sinking into his wasted chest. But now he could peer past Jack, and he stared at her with those bulging eyes. "I could've done it," he moaned. "I could've had kids. I loved her, you bastard. *I loved her.*"

"You're not dom enough to breed with a skin." Jack sighed, still balancing easily in a crouch. His coat's hem lay along the padded floor. "If you were serious, though, you could've brought her to meet your parents. You could have come to Dad for help and protection, to Allison, to me. To anyone, at any time. But you chose this instead."

Greg's lips pulled back again. "*Amber*," he hissed, and Zoe took a blundering, blind step back. "Amber Harris. That's what you called yourself, right? Smart move. They weren't sure you were Rouje's lost daughter, but by now they are. Oh, you *bet* they are."

What. The fuck. So someone *else* knew about who she'd been in Akron? That changed things, but only for the worse.

"Okay." Jack unfolded, a leisurely movement, controlled at every moment. "We're done here."

But the man on the floor wasn't done. "Amber," he chanted. "Amber, Amber, *Amber*. If I hadn't been caught—"

"But you were," one of the male Kith behind Zoe said, a little too loudly.

The skinny, jaundiced scarecrow on the floor waited until Jack was midway to standing, and exploded into motion. He pushed off from the wall, slithering along on his side so fast his T-shirt tore, and launched himself straight at her.

❦

Zoe had enough time to think *this will hurt* as she stood frozen, as if Bea was in one of his furious moods again. The rushing filled her ears, and that had always infuriated him even more—Zoe could slip out of her body, leave it behind for a short while, and lock the most important part of herself behind an impenetrable shield of that slip-stream sound.

It drove men crazy to know you could check out and ignore them.

The collision never happened. Jack was suddenly *there*, right in front of her, and she blinked at the back of his coat as his right hand whipped out, the force precisely gauged. There was another solid, meaty sound, a punch instead of a slap, and Greg spun, falling and sliding once more along the mats until he hit the padded back wall. He curled up again, his heaving ribs plainly visible through the black T-shirt's rags.

The scarecrow was laughing. The three other Kith males in the room growled, a low hum sinking into Zoe's bones. Her lungs burned afresh because she wasn't breathing, and for a moment she wondered what would happen if she just turned around and ran.

She didn't know if Greg would keep them occupied long enough for her to escape. Of course she could get out of the warren of passages, since she'd paid attention on the way in and it was easy enough to retrace your steps in any labyrinth. But then there were Gessel and the others to get past, and once she was out on the street, then what?

No, Zoe was trapped just like this skinny wreck of a Kith, except her cage was larger and much more comfortable. All the waiting for the inevitable was over.

Now she had to deal with the fallout. Again.

Wait until you have a better shot. It was probably the voice of the devil inside her skull but it had a good point, and she had the oddest sense that time had stopped, that she had plenty to make a decision and paradoxically none at all, like waiting in the church cellar for Bea to come back because she knew he would. He *had* to, because it was

all part of a pattern, and the rest of them—even her beloved Mama
—were blind to its loops, knots, and straightaways.

Even if she managed to shut Royal up and keep him happy,
someone else knew she'd been Amber. It was only a matter of time
until her father—and Jack—found out.

There was a subliminal, glass-crunching *snap* and the world
slipped back into normalcy, or whatever was passing for it in her life
these days.

Greg coughed, choked, and continued to cackle. Jack half-turned,
and even though she knew he wasn't going to, Zoe flinched as if he
meant to strike her as well.

Instead, his left hand curled under her braid, warm and sure
against her nape. He pulled her close, ignoring the Kith on the floor.
Jack's chin touched her hair and he inhaled deeply. The twinbond
buzzed like a warning rattlesnake, and for a dizzying moment she
was inside his skin and her own as well.

It's all right. The spark leapt between them, the contact she
longed for and feared all at once. *I'm here.*

Which was great, but how long did any protection last?

I'm so scared. Unbidden, her reply bridged the gap, a bright star in
a still, dark wasteland. She breathed him in too, a slight tang of after-
shave and clean clothes, fresh air and the indefinable warm haze that
was *him*, her twin, the only person in the world who could possibly
understand.

But he didn't. She was alone, not to mention living on borrowed
time. As always, and as usual.

No, you're not. He lifted his head slightly, and his physical voice
lacked the intimacy and infinite nuance of the inner one. "He's about
to go into the bend. Call downtown and let Pindar know so we can
get his parents out here, if they want to see his passing."

Greg stiffened, curling into an even tighter ball, and his shuddering laughter took on a terrible, jagged edge, a whine lingering
behind heaving gasps. His eyes had rolled back, slivers of darkened,

tainted sclera showing between wet matted lashes, and his mouth was a rubber *O*, contorting, greased with spittle.

"Yessir." Big brunet Syl had gone pale. "I'll stay with him. Marcus, go ahead and lock me in."

"You sure?" Marcus watched Greg, every line expressing tense readiness. "You know how they get."

"Someone has to take care of him." There was no anger in Syl's tone, just weary resignation. "Go on."

Jack bumped against her, and a deep rosy flush swallowed Zoe whole, beating back the terror for one endless, precious moment. She found herself backing up, her twin moving along as if they were dancing, and when the heavy door closed Greg's keening laughter was muffled.

But it could still be heard, especially with Kith-sharp ears.

63
MATTER OF DEFINITION

No, HIS *DEMIE* SAID, HER EXPRESSION SET, SO PALE SHE WAS ALMOST transparent, she didn't want to visit any library now. But she consented to go into Manhattan with him.

So thickening traffic swallowed the SUV, a winter afternoon brightening with forlorn hope before dusk and looming snow descended. Gessel hummed along with some kind of Muzak, turned down so low barely anything could be heard. Zoe hugged herself, huddling in her seat, and his sweet, beautiful *demie* was still trembling.

He wished she hadn't seen the ending stages of skate addiction, but at least his last nagging questions about Greg's precise value to the skin hunters were answered. And at least Zoe had witnessed the fact that her *demi* wouldn't allow any harm or insult to her, underlined and in glaring neon.

Unfortunately, it didn't seem the lesson had been a comfort. At all.

"I just have to check in with Dad," he repeated. The twinbond was taut between them, and full of strange half-seen thoughts behind fluttering veils. "Since Greg cleared up a couple things."

Simply calling on the phone wouldn't cut it, not with what he now knew.

Whatever timetable these hunters had been on before, Greg's capture and Zoe's return had moved it up. The attacks overseas were unconnected, but useful cover. The real danger now was those damn tranquilizers, and whatever intel the hunters had—especially if they still had telltales, nags, or backdoors hidden in the Pride's systems.

Zoe nodded, staring past Gessel and doing her best to mute the bond. Maybe the display of aggression had unsettled her; maybe she didn't want to look at him. Maybe the idea of visiting Dad made her nervous.

Amber Harris. The last name in the skin hunters' dossier before the Martha Smith identity in Marquette. If she'd worn other monikers between Akron and Texas, nobody knew. She'd shifted enough to claw a skin and left Ohio right afterward; no wonder the reminder upset her.

The news that skins were looking to experiment on and autopsy her couldn't be welcome, either. "You realize what this means, right?" He watched her profile, wishing she'd look at him.

"Mm-hm." Zoe gave another small nod, but he thought it very unlikely she did in fact grasp that the situation had undergone a dramatic change.

"Are you sure? Because there are ramifications, Zo."

"I'm sure," she murmured, and there could have been a tinge of sarcasm to the words. She shrank further into herself, and a stray curl had escaped her braid as it dried. It bobbed as the car moved, and his fingers ached to touch, perhaps tuck it behind her ear.

Gessel wasn't as gifted a driver as Hermann, but at least the vehicle never stopped moving even in thick traffic. Zoe shifted her attention out the window on her side, and the muffled echoes through the bond were concerning, to say the least. She was winding tighter and tighter, nervous and edgy. Who wouldn't be, hearing that a shadowy collection of skins was willing to murder and kidnap in order to study and dissect you?

He wanted this over, so he could settle to teaching her more pleasant things. And he wished they were alone, but if the skins came after what was evidently their highest priority target, a myrmidon might be the deciding factor in the equation. Jack would protect his *demie* while Gessel taught any attackers the folly of their ways—and if necessary, the myrmidon would use his own armored hide as cover for a shaman to retreat.

Jack's arms ached, but the sensation was hers, filtering through the bond. She hugged herself harder, gloved fingers sinking into the wool coat's upper sleeves, and Jack couldn't take it anymore.

He unclipped his seatbelt and slid across the bench seat, settling in the middle and getting his left arm around her. She was stiff as a poker but didn't actively resist, and the contact pushed back his bleak, impending rage.

"It's all right," he said, softly, wishing he could guess the right words to unlock her agony, strip it away. "They've done things like this before. Idiot skins thinking that if they dissect us they can find immortality."

"Immortality?" At least that piqued her interest, but she still wouldn't look at him.

"We live longer. The more dominant a Kith, the longer we endure." And *usanaugh* lasted longest of all. Seventeen years of missing her were too many, true—but they were also a drop in the bucket.

"Are we a different species? Is that what that means?" The sharp rise in her tone was perilously close to fear. She hadn't used much Voice yet, but he suspected soon she'd be able to pin a fellow Kith to the floor with sound alone.

He couldn't wait to see it.

"We don't know." Now Jack had her engaged, and talking. A fraction of the tension in the bond drained away—not nearly enough, but every little bit was a victory right now. A horn blared, and Gessel murmured something amused in response. The windshield wipers began, brushing glass clean. "Some of the shamans think so. The geneticists are still arguing it out." It seemed to be mostly a matter of definition, like a lot of things in biology.

"Great." His twin sagged all at once, leaning into him. "I'm an alien."

The way skins act, that's probably a badge of honor. But he suspected that observation would be unhelpful at best. He settled for something a little more comforting. "Which makes me one too. Don't forget that."

"Jack..." She made a small, restless movement, and he longed to take her home, close her in safety and quiet. His *demie* shouldn't have to deal with this.

"They're not going to get you." That was it, in plain English. He wished he could believe her earlier dizziness was simply the Gene warning her of this revelation, but something was *still* off, and whatever it was lurked in the skin hunters' plans. Jack was deadly certain they weren't finished with the Kith yet, and especially with the Rouje Pride. "We have you now, you're safe. All right?"

"Safe." The word was lost in a tiny, colorless laugh. "What does that even mean? Nothing's ever safe."

Except it is, and you'll find out. There was no changing her mind at the moment. At least he could tell that much about his stubborn *demie.* Manhattan swallowed them, familiar buildings rising to blot out the sky. "You're not alone anymore, that has to count for something. We're almost there, okay? We'll just pop in and talk to Dad, then go home. He'll be thrilled to show you his office."

"Take your child to work day," she muttered, and Jack had to laugh. It was unreal, how easily she could cheer him up.

He hoped the feeling was mutual.

Concrete towers scraping the clouds, crowds of skins hurrying on shoveled and salted pavement, bicycle messengers whizzing between lines of cars with reckless disregard for ice, life, or limb—

the pulse of the city was frantic here during afternoons, especially just before market closing. Horns blared and imprecations were shouted through windows rolled down despite the cold, cars and buses and garbage trucks all crawling resentfully along under thickening snow. Gessel knew the tangle of one-way and traffic-choked streets well, and his instincts were spot-on as usual. The parking levels of the Rouje building swallowed them, a relief from the chaos outside, and Jack wished they were visiting under better circumstances.

The private elevators on the third underground level were just the same as usual, and in short order they were whisked up, up, and even further up. Zoe stood stock-still in the corner of a steel box as it whispered, lifting its cargo on greased cables. Her eyes half-closed, she was so pale she was almost translucent, and the link was full of static and deep, almost inarticulate misery she was probably trying to protect him from.

She was even afraid to help her twin, and his beast was painfully awake, scanning their surroundings for whatever had disturbed its other half so badly.

When the doors opened on the seventieth floor, Jack knew something else had happened, too. The offices of the Pride's most powerful echelon were humming with activity, the reception area with its pale wood floor and potted plants not only holding two regular Kith admins but also an additional pair—myrmidon and jäger—for security, one lounging elegantly on a leather couch and the other at the coffee counter, glancing at the new arrivals and nodding slightly. All of them were brimming with energy from last night's Moonfall, either at the shamans' estate or the smaller, private celebrations.

They knew him on sight, and thus Zoe was known too. The admins leapt to their feet, but he waved them back down, shepherding her past the desk, through frosted-glass doors, and plunging into yet another warren. Gessel disappeared down the hall to visit his aunt; she worked in requisitions.

It was much nicer than the warehouse. The scent of paper, the clicking of keyboards, the whirring of printers—all familiar, all soothing. Dad had a show office in the penthouse five floors above, but the real work was done here. And Jack's instincts were spot-on, too, because there was Hermann leaning over Daniel Shale's shoulder as they studied a flatscreen monitor; the hushed tones of Dad's work secretary and his personal retainer conferring were also deeply familiar.

Hermann caught Jack's eye and motioned him past, betraying no surprise at the heir's appearance. He would probably assume Zoe had known, in a shaman's soft silent way, that the Rouje twins were needed.

"Jack?" Zoe whispered, tugging at his coat sleeve with her free hand. He had her other one safely imprisoned in his own. "I'm sorry, but is there a restroom?"

"You can use Dad's." He pushed open and held the door for his *demie*, happy to finally have that one small duty. "It's even got a shower; he used to weekend here sometimes. Won't do that now that you're home, thank God." It probably irked Trevor to spend time in-city instead of at the home office, where he could simply take a stroll and reassure himself that his precious daughter was indeed safely returned.

Of course Dad would take this news dispassionately, but that calm would merely be a mask. This crop of skin hunters had committed a capital goddamn error, as Amerlane the elder would say.

Another set of glass doors opened, a heavy thrumming of Voice filled the air, and Dad straightened. Allison was near the vast window looking over the darkening city, listening to McKenna, whose hair was slicked down and unruffled though his hazel gaze burned.

Jolie leaned against the massive teakwood wet bar, her phone clamped to her ear and her expression full of devouring sadness. She'd no doubt already alerted the Jaspersons that their son was rapidly going downhill, and was probably prepping transport and an honor guard for them to visit the warehouse.

Greg was a waste, but at least his parents would have closure and all the help the Pride could give.

Dad was at his desk, and Sondra Amerlane, one arm weighed down with manila files, brightened as she saw the new arrivals. "Speak of the devil," the lawyer said, and Zoe stiffened.

Bad choice of words. Jack winced inwardly.

"I was already here." Trevor's smile was instant, and warm. "Always arriving just as needed, Jackson. And good afternoon, little dancer."

"Restroom's that way." Jack would have liked to take his *demie*'s coat, but she simply dropped a hurried curtsy—like the little ballerina she was—in Dad's direction and hurried for the indicated door. "We just came from visiting the traitor. You're not going to like this."

That caught Mac's attention. "Checking up on my work?" His forehead wrinkled; despite Jolie's proximity he nearly vibrated with anger. His beast ran under his skin, twitching as it turned over and settled, resentfully, back into quiescence. "I *knew* that little misbegotten was holding out."

"You did all you could." Jack set himself to the business of handshakes and greetings. It was a luxury to no longer be a ghost in the Pride; Sondra didn't give him any cautious sideways glances at all. "Greg wasn't just giving them any old information he could get his paws on. He admitted they were after my *demie* specifically, and he knew the name she was in Akron under."

This bombshell was greeted with grim looks. A door closed softly behind him; Jack watched his father's face.

"Well," Trevor said, quietly. "We just got word from Amelia. They tried the house again—a daylight raid this time, complete with tranquilizer guns, restraints, and some more traditional firepower."

Son of a bitch. Was that why Zoe was so wound up? Prickles slid down Jack's arms, fur seeking to poke free. "We slept in, left right after a late breakfast. When did they hit?"

"Less than an hour ago." Dad's welcoming smile, worn entirely for Zoe's benefit, had vanished. His wine-red tie was a little looser than usual, and his eyes glittered with well-banked fury exponentially deeper than McKenna's. "A twelve-man crew, all dolled up in riot gear. Their body armor's a new type, Amelia said it might stop a clawswipe but their bones still break inside it just fine."

"Did she leave any alive to talk?" Jack's brain raced, furiously. Zoe was still shutting him out, the bond trembling like surface tension on an overfull glass of water.

"Two. Lev and the regular staff are handling repairs, the others took their transport for processing. Sarah just called and said the last of their vehicles is being searched and chopped." McKenna's hands were tense; he stepped to his usual spot at Jack's left shoulder and the hazy heat coming from him was familiar, welcome. When Zoe returned she would stand at his right, and he would be able to take her under his wing again, feel her soothing warmth against his side. "But these guys were still just mercs, from what Amelia can tell. They weren't ready for Kith the way real hunters would be."

"This must've been planned before we drained their financial streams. We still haven't found the individual players' bank accounts, but we will." Trevor looked thoughtfully over Jack's shoulder, blue eyes narrowed. "What was Greg's clearance level again?"

"Not very high, but he had friends." Sondra's expression could best be described as *sour*. Her lipstick was tawny, and her mouth was pursed; her silver earrings gleamed as she shifted the files, clasping them to her chest like a schoolgirl's stack of books. "And who wasn't pitching in with the search, after all? All he had to do was ask."

"In the old days..." McKenna shut up as soon as Trevor's gaze fell upon him.

"His parents aren't responsible." Jack stepped in, as usual. "And in any case, Greg's almost in the bend. He'll be reborn as a worm or something, it's not our problem." He took a deep breath, wishing his twin would finish in the restroom—but she probably needed a few moments to herself, and he wanted to give her everything he could.

"These hunters think one of us raised as a skin will be easier to catch and study. Not to mention dissect, once they've finished."

A short, shocked silence filled the office. It was a blasphemy, and both Dad and Allison would know the autopsy part of the hunters' plans wouldn't come until the skins had tried breeding their captive, with all the damage that implied.

It had been attempted before. More than once.

"Makes the Plainswalker mess look like easy knitting," Sondra muttered, finally. "I'm glad to be home."

"That's another thing." Dad picked up his suit jacket from the ergonomic chair at the huge, shining-polished wooden desk. "George Fantome's dead, but not by his sister's hand. They made an attempt on the Howler today too."

Jack absorbed this. There were ramifications he could sort out at leisure about the McFisk affair, but that wasn't the most pressing concern at the moment. This meant the hunters' timeline had indeed been compressed—but not by much. "We moved not a moment too soon. We'll have to go scorched-earth, Dad."

"*Thank* you," McKenna muttered. "I've said it three times, but nobody's listening."

"Probably because burning everything down is your default setting." Jolie joined the group, tucking her phone in her blazer pocket. "The Jaspersons are on their way to bid their son farewell. I warned Clementine, but I don't think she really understands."

"What mother could?" Dad's sigh was a heavy, familiar sound. There were some things even a Pride leader couldn't mitigate for those under his care. "It's a good thing you two were out of the house, Jack. Even if it meant my daughter had to see a traitor's penance. How did she take it?"

"She..." Jack paused. His mounting discomfort was usual after seventeen years, suppressed with a reflexive habitual effort, and he hated it. "She didn't like it." The understatement was laughable.

Wait. He shouldn't be feeling this particular sensation at all, since his *demie* was just in the next room. His attention turned inward, sensing a critical lapse in an analyst's awareness. *Zo?* The call echoed down the bond, a penny dropped into a dark well. *Zoe, answer me.*

Allison and Jolie had both stilled, watching him intently. Jack whirled, and replayed the last few moments' worth of mental footage.

The sound of a door, closing softly. It hadn't been to the restroom; no, it had been to the outer office.

Oh, fuck. "She thinks she's responsible," he said, numbly. It was the only theory that made any sense. "For the attacks."

"What?" It was the first time in years Sondra looked outright baffled, and Jack couldn't even enjoy the experience.

Because his *demie* had vanished, and twinbond resonated painfully with her absence.

64

A CLEAN BREAK

IT WAS SURPRISINGLY EASY. ALL ZOE HAD TO DO WAS PUT ON A RETAIL worker's fixed smile and walk as if she was on a mission. It was just like the invisible *don't touch me* you learned to ward off pesky customers with—head up, brisk pace, not flinching from eye contact but not seeking it either.

At least the elevator didn't need a keycard or anything. Most places only controlled entry; prisons and schools watched their exits more vigilantly but this place was neither, thank God.

The lobby on the ground floor was glass, full of fading grey winter sunlight, and there were only a few scattered Kith in the milling business-clad folk. Of course the entire skyscraper couldn't be full of her kind, and they studiously ignored her since she was still moving with purpose.

It was weird to be among normal people again. She'd almost forgotten how washed-out they smelled, their watered-down emotions still clearly decipherable through her sensitive nose. A giant revolving glass door spat her onto the street, and she was in New York for the second time in her life.

Maybe it counted as the first despite the New Year's Day trip, because she was now alone. Zoe walked swiftly, barely feeling the cold. At least she wasn't in a skirt, and even though her slacks were thin the long black wool coat would be a blessing once night fell. Her instinctive choice of brogans instead of heels this morning made sense now.

Some part of her, as always, had known this was coming.

It was also deeply strange to be walking in a city again, to feel the old nerve-scraping, weary panic, her only real friend. How many of the people hurrying around her had any idea the Kith existed? None gave her a second look, and of course, in this part of town her clothes would fit in.

It wouldn't be the same elsewhere. Even the long black coat screamed *money*. She'd have to move carefully.

An emptiness dilated in her chest, the twinbond attenuating as she walked. Jack would be fine; he was part of the Pride now. He and Trevor would be glad to have one less problem to deal with—it sounded like they had no shortage—and if she worked this right, they wouldn't even have to know about Royal.

Always assuming he didn't have Jack's number, or Dad's, like he'd gotten hers. How in the hell had he done *that*?

Well, soon enough she'd find out, and it didn't matter anyway since the hunters knew all about 'Amber'. And to think she'd only been worrying about Roy while other, invisible dangers loomed.

It figured. She would never win. Maybe it was time to stop trying altogether, and just do what she could to mitigate damage before... well, she'd figure that out in a bit.

Zoe took long swinging strides as if she had somewhere to be, the black coat's collar popped and a few stray curls lifting on a frigid, snowy breeze from the river. Go figure, she was now in the Big Apple itself, and she had only the clothes on her back.

The new leather purse was in the building she'd just left, placed neatly next to the sink in the palatial restroom off Trevor's office. She'd left the princess signet right next to it. The ring hadn't cried out when it left her finger and slipped her still-warm glove back on. It had glittered once, sharply. That was all.

No ID, no credit or bank cards, and no phone either. But she had two hundred in cash stuffed hurriedly into a trouser pocket—she'd landed in other cities with far less, really, and could make this work. The fake Martha Smith card and eleven dollars she'd brought from Marquette were back in the blue suite, but it was probably better that way.

A clean break was harder to trace. Though they'd tracked her before, she couldn't forget that.

Amber, Amber, Amber. If I hadn't been caught...

Well, she was warned now. Chasing a terrified kid who thought she was a skin was one thing, but Zoe suspected chasing a fore-warned Kith shaman—even one who largely didn't know what the hell she was doing—was whole 'nother ball of horsepuckey, as Auntie Scarsdale would say.

All she had to do was not get caught. Easy-peasy, especially once she dealt with a nagging loose end.

She couldn't do anything about the hunters. But Roy? Oh, he was entirely *her* problem, and she would solve it.

Zoe tucked her chin and halted on a corner, waiting for the light to change. Some pedestrians simply darted into the road with magnificent disdain for their own safety, but more of them seemed content to wait, given the volume of big metal beasts chugging by. A bus lumbered past on a cloud of diesel stink, and instead of calling it *following her nose* she could call the tugging of intuition *shaman-stuff* and trust it to work.

It had never let her down before. But her chest ached, and now that she understood what that feeling meant she wondered how Jack had stood it all those years.

Knowing what you were missing was always the hardest part. Ignorance wasn't bliss, but it also wasn't as painful as being able to call the loneliness by its proper name.

The light changed, Zoe's fingers—stuffed deep in her coat pockets—began to tingle, and she followed the subtle inner prompting without hesitation.

Public libraries were best for what she needed, but she didn't have a card or ID and didn't know if the systems around here required either for internet access. Shaman-instinct poked and prodded, pulling her along. At one point she descended into the subway, moving aimlessly on the stairs until she saw a kid with a heavy backpack jump the turnstile while a pair of bored cops were busy looking the other way. Zoe followed suit as their attention waned still further, and thanks to the New Year's expedition she knew how to blend in even here.

Dusk had fallen by the time she surfaced from roaring tunnels full of whooshing air and bad smells, the snow had halted, and the tingling of instinct became almost unbearable.

Bingo. She spied, with her little eye, an internet café across four lanes of busy traffic. This time she started across without waiting for the light, and despite a blaring horn and blast of shouted cussing she was nowhere close to being hit.

A single victory on a day of defeat; she hoped she could make it count. And that it wasn't her entire ration of success for the foreseeable future.

In a close fug of humid, coffee-scented warmth, she paid for a plain latte and half an hour of access on a public computer. The coffee's warmth was welcome, even though the drink itself wasn't nearly as nice as Amelia's magic with caffeinated beans.

Zoe settled into a squeaking chair, glancing at the skins around her. Not one of them noticed a Kith in their midst. Even the kid at the counter who signed her in had been more interested in his own phone than anything else, and being anonymous again was a deep, almost unalloyed relief.

She decided to keep her gloves on. *Leave no trace* was the order of the day. If her stupid heart would quit hurting, if she didn't feel so empty and lost, it would've been a piece of cake.

Where are you? The call was faint but definite, rising in the distance. She'd felt it even in Hall City, but maybe half a continent wasn't enough to break the *usanaugh* bond. Would the whole one do it? She could head to Los Angeles, but if that didn't work...

Well, really, she could go anywhere. Crossing a border was a lot easier when you could run for miles without getting tired, and she could experiment to find her new limits now that she knew what she was.

Kith, a whole separate species. A shaman. A twin, even if she never saw him again.

We can't be apart. It's...destabilizing.

Well, it was better than being shackled to *her* dumb ass, and pretty soon Jack would realize as much. Especially if Royal was busily sending him and Trevor pictures of her on the pole, or worse.

Her eyes stung. She'd done it to survive, and because she'd thought Royal loved her. She was a creeping, cringing bitch, so hungry for affection she'd let him do whatever he wanted in return for a little warmth. But she was older now, she'd survived—and her wrists twinged a little as her claws sought release.

I'm not a kid anymore. It was a goddamn relief.

Zoe took a deep breath, and the sensation in her wrists faded. Then she pulled the keyboard a little closer, tapped the mouse to make the monitor cable-tied to the table light up, and began typing.

65

FREED BY TENSION

Dad's office door swung open so hard it hit the wall with a solid, unhappy sound. Bella hurried through, Dimitri in her wake. The pair wore identical expressions of concerned alarm, and Bell's auburn bob was gemmed with sleet-jewels. Their boots held traces of snowmelt, and if he cared to, he could probably figure out from where.

But he didn't. Jack suppressed a snarl. "I don't *know*," he repeated. "I thought she couldn't block the link. Not at this point."

"Well, she's had a few shaman lessons. But it's going to take concentration to keep it up, however she's doing it, and she can't keep that up forever." Jolie's calm spread in concentric rings, and under any other conditions it would have been deeply soothing.

Right now, though, it was purely and simply maddening. He didn't want a sodding shaman's calm, he wanted his twin.

Sondra had disappeared to handle yet more diplomatic details with the Plainswalkers. Daniel was manning the phones from his desk outside; Hermann lingered at the door, ready to run any errand. Allison sat cross-legged and sockfoot on the couch, her eyes closed and the pale streak over her temple glowing. Her empty boots sat neatly on the floor, waiting. All her attention was focused inward, attempting to unravel whatever trick Zoe had learned to throw shamans off her trail since childhood.

Dad, his arms folded, was behind the desk, staring out the window; nobody dared approach him just yet. There was no need; he'd given his orders.

Lock down the city, and scour every inch of it. I want my daughter found.

The Pride was leaping to obey. Every in-city jäger—except those with critical support roles—was ready to hunt, and teams of regular Kith were already dividing up the boroughs. She had a ten minute lead, and it only got bigger the longer Jack was trapped here. Intellectually he knew preparing himself and letting the Pride cordon off the island as well as the rest of the city before he began his own pursuit was the best strategy.

The rest of him was having a great deal of difficulty with the notion.

"We've got news, and—oh, dear." Bell fairly skidded to a stop. So did Dima, and it irritated Jack even more to see the two of them working in concert so beautifully. "What now? How can we help?"

"She can't get far with Allison looking for her." Jolie was still attempting to defuse him. "It will be all right, Jack."

What did I do? How did I fuck this up? He kept reaching for his *demie* and finding nothing but empty air, and his beast was seriously unsettled.

Not to mention aggressive.

Jack pried his fingers open. The princess signet gleamed in his palm amid a collage of tiny, quickly healing cuts; he kept clenching at the ring as if it would make her reappear.

McKenna was downloading to Bell at high speed, *sotto voce*. Jack turned away from Jolie—she was trying to be kind, but that only made the consciousness of his own failure deeper.

Not to mention more painful.

"But she can't." Bella sounded truly horrified. "Not without Jack."

Yeah, try telling her that. He skirted the desk and reached his father's side.

The city glimmered as the westering sun fell behind thick cloud; the snow had stopped. Evening lights were coming up all over New York, jewels strung across dark abysses. Somewhere out there was his *demie*, alone again. Maybe she found it preferable to his company. Maybe he'd pushed her too far, or not far enough.

Maybe Greg had frightened her worse than Jack had thought. The urge to go back to the warehouse and tear the traitor to pieces fought with the conflicting imperative to leave, right now, and start tracking his *demie* like a Broken.

And when he found her…"I should go," he said, quietly. He didn't dare look at his father's expression; seeing disappointment there stood a good chance of driving him right over the edge. The ring was a hard lump in his fist again, tiny pain-claws digging in.

"We'll find her." Soft, and thoughtful, Trevor's tone nevertheless held a deep thrumming of Voice. "I promise you that, son. We *will* find her."

"Sir?" McKenna, quiet and respectful, which was a warning in and of itself. "Uh, you'll want to hear this."

Bella, of course, didn't see the need for any preface. "There's a breach. A serious one." She stood on the other side of Dad's desk, leaning over and flattening her palms on the well-polished surface. Dimitri hovered at her shoulder, and there was no trace of his usual good cheer. "Maura over in Security found it, she's bringing Gibs and Awen and the other hackers up to speed. Jasperson the younger didn't just give them information, he somehow got access codes well above his clearance and handed those over too."

Silence fell. Even Voice halted, the low rumble dying as if sliced by a knife. It was faint comfort that Jack had already alerted the Pride to the possibility; they would have found this out eventually, probably within an hour. Good luck and the Rouje habit of building in redundancies had granted them an opening, and now they could pursue the skin hunters far more easily.

It was a good start, but not nearly enough.

Trevor turned, with slow, irresistible grace, and there was nothing skin in his face. His golden mane stiffened, swelling along with the tiny flickers under hide as the beast rippled through him, mastered in less than a heartbeat. "How bad is it?"

"Don't know yet. They've certainly got names and contact info, but Gibson's white hats think the other firewalls have held. They're mole-hunting right now; Gibs says we should get everyone new phones and numbers. It was luck that we caught them, or their own greed—they were trying to get into the financials proper, and Maura flagged it."

Contact info. The shape of the situation changed inside Jack's head.

The skin hunters had a whole file on her, and Greg knew the name she'd been in Akron with—where she'd clawed the skin and fled. Of course Zoe's phone was listed with his and Dad's, and the number was new; all they had to do was run a later-than date search.

Now the morning made more sense—Jack had thought her simply disoriented and slightly hungover from her first Moonfall. But she'd been looking at her phone before that wave of emotion crashed into him, so it hadn't been a physical reaction to the communal run.

No, his twin's response had been pure, unadulterated terror. And she'd asked for a restroom at the warehouse too, but was no doubt unable to slip away. So she'd waited, picked her moment, and tried again.

Viewed this way, the entire tangle was laughably simple. "Ah." A single syllable escaped him, the verbal equivalent of a light bulb turning on over his head.

If only he'd pushed harder, forced the twinbond more instead of cautiously building it, thread by careful thread, while she slept—if he hadn't been so reticent, he would have seen this coming and forestalled it.

"I know that sound." The second, stronger ripple passing

through Trevor was his beast's attention settling, unblinking, upon his son and heir. "Tell me."

"Akron." The impatience of dealing with non-analysts threatened to choke him, ran up against the urge to simply bolt from the room and start hunting, and between the two he could be torn in half, or he could set the warring impulses against each other and use the space freed by the tension to think clearly. "She had contact with a skin there before she ran south to Marquette. Ended up clawing the bastard—it was in the dossier."

"I read that part." Dad nodded, encouraging. "Continue."

It was the same as any other hunt, except this one was far more important than pursuing a Broken or a skin with pretensions to troublemaking. And Jack couldn't afford to make any further mistakes, even small ones. "This batch of hunters had access to our intel through Greg, but I'd wager they've had a watch on hospitals and emergency rooms in major cities for a long time while they looked for a way in or cultivated him. They must have flagged the skin's wounds as Kith-made. They made contact in the two years since she left, realized what they had, probably indoctrinated the skin she clawed, and now they're using him as bait. She's not running blind; she might be returning to what she knows." Everything made sense now.

Profoundly uncertain, thrust into an entirely new universe, learning her entire childhood was a lie, Zoe was deeply confused and vulnerable. Used to loneliness and longing, racked by Angelina's noxious guilt-tripping, his *demie* was a walking target.

She wasn't even capable of trusting her *demi*, thanks to their so-called mother's tender care. She was thinking like a skin, and she'd be caught like one.

Unless he could somehow track her down before these murdering skin bastards did.

"What do you need?" The tiny movements under Dad's skin stilled, and the air in the room changed, hot and tense.

It was good to be a Kith, and even better to be part of the Pride.

Even without his *demie*, he was still a valued member of the family. There was never any question that any help a Pride member required would be given; just how Greg could have ignored that fact was beyond all comprehension.

Call your shots, Jack. Start the hunt right. "Keep the city sealed, and keep looking for her. Get everyone new phones, but have the hackers hive the old numbers and keep regular comm patterns going until we find her—then we can strike and lock them out. She'll try tangling up pursuit the same way she did before, so have the shamans direct the jägers." Jack paused. "Does Belmario have that counter to their new tranqs yet? I know she was testing it."

McKenna cleared his throat. "She's working on it. Says it's close —but the good news is, a dominant Kith will burn it off pretty quickly even with the skate admixture, at least the samples we've acquired so far. They've been testing, so that could change with the new crop from the attack on your house."

That was either very good news, or very bad. "Well, then." Jack rolled his shoulders, stretched his neck—first one side, then the other. It was his usual pre-hunt ritual, and he didn't have to look at Mac to know the other man had tensed. "Give Mac a supply of the counter as soon as she's got anything even mostly viable, and let him come find me."

"Oh *hell* no." McKenna's objection was immediate. "You're not leaving me out of this one."

Dad said nothing, but a rattle went through the room, a single irate vibration, and Mac subsided with only a single mutinous glance.

Jack held his father's gaze. After a while, his *demie*'s might take on the same piercing intensity, and Jack very much wanted to see that. First, though, he had to find her again.

If the skin hunters managed to capture her, she would even further traumatized. And he would personally eviscerate every single one of them he could find. He could make it the work of a long life to hunt their descendants too, if his sweet *demie* would let him.

Where are you, Zo? Let me in. Just give me a single clue. Please.

No answer. Only that terrible, maddening *absence*. He'd borne it for seventeen years, and its reappearance could very well break him.

"Hermann?" Dad's tone was mild, but every Kith in the room stiffened slightly. "Get my son and McKenna a pair of burners." The retainer hurried out to do so, probably glad to have an actionable order, as Trevor continued. "As soon as Belmario has something or Allison has her location, Mac will contact you. Go." He turned back to the window.

"Sir." Jack set off, McKenna falling into step behind him, and by the time they passed Daniel's desk Hermann was already hurrying up with two brand-new, preloaded burners.

"I've put the numbers in both," the retainer said, anxiously. "Sir..."

"I'll bring her back." Jack didn't know if that was the answer he was looking for, but it was the only one he could give. His fist throbbed, the ring clutched in his palm skin-warm and painful. "See you soon, McKenna."

He received a curse in reply, clapped Mac on the shoulder, and left.

66

GREAT TRICK

It was no great trick to find a hotel.

Instead, the problem was finding one cheap enough not to care about ID but expensive enough to keep her from being stabbed or assaulted while she was trying to sleep. Zoe had her claws, certainly —but it seemed far better to fly under the radar, especially since she didn't know where Royal actually was.

She suspected he was also in New York somewhere, crazy as that sounded. It wouldn't be like him to simply stalk her from Ohio; he'd want to see her fear up close. But how, in God's name, had he found her new phone number? It couldn't be listed publicly.

Still, where there was a will, there was a goddamn way. She knew that better to anyone, and though she'd spent years avoiding any real digital footprint she still knew how you could find anyone who even dipped a toe in social media waters. Her old social media profiles as Amber had been temporary, skins shed as soon as she wriggled free, and any email account she'd ever had was the same, only accessed through public machines and left behind the instant she moved on—but it looked like it didn't matter, Royal had found her anyway.

How long had he been looking? Probably the minute he got out of the hospital.

Going back to living on the run wouldn't be too hard. Of course she'd miss the blue suite, Amelia's cooking, the luxury and warmth and quiet. Most of all, she'd miss Jack.

But they were all better off without her, and she could even be relieved at the release of pressure. In the Kith world, she was an interloper, a foreign object. Mentally adding up how much cash she had left and planning her next escape was far more familiar.

It felt, in fact, like home. She'd had a lovely dream, but now she was awake and the world had her in its own claws all over again.

Consequently, she decided not to settle in a hotel room just yet. Restless motion was better, especially since she was...uneasy. Her nape tingled off and on, a familiar tickling sensation, and now that she'd had a few lessons she knew what it was.

A fellow shaman was trying to find her. Every once in a while the sensation would crest and Zoe would have to take a deep breath, unfocus her eyes, and tune her thoughts to a meaningless, static-laden hum until it moved on.

No city worth the name ever truly slept, but this one, as Bell said, took insomnia a few miles further. She rode the subway for a long time, learning the pattern and rhythm of subterranean arteries, then surfaced in Times Square to watch the bright lights, flocks and schools of skins swirling around her all intent on their own business, unaware of her essential difference.

Zoe spotted no other Kith, but sometimes she paused, stepping into a doorway, or changed direction entirely, sensing others like her moving purposefully through the whirl. Sometimes a random vibration—car wheels over metal plates laid where road work was being done, the thrum of the subway, a storm drain full of foaming melt—rubbed her skin like sandpaper and she moved quickly in a different direction, a virus dodging T-cells, a stray cat escaping notice.

Somehow that night she also ended up in Greenwich Village, ducking into a 24-hour café where she bought two panini and enjoyed every bite despite the fact that they were overpriced and overprocessed. Amelia would have been horrified, but they were packed with good hot calories, and Zoe licked her fingers before pulling her gloves back on and hastily leaving because a flicker of motion outside the café's window had bright eyes, moving with fluid grace she recognized.

She was sensing Kith everywhere, now. Either she was paranoid, or there were a lot of them in the area.

So she tried something else. Even in a place this built-up and crowded, there were waste lots, green spaces, and parks. All were quiet and dark, though the homeless burrowed wherever they could find purchase, the rumble of traffic was never far away, and any truly wild areas were buried in snow.

She knew the trick of balancing on a frozen crust now, and there was a surprising amount of wildlife for such an urban area, too. The rats left her alone, the feral cats noticed her, but they could tell she didn't want company and so turned their shoulders, going about their business. Stray dogs regarded her with bright interest, waiting to see if she wanted to talk or possibly share a bite of something, and Zoe's heart hurt every time she realized she had nothing to give them.

It was just one more pain to add to the others. She caught herself reaching internally for the twinbond, desperate for some kind of comfort, and each time snatched her mental fingers back at the last moment.

Leave him alone. You're fucked up beyond repair, he doesn't need that.

Sometimes she thought they probably hadn't even realized she was gone yet, then she would feel the shaman-attention moving over the city again, intuition seeking her trail. Around midnight, deep in Central Park, Zoe balanced on a snow-covered boulder amid a tangle of bushes and thorny vines, listening intently, and the loneliness rose again to suffocate her.

She crouched, gloved fingertips trailing over ice-edged leaves, and knew she should have fled the city outright. Waiting around for Royal to reply was a dumb move.

But she wanted to know. She'd signed into Amber's old email and found three more demands from him, every blessed one ending with **"ANSER ME"** in all caps.

It hadn't taken very long to figure out the reply that would irritate him most.

It's spelled "answer", dipshit. What the fuck do you want?

She'd pressed the send button with equal parts trepidation and exultation. Two years ago—or, hell, even up the day before Jack found her in Marquette—she would never have dared, simply taken off for the hills. Dodging, flight, avoidance, those were her usual tools.

It was time to sharpen new ones. Even a failed Kith—broken, misbegotten, whatever they would call her now—was stronger than Roy could ever dream of being. She could be grateful she knew as much, even if she had to leave the fairytale behind.

The house, the Kith, and her brother were a pretty story, for all the danger of claws and skin hunters. Roy was the ugly reality, and Zoe couldn't take back anything she'd done while struggling to survive.

She could damn well make sure he wouldn't hurt another young girl ever again, though. Either by scaring the stuffing out of him—though he was apparently too stupid to be cautious of a girl who had somehow sliced him up like a log of deli meat—or with something more permanent.

It was official, she was going to hell. But Zoe Rouje couldn't find it in herself to care. Especially if she sent a certain small-time, woman-beating hoodlum there first.

That would be the best trick of all.

67

ANGRY EEL

MOST OF HIS LIFE HAD BEEN SPENT SEARCHING FOR HIS *DEMIE*. THIS HUNT was no different, except he *knew* beyond a shadow of a doubt she was alive, and furthermore that she was still in the city. He didn't have a whole globe to search, or even a whole continent. Just a single urban sprawl of densely packed skins, also being ransacked by every Kith not occupied with a truly critical task.

The security feeds inside the Rouje building showed her walking right out the front door, turning to her left, and reaching the end of the block. Hackers who could be spared from mole-hunting were searching other CCTV and security camera footage all over the Big Apple, scanning it with hush-hush biometric programs skin governments or law enforcement would have killed to lay hands on.

Every resource not absolutely necessary for the Pride's defense was turned toward finding a lost *demie* in this concrete wilderness.

There was a faint thread of her on cold, snow-laden air, flaring and fading maddeningly, crossing and recrossing itself. The twin-bond quivered inside his chest, a ceaseless questing motion; sometimes he caught a distant echo and stopped, his head tilted and hands thrust deep in his coat pockets, her signet still clutched in his right palm.

It was a freezing night, but that didn't stop the skins from venturing out in search of jobs, food, entertainment. It didn't stop him either, and he hoped she was warm enough. He hoped she was staying far ahead of the skin hunters, and hadn't already been lured in by a two-bit skin pimp with fanatical pretensions. He hoped he could find her, and he also hoped it would be soon, because each passing hour made the restless aggression of his beast worse.

If he finally managed to catch sight of her—no, *when* he managed to, he wouldn't allow the possibility of failure—he would run her down like a Broken pursuing prey, and that might frighten her even more.

It would also end with her safe, and he would only be hoodwinked like this once. If she wanted to leave so badly, fine. He'd simply go with her, anywhere in the world, and he had no problem applying the lesson as many times as it took to sink into her stubborn, beautiful head.

New York was a familiar pavement wilderness, Times Square blaring with electric light and throbbing like a bad tooth with skin desire. They wanted what they didn't have, always; he only wanted what he was born with. The difference was ontological.

Bodega cats blinked at him, too well-mannered to show either surprise or recognition. Rats scurried in dark corners, snow and ice no bar to their constant hungry quest for survival. Other strays avoided him and the harsh scraping scent of *predator* leaking from his pores. They kept moving like he did or found warm boltholes to huddle in, hibernating as the mercury plunged.

He finally descended into the subways, and had to shake his golden head at his *demie*'s quick, instinctive intelligence. The interference in the tunnels would keep her camouflaged for a while, and she could ride in relative warmth and safety. In those close quarters, a capture team of skins—even in their new armor—would have a great deal of difficulty with a wary Kith, even one who didn't know half her own strength.

Unless they managed to get one of those tranquilizers in her, and had found a formula that worked.

Be safe, babygirl. Just be safe until I can get to you, and then we're going to have a talk. Her stubbornness had probably kept her alive, true, but now it was working against her self-interest. If he could just get to her before the skins did, all his problems would vanish.

She no doubt feared his temper, though absolutely nothing about this was her fault. Jack climbed to street level near Greenwich and sniffed deeply, following what could have been a false trail. Two other hunting teams were in this area, both giving him a wide berth; anyone coming across a *demi* in his state would be wise to do the same.

His nose twitched. He swung aside, darting through the door of an all-night café with a merrily jingling bell; the place held a definite tang of her. The smell of fried butter enfolded him, and he found the wooden stool she'd perched on at the corner of the counter.

Finally. Why were you here, Zo-baby? Just looking for something to eat? At least she had some money, though she'd left all her ID, the cards, her phone—well, she traveled light, it was what she was used to.

Jack wasn't hungry, but he ordered anyway, paying with cash because *she* would have. Thinking like your prey was always the best tactic. Unfortunately, he didn't know nearly enough about what went on inside her head.

Where are you? Just give me a sign, anything. Please.

The bell over the door jingled once more, and Jack tensed.

But it was only McKenna, shaking small bits of ice from his dark hair. Jolie glided behind him, her great dark eyes slightly unfocused; she kept a hand tucked in the crook of Mac's elbow, trusting him to steer her physical self while the rest of her used shaman's intuition.

They were most probably tracking Jack instead of his *demie*. All the same, a burst of relief filled his chest, warring uneasily with the nagging, aching loss.

"There he is." McKenna guided Jolie to the counter. "Good work, kitten."

The shaman blinked a few times, sense returning to her dark gaze. "Hungry," she murmured, and Mac gestured for the tired, shuffling skin waitress, who was even now bringing out Jack's order—a panini with sundried tomatoes, basil, and bubbling mozzarella, since he suspected it was something his twin might like.

He'd have Amelia make her a better version of this when they got home.

In short order the Kith trio were alone again, the waitress in her pink polyester uniform ambling away. Jack decided manners could go to hell and took a giant bite. It wasn't bad, but he longed for some of Meel's cooking instead. "Please tell me you have something."

"Why else would I come look at your ugly mug?" McKenna's grin was a simple baring of teeth; he settled on the seat to Jack's right, carefully keeping himself between the Pride heir and the shaman. "I could be at home, sleeping. Or out stealing cars."

Jolie climbed onto her own seat, pausing midway through the motion. When she finally settled, she reached for her water glass with a frown of concentration, winced as her fingers closed around it, and took down half the liquid in one long series of swallows. "Ouch."

"What do you need?" Mac's smile died, and he leaned possessively close. For once, Jolie didn't demur, resting her dark head on his shoulder even though his coat was damp.

"Just some food. It's like trying to hold an angry eel; no wonder we could never find her before." Jolie sagged. Her big dark eyes were brighter now and a shaman's calm spread from her once more, a lake of stillness. "But Allison's right, it's a child's trick. Once you know how she's doing it, everything's easier."

Get on with it, then. Jack squashed a flare of impatience, and waited.

"Must be like trying to track *this* asshole." Mac shook his head, but carefully didn't elbow the heir. Jack was clearly not in a mood to be touched at the moment, even by his best friend. "Belmario sends her regards. She's solved the tranqs, I've got some inoculations in my coat pocket that should work no matter how they tinker with the base recipe. Even the best of their recipes only put a Kith down for a short while, and the more dom the shorter that while is."

"Good news." Jack kept to his work, without really tasting the food. It was simply fuel.

"That's not all." McKenna settled his elbows on the counter, frowning a little at its stickiness. "Amerlane the younger talked your dad into going through your sister's phone, and what do you know? Texts from someone calling her Amber and threatening blackmail."

"It's a privacy issue." Jolie's mouth pulled down sourly at the corners, breaking her calm for a single instant. She toyed with her water glass, sensitive fingertips sliding through condensation. "But I can't see any way around it."

"Which is just what Trevor said." The light from buzzing fluorescents overhead glittered in Mac's hair, and didn't quite manage to turn him sallow as a skin. None of the other patrons would hear their murmured conversation, but this was New York. They'd probably ignore it even if they *did* hear. "I should've worked Jasperson harder. Motherfucker."

"You did all you could." Jolie sighed. "*I* should have—"

"Did they find out precisely who's blackmailing my *demie*?" Jack kept his voice low, but there was an edge to each word.

"Some guy named Petterson, texting her. And get this, he's in town, or the phone sending those texts is." Mac didn't fidget, but the eagerness of a hunt buzzed in him like a rattlesnake's warning. "She didn't reply, and there's no voice calls between that number and her phone. In fact, she never called anyone at all, just texted."

"Modern times." It only cheered him for a moment, his talent taking in that data point and serving up logical ramifications. "There's got to be some other method of contact." Since, of course, there was no meeting information, or they would have already been en route to the location.

Petterson. The moment he had his *demie* safely returned, Jack was personally going to hunt this particular skin down. Maybe she'd even help him, once her twin explained, once and for all, that *nothing* she had been forced to do as a skin mattered.

If she had simply trusted him, a blackmail threat would have had no effect at all. But seventeen years apart meant she couldn't even trust herself, let alone her *demi*.

And he hated knowing as much.

"Well, Gibson himself cracked his knuckles and started swearing." McKenna's tone was tinged with unwilling awe; Gibs was one of the few Kith he never teased or poked. It just wasn't worth it to piss off the Pride's best hacker. "He's breaking into phone company databases and has his crew triangulating from cell towers. We might be able to find the entire nest and clear it out before they even get near your *demie*. Oh, and get this, your dad says I'm supposed to restrain you if necessary."

"Good luck with that." Jack indicated his plate; half the second panini was untouched. "Pindar? You want some?"

The shaman finished another sip of water; she was pale, but determined. "I'll wait for mine, thanks. She keeps moving, won't stay anywhere to rest."

"Smart girl." McKenna even sounded grudgingly admiring— twice in one night, it was a banner event. "Still...we can't keep every exit closed for long."

"She's not leaving the city." It was an elementary deduction; Jack bent back to his work of consumption. Now he needed the calories; with Jolie tracking her they could run instead of sticking their noses in each corner, and that required fuel. "Not yet, at least. I think my *demie* might be planning to face one of her demons."

"Dangerous work, even for a shaman." Jolie brightened as the waitress reappeared bearing full plates. Their small group was half the total customers at this hour, but that wouldn't last long. A crop of hungry drunks would descend soon; the pulse of the night was strong and sure even if the streets were frozen.

Just stay safe. Jack's impatience tasted like metal. He couldn't enjoy the sandwiches, or anything else. The only thing that would help the fury mounting in his bones was his *demie*.

Against all the odds, they'd both survived the years apart. It would be particularly cruel to lose her now, and McKenna was probably the one who would have to kill Jack when the shock turned him into a Broken. That was the other reason Dad had given Mac this job, and knowing it would be a friend tearing his throat out was almost a relief.

Almost.

Be safe, Zo. Keep moving, stay warm, and don't let the skins get you.

They would find her. They *had* to.

There was no other option.

68

BREAKFAST RUSH

BY THE TIME A BLEARY RED SUN ROSE OUT OF THE ATLANTIC, ZOE WAS already three cups of over-boiled coffee deep, gazing out the window of a Brooklyn diner specializing in crêpes both savory and sweet. A striped awning fluttered over the door and the place was far too expensive for a girl on the run, but the internet café across the street didn't open until nine A.M. and at least her clothes—disheveled as they were after a night in the open—still said *I have money, I belong.*

She'd keep the coat, certainly. The rest of her outfit would have to go, except maybe the footwear. Good shoes were hard to buy on a retail worker's pittance, and most of her remaining funds would have to go for a bus ticket, *if* she managed to deal with Royal and *if*—another big condition, probably the biggest of all—she could find some kind of ID that would pass cursory inspection. That took time and connections, not to mention more cash.

Of course, she was Kith. She could probably sneak onto a train, avoid the conductor with shaman-sense, and travel that way. Maybe she could even stow away on a bus, if she was daring enough.

Still, she was tired and all those were a tomorrow-problems. She had all she could handle today, especially if Roy had replied.

If he hadn't, well, he would have to stalk a ghost. Spending another night wandering a freezing city, dodging Kith and mounting panic, wasn't an option. She was certainly being chased—but surely they had to see they were better off without her?

Maybe the pursuit was the shadowy skin hunters instead, with their rifles and riot gear. She'd known she was being tracked even in Marquette, and nothing said it had to be just Trevor and Jack trying to find her. The idea that Royal might have hooked up with paramilitary assholes hunting Kith who were just minding their own business was outlandish, but so was everything else about the entire situation.

Zoe was even wondering about Mama's constant fear of being discovered. What had her mother known about skin hunters? Even if Angelina was still alive, she probably wouldn't answer a question like that.

Mama, I'm scared. I wish you were here. It was a useless thought, since Mama would only hiss at her to stop being dramatic.

Zoe smiled as the waiter approached, a nice normal mask. "You're about to cash out and go home, aren't you."

"How did you know?" He was handsome enough, tall and blond, and the interest in his hazel eyes wasn't predatory at all. He laid down a scrap of paper bearing the bad news. "It's okay, though. I can just hand you over to Libby, she's on shift next."

"No, I'm about to get going." Zoe glanced at the bill, digging in her pocket. Soft guitar music noodled through the diner's speakers, looping endlessly. "They're about to open up across the street."

"We've got wifi too." The waiter folded down in a crouch, not nearly as gracefully as a Kith could, and rested his crossed arms on the table. It was a good strategy to get a bigger tip, one she might use herself. "I can give customers the password."

"I'm good, thanks." She added a very nice tip—there was no reason not to be generous, even if she only had what was in her pockets until she could get out of the city. This guy was just doing his job, and hadn't tried any of the usual male bullshit. "The breakfast rush should be in soon, and you guys'll need this table."

"That's the voice of experience talking." He tilted his head, his smile softening, and she was reminded of Jack. "I can tell."

Where are you? The call had faded; there was a scratchy sense of impending thunderstorm in its place. The twinbond actually hurt, a sharp precise agony leaking into her ribcage, and that was new. *Just tell me where you are.*

"I've done my share of waiting tables." Zoe laid the money down carefully. She felt slightly greasy, and even if the cold didn't really touch a Kith she still felt a layer of it deep inside, where not even a good meal could reach. "No change."

He gave the cash a quick glance, and his eyebrows rose. "You sure?"

"Very." *I'm not sure about any of this, my friend, but that's not your problem.* "Thank you."

"My name's Zack, by the way." He lingered, slowly gathering the bills.

Christ, now she had to come up with a fake name, and offer her hand for a shake. "Jolie." Maybe she could use that one for a while, and pretend she was as calm as the other shamans always appeared. "How do you do?"

"How do I do *what*?" But Zack laughed, and didn't squeeze her hand too tightly. "I'd ask for your number, but I think you're out of my league."

Buddy, you have no *idea.* A shiver of distaste went down her back at the physical contact, though his skin was warm and perfectly unobjectionable. She wished Jack was here, but that was pointless. "I'd ask for yours, but I'm leaving town. Thanks, though. It feels good to be appreciated."

"I'll tell my boss and see if it makes him practice a little in my direction. Have a good one, Jolie." He gave her plenty of time to change her mind while he sauntered away, too, but the OPEN sign flicked on in the café across the street and Zoe rose, heading for the tiny customers-only restroom.

Splashing a little cold water on her face worked wonders. Her braid was coming loose, curls blooming every which way, and the only thing keeping her from cutting the whole mop off was the fact that Mama had threatened it as a punishment so often.

So much of life was just enduring what you had to. In this one small way, Zoe would still resist.

By the time she left, Zack was nowhere in sight and a red-haired waitress with a pixie cut—presumably Libby—eyed her curiously. The table had already been cleared, and the front door was opening and closing regularly as the first bit of the breakfast rush began to dribble in.

It was going to be a busy day.

The internet café started filling up as soon as it opened and had better coffee than the diner across the street, though not nearly as good as Amelia's. A huge vintage neon sign on one wall proclaimed that Pabst beer was best, and Zoe was content to let that assertion pass unchallenged. She paid for a half-hour on one of their machines, and chose a seat where she could watch the door.

And, not so incidentally, the street outside, mountain ranges of plowed snow piled high on either side, striped with dirt and losing the ruddy flush of dawn.

Royal had indeed replied. His email contained an address she discovered was nearby—they were both a long way from Akron, go figure—and a grainy picture of a sagging industrial building.

COME ALONE, the email said. Anytime. BRING MONEY OR I'LL SEND YOUR NEW DADDY PICTURES. YOU KNOW WHICH ONES.

So it *was* blackmail, which figured—Roy never saw the value in working if he could just take someone else's cash. At least he spelled everything correctly this time, though, and even used punctuation. Zoe considered this, chewing meditatively on her right index fingernail as she slouched in a squeaking office chair a hundred skins had lounged in before her, and hundreds would after.

She could just...leave, she realized. Extortion didn't work if your target simply vanished, right?

But if he'd found her here, he would find her elsewhere. Someday Zoe might want a real job or something, albeit under a different name somewhere far away from any Kith. She had to deal with this now; as Bea sometimes said, there wasn't any use in trying to avoid a test God had set in front of you.

Zoe wondered if Bea had enjoyed meeting Mama's Jesus, or the other guy. For that matter, had Mama enjoyed going home to glory? There was no way to tell, and if she started down that mental path she might lose her nerve and simply run away. She'd spent her whole life running, avoiding problems, trying to slip under the radar, pass unnoticed.

It was high time to change that, if only once. Besides, she couldn't make the world a tiny fraction safer for the other girls Roy would prey on if she just vanished.

On the bright side, it didn't feel like other shamans were looking for her anymore. There was only that prickling storm-sense, and that could have been her own nervousness.

Get it done before you lose your nerve.

Zoe spent a few more minutes looking up directions to the weird, shabby building. It was in Newark, and she was looking at some travel time to get there. The weather report said it would snow again later in the day.

Get going, Zo.

She logged out, stretched catlike with a sigh, and was gone before the screensaver came on, back out in the cold.

69

SIMMER DOWN

IT WAS NO SMALL FEAT TO ELUDE AN ENTIRE PRIDE TURNING A WHOLE CITY upside-down to find you. Once she was safely back where she belonged, Jack could even feel proud of his *demie*'s achievement.

Right now, though, having found only another dead end in Brooklyn, he was having difficulty keeping his claws sheathed and his beast's fury properly leashed. The grumble of irritation was cresting at progressively shorter intervals, almost breaking the surface of his outward calm with spikes of Voice that would rub any fellow Kith's fur crosswise.

He was also doing his best not to reach through the twinbond. Jolie leaned against an alley wall, her eyes half-lidded; their prey was close, but she apparently couldn't pin down the location any further without alerting an exquisitely sensitive *demie* to pursuit nearby, and once she did they would have to move swiftly enough to reach and contain a wary shaman.

Which meant Jack had to stay buttoned down too, in case he spooked his *demie*. And it also meant McKenna had to get off the goddamn phone.

"Got it." Mac hung up and turned back to them. His coat collar was popped, and a faint blush of chill and excitement touched his stubbled cheeks. He, at least, was in completely control of his beast; the completely aesthetic scruff showed as much. "No more activity on Petterson's phone, but our hackers are worming into their comms even further. They're getting nervous, probably because the attack on your dad's house didn't go well."

It was the understatement of the year—Amelia had indeed kept two of the attackers alive for interrogation. Allison had questioned them as only a shaman could, and found out the group actually *weren't* mercenaries but hunters, albeit complete neophytes.

As far as the skins would be able to discern, the entire jumped-up strike team had simply vanished just like the one before Christmas. So had the ones sent after the Howler, and though George Fantome had been taken down—apparently a flamethrower had been involved—none of *his* attackers had survived the attempt.

There would be no police alerted, no news cameras, nothing but a vast silence swallowing the men they'd sent to kill Kith.

And it would haunt them. Skins didn't deal well with ambiguity.

The overseas Kith were chasing down their own tormentors with likewise success, and had verified that they were unconnected to this batch. Which gave the Rouje Pride one less overarching worry to deal with at the moment, a welcome change from the usual. A hot wire of satisfaction curled inside Jack's chest next to the mounting pain of the blocked twinbond, his *demie*'s absence bleeding like an open wound.

"But the big news is a burst of activity over in Jersey," MacKenna continued, leaning closer to Jolie. All night he'd been moving to shield her from the wind, shepherding her as the shaman turned inward, trusting her protectors to take care of everything else while she painstakingly pursued Zoe through the shifting inner landscape of the Sorcerer's Gene. "Their chatter was encrypted, but Gibs set Awen on it and they broke the entire thing near dawn. It's a trap."

Of course it's a trap. "In Jersey?" Jack longed to be moving instead of engaging in all this stupid chatter, but that was the beast's urge.

Once he got close enough, he could batter through any reticence in the bond—but that would frighten her more.

They had to find her without triggering wild, reckless flight, and Jolie was the best chance of doing so. But it tore at him, and his beast strained the chains holding it to good behavior

"An abandoned factory in Newark, to be precise." McKenna scrubbed at his cheek with blunt fingertips, and glanced at the sky, checking the weather. All three Kith were damp to the knee, their coats heavy with melted sleet. "They're moving into place now, and they seem pretty sure our girl's going to show."

"Newark." *Don't go, Zo-baby.* But if she didn't, they would lose their own best chance to catch her. Jack hoped someone would at least glimpse her at one of the stations or crossing one of the bridges, but morning rush hour meant a lot of people moving past Kith, who could not, after all, close every exit indefinitely. And there were the tunnels to consider. "Guess we're crossing the river, then."

"Jersey isn't so bad." Still, Jolie grimaced, rubbing at her temples. Her boots were outright sodden, and ice clung to the tips of her sandalwood mane. "Maybe we can even get a snack on the way."

It wasn't a bad suggestion—using the Gene took fuel just like running did, and all of them had passed a sleepless, nerve-wracking night chasing a ghost from one end of New York to the other. "Or we can get there, put their heads on spikes, and collect my *demie*." A hint of snarl rode the words, and Jack clamped back down on his temper.

"Easy, Jackson." Mac bristled. "She's been working all night too."

"*Both* of you simmer down." Jolie's sigh was as deep as Allison's, and probably an unconscious imitation. She even touched McKenna's shoulder, gloved fingers smoothing black wool, and he leaned into the contact.

Jack had to look away. "Who else is heading that direction?"

"Two groups under Smythe and Traleski." McKenna's growl faded; the man was enjoying his beloved's attentions almost too much. But then again, he had clearly set his sights on a mate, and that steadied even the most recalcitrant and wild of Kith. "Sam

Coughlin's going too, but the rest of the shamans have to to stay in place."

In other words, Dad was still keeping the Pride's grip on the city's exits as far as they could, just in case his daughter decided not to visit a trap. "Good. I presume we have transport?"

"No stealing cars." Jolie perked up enough to fix McKenna with a baleful glare. A single pinprick of shamanlight showed in her pupils for a moment, and she stilled again.

"You never want to have any fun. But don't worry, kitten, that kid Freitag will meet us en route." Mac shifted uneasily, glancing over Jack's shoulder at the alley's mouth. "Smells like more snow."

Jack's limbs burned with the need to run, to tear through the daytime city no matter how many skins saw him shifting through his beast. He longed to gallop over icebound bridges, plunge into tunnels, hop over cars, and tear through anything else in his way to find his *demie*.

Control. The long-ago feel of his father's fingers clamped on his nape helped, but not enough. *You are my son, and you* will *use proper control.*

"—Jack?" Jolie sounded anxious.

Of course both of them would sense his tension, and smell the red rush of rage. He was right back where he'd started, but this time his *demie* had left of her own accord instead of being stolen.

It hurt. "Fine," he muttered. Did she feel like this when she insisted she was all right? Why hadn't he seen it before, done something better, somehow forestalled this? "Just fine."

"Liar." But Mac was only bantering, and he even bumped Jack on the shoulder with a loose fist, a rough, casual contact any other Kith wouldn't have risked with an edgy *demi*. It was a vote of confidence, one Jackson could appreciate even as it threatened to snap the ropes holding his beast in check. "Let's go."

70
ONE WAY OR ANOTHER

THE TRAIN DIDN'T FEEL RIGHT, SO A SNORTING, HEAVING BUS CARRIED HER over a famous bridge and through Manhattan while she hunched in her seat, sensing Kith activity. Fortunately, she passed unremarked and switched to another bus, chugging through an underground tunnel.

Then, hey presto, Zoe was in New Jersey, watching smokestacks rise and adding another state to the list of those she'd visited since leaving Nebraska.

Anything earlier didn't count, since she'd been traveling with Mama. The bus swayed, belching, and blundered to its stops like a snuffling, roly-poly pig sampling different feed troughs. Her stop was coming up.

She was used to—and good at—navigating cities without GPS, but now Zoe wondered how much of her success was shaman-stuff, and how much just plain old common sense. It was an almost-unanswerable question, like why hot dogs and buns were packaged in different quantities or why people stayed poor if Jesus truly loved them.

She could probably get close to figuring her sense of direction out with some experimentation in a different city, though, assuming she could deal with Royal and get out of this icy wasteland without further problems. A tremor had settled in her bones, and she had to wipe at her cheeks more than once because her eyes were leaking. Trying to blame it on the change from freezing outside to the bus's muggy warmth didn't really work, any more than it had helped when she was a child and the sadness would descend for days on end.

Stop that blubbering, Mama would snap, but Zoe was never able to. She often didn't even know *why* she was weeping, but now she had a name for the pain.

It was missing her brother, and the feeling only mounted over time. Her heart hurt, and so did the rest of her, including her head. All the coffee she'd taken down boiled, an acidic whirlpool in her stomach, and the fidgets had her, too. If she wasn't careful people would start to stare at the girl twitching like a junkie, her cheeks gleaming with salt water.

Or maybe they wouldn't. Zoe shifted uncomfortably on the hard plastic seat, staring at the heavily fogged window. It was New York, after all, and everyone here avoided eye contact like it was a disease. The Midwest would have called it cold and unfriendly, but there were so many people around you couldn't smile at them all. It was impossible, so why bother?

The crowd was another problem. It had only taken a few short weeks to become used to Jack's steady warmth beside her, a shield against the constant, withering scrape of so many other thinking, breathing creatures against her bare nerves. Maybe pretending to ignore everyone else was actually a politeness, a social fiction that helped people get along without running amok and murdering each other more than they already did.

She didn't know how much longer she could stand the emptiness in her chest; her nose tingled, too full to smell properly. She hated not being able to scent danger; it was as if half the world's colors had drained away and the rest had turned pastel, leached by steadily mounting pain.

Maybe the longing would ameliorate if she could travel far enough. It was worth a shot. And when the bus next began to slow and nose toward yet another Plexiglass cube where shivering people waited to climb aboard, she rose easily, her knees loose as she strode down the aisle.

Clambering down dirty, slippery metal steps and hopping onto an ice-rimed sidewalk was a relief, but she was a long way from her destination and had yet another bus to catch. She was even fairly sure she wouldn't have to pay a separate fare, since it was the tail end of the morning commute.

So Zo turned up the collar of her coat once more, sniffed heavily, and set off into a bruise-colored winter afternoon.

The first few flakes of snow fluttered down, vanishing into filthy slush.

It was a relief to be near the end of even a short journey. She'd lost not only her hard protective carapace but also the habit of traveling in the past few weeks; her toes were numb despite a Kith's high metabolism providing warmth and there was nothing to eat in this part of town unless she wanted gas station nachos. Which she wouldn't have minded, really, but the sooner she got this over with the sooner she could turn to the problem of her next move. South would be warmer, but someone...

Jack.

...someone else might guess she'd think like that. So it was north or west, and no matter how she mulled it over, even with the help of steady walking, she couldn't decide. West meant traveling close to Roy's old stomping grounds, not to mention Bea's, but if both of them were out of the picture what did she have to lose?

Still, she hated the thought of even passing through Akron, though she could probably avoid Hall City for the rest of her natural born life without any trouble at all. Mama's grave was there, and now Zo wondered if Bea would be buried next to her.

Mama might enjoy that. She'd thought Bea hung the moon. Had she seen that he was Kith?

Don't think about that. There's no point. North was probably the best bet, though the snow was even worse that way.

There weren't any pedestrians now; the sidewalks were mostly unshoveled or nonexistent. Zoe picked her way along, sometimes walking on the snowy shoulder. Weedy waste lots sat quietly under blankets of white tortured into strange shapes—animal footprints, the vagaries of short thaws, the buckle-and-heaving of refreeze all left their marks, and the constant sawing wind sculpted anything remaining. Plenty of windows were boarded up, and one or two of the warehouses even looked like good squat material, especially in summer. The sound of traffic retreated the further she walked, and while some of its fading was due to distance the rest was the peculiar silence of new snowfall.

The flakes thickened, turning wet as the temperature crept a few degrees upwards. The twinbond ached like a broken bone or abscessed tooth—Zoe had never experienced either, but she could *imagine*, and had winced in sympathy at other people's injuries all her life.

At least the weird staticky sense of shamans looking for her had faded. It had only taken a single night for them to realize they didn't want her, despite all their welcome and kindness.

It was for the best. Especially with what she was contemplating.

She stopped next to a listing construction fence, originally meant to be temporary but solidifying into permanence with a heavy coat of graffiti. Her legs simply refused to take another step, locking in place, and her head came up, blue eyes narrowed as she scanned her surroundings yet again.

An empty street, only indifferently plowed, with great craggy peaks of stained snow on either side. The sidewalk had been scoured by wind, so it held only a packed sheet of ice quickly vanishing under fresh white flakes. A Pilot station crouched listlessly a block behind her, its sign glowing in the storm-dimness of a winter noon with heavy weather moving in. A warehouse, its parking lot half-cleared and holding several relatively snow-free cars—people at work, while she was an alien getting ready to...what?

What *precisely* was she going to do to Royal? And why would he drag her all the way out here?

Power, of course. It was the drug every petty little jackass craved, like Mama and her medicine. Zoe had run right from Bea to a junior version of the hypocritical, bullying, misbegotten pastor, and she'd thought she was so *smart*.

Well, at least she'd learned a thing or two since clawing the shit out of Roy. A chill spilled down her back. It wasn't from the snow, or the rising knifelike wind.

Something's wrong. Run.

But she'd been running practically her entire life. When would it stop? The Kith were a good dream, the bright fairytale, the movie montage. Bea, Roy, the men in their bulletproof vests and goggles, determined to shoot and smash just to prove they could—*they* were the reality, and they kept kicking and beating and breaking until they were stopped.

What are you going to do? Kill him?

Well, she had claws, didn't she? Kith were stronger, faster, and Jack said smarter too. No wonder the skin hunters were terrified. They wanted to murder what they didn't understand, what they couldn't control.

It was only human, and you could even argue it was the way God wanted it since humanity had clearly been *made* that way.

If she was an alien, did God and Jesus and hell even apply? It was a fine time to be having an existential crisis. Royal couldn't even leave her alone long enough for Zo to truly discover the limits of what she was—but it was probably for the best, since tearing herself away from her twin and the warm, comforting blanket of the Kith on her own terms instead of being kicked out might have been impossible if she'd had more time to get used to the seductiveness of comfort, of acceptance.

Soft, stealthy sounds tiptoed through the snow-silence. Zoe eyed the other end of the street; the roof and dead dark double smoke-stacks of the ramshackle building Royal wanted to meet in were barely visible two blocks down. She was very, very close. Her right hand rested lightly on the fence, vibrations communicating through cheap plywood, chain link, metal stands, plastic netting, and her glove.

The part where lined leather had been cut to fit over her signet sagged, and Zoe swallowed, hard.

Tires crunched on ridged ice. A dirty white delivery van hove into sight, and the chills were coming in waves now. Her teeth all but chattered. The old familiar slipstream threatened to fill her straining ears, drowning out small creeping sounds all around her.

What the fuck is going on?

More crunching sounds behind her, as if someone had left the Pilot station and was cautiously driving west, the street empty just a moment ago now feeling uncomfortably active—and unfriendly.

Very unfriendly indeed. Zoe's hand dropped back to her side and she tilted her head, a snow-freighted strand falling in her eyes. Cold wind made the single curl bounce heavily, weighed down by frozen water, and she realized what the tiny creakings and slitherings all around her were.

Feet. Normal people, attempting to wade quietly through snow.

She was surrounded.

71
WORKING OVERTIME

KIERAN, THE OLDEST OF THE FREITAG CUBS, DID INDEED MEET THEM EN route with a silver Jeep Cherokee, its snow tires gripping sure as a jäger's footing. McKenna rode shotgun, probably so Jack wouldn't make the young Kith nervous. Freitag also had new phones to hand out, each with a small printed card for the password manager's master log-in since every single one of their digital keys had been changed.

The hackers were working overtime, but Gibs and his crew enjoyed that sort of thing. The tech support crew was probably glad to have something to sharpen their claws on that wasn't *did you turn it off and back on again?*

"I have the location right here." Kieran tapped the phone in its dash holder; their route was a bright red line on a constantly updating map. "Good thing I was on this side of the river already, the bridges are fucked and the tunnels aren't far behind."

"Language, kid. There's a shaman present." McKenna grinned, thumbing at his new phone, and exhaled a satisfied sigh. "Thank God for this. Worse than running in fog."

"You know there was life before smartphones, right? There was even a time before the internet." Jolie sounded relieved as well; she leaned forward eagerly, peering out the windshield. "Please tell me you brought something to—"

"Snack on? Sure, just reach over the back seat, there's granola bars and Gatorade. I'd've stopped for something better, but Mom said speed was more important." Kieran feathered the accelerator, and Jack began digging through messages on his own small brick of plastic, metal, and circuitry.

None of them were from his missing *demie*, so he hit the side button, watched the darkened screen for a few moments as the Jeep rocked over corduroy-packed snow, and tucked the phone away. Impatience beat under his heart, right next to the bond's steady painful bleeding, and he stilled.

There. "We're getting closer." *Thank you.* He could feel his *demie* now, the faintest suggestion of distant music, a concert on the other side of a hilly park audible when the wind veered.

"I can feel it too." Jolie slid her phone into her coat's breast pocket and patted at her hair, tangles separating smoothly under sensitive fingers. She betrayed no unease at being next to a disturbed *demi* in a confined space, but then again, she was Allison's chief protégé. "She's not even bothering to block now. How close are the other teams?"

"A few minutes." Mac exhaled sharply, a familiar sound—the hunt was about to break loose. "Although I don't—"

Jolie gasped, and Jack stiffened as a sudden, grating shock slammed into him. The twinbond turned red-hot, a tangle of glowing razorwire clotting around Jack's heart, and a flood of stinging sensation poured through it, a nova exploding.

A deep warning growl filled Jack's throat. Jolie flinched, inhaling sharply once more, because the invisible wave smashing through the Jeep was made of pure fear. It was a shaman in distress, broadcasting wildly.

It was also his *demie*.

Her body knew before she did; Zoe coiled herself and leapt, catching the top of the flimsy fence. She was over in a flash, landing light as a butterfly—a Kith trick. Plywood shuddered and icicles were shaken free, shards plopping into fresh snow. A silver glitter flicked past her, hitting the fence and skittering away, and for a moment she thought it was a huge metal insect.

What the hell?

She dodged another weird silvery missile, instinct and reflex yanking her body aside before the rest of her caught up. This one sank its long wicked point into the icy fence, and she realized what it was from television shows.

A tranquilizer dart.

Jesus Christ, Roy wants to roofie me? A disbelieving laugh slipped through her chapped lips and she dodged again; another dart smacked into a drift near her feet. It was almost ridiculously easy to avoid them, and she took off parallel to the fence, running like Jack had taught her.

Except she'd already known. He'd simply encouraged her into discovering it for herself, and she was downright glad he wasn't here now.

This seemed too dangerous, and she didn't want her twin hurt. Ever.

What the fuck, Roy? She could figure it out later. Shouts—heavy male voices only barely muffled by the rapidly thickening snow— and the crunching of tire chains digging through packed ice filled her ears.

Zoe cut across the corner of the lot, snapping a glance to her right. Her pursuers on this side of the fence were in puffy white suits, and she thought they were snowmen granted temporary life for a brief terrifying moment before she realized it was simply camou- flage. Behind them, a half-constructed building had been left to rot, naked rebar vibrating slightly, musically, as the wind slipped through its claws.

More pop-pocking noises, more silver missiles. They were

shooting *tranquilizers* at her; it occurred to her that these were the skin hunters. How did these people know about Royal? Or was he one of them?

Well, don't I feel silly now. She should've known he'd shack up with that kind of crowd, it was *right* up his gangsta-wannabe alley. Every pimp liked to pretend he was a for-true tough guy. Zoe dodged again, and it occurred to her that Roy probably wanted revenge for the scars, too.

She had to decide which way to bolt, but the twinbond pulsed inside her chest. The welter of sensation confused her for a moment, and she froze.

Thwip. A spear of ice buried itself in her right thigh, and Zoe screamed. It was the same high glassy cry shamans gave during Moonfall, the same noise she'd made when she burst from the church cellar, clawing wildly at Pastor Bea who turned out to be plain old Leroy McFisk, a misbegotten Kith.

Was that why he'd hated her so much?

Her leg went numb, and the world turned over. Zoe landed hard, suddenly floundering in ice-crusted snow that had held her up without complaint just a half-second before.

Oh, shit.

72
SHORT DURATION

"No." Jolie's hand was an iron clamp. Her fingers couldn't reach all the way around Jack's upper arm, but they sank in with a shaman's undeniable strength, and instead of tracking Zoe she was now wholly occupied with keeping him still. "Not yet."

"Let *go*," Jack snarled, Voice bouncing through the Jeep's interior. The windows flexed, condensation crawling up in venous patterns. "Fucking *let go!*"

His *demie* was still alive, he could sense that much. But she was either injured to unconsciousness or sedated, and there were skins boiling around the waste lots and an abandoned factory, its dead cold smokestacks leaning just a few degrees off true.

Looked like the meet had been a success. An off-white delivery van crept in front of Freitag's Jeep, its right turn signal blinking for an eternity before it wallowed through a break in chain-link fence. Two bundled-up skins hurried to close the gate, and even one of their own oblivious kind would have seen the rigid shapes of body armor under their heavy parkas.

"Keep him contained." Mac leaned forward in his seat, staring intently; his beast rippled under his skin. "They have to be taking her there. *Don't* slow down, kid."

"Wait, we're not gonna go after them?" Kieran was having a little trouble focusing, but then again, he had McKenna snarling on one side and an enraged *demi* sitting right behind him, restrained only by a junior shaman.

"Just drive casual." McKenna clapped his phone to his ear. "Like you don't notice anything wrong. Yes, hi, it's McKenna, they've got her, there's a lot of them, *get here.*" He jabbed at the disconnect button, stuffed his phone back into his breast pocket, and hit his seatbelt release. "Son of a *bitch.*" It was the conversational tone he used when the cops became involved, amusement mixing with disdain and a tinge of good-natured mockery. "I said keep going, kid."

"We can't leave one of our own, can we?" The cub had the right idea, but McKenna's only answer was a short growl, a hot wave of dominance spreading from him, enforcing obedience.

Jack surged against Jolie's hold, and almost slipped free. Muffled, agonizing fear poured through the twinbond, a stinging in his right thigh, his terrified *demie* nearby and unable to shut him out as she fought an entirely different battle.

"Calm down," Jolie hissed. "Dammit, Jack, *help me.*"

He didn't want to help her. He wanted to tear the car door off its hinges and run straight to his *demie*, whose shock and panic struggled against a sickeningly warm chemical haze.

Looked like the tranqs did indeed work in the short term.

"Let go of me." He didn't recognize his own voice. Jack sounded like his father, Voice and dominance riding every syllable. But Trevor had never sounded this furious, not in Jack's memory, even that terrible day his wife and daughter disappeared. "Let go of me, or *I will kill you.*"

"Don't be an asshole," McKenna snapped from the passenger seat. His beast was nervous too, by the way his flesh was rippling and his hazel eyes glowed. "Go another block, Freitag. Take a right there, and pull in. Can't let them think we're anything other than a random passerby."

"How far is backup?" Like most young creatures, the cub settled as soon as he had proper direction. He feathered the accelerator, the tires bit packed, rutted snow, and they were drawing away from Jack's *demie*. "Those are them, right? The hunters everyone's talking about."

"Don't worry about it." Mac twisted to look into the backseat. "None of those skin bastards are going home. Jack? Jackson, look at me."

I don't fucking want to. But Jack's gaze snapped to McKenna's, dark and familiar, and his best friend smiled, baring strong white teeth. It was a bloodthirsty grimace, Mac's canines swelling as the change struggled for release.

"Backup's on the way," Mac continued, soft and matter of fact. "We're going in first, but for God's sake, Jack, don't tear the door off this kid's car, all right? He saved up for it."

"It's not like it matters—" Kieran piped up, somewhat anxiously, but then Jolie's hold slipped.

Not much, a mere hair. A single, tiny fraction. And not for long, either—only a small slice of a second, less than a heartbeat.

Jackson Rouje exploded into motion.

For the first time she could remember, Zoe's body simply wouldn't obey her. Her arms and legs were heavy, inert sausages; her head lolled and her pulse was a sluggish murmur. Even her eyes unfocused. She drifted in a chemical soup the temperature and consistency of blood.

At least her ears still worked. She heard them—all male, and all with the strange flatness that meant skin. No depth or rich timbre; even their voices were pale in comparison to Kith.

"I can't believe it." A young man's voice full of excitement, echoing off hard surfaces. "Walked right in."

"Well, they're animals." Another man, a little older. "What did you expect?"

She was lifted, dragged. Tossed onto something hard, like a table. Metal clanged, and she heard a shapeless moan.

It was her own. Her throat didn't want to work properly. A bubble of drool was collecting at the corner of her mouth, and her wet cheeks stung with faraway pain.

"Good work, son." There was the sharp sound of a hearty male slap, the crowd full of congratulatory testosterone, each syllable echoing as if they were in a locker room.

And suddenly, a familiar whining tenor pierced the hubbub. "Thank you, sir. It's an honor to help."

I know that voice. It was Royal, fawning like he did when a high roller came into the club.

All the running, all the hiding, and it all came back to this. She might as well be back in Akron, breathing cigarette smoke, feeling the stickiness of spilled alcohol under platform heels, and listening helplessly while men discussed the girls on display. *Nice tits, but skinny...looks like a schoolgirl...whatta wildcat...*

At least the sedation quieted the whirling inside her head, relieved the awful pressure, and deadened the aching in her chest. Was this what getting drunk did for Royal's other girls?

No wonder they liked it so much.

More sounds of motion, clanging, shouts and cryptic muttered exchanges. They were doing something with her arms, her wrists pressed together. Her legs were heavy clay, useless and dead. The hardness underneath her felt metallic, and though she knew it was snowing sweat prickled all over her.

Her nose began to work again. She smelled iron, industrial-grade dirt, and a weird brassy note that somehow made her think of guns, all mixed with a collage of different males. The skins were sweating too, but with excitement instead of terror, and small creaks from their equipment mixed with static-popping babble from radios.

Are they cops? That would explain a lot.

A cool draft touched her face, freighted with a terribly familiar odor. He was still using the same aftershave.

"Hi there, honeybun." It was Roy's usual greeting for one of his girls when he was in a good or expansive mood.

Oh, God. Please help me. The calculations began to whirl inside Zoe's head, each thought trudging through thick mud instead whizzing along at normal speed.

Did he sound upset, or pleased? How bad was it? Would she have enough money to make him happy for the night, or would he tell her to go out again?

Something caressed her cheek, hard and cold.

"Get that away," an older male barked; it was the voice of a man in authority, very used to instant obedience. "We want her intact. At least to begin with."

"Let him have some fun." This was another youngish man, and something in his tone made frantic, drugged loathing prickle all over her along with the sweat. Clicks and banging, and the sound of a zipper, going up or down—she couldn't tell. "I mean, look at his face, man."

"Bet you never thought you'd see me again," Royal whispered. "Oh, Amber, honey, you have fucked the fuck up."

Everything inside Zoe stilled. It didn't hurt anymore, and she was grateful for that. It was probably a mercy of short duration, like every other lucky break in her misbegotten life.

Then, in the silence, a bright, white-hot flower bloomed. The twinbond blazed into almost-painful life, not a spark but a flood as any objection, any barrier was brushed aside and her brother poured into her.

I'm here, he said, silently. *I'm right here, and you'll be safe soon.*

A sob caught in Zoe's throat. The sound must have attracted her captors' attention, because she heard more than one skin crowding close, and a mutter of male laughter.

"Where's our transport?" An official-sounding bark from the older man, the one clearly used to everyone around him jumping when he demanded. He too smelled of aftershave, just far more expensive than Royal's generic drugstore reek, and the burr in his voice as well as the tinge of burning to his scent said he liked a good cigar every now and again. "Darnell?"

"Should be ready, I sent Mark out to..." That reedy, youngish voice, the one she immediately disliked. "Come on, don't let him spoil the merchandise."

Zoe's head snapped aside, her cheek stinging. It didn't truly hurt, but it did send a shock down her entire body. Pins and needles crawled over her, limbs waking up from nerve compression.

Someone had hit her. Well, she'd expected that. The bond went still inside her too, Jack's welter of emotion shrinking to a single small, still, undeniable point.

Don't, she pleaded, silently. *They have guns, they'll hurt you. Just leave me alone.*

A sharp bolt of utter negation. Wherever he was—and she suspected it was close, which was surprising but not entirely unbelievable—Jack had no intention of going home and leaving her here.

Which meant she had to do something, if she could just get rid of whatever they'd roofied her with.

"Oh, honeybun." Roy was getting excited, if his breathing was any indication. His fingers were on her face, digging in, and his breath smelled like peppermint and rancid coffee. "We're gonna get it through your head, and the rest of you, too."

You are such an asshole. Fury mounted in Zoe's bones as the animal in her stretched, lifting a sleepy eyelid. So much striving to keep it contained, to keep herself locked up in a little box, slinking in shadows and hiding in corners.

What was the point? It never worked, they still came after you no matter how well you hid.

A series of shattering bangs echoed through the space, padded sledgehammer blows so loud she felt them all over.

Gunfire. The twinbond dilated, and a stinging in her arm was Jack's. He was hurt, a bullet tearing through flesh.

Oh, hell no.

Zoe's eyes snapped open. The plastic zip ties at her wrists sliced cruelly before breaking, the pops unheard in the sudden cacophony. More shots, terrible screams, light strobing because her eyelids were fluttering, and blood flew. Her left hand flashed out, and Royal—his dark hair ruthlessly sheared as if he'd joined the military, wearing some kind of black body-armor like the assholes who had invaded the Rouje mansion before Christmas, and leaning over what he thought was a helpless woman—let out a choking gurgle as her claws once again bit deep into his flesh.

73
SPEED OF THOUGHT

Of all the places for skin hunters to hide, they had to go and pick New Jersey. It boggled the mind.

The factory—God only knew what it had originally been in the business of creating—had been hollowed out and turned into a warren, albeit with two satellite dishes on its roof and a cell tower rearing from its backside, taking advantage of the dead smokestacks. An indifferently paved parking lot, hidden from the street and ringed with privacy fencing, held a collection of vehicles including a glossy black BMW sedan and a decommissioned armored truck.

The truck—once used to take bags of cash between banks—had been backed up to a receiving bay, its rear doors wide open, and a glance inside showed what it was meant to haul. There was a long narrow metal shelf with restraints laid carefully aside, ready to cinch down a drugged, helpless Kith. Medical equipment and seats for skin guards to perch and watch the cargo took up the rest of the space.

McKenna took the stocky, body-armored skin who was readying the thing with a quick snap of a neck like a green stick breaking, and his friend's silent snarl found its answer vibrating in Jack's own chest. Neither of them were armed, but then again, they didn't need to be.

Guns, while useful, had no place on this particular hunt.

Jack plunged through the loading bay doors, sensitive ears picking out individual skin heartbeats—at least thirty if not more, and all male. His nose twitched, and his beast caught an elusive, maddening, very welcome scent.

If he hadn't already known his *demie* was here from the twin-bond's pulsating inside him, filling him with clear red fury, that thread of fragrance would have told him so. The entire world caught on that single invisible filament, keeping him from the abyss.

Gunfire boomed, bullets spattered, and the smoke of propellant was an acrid smoky reek as Jack collided with a relatively tall, muscular blond skin in body armor, his claws flickering to open the man's throat almost as an afterthought. Arterial spray blossomed, the skin hunter gurgled as he collapsed, and a ricochet stung Jack's arm, careening away through walls, zinging off iron support beams.

It would heal almost instantly, but his *demie* was suddenly inside him, the link resonating with powerful, protective fury. Two plucked strings, a single sweet piercing harmonic, and he felt the shock as her smaller, razor-sharp claws sliced through a tormenter's face, catching on bone before shearing through as her wrist tensed. A gorgeous soprano howl thrilled through the entire structure, a shaman's battle-cry, and it drew him after it like a silver needle carrying crimson thread.

McKenna howled behind him, the sound of a dominant Kith in a hunting rage, and there was another jolt of gunfire—sounded like an assault rifle, the most American of bird calls—cut off on a scream ending with another dying gurgle. More crashing, wood snapping and metal shearing, but Jack turned away.

Mac could take care of himself.

Where are you? The question leapt from him at the speed of thought, and a wordless flood of information filled him in reply. His twin was close, and terribly frightened. Her voice rose once more, thrilling into ultrasonic. Her beast, at least, understood he was here to help.

Blood exploded again. They were indeed using the new body armor Amelia had reported on, and it was easy to simply bounce between them like a pinball, transferred momentum crushing them inside their ridiculous shells. Two more skins died, one having time to fill his pants as sphincters released at the moment of crisis, and Jack burst into a relatively open space filled with portable half-walls like a cheap office fishbowl. The structures were so flimsy even a skin could walk right through, but few of them ever thought of doing so. They were blind, both in eye and nose, weak wriggling worms knowing only mindless chewing destruction.

Jack's kind would never be this goddamn *crude*. Even a Broken's cannibalistic rage was cleaner than the skin hunters' deep-seated desire to torture, to mar and break victims before killing.

When a Kith killed, it was because they had no other choice, and it was done quickly.

But if they hurt his *demie*, or robbed him of her life, he would make an exception. He would rage worse than a Broken ever could, and his only regret would be that he could not make the entire world suffer in return.

Some of the 'offices' had metal autopsy tables, and the smoking odor of fresh blood was laid over a deep rancid well of old death. They obviously had other victims, but figuring out who else had fallen foul of these bastards could wait.

Jack plunged through two of the cubicles and skidded to a stop in a third. Monitors glowed, and a freckled, carrot-haired skin male busily tending to a bank of keyboards and other equipment turned, staring at him with wide blue eyes. Whatever he saw made the skin's face turn cheesy-pale, and Jack tore the life out of the man with reflexive ease, taking in the setup with a glance—a comms hub, police scanners and some CCTV feeds of the factory's outside, along with a rack holding two pistols, ammo in neat clips, and a well-maintained but probably never-fired AR-15.

His arm twitched as a final chunk of bullet was expelled, and the hole in his flesh closed almost instantly. The beast in him laughed at such things, or it would have if the deadly serious business of finding his twin wasn't occupying every inch of its awareness.

Jack took off again, and walls crumbled before him.

Hold on, demie. *I'm almost there.*

74
FLOCK TOGETHER

O<small>NCE SHE STOPPED FIGHTING HER OWN NATURE, EVERYTHING BECAME SO</small> much easier.

Zoe spun, snarling, and her left hand whipped out again. The zip ties had cut her wrists badly, but the slices were healing in fast-forward and the smell of her own blood hit the back of her throat like a slug of bourbon, napalm-potent where skin alcohol was merely a weak pleasure. The metal gurney she'd been laid on clattered, but its wheels were locked. Zoe hopped down from temporary high ground, her brogans untied and her torn sweater flopping.

Her coat was gone, and they had been trying to take her shoes off. For some reason, the thought filled her with another burst of clear, clean rage.

Royal's body was a collapsed, savaged lump. A wheeled cart with stainless-steel dishes of weird implements—saws, forceps, scalpels, other things—spun away as Zoe's hip brushed it, crashing into a heavyset older man in black body armor, his mouth working fishlike under a greying goatee. He was the one in command, the one the others obeyed, but at the moment he was screaming while he fumbled at a holstered pistol, his fat fingers suddenly slippery with fearsweat.

Their terror was all around her, wine-red and intoxicating, and though her right leg was still a little weak the rest of her seemed to have shaken off the chemical soup just fine. Which was good, because she was surrounded; Zoe snarled, the animal caged in her bones finally, exquisitely free. Her teeth tingled because they had *changed*, longer and sharper like her claws, and the quivers under her skin turned to hot stipples as black fur bristled and receded in waves.

Male skins were visible on CCTV feeds coming through a bank of old-fashioned monitors with heavy glass faces, all the men running around like headless chickens in black body armor or those puffy white camouflage jumpsuits. They'd thought they were going to watch a lab rat's torture, and found themselves facing an angry Kith instead. Zoe uncoiled like a striking rattlesnake as a screaming blond man, tiny dewdrops of blood clinging to his golden stubble, leveled a rifle, its muzzle a deep black hole.

He yanked at the trigger, a spasmodic motion accompanied by a deafening roar, but she was already moving, bullets plop-popping in a stream behind her as she leapt, crashing into him. The gun went flying and so did he, spinning in midair before hitting a concrete support pillar with a sickening crack.

Zoe's left foot flashed up, and the grey-haired man with the goatee, struggling out of the ruins of the medical cart, went flying. He hit the monitors with another terrible crunching noise.

The floor was concrete too, stained with God only knew what, and the walls were rippling as if brushed by an earthquake because they were cheap movable cubicle containers, some covered with blue nylon carpeting. She'd done call-center work in Ohio for a short while before meeting Roy, and maybe she was dreaming because the 'offices' there had been *exactly* the same.

Well, without the armed men, bare concrete floors, guns, and torture implements, but still.

Shadows swayed crazily as the hanging lamp over the gurney spun and whirled, its cord vanishing into a shadowed immensity overhead. The ceiling looked industrial, great beams and girders crossing at precise angles, and she ducked as another man managed to squeeze off two pistol shots. He dove behind the still-rocking gurney, clearly hoping it would provide him cover, and landed on Royal's mangled corpse.

Roy would never get anything through another girl's head ever again. He would never pinch, or slap, or shout either; he was a rag of shredded meat and chipped bone.

And Zoe, for once, didn't care that she'd hurt someone. In fact, scorching satisfaction filled her, and her only regret was that she'd waited so long to rid the world of such a shithead.

He had friends, though, and her fury was not yet spent. She heard them all—men crawling through this building, the explosions of gunfire, skin heartbeats and heaving lungs, their footsteps and the creaking of their gear. Of course they'd gotten all dressed up to go hunting one exhausted, confused Kith girl who just wanted to be left alone.

Assholes and fascists always had to wear their little costumes. It was, like exercising power and causing pain, what they got off on. It wasn't any wonder Roy had found them or the other way 'round; birds of a feather were gonna flock together, as Pastor Bea often intoned.

The animal inside, the thing that had saved her, felt the tingling as the dregs of whatever they'd dosed her with was cooked off in her veins, and for moment it—and Zoe herself—wished Bea wasn't already dead.

Because it would have felt good to sink her claws into *him*, too, and take sweet vengeance for every single thing he'd done not just to her but to the congregation under his care.

I'm going to hell. It was the only sane thought in a whirlpool of confusion, and she clung to its familiar pain. There was another body on the floor—the reedy-voiced guy, she thought—and though she didn't remember tearing into him, she indubitably had. The brassy, sickening smell riding the air was death, mixed with smoke, shit, cold fresh air, and a tang of medical disinfectant.

More crashing, more thumps, more explosions, more zinging sounds as bullets bounced off metal and concrete. Under the confusion, a thrumming growl resonated—no, two deep growls, and one was a voice every inch of her recognized.

Her brother was here. He'd found her. Again.

The blond behind the gurney whimpered, fiddling with his gun. Something had jammed; he rolled away from the mess that had been Royal Petterson and his terrified blue eyes—not nearly as vivid or piercing as Trevor's, or her own—peeked through metal struts. He pointed the malfunctioning weapon, and Zoe's chest vibrated as her lip lifted, the change bathing her like sizzling oil.

After she took care of him, she could leave this nasty little room and find the other skin hunters.

Kill it, the animal in her keened. *Kill them all. It's what they'd do to you.*

Caught between that urge and the equally intense instinct to simply flee, get the fuck *out* of all this chaos and run howling into the snow, Zoe hesitated.

The blond man squeezed the trigger, and his gun was no longer jammed.

A single shot rang out, lost in the jumble of competing noise.

75
MONSTERS

THE LAST WALL BETWEEN HIM AND HIS GOAL DISINTEGRATED WHEN JACK HIT it, and he barely noticed the blond skin bastard taking cover, prone, behind a gurney to his left. The smell of old blood was thick here, and the reek of freshly spilled claret overlaid it in a heavy copper wave. A skin with a greying goatee had been tossed into a bank of monitors, leaving a clear imprint and ending up draped over a single lazily spinning office chair; medical implements lay scattered amid two other bodies. There was a rag of flesh and bone near the gurney, right next to the blond, who was taking careful aim.

Amid the wreckage, Jack's *demie* crouched, her hair a wild tangled raven glory, her eyes burning and the change blur-buzzing through her in waves precisely echoing its passage through his own larger frame. A bullet dug a shallow furrow in concrete near her left knee and fled, screaming, into the rest of the battle.

Jack leapt, landing with a jolt as the blond bastard on the floor managed another shot. A hammerblow to his chest, ribs snapping, and the pain was a spur. The Kith snarled, lunging for the gurney, and kicked it aside with one swift motion.

Zoe screamed, a red jolt of electric fear goading his beast.

Jack tore the life from the skin on the floor and whirled, his boots slipping in greasy blood. A burning poker in his chest—he bent slightly, coughed, and spat a bright crimson wad. Another wringing effort as the blond skin convulsed, a geyser of internal fluids finishing its gush from a terribly fragile body reduced to mincemeat, and a deformed lump of metal caught in Jack's throat.

He spat the still-hot bullet aside, contemptuously, and straightened, wincing a bit as his ribs crackled. His gaze settled on his *demie*.

Paper-pale, her blue eyes huge, Zoe trembled. Waves of shudders passed through her, and it was a good thing *demie* couldn't be Broken because shock and pain filled her to the brim, echoing down the link and cracking his heart as the bullet had failed to do.

Her chapped lips, tinged with flecks of blood, shaped his name. The word was lost all the chaos—more growling, and a shaman's clear high call bouncing through the factory's gutted cavern.

Backup had arrived. Which was great.

Zoe's coat and gloves were gone. Her slacks were torn, and her sweater had been sliced, maybe by her own claws but maybe by the skins. Of course they couldn't restrain themselves, of course they would try to rip, violate, destroy the most beautiful thing in the world.

Had they truly hurt her? If they had, he was going to kill *all* of them, and—

"Jack," she repeated, barely audible, and hunched as if afraid. What on earth did she think he was going to do?

He swung into motion again, two stamping steps leaving bloody footprints on stained concrete, and dropped to his knees. His hands shot out, grabbed her shoulders, and he dragged her into his arms.

I thought you were dead, she whispered into the twinbond's vast internal hush, and he buried his face in her hair.

"Not while my sweet *demie* needs me," he whispered back, and held on for dear life as Kith swarmed the abandoned factory, hurrying to rescue one of their own.

"In *Jersey*," Mac repeated, grimacing, and scrubbed at his face, freeing dried blood with a crackle. His coat would never be the same, holding a peppering of bullet holes; his beast for once had its fill of bloodlust and was sleepy, heavy-eyed. "They even have a T1 line run out here."

The snow had begun again, with a vengeance. So far, nobody had taken any notice of a pitched battle, but that was why the skin hunters had chosen this place—for a space resting its cheek on one of the world's biggest cities, it was surprisingly isolated.

"You're not going to believe this." Jolie's long sleek mane was disheveled, for once, and there were marks of strain around her large dark eyes. "There's a walk-in freezer too, and that's where they stored their victims."

Victims, plural? Jack listened with half an ear, the analyst in him collecting and collating information. The rest of him was too busy to care.

"Kith? But nobody's missing." Allison was dewed with melting snow; she'd apparently run all the way from the Lincoln Tunnel. More Kith were arriving every moment, even as the snow thickened. Kieran Freitag clamped his phone to one ear, nodding vigorously as though whoever was on the other end could see him, white flakes frosting his curls.

The kid was pale, but holding up well. His Jeep Cherokee stood patiently, waiting, and Jack had *not* torn the back driver's side door free of its moorings.

All things considered, he'd been a marvel of restraint.

"As far as I can tell, they're skins." Jolie shivered. She was untouched, her arms crossed tight over her midriff. "Why would they kill their own?"

"Because they're monsters." Mac edged closer to the junior shaman, sliding an arm across her shoulders and pulling her into his warmth. She didn't demur, simply leaned into the offered comfort. "Jack? How we doing?"

"It's all right," Jack said again. The princess signet slid easily over his *demie*'s knuckle, and he snugged it back at the base of her left third finger. The ring glimmered, happy to be back where it belonged. "Just stay still, Zo. I've got you."

Zoe perched on the back passenger seat of Freitag's car, wrapped in her black woolen coat rescued from a storage area inside the abandoned factory. Other clothing, folded and stored in neat rows, filled the heavy metal shelving in that space, and all of it was civilian.

Some of it bore bloodstains.

"I'm s-s-sorr—" His *demie* kept trying to apologize, the words chopped into tiny pieces by chattering teeth. She shivered like a skin, but it was pure shock instead of cold.

"Nothing to be sorry about," Jack soothed again, and glanced over his shoulder. "I've got to get her out of here. Has Dad been notified?"

That caught Kieran's attention; the cub gave a thumb's up with his free hand. That explained his excitement—he was on the line with the Pride leader, a high honor for any Kith.

"By the *Moon*." Allison peered the loading bay, her nose wrinkling as she studied the metal shelf, the restraints, the medical equipment. "How...what..."

It smelled like death inside the armored car, not a kind easing of burdens into restful sleep but long, tortuous, drawn-out murder. It reeked of agony, of hopelessness, and a dull copper note of sadistic enjoyment.

This group of skins didn't deserve the title of 'hunters'. They were, true to form, worse than Broken could ever hope to be.

"Are we cleaning this up?" Mac was already anticipating the next problem. He pulled Jolie closer, and again she didn't resist, burying her face in his shoulder to block out all the hideousness. "Or...?"

A whoosh, a soft burst of snow, and Bella came to a halt, bearing the same drops of snowmelt Allison did. Dimitri followed a half-breath later, and shadows amid the falling snow were yet more Kith arriving. "Hey," the *demie* gasped in greeting, and caught sight of Zoe. "Oh, thank *God*."

A single glimmering tear slipped down Zoe's cheek. "Roy," she whispered. "I killed him."

If you hadn't, I would have. The thought leapt between them—there was no bar to communication now. For better or worse, he was firmly inside his *demie*'s head, and had zero intention of ever giving her enough space to repeat this terrifying incident.

But it was over now, and she was safe. His beast could barely believe it, and he seconded that emotion. "Good," Jack said, shortly. "Give me a second and we'll be out of here, babygirl. Just keep breathing."

Even Allison stilled when he half-turned, keeping Zoe's hand firmly imprisoned in both of his. Dimitri stepped in front of Bella, peering past Allison into the loading bay, and his usual grin was gone. The dark-haired *demi* wore a look of mixed concentration and disgust as he bumped his twin, subtly herding her away from the opening.

Jack cleared his throat. "We might not have to bother cleaning everything up," he continued, pitching the words to carry. It was so much easier to think now; the contact with his *demie* was wonderfully soothing. "Just get all the intel off their electronics and make sure nothing Kith remains here, then get home. We can always monitor the skin authorities when and if they start investigating. Might as well let them chase their own kind."

"But...why?" Jolie raised her head from McKenna's shoulder. Her eyes glittered with unshed tears. "Why would they...there are so many bodies, Jack."

"Testing." It was simple, and obvious. Still, Jack hated saying it aloud. "Our metabolisms and structures are a little different, but the basic biology's pretty much the same. And if they can't catch one of us they would have to experiment to have something to extrapolate from."

And Greg Jasperson had been *helping* them.

He hoped the traitor was dead by now, torn apart by the seizures accompanying the last stages of skate addiction. Because if not, Jack might visit the warehouse again, and help that process along.

It would be a cleaner end than that inflicted by these...creatures, these things. *Human* was too good a word for them.

"Fucking monsters," McKenna repeated, and Jolie made a restless motion. Of course she'd want to soothe the baffled pain of any Kith witnessing this ungodly mess.

"This has to be cleansed," Allison said, softly.

"Fine, just make sure the hackers get everything we can scrape from here." *Now get to work so I can take my* demie *home.* For a moment, Jack resented the burden of command, and wondered if his father felt the same. "And make sure nothing Kith is left even if you want to clean this up. I don't know if this place'll burn, but we can try."

"We'll take care of that." Allison was pale too, and she stuffed her hands in her coat pockets, though she was most likely perfectly warm. "Kieran, is it? I presume that's Trevor on the line."

"Yes ma'am." The cub straightened even further. Snow was beginning to clot in his hair. "You want to talk to him?"

"Tell him you're needed to drive his children home, and I'll call him in about ten minutes when I have a better idea of things here." The shaman's face set, and foxfire sparks glimmered in her pupils. "Dima, Bell, run the edges of this place and keep watch for skins wandering by. They could have reinforcements too, let's not forget that. Jolie, start directing whoever else arrives to help; McKenna, get a handle on what we can strip from the electronics inside this building." Quickly, with her usual serene grace, Allison took charge, and the Kith scattered except for Freitag, who hung up after an exceedingly polite farewell and hurried for the driver's side of his Jeep. "And as for you..." The shaman took a few brisk steps, ending up at Jack's shoulder, regarding his *demie*. "Oh, little kitten. You've had a dreadful day."

Zoe flinched as if struck. She was expecting anger, punishment, quite possibly more violence. Jack held her hand, making himself a wall, flooding her with reassurance through the raw open wound of the twinbond.

"Here." Allison attempted to shoulder him aside, but he didn't move much. The shaman caught Zoe's chin in her cupped palm, and his *demie*'s tearstreaked face was lifted to fading afternoon snowlight. "I told you this before, but it doesn't seem to have sunk in. That's all right—we know how strong you are now, my dear. Now listen. Hear only my voice, and trust..."

When the feartaking was over, he climbed into the car next to her, buckled his *demie*'s seatbelt and his own, and sat next to her all the way back to the Rouje manor, murmuring reassurance in her ear as she alternated between trembling, nervous silence and weeping as if her heart would break.

His own chest ached, too, with every muffled sob.

76

IN TIME

THE BLUE SUITE WAS JUST THE SAME, AND IT ACCEPTED HER AS IF SHE'D never left. Amelia made a short coughing sound of relief as soon as she saw Zoe and hurried about, her footsteps feline-soft. She clucked over the state of the black woolen coat, whisked away the ruined clothes, and chivvied Zoe into a hot bath as if she was five years old and needed help. Jack lingered outside the bathroom door during *that*, and Zoe's cheeks were scarlet not just from the heat of the water. He was *in her head*, the same way she was in his.

The twinbond had been ripped open, every inch laid bare. There was no place to hide, now.

Bundled into pajamas and the fluffy indigo-striped robe, Zoe perched on the couch in the blue sitting room, holding a thick white china mug of hot chocolate. There was a mound of buttered toast on the tray, too, and Amelia promised dinner soon before she bustled away, sniffing once, deeply, and hurriedly brushing at her cheek. Outside in the hall, there was the faint rumble of Hermann asking a question and her lighter reply as she shooed him along. A heavy, slumbrous winter evening pressed against the windows, fluffy snow falling with a vengeance.

"Clint Barclay," Trevor said, his hands clasped behind his back as he pretended to examine one of the bookcases. Zoe hoped it held up to inspection, and another wave of shivers passed through her. "Pharmaceuticals, if I remember correctly. He always was a pathological little sleaze."

"We've done fundraisers with him." Jack shook his golden head; he'd toweled off and changed, somehow, while she was being bossed into clothes by Amelia. "And all the time he was bankrolling skin hunters?"

"Pretty much. They apparently didn't even know the overseas hunters existed, so they didn't get any funding from our favorite sector of the Vatican. These bast—ah, this *organization* was trying to expand too quickly." Trevor turned, and studied his son. For some reason, he wouldn't look at Zoe, and she was too exhausted to feel anything other than a weary lack of surprise.

"The downfall of many a skin company." Jack's gaze rested on Zoe, and she tried a sip of cocoa.

It was too hot, but even that was a gift. Just when she thought the tremors were fading, another batch of them raced through her.

They were getting weaker, though.

"Clint wasn't a religious fanatic; he apparently thought stem cells from a Kith were the key to eternal life, or some such foolishness." While Trevor's gaze was locked with Jack's the similarity between them, father and son, was clearly visible. "They were very excited at the prospect of capturing one of us so soon; they cut too many corners. It'll take a while to get through all their data. Gibson's crew are doing damage control, cleaning up any traces of our cell phones in that area, and sharing intel with other territorial leaders. The Howler's teams have run a few of their cells down, the West Coast is cleaning house, and Fantome's sister has declared open season on any skin hunters within her borders. Trenckow sends his regards from Florida."

They were talking about this right in front of her, and nobody had started yelling yet. Zoe couldn't figure out how to feel, or even what to do next. Each time the panic threatened to return, Allison's shaman-stuff swamped her with calm.

It was cleaner than the skin hunters' chemicals, but Zoe wished she could feel her own fear again. Without it, she ran a very real risk of turning into a puddle right here on the couch.

"What about the site?" Jack dropped down next to her, collecting his own mug of hot chocolate. There was no cup for their father; he didn't often indulge his sweet tooth.

Trevor shrugged, a supple, controlled motion. "Allison didn't think that place would burn completely, but McKenna said there was no reason it wouldn't, just give it a shot." Both he and Jack spoke softly, moved slowly, as if someone was asleep beyond the half-open door to the blue bedroom—perhaps the girl she should have been, if Mama hadn't taken her.

Jack snorted, quietly, and a sardonic grin flashed across his face. "Trust him to take it as a challenge."

She could feel his amusement, and it had an edge. Hopefully that sharpness wouldn't be directed at her. She wished one of them would just get it over with, tell her how disappointed they were, *do* something so she knew the worst was over and could finally relax.

"He appears to be right, too." Trevor eased into motion, stalking for the couch, and Zoe's throat was full of something heavy before Allison's voice echoed in her head again.

You will trust your demi, *and you will not fear.*

And Jack's followed, echoing down the link. *You're not in trouble, I promise. I swear.*

Which was nice of him, and she wished she could believe it. Even if the usual panic didn't rise to swamp her she still *felt* like it would, and braced herself for a punch that never came.

Their father lowered himself gingerly to sit on her other side, not too close, but not too far away either. "I'm sorry, little dancer." He offered his hand, a big warm cupped palm, surprisingly dextrous fingers hiding claws just like hers. "We haven't done a good job of protecting you. Forgive me."

Her jaw threatened to drop. Zoe was hard-pressed to scrape up any words at all. "I sh-shouldn't have..." If they would just shout, or hit her, she could handle it.

The kindness was disarming, and overwhelming as fuck.

"You were trying to protect us." His blue gaze, so much like Zoe's own, bored into her. It had always unnerved Mama, her daughter's steady stare. "And yourself. Correct?"

Zoe nodded, and cringed internally.

"No shame in that," Jack weighed in. "And if anyone has a problem with it, they'll answer to me."

Even more disconcerting was how he meant every word, his certainty burning in her own chest. "I'm sorry," she whispered once more, unable to stop. The two words would probably follow her into the grave, and straight down into hell, too.

Would Jack accompany her that far? To be honest, he already had.

"I know. But you don't have to be." Trevor sat there as if it were perfectly normal to just let your hand hang in midair, waiting for another's. "It's a good thing this Petterson fellow is already dealt with. Nothing he forced you to do matters, Zoe. You don't believe it yet, but you will. In time."

He didn't force me. That was the most shameful truth of all. She'd *wanted* to work, to help him. And it had all ended up with a ravaged corpse on stained concrete. She couldn't even feel bad about that—Royal would never slap another terrified woman, never take the lion's share of a working girl's money ever again.

She still couldn't wrap her brain around the rest of it. Murdered people, medical research, a coast-to-coast network of hunters?

The fairytale was darker than she'd ever imagined. One of the originals, before the Grimm brothers got around to cleaning things up for their audience.

"I didn't mean to...I thought..." God, she couldn't even form complete sentences. She was a sorry excuse for a Kith, even if they seemed not to care at the moment.

"I know." Trevor was patient, and completely calm. "All will be well, little dancer. Will you try to trust us? That's all I ask."

"Yes." Her vision blurred once more, stupid useless tears. Zoe freed her fingers from the mug's comforting warmth, and laid them hesitantly in her father's palm. "Uh, yes, s-sir."

"Good heavens, don't *sir* me." A hint of a smile touched Trevor's mouth, and he squeezed her hand gently. "It makes me feel old, coming from you. A simple *'yes, Dad'* will do."

"Yes." Her throat was dry. "Dad."

"Good." He nodded briskly, patted her knuckles with his free hand, and rose in a graceful, coordinated wave. "Dinner will be soon, I hope to see you both there. Amelia will need to stuff you like partridges; don't disappoint her. I'll be in my office, should you need me." And with that, he left without a backward glance.

Which left her alone with Jack. Her twin took down half his own hot chocolate and winced at the burn, but it was over just as quickly as liquor's transient bite. "I'm starving," he said, and it was almost as if she'd never left.

Almost. And she couldn't stop crying, slow tears and sniffles, even when her *demi* took her mug, set aside his own, and gathered her into his arms.

The snow continued to fall all through the night, and in the depths of cold darkness well after midnight she woke from a nightmare of a bleeding Royal shambling after her, a croaking *gotta get it through your head* rising from his ruined, shredded throat as gunfire echoed in concrete halls.

She lunged into consciousness with a stifled cry, and her twin's skin was warm and comforting against hers.

"Shh," Jack whispered into her hair, and the link blurred between them until she couldn't tell whose fear was choking them both. It faded as he held her; some time later, both of them dropped back into the river of sleep without a murmur.

77
PINK ROSES

THREE MONTHS LATER

It was a bright, beautiful day, the kind that explained why anyone had bothered to settle Nebraska in the first place. Fleecy clouds sailed through an achingly blue sky, the prairie was alive with birdsong where it wasn't scarred by buildings or roads, and crops stretched skyward from rich earth, basking in bright yellow sunshine.

The rolling, overwatered green of the Haslip Lane Cemetery was studded with monuments, a windbreak of firs drawing a dark shaggy line along one side of the verdant expanse. The wind was full of the good scent of growing things and a tang of exhaust.

Even the dead could be lulled by the constant hum of traffic in the near distance.

Angelina Simmons, the small flat rectangular stone said, with the wrong birth year chiseled in. Of course Mama had often lied about her age, holding it to be a lady's prerogative, and Bea probably hadn't cared what was on the tombstone as long as the date was right on the paperwork so he could cash in the death benefits.

Zoe didn't know where *he* was buried, and didn't want to. She regarded her mother's grave, her hair combed by a sweet soft breeze. Mama's long-ago funeral had been a blur, Bea's fingers digging cruelly into her shoulder whenever Zoe's lip trembled—*don't you dare cry, girl*—and what had come after still returned on some nights, bad dreams rising from the tiny locked box they lived during daylight.

But each time, Jack woke her up and held her close.

He stood at her shoulder, a lean tall young man with a shock of golden hair, scanning the horizon fiercely as if daring it to try some mischief. Occasionally he glanced at the remembrance chapel, a long low brick building with a white spire impersonating a church's.

Everyone had gone to Righteous Savior for the service before and the potluck after the burial. She could remember every minute of that dreadful day, even Auntie Scarsdale on her way out the door, pinching Zoe's cheek and sniffling a little before cautioning her granddaughter's friend to be good.

Your mama is looking down from heaven, honey.

Well, Zo had her doubts. Especially considering what had happened after the last of the cleanup ladies had gone home, and it was just her and Bea.

Still, the grave was neat, well-maintained, and Zoe could afford to have flowers delivered. The bouquet she'd brought this time, tucked into a small plastic cone on a listing metal spike driven deep into willing earth, was baby's breath and pink roses—Mama's favorite, and they smelled just like rose soap in small metal tins.

Maybe Angelina's ghost would be happy about that, even if her children were everything she'd feared.

Zoe's hands twisted together, clenching hard on the edge of pain. The princess signet glittered, and Jack reached down to untangle her fingers, slide his through, and hold fast. He didn't ask if she was ready to go—he could tell she wasn't, and was perfectly happy to stand here for as long as it took.

It was strange to travel first-class, every possible obstacle smoothed over and handled before she was even aware of its existence. Doubly strange to have an entourage, since this was Louisa Fantome's territory now and diplomatic etiquette had to be observed. Sondra Amerlane was kind of terrifying—butter wouldn't melt in the lawyer's mouth, but every once in a while she made a soft observation and Zo realized she'd been thinking eight steps ahead of everyone else, just like Jack.

Jolie and McKenna were back at the hotel, and Jo was still leading Mac a merry chase. They'd end up mated, Jack said, and that was nice to think about. Apparently Kith weddings were more like week-long parties.

There was an office building being constructed over the scraped-flat remains of Righteous Savior. Apparently Ms. Fantome—she was, by all accounts, *definitely* not a Miss or Mrs.—was Leroy McFisk's mother, though he'd been taken away from her for some reason probably involving her dead brother George.

Now she ruled this part of the country, like Trevor ruled his. Zoe was content not to know any more. It was weird to think of Bea as someone with a mother of his own, but even the worst people imaginable had to have one.

It was enough that Zo didn't have to meet the woman. Sondra and McKenna handled all that. And while there were still skin hunters lurking—there had been an attack in Seoul just last week—the Kith handled that danger as they always had, with swift, collective action.

Zoe tipped her face up to the sunlight, closed her eyes.

She could visit Jenny, she supposed, or take the silver Lexus sitting patiently on the cemetery-access road and drive through Hall City instead of walking or taking the bus. She could see Joplin High School again, the Piggly Wiggly she and Mama used to shop at, or the rundown building she and Mama had first lived in when they arrived all those years ago—assuming it hadn't also been knocked down for something else.

"Anywhere you like," Jack said softly.

She was getting used to him answering things she hadn't said aloud, and vice versa. Bella was right, thinking inside your *demi*'s head was powerfully comforting, and Zo didn't know how she'd ever lived without it.

Bell called every night after dinner for a video chat; she was bubbling over with plans for Zoe's return. There were classes to attend—a degree was a distinct possibility, even if she had to get prerequisites out of the way—and more of Janine's mood boards to look at, shopping to do and shaman lessons all waiting for her as well. Best of all, she could go back to dancing, and even when everything else was overwhelming the peace and order of ballet class never varied.

Her phone chimed, the notification sound for Dad's texts. He was a little anxious over her being here, but as far as the regular authorities were concerned, the rich man in charge of Royal's skin hunter friends had ties to organized crime and probably double-crossed someone he shouldn't. The factory in Newark had burned to the ground, its attendant cell tower holding the only record that he'd been there at all because any body in the wreckage was near-unidentifiable.

Jack found that amusing, in his own particularly sardonic way. They hadn't identified Royal's body yet, either. Apparently the fire had been...intense.

Just like the one at Righteous Savior.

Daylight dimmed as a cloud wandered in front of the sun. Jack's hand was steady and sure in hers, and Zoe exhaled shakily, opening her eyes. They smarted, but didn't overflow.

Maybe she'd finally cried enough.

Goodbye, Mama.

She didn't have to say anything. Jack knew she was done, and turned with her. They ambled back to the car, hand in hand, grass cut yesterday simmering under her black heels and sending up a faint good smell. The edge of her skirt fluttered as the breeze swirled around them, and there were voices in the air, if a shaman wanted to listen to them.

"I'll call Mac," Jack said, knowing she wanted to leave.

When you were Kith, you could do that—simply decide, and walk away. "Which means you want me to call Dad." It was probably a sin to smile near Mama's grave, but she couldn't stop it any more than she could keep her *demi* out of her head anymore. The twin-bond pulsed between them, soft undeniable strength.

"He'll start asking about work if I call." Jack dug for the car keys with his free hand, and a laugh bubbled up in Zoe's throat. It pushed aside the sadness, and she squeezed her twin's fingers.

"Work?" she said. "God forbid."

Jack's laughter matched hers, and the cloud over the sun fled, deciding it had better things to do. Spring would turn into a hot summer soon enough, and the cemetery would drowse through it like every other season.

And Zoe Rouje, at long last, found out she couldn't wait to be home.

ABOUT THE AUTHOR

A.C. Delauncey is a pseudonym.